The Moving Castle

THE MOVING CASTLE

Hwang Sun-won

translated by
Bruce and Ju-chan Fulton

Si-sa-yong-o-sa, Inc., Korea
Pace International Research, Inc., U.S.A.

Published simultaneously in KOREA and the UNITED STATES

KOREA EDITION
First printing 1985
Si-sa-yong-o-sa, Inc.
55-1 Chongno 2-ga, Chongno-gu
Seoul 110, Korea

U.S. EDITION
First printing 1985
Pace International Research, Inc.
Tide Avenue, Falcon Cove
P.O.Box 51, Arch Cape
Oregon 97102, U.S.A.

ISBN: 0-89209-322-6

This book is a co-publication by Si-sa-yong-o-sa, Inc.
and The International Communication Foundation.

Translator's Preface

In this translation we have used a slightly modified version of the McCune-Reischauer system of romanizing Korean words. McCune-Reischauer has long been the preferred system of romanization in Western scholarly writings on Korea.

For the convenience of the reader, we present the full names of six of the major characters, whose surnames are infrequently mentioned in the novel: Yun Sŏng-ho, Song Min-gu, Ham Chun-t'ae, Nam Chi-yŏn, Han Ŭn-hŭi, and Chang Ch'ang-ae.

We are indebted to several individuals whose efforts have substantially improved this translation. Steve Hopkins, Rick Davidson, and Suzanne Crowder edited the manuscript and offered many useful comments. Fred Lukoff, professor of Korean language at the University of Washington, made several insightful editorial suggestions. Finally, the author himself spent many hours with us, elucidating phrases and passages that we would never have been able to bring to life on our own. We are deeply grateful to this most gracious man for his constant interest and encouragement. Of course none of these individuals is to be held responsible for the shortcomings of the finished product.

This translation was made possible by a grant from Si-sa-yong-o-sa, Inc. We wish to thank Min Young-bin, chairman of Si-sa-yong-o-sa, for coordinating this project.

MAR 1987

If through this volume we are able to share with others our delight in the rich literary world of Hwang Sun-won, and if we can thereby stimulate a broader interest in modern Korean literature, then our efforts will have been amply rewarded.

BF
JCF

Introduction

In 1930 Hwang Sun-won began publishing children's stories and poetry in newspapers in P'yŏng-yang, capital of present-day North Korea. His most recently published story as of this writing was completed in November 1983. Encompassed within this half century is a literary output of sustained high quality unmatched in modern Korean literature—more than one hundred stories, seven novels, and two volumes of poetry. Hwang has been honored with every major Korean literary prize, and his works have been made into films and translated into at least five languages. Columnist Peter Hyun's evaluation of Hwang is perhaps not overstated:

> He is...one of the finest novelists writing in the Korean language today.
>
> In many ways, he reminds me of William Faulkner—introverted, introspective and totally dedicated to the perfection of his craft.
>
> More important,...like Faulkner and Dostoevsky, he has the knack of crystallizing ordinary everyday events and people into his own universal perspective, a perspective that is so timeless and placeless and yet so lucid that it can be easily understood by any literate reader.[1]

Curiously, Hwang Sun-won appears to be somewhat underestimated in Korea. This is in part the result of the tendency in Korean literary circles to identify authors by their "representa-

[1]Peter Hyun, "Portrait of an Artist," *Korea Herald,* February 26, 1984, p. 6.

tive works" and in part the result of the interest taken by younger readers in authors who are more outspoken in their treatment of social and political issues. Although most Koreans with a middle school education can identify Hwang Sun-won, most will do so in reference to a single story—"Shower," a fixture in most Korean middle school literature texts. This bittersweet tale whose pastoral setting conceals darker overtones is deservedly popular, but to identify the author with it, as a great many readers do, would be somewhat akin to remembering Ernest Hemingway as the author of, say, "A Clean, Well-Lighted Place."

In the 1970s a new generation of Korean authors—Hwang Sŏk-yŏng, Yi Mun-gu, and Kim Chi-ha, for example—became popular not only for their literary excellence but for their stands on various social and political matters. Perhaps because Hwang Sun-won's aims have always been literary more than political, his works seem to be regarded as somewhat less relevant and up-to-date than the literature of this younger group. In fact, though, Hwang Sun-won has never shied from a direct confrontation with the social realities of his times. *The Moving Castle,* for instance, touches on such issues as the exploitation of laborers, mine safety, and government treatment of urban squatters.

In the end, though, it is Hwang Sun-won's uncompromisingly high standards of literary craftsmanship that have secured him his place in the short history of modern Korean literature. As Kim Chong-un, professor of American literature at Seoul National University and a translator of both English and Korean literature, has remarked,

> Not only is [Hwang] a good story-teller but his style is...natural and convincing. In fact, he has all the good qualities of a timeless, classic writer, and it is precisely this timelessness that is mistaken for "old-fashionedness" by some sophomorish critics and younger readers. In their somewhat distorted thinking, rampant avant-gardism is equated with superiority. Then, too, some younger students of literature tend to place much

value on the "trendy" social realism which usually has no place in Hwang's solid, staid, and pure literary world.[2]

Hwang Sun-won was born in March 1915 near P'yŏng-yang. He was educated there and in Tokyo, where he graduated from Waseda University with a degree in English literature in 1939. The next year his first collection of stories, *The Marsh*, was published. In May 1946 Hwang and his family moved from the Soviet-occupied northern sector of Korea to the U.S.-occupied south. He began teaching at Seoul High School in September of that year. Like many Koreans, Hwang and his family were refugees during the Korean War (1950–1953).[3] Since 1957 Hwang has taught Korean literature at Kyung Hee University in Seoul and has been a member of the National Academy of Arts.

The Moving Castle (움직이는 성) was completed in August 1972. A penetrating examination of the confrontation of Eastern and Western culture that is taking place in South Korea today, the novel is at the same time a study of the ambivalencies within the human soul. At once hard-boiled and lyrical, rooted in the workaday lives of slum-dwellers as well as the bizarre dreams of the affluent, pervaded with individuals both strange and familiar, alive with the vibrant smells, colors, and sounds of the metropolis of Seoul and yet the silence of the immemorial countryside—the other Korea—*The Moving Castle* is, in a word, the embodiment of Hwang Sun-won's manifold style.

The moving castle may very well be a metaphor for the nomadic mentality that Chun-t'ae speaks of throughout the novel. At the same time, the movement of a castle—which, as Yi Sang-sŏp has noted, is the epitome of stability[4]—suggests

[2]Personal correspondence, January 10, 1984.
[3]The Hwang family's refugee life is treated in "Pierrot," in *The Rainy Spell and Other Korean Stories,* trans. Suh Ji-moon (London: Onyx Press, 1983), pp. 129–46.
[4]Yi Sang-sŏp, "'The Nomadic Mentality' and 'The Eyes of the Creator,'" afterword to *Umjiginŭn Sŏng* (The Moving Castle) (Seoul: Munhak Kwa Chisŏngsa, 1980),p.449.

many of the contradictions to be found in Korea today and in the past. One of the most homogeneous ethnic groups in the world, a fiercely independent people, possessors of a rich and ancient culture, Koreans yet emigrate by the tens of thousands each year, and the growth of Christianity in Korea is almost unparalleled elsewhere in the world. Shamanism, which along with Christianity figures so prominently in the novel, is regarded with amusement by many Koreans, but it continues to enjoy widespread support, and mediums, exorcists, fortune-tellers, and geomancers continue to make a living. Indeed, in recent years, Korean shamanism has become the object of considerable scholarly investigation by both Koreans and Westerners.[5] These are only some of the more obvious examples. This moving castle of inconsistencies is no doubt due in part to the buffetings Korea has taken throughout history at the hands of its more powerful neighbors—first the Chinese, then the seminomadic pastoralists to the north, and more recently imperial Japan. But there is more to the moving castle than external influences, and it is to the Korean mentality itself that Chun-t'ae addresses himself with a forthrightness rare in modern Korean literature.

The history of modern Korean literature is generally considered to date from the end of the first decade of this century. At that time Yi Kwang-su, still in his teens, founded the literary magazine *Youth* and began campaigning for a Korean literature composed in the vernacular (prior to that time, Chinese was the written language of the educated Korean author) and addressed to contemporary themes rather than stock formulas. Since then several literary movements have surfaced in Korea.

[5]See, for example, Youngsook Kim Harvey, *Six Korean Women* (St. Paul: West, 1979); Jung Young Lee, *Korean Shamanistic Rituals* (The Hague: Mouton, 1981); Roger L. Janelli and Dawnhee Yim Janelli, *Ancestor Worship and Korean Society* (Stanford, Calif.: Stanford University Press, 1982), Ch. 6; and Laurel Kendall, "Wood Imps, Ghosts, and Other Noxious Influences: The Ideology of Affliction in a Korean Village," *Journal of Korean Studies*, 3 (1981), 113–45.

There has always been a strong current of realism, and as we noted above, some younger writers have addressed themselves more explicitly to social and political issues. In the 1920s and 1930s a proletarian literature emerged briefly. On the other hand, there have been practitioners of a pure literature, such as Yi Sang. Hwang Sun-won, a central figure in Korean literature for fully two thirds of its brief history, has tenaciously resisted categorization in any of these movements. Indeed, as Edward Poitras has pointed out, Hwang has experimented successfully in a variety of styles.[6] Yet at the core Hwang remains a consistently satisfying author—a master craftsman, an engaging story-teller, a writer of Korea who yet can speak to those outside Korea. He is, in short, a writer for the ages.

Hwang Sun-won has been publishing poetry since 1930, short stories since 1936, and novels since 1950. His published works are as follows:

Poetry: *Wayward Songs* (1934)
      Curios (1936)
Short Story Collections:
      The Marsh (1940)
      The Dog of Moknomi Village (1948)
      Wild Geese (1951)
      Pierrot (1952)
      Cranes (1956)
      The Lost Souls (1958)
      Time for You and Me Alone (1964)
      The Mask (1976)
Novels: *She Lives With the Stars* (1950)
      Descendants of Cain (1954)
      Human Grafting (1957)
      Trees on the Cliff (1960)

[6]Introduction to Hwang Sun-won, *The Stars and Other Korean Short Stories,* trans. Edward W. Poitras (London: Heinemann Educational Books, 1980), p. 36.

> *The Sun and the Moon* (1964)
> *The Moving Castle* (1973)
> *The Dice of the Gods* (1982)

Hwang has been honored with the following literary awards·

1955: Asia-Freedom Literature Prize (for *Descendants of Cain*)
1961: National Academy of Arts Literature Award (for *Trees on the Cliff*)
1966: March First Literature Prize (for *The Sun and the Moon*)
1983: Korean Literature Grand Prize (for *The Dice of the Gods*)

Hwang Sun-won's fiction has been translated into English more than that of any other twentieth-century Korean author. Among the translated works are two novels, two collections of stories, and various stories published in anthologies, newspapers, and journals.

Novels:
The Cry of the Cuckoo (카인의 후예), trans. Youngsook Chang and Robert Miller (Seoul: Pan Korea Book Corporation, 1975). This novel (listed above as *Descendants of Cain*) is no longer in print.

Trees on the Cliff (나무들 비탈에 서다), trans. Chang Wang-rok (Larchmont, N.Y.: Larchwood, 1980; available from the Korean Literature Foundation, 1-48 Sajik-dong, Chongno-gu, Seoul 110, Korea). This volume also contains the stories "Shower" (소나기) and "The Night He Came Late" (이날의 지각).

Collections:
The Stars and Other Korean Stories, trans. Edward W. Poitras (London: Heinemann Educational Books, 1980). This book contains an excellent introduction and consists of the following stories by Hwang, composed between 1936 and 1974:

"A Matter of Custom" (풍속)

"Conch Shells" (소라)
"The Sacrifice" (닭제)
"The Stars" (별)
"An Old Man's Birthday" (황노인)
"The Old Potter" (독 짓는 늙은이)
"The Cloudburst" (소나기)
"The Crane" (학)
"Coarse Sand" (왕모래)
"The Diving Girl" (비바리)
"The Calf" (송아지)
"A Numerical Enigma" (숫자풀이)

The Drizzle (Seoul: Si-sa-yong-o-sa, Inc., 1983). About half of this collection, volume 2 in the series *Modern Korean Short Stories,* is devoted to stories by Hwang, all of which originally appeared in English translation in *Korea Journal,* a monthly publication of the Korean National Commission of UNESCO:

"The Drizzle" (가랑비), trans. Kim Chong-un
"Time for You and Me Alone" (너와 나만의 시간),
        trans. Kim Chong-un
"Acorns" (도토리), trans. Norman Thorpe
"Stars" (별), trans. Choe Chol-li
"Life" (목숨), trans. Kim Se-yong
"The Weighted Tumbler" (원색 오뚜기),
        trans. Kim Chong-chol
"For Dear Life" (온기있는 파편), trans. Song Yo-in
"The Moon and the Crab's Legs" (달과 밭과),
        trans. Edward W. Poitras
"Masks" (탈), trans. Edward W. Poitras
"The Children" (아이들), trans. Edward W. Poitras

Miscellaneous Translated Stories:
"The Lost Ones" (잃어버린 사람들), trans. Chu Yŏ-sŏp, in *Collected Short Stories From Korea* (Seoul: Korean Pen Club, 1961)

"Cranes" (학), trans. E. Sang Yu, *Prairie Schooner,* Fall 1963

"Crane" (학), trans. Kim Se-yong, in *Modern Korean Short Stories and Plays* (Seoul: Korean Pen Club, 1970)

"Cranes" (학), trans. Peter H. Lee, in *Flowers of Fire,* ed. Peter H. Lee (Honolulu: The University Press of Hawaii, 1974)

"Shower" (소나기), trans. E. Sang Yu, in *Flowers of Fire,* ed. Lee

"The Old Jar-Maker" (독 짓는 늙은이) trans. Norman Thorpe, *Korea Times,* November 1, 1975

"Snow" (눈), trans. W. E. Skillend, in *Modern Far Eastern Stories,* ed. Chung Chong-wha (London: Heinemann Educational Books, 1978)

"Cranes" (학), in *A Washed-Out Dream,* trans. Kevin O'Rourke (Larchmont, N.Y.: Larchwood, 1980; available from the Korean Literature Foundation, 1-48 Sajik-dong, Chongno-gu, Seoul 110, Korea)

"Retreat" (너와 나만의 시간), trans. Chung Chong-wha, in *Meetings and Farewells,* ed. Chung Chong-wha (New York: St. Martin's Press, 1980)

"Pierrot" (곡예사), in *The Rainy Spell and Other Korean Stories,* trans. Suh Ji-moon (London: Onyx Press, 1983)

Bruce Fulton

The Moving Castle

PART I

Chapter 1

A girl of four or five, sitting in a path between some houses, is playing with mud. She wears only a pair of underpants, stained deep red from the moist soil. She isn't even wearing shoes. The dark line of her fleshless, bony spine reflects the sheen of the sunlight slanting through the gaps between the houses. Sensing someone's presence as she fashions mud cakes from the earth, she lifts her head.

A blind man feeling about with his cane is coming around the corner and into the path. He is middle-aged. His misty eyes blink continuously beneath a forehead strewn with dry, dusty hair.

The girl jumps up. The blind man is pecking about with his cane in a puddle of water thrown out on the street; his feet won't move. The girl goes to the blind man. With her thin, earth-stained hands she grasps the middle of his cane and positions it so that he avoids the place where the water has collected.

Beside the shallow well in his yard Sŏng-ho was doing some laundry that had been piling up. Using a nickel-silver dipper he scooped fresh water into a tin basin, where he rinsed the roughly washed clothes. He was quite proficient at drawing the

1

clothing back and forth in the water and then wringing it out.

He hung the laundry in an orderly line, finishing with the socks. Then he heard a guttural voice.

"You're really caught up in that. You don't even know when you've got a visitor."

The flat, broad, well-complexioned face of Min-gu drew near among the articles of clothing on the line.

"Hey, who's this? I haven't seen you in ages."

"I oughta take a picture of this. What a miserable state of affairs. Why don't you keep a maid?"

"I don't have that much to do. What are you talking about, keeping someone?...You got the day off from school?"

"No, my classes were all this morning—I'm on my way home now. Boy it's hot! Here we are in September and the sun's still not letting up. Let me wash up with some of that spring water of yours before I do anything else."

Sŏng-ho rinsed out a washbowl, poured it full, and gave it to him.

Min-gu took off his shirt and threw it on the stoop of the porch. On his way over to the washbasin he looked into the well water. "Yup, this is *ammul*[1] all right."

The water was milky white, like boiled clam broth.

"I don't know whether it's *ammul* or *sumul*.[2] They say the taste is good, so even the people from down below come and get it."

"I thought so,"said Min-gu."*Ammul* is generally soft water, not hard. The taste is sweet, it makes good lather, and the laundry turns out well."

"Since when have you become an expert on the quality of water?"

"I've been bumming around the countryside too much. This is the kind of lore I've picked up along the way. The only time people don't use *ammul* is when they're praying to the spirits."

---

[1] *Ammul* (literally "female water"): well water that has a milky color.
[2] *Sumul* (literally "male water"): a word coined by Sŏng-ho as a joke.

"That's something I've been meaning to bring up," said Sŏng-ho. "Can't you stop chasing that shamanism business? Why don't you get back on the right track and start collecting folk songs again?"

"Now wait a minute. The shaman culture's what I'm most interested in now. Frankly, the more I look into it the more absorbed I get. I can't help it."

"Come on, wash up."

Min-gu washed his face noisily, all the while saying how refreshing it was. Then, while wiping his face with the towel Sŏng-ho had given him, he turned to look at the church standing directly before him at the left side of the yard. The lower part of the block wall had crumbled in places and become pockmarked. The tin roof was losing its paint and getting rusty. It was coming loose here and there, and its slant was uneven.

"Doesn't it leak, the shape it's in?" asked Min-gu.

"Not yet...it'll need some fixing up next spring, though."

"How long's it been since you took over here? Over a year, isn't it?"

"A year and a half."

"A lot more *yesujaengi*[3] during that time?"

"Not to speak of."

"I'll bet there're a lot more shamans and fortune-tellers down there in the lower village since last time," said Min-gu. "After all, you can't beat poverty as a hotbed of shamanism. I would guess it isn't easy being a clergyman in a place like this. You're bound to be running up against shamanism pretty soon." Min-gu picked up his shirt and put it on. "I came over today because I have a special favor to ask you. We've made up our minds now."

"You've made up your mind?"

"We figured it's time to get engaged."

"Hey, that's good news. No use letting it drag on. But what's

---

[3] *Yesujaengi:* a derogatory term for a churchgoer. *Yesu:* Jesus; *-jaengi* (a colloquial variant of *-jangi*): monger, dealer.

this favor?" asked Sŏng-ho.

"I'd like you to officiate at the engagement ceremony."

"Who me? What about the minister at Elder Han's church?"

"I was thinking about asking him to do the wedding."

"If the same guy does both ceremonies, what's the problem? I'm still nothing but a preacher, and a sorry bachelor to boot. You know that."

"Does that mean you'll refuse if the people here at the church ask you to officiate at something?"

"That's different. They're my flock."

"Hey, I'm a decent baptized Christian too, even though I go to a different church. Don't say another word. It's this Saturday—today's Tuesday, so it's four days away—seven P.M. We'll all meet at the Hosim Grill, second block down Chongno."

"Brother. Why on earth does it have to be me..."

"It would be better, kind sir, if you understood that I decided on this after considerable thought."

"Huh—that means I'm the chosen one," said Sŏng-ho.

"No ifs, ands, or buts about it. I'll even send someone to pick you up. Miss Han's family have a car."

"Hold on now. If I'm really the one you picked, then I'll be honored to do it. Forget about the car. I'll be there on time."

"Maybe this engagement'll turn out to be an engagement between Christianity and shamanism." Min-gu clamped his large lips together and grinned.

"You're just plain crazy about shamanism," Sŏng-ho said with a laugh. "I'd rather you took this opportunity to get rid of that craziness."

"I don't think that'll happen," said Min-gu. He stole a look at his wristwatch. "Well, that's it for today."

"Just a minute. I'll go with you. I've got to make a visit somewhere."

Sŏng-ho went in and changed and came out carrying a bag with his Bible and hymnal. He would be calling on a young woman named Myŏng-suk, who was laid up with an illness.

They went out the front gate, where the row houses of Stone

Village could be seen at a glance. These houses had been put up in the basin created between the original village, at the foot of the hill where they stood, and the mountain opposite. They were in neat rows and looked very tidy. Slightly to the left of the row houses a big tent had been pitched. It was the elementary school. A road stretched between the school and the row houses.

A couple of steps before them on the lane that descended the hill, a small, faint shadow moving back and forth on the ground caught their eye. First Min-gu then Sŏng-ho lifted his eyes to the sky. A couple of paces away a dragonfly was flitting to and fro. Going off to one side and turning back sharply, then to another side and turning back again, it moved swiftly and vigorously. At every sharp turn its body glittered in the sunlight.

As they passed by the tent schoolhouse a roar from the children came surging out. Min-gu stopped and his black eyes opened wide.

"What's that all about?"

It was the girls coming out onto the playground. They squatted down with a hop, and various faded skirts settled over the ground, like small parachutes.

"You'll find out soon," Sŏng-ho said as he stopped beside Min-gu.

The girls rose in ones and twos, leaving the ground blotted with water.

The boys ran to the side of the playground, whipped down their pants, and stretched out lines of water.

"No toilets?" Min-gu asked, starting up again.

"They have 'em, but it seems they can't accommodate everybody at the same time. Must be handing out rations today, judging from all these kids. Every few days they serve 'em corn gruel, and that's the only time you see a whole bunch of 'em; the other days they don't come to school."

At the junction with the main road, Sŏng-ho left Min-gu and entered Stone Village. That name had been attached to this village, some thirty *li*[4] northeast of Seoul, because there were said to be many stones in the vicinity. Its row houses had been set up for flood victims and squatters whose unauthorized houses had been condemned by the government. The buildings consisted of block walls roofed with Japanese cement tiles; each contained five units in the front and five in the rear. They were arrayed in five rows of twenty buildings each.

At first the destitute had come here to live, but soon there were changes. For the most part, the people who sold their houses and left the area were those who lacked even the money for commuting into the city to do odd jobs; those who bought and moved in were low-income working stiffs who thought that a house of their own, even in an area like this, was preferable to taking out a long-term lease in Seoul. The going price was seventy thousand *wŏn* for a one-room unit.

If one were to walk into one of the narrow alleys between the buildings, he would find their filthy appearance completely different from what looked clean and tidy from the hill.

Bending over to pass under some raglike laundry hanging from a line, Sŏng-ho discovered a young woman standing with an infant in her arms. She looked fifteen or sixteen, but she wasn't babysitting for a sister. Her breasts, which made Sŏng-ho's eyes bug out as he brushed against her in the cramped alley, were those of a mother. Sŏng-ho was startled, even though it was not a novel scene. He had heard several times from his parishioners that as soon as it gets dark the hill at the back of the church and the hill in front of Stone Village become places for illicit meetings for young couples, from early spring to late fall. Naturally these young women, who lacked the money for an abortion, were destined to give birth without the baby's father. Sŏng-ho recalled his past. He and Mrs. Hong had aborted a fetus not quite four months old. Perhaps they were inhumane to have done so. But at the time there was no

---

[4] *Li:* a unit of distance, usually computed in tens or hundreds; 10 *li* equal 3.9 kilometers, or 2.4 miles.

other way. Once again Sŏng-ho's heart ached.

Sŏng-ho first dropped by the house of Deaconess Cho, who always accompanied him when he paid a visit to one of the faithful. She wasn't home. Sŏng-ho had no choice but to go by himself.

Myŏng-suk was lying by herself in the room. Perhaps her mother had gone downtown to sell flowers, and her younger brother to the tent school.

Myŏng-suk was a Sunday school teacher. She was the daughter of middle-class parents, and until her father lost his job, fell ill, and died, she had gone to school downtown and even studied classical dance. After her father's death the family's life - stagnated, and they had eventually drifted into this row house. Now Myŏng-suk's only joy was to go to church. At odd moments at Sunday school she taught the children to dance and play the organ. This may have been why she guided more of them to church than anyone else. She had been lying in bed for several days now.

Myŏng-suk was motionless, as if she had fallen asleep. Her face looked worse than it had two days before. Her eyes, surrounded by dark shadows, had sunk more deeply, and her lips were parched and black. Even so, there was no place in particular that pained her, and not even a fever—she merely lay without eating. The illness couldn't be diagnosed even at the hospital.

Sŏng-ho sat quietly at the sick woman's side so as not to wake her. After a while Myŏng-suk suddenly sat up in her terrycloth nightgown, looked around at the walls, and began trembling all over. The trembling didn't seem about to stop, so Sŏng-ho took hold of her shoulders and made her lie down. Myŏng-suk followed obediently.

Sŏng-ho placed his hand on Myŏng-suk's and prayed. The spasmodic trembling of her cold hands gradually faded away. At the same time, sweat oozed out their backs.

Even after the prayer Myŏng-suk looked around at the walls with her cavernous eyes, struck with fear.

"Reverend, I was really scared just now. There were black snakes swarming all over the walls."

"You were dreaming."

"It wasn't a dream. I saw it clearly with my own eyes. Black snakes crawling right down toward me." Her voice was barely able to squeeze out the words.

"If it wasn't a dream then it was an illusion. Your nerves are shot; that's why. There's nothing in the least to be frightened about."

"If you hadn't come, Reverend, it would've been awful."

"From now on, if anything like that happens, imagine the cross. If you do that, everything'll go away."

The door opened and Myŏng-suk's little brother Sŏp-i[5] entered. After greeting Sŏng-ho with a bow, he placed a dented aluminum bowl in front of his sister. He had come home with the corn gruel that had been rationed out at the tent school.

"You're early today." Myŏng-suk looked at her brother and with difficulty displayed something like a smile on her parched black lips. ·

"I've gotta go again. We're gonna get some wood."

At the tent school the teachers were having the children fetch wood before winter set in.

"You little rascal—this is for *you* to eat. Why'd you bring it to me again? I still have some rice gruel left over from breakfast...Could you give me some water?"

"What's gonna happen if all you drink is water?" While saying this the boy goes out, fills a large nickel-silver bowl with water, and comes back in. Myŏng-suk takes the bowl and gulps it all down.

"Eat that too," says the boy, as if angered. Then he disappears. The sound of his running soon dies out.

"He made a point of bringing that," says Sŏng-ho. "You've got to eat it." And to encourage the sick woman he adds, "Even

---

[5]The suffix -*i* attached to a name is a diminutive, like -*ie* or -*y* in English.

though it's force-feeding, you'd better eat it and get right up. Do you realize how much the kids at the Sunday school have been waiting for you?"

Myŏng-suk reluctantly takes the spoon from the empty bowl she uses for her thin rice gruel, scoops some corn gruel from the aluminum bowl, and brings it to her lips. She frowns as if she has eaten something bitter. Unable to eat even three scoops, she puts down the spoon.

The voices of two women came from the room to the right.

—— Y' know that *pang-ul* shaman[6] livin' over there at the corner? She's a good one, said one of the women in P'yŏng-an Province dialect.

—— The shaman who moved here a few days back? asked the other woman.

—— Yeah, that's the one. I heard that a woman in a village about ten *li* back came here yesterday and asked her to do an exorcism. So she went. Every time this woman has a baby boy an evil spirit latches onto it and kills it. How about that?

—— Oh the poor thing. What's she gonna do?

So that Myŏng-suk wouldn't hear this conversation, which was so close it seemed to be in her own room, Sŏng-ho raised his voice and began to pray again. As soon as he does this, Myŏng-suk's stale, weak voice breaks in.

"R—Reverend, I can't hear the prayer." Her trembling eyes are looking up at Sŏng-ho. "Could you please try to hear what they're saying? I'm sure it's something they want me to hear. Night and day it's that kind of talk. At first I tried not to listen, but the more I tried the more scared I got."

Sŏng-ho said nothing. After a moment he gives her a nod. She might be right, he thinks.

The voice of the P'yŏng-an Province woman next door was becoming more animated. Sŏng-ho studied Myŏng-suk. She had closed her eyes, and her dark eyelids were vibrating

---

[6]*Pang-ul* shaman: a shaman who utilizes *pang-ul,* a set of seven chestnut-sized bells whose sound is thought to attract the spirits.

faintly.

The conversation next door continued. The listener seemed utterly absorbed, fitting her replies to the rhythms of the other's speech.

Myŏng-suk kept her eyes closed. Her parched black lips trembled, and the low voice that escaped from them seemed rather to be crawling into her throat.

"The cross...the cross...I can't see it."

Sŏng-ho sat beside her until she went to sleep again.

"Asking my friend to take care of the engagement ceremony is like killing two birds with one stone. You see, it's a good opportunity to introduce him to your father. It'll help him get a foot in the door at your father's church some day. He's being wasted where he is now. I'm sure your father'll like him."

"Do you think my father's the only elder in the church?"

"Doesn't he have the strongest voice on the church board?" Min-gu stirred his coffee. "I'm not asking for special consideration—moving him to a top-notch position or something. I'm just suggesting we help him along. After all, he's an outstanding clergyman. And he's a man with a mission. You know what that means?"

"A man with a mission?" Ŭn-hŭi stopped splintering the match she had picked from the matchbox on the table.

"We both majored in Korean literature at the same university, right? After that he turned down a job at a high school, and he wasn't even interested in helping out in that big business his father runs in Pusan. He just bummed around for a while and then he enrolled in divinity school. Something must have given him the urge to do it. He didn't simply become a clergyman because his father was a minister or choose divinity school for the sake of a job. That makes a big difference. It's the same with shamans. There are people who study to become shamans, people who are born into it, and people who are called by the spirits. And as a rule, it's the ones who receive the call who are most effective."

"Always talking about shamans! Are you saying ministers are the same as shamans?"

"No, it's just that you can compare them like that." As Min-gu said this one of hands went into his pocket.

"There you go again!" Ŭn-hŭi promptly said. "You're looking for cigarettes, aren't you?"

"Oops." Min-gu shook his head vigorously. "Nope."

In fact, before he was aware of it his hand has gone into his pocket in search of cigarettes, as Ŭn-hŭi had said.

"If you've got cigarettes, give 'em here!"

"Don't have any, see?" Min-gu slapped his pockets. For several days now he had not been carrying around cigarettes. He had decided to follow Ŭn-hŭi's advice that as a baptized Christian he shouldn't smoke. But out of habit his hand still moved toward his pocket.

One of the waitresses comes over and tells Min-gu there is a call for him. Min-gu, who had taken a job teaching folklore at a university downtown, had told people that this Uju Tearoom was a place outside of school where they could get in touch with him. The cashier told him the same person had called before.

It was Pyŏn, a male shaman. He was one of the people who had helped Min-gu in many ways in his research in shaman culture. He was calling today about a *ch'angbu* costume, which shamans had worn in the old days; he had come upon one of them, and wondered if Min-gu wanted to buy it. Min-gu had been collecting various shaman clothing and paraphernalia, either by photographing them in color or by buying them. Among all the shaman clothing, the *ch'angbu* costume was the most difficult to obtain. Min-gu became impatient at the thought of getting hold of one. But he asked whether he could postpone seeing it until the next day. He and Ŭn-hŭi had decided to see a movie. Min-gu sensed Pyŏn was thinking it over, and finally Pyŏn said he hoped Min-gu would come over then if he weren't too busy.

Looking troubled, Min-gu returned to his seat.

"Sorry. We'd better postpone our plans until tomorrow."

"What's this all about? Who was it?" asked Ŭn-hŭi.

Min-gu told her he had to meet Pyŏn about something.

"Oh I could die! What's the use of buying all that ghost stuff?" A frown creased Ŭn-hŭi's brow. She disliked even the sight of the shaman clothing and paraphernalia in Min-gu's apartment.

"I keep telling you if I'm going to research it thoroughly I have to bury myself in it."

"And I've told you I don't like it. If you keep on like this and end up getting completely carried away, what's gonna happen?"

"Well, maybe I won't be a male shaman. And even if I did, it could only be through study, so I probably wouldn't be very effective. Well, let's go. I'll take you as far as your house."

"If you're already taking our plans as casually as this, then I'd better think things over again."

"What are you talking about? Tomorrow I'll do anything you say, come hell or high water. As far as I'm concerned, there's nobody but you—honest." One of his eyes winked under its dark eyebrow. "How's this wink?"

Ŭn-hŭi can do nothing but laugh. "Pretty sly. But that's no wink. It's a twitch."

"A while back you said something was wrong with my eyes— they must be better now. Okay, let's get going. I'll take you home since it's on my way."

After they left the tearoom it was a good while before they were able to catch a taxi.

After passing Tonhwa-mun their taxi became hung up in traffic at a red light at the Wŏnnam-dong rotary. Min-gu looked out the window. "Isn't that Chun-t'ae's wife?" he said, leaning forward.

"Where?"

Min-gu pointed to the sidewalk on their left where a woman was trying to catch a taxi. She was wearing a cobalt-blue suit and brown high heels and carrying a brown handbag.

"You're right. But she's alone. Looks like Chun-t'ae didn't come with her," said Ŭn-hŭi.

"Is there any rule that says they have to stick together even if they came up to Seoul together?"

"Since her family's in Seoul, could be she came by herself. Who knows?"

Chun-t'ae worked at the agricultural testing station in Suwŏn, and when he came up to Seoul he would generally look up his army buddy Min-gu. So Ŭn-hŭi already knew him. Last spring Min-gu and Ŭn-hŭi had gone to Suwŏn during strawberry season and become acquainted with his wife also.

"She really has the face of a beauty, and her figure and the way she dresses are so stylish," said Ŭn-hŭi. "It's been four years since they got married, and do you think she looks like a married woman? Do you suppose that's because she hasn't had a baby? Yeah, by the way, why hasn't she had one?"

"How do I know? Maybe they're preparing a select breed."

Some time ago Min-gu had gone to see Chun-t'ae at the testing station. That day Chun-t'ae was working on a salt-resistant hybrid variety of cotton in order to obtain seeds that would thrive in soil as salty as reclaimed land. The imminent blooming of the cotton-flower bud can be easily distinguished by the rapid enlargement of its petals that takes place for two or three days. The day before it blooms, the bud is covered with a paraffin envelope after the stamen has been removed with scissors and tweezers. The next day, pollen from the stamen of another variety of cotton is applied to the head of the pistil and the bud is again covered with paraffin. Ten days later the paraffin envelope is taken off. It was this application of pollen that Chun-t'ae was busy with the day Min-gu dropped by. There was enough pollen for a great many pistils. Chun-t'ae told him that obtaining one of these hybrid varieties required at least seven or eight years of research on its particular qualities and a test of its productivity. It was because of this recollection that Min-gu had joked that perhaps Chun-t'ae and his wife were preparing a superior strain of child for the future.

"They're both cultured," Ŭn-hŭi replied, "and they're smart—I'm sure they'll have some fine children."

"Of course." Min-gu feels proud thinking about Chun-t'ae and his wife. They will be at the top of the list of his friends to be invited to the engagement ceremony.

That same day Chun-t'ae had also come to Seoul, and was toting a bundle of books in and out of second-hand bookstores on Ch'ŏnggyech'ŏn.[7] Because of some remarkably lavish expenditures by his wife, Chun-t'ae did not have enough pocket money these days. Finally he had felt compelled to sell some books. But the prices being offered him were ridiculously cheap compared with what he had paid, so he continued to look around for a better deal. He had counted on obtaining six or seven thousand *wŏn*—perhaps as much as ten thousand. But what he was being offered was less than four thousand. Some of the shops advised him to forget about books on agriculture and to deal only with such things as dictionaries and books on philosophy. There seemed no other choice but to dispose of these unwanted books at a giveaway price. So, making up his mind to sell the lot of them at once, he looks for the next shop.

Chun-t'ae was about to wrap up his books again. He couldn't remember which store it was. He had untied the cloth wrapper, and the proprietor had first offered him thirty-eight hundred *wŏn* and then four thousand. Chun-t'ae had demanded five thousand. Suddenly someone behind him said, "I'll buy them." Turning around, he discovered a woman he had seen in one of the other shops. She had been looking among the bookshelves as if she were shopping, and had then watched disinterestedly as Chun-t'ae bargained with the shopowner. Twenty-six or twenty-seven? he wondered. She was wearing a black, short-sleeved sweater and a black, narrow-pleated skirt. She counted five thousand *wŏn* from a white

[7]Ch'ŏnggyech'ŏn: a major thoroughfare in Seoul. Unlike most of the other major avenues in Seoul, whose names end in *no, lo,* or *ro* ("street"), Ch'ŏnggyech'ŏn is named in part for the stream *(ch'ŏn)* that used to flow in its place.

handbag covered with beads, gave it to Chun-t'ae, and without a word tied up the wrapping cloth and left with the bundle.

Chun-t'ae felt slightly ashamed, but not especially displeased. Perhaps this was because the woman had acted as if she had come across books she needed rather than buying them out of sympathy for him.

As Chun-t'ae is about to go out, the proprietor stops him. He demands a ten-percent commission, since the transaction took place in his store. Chun-t'ae is flabbergasted. Lacking a retort, he simply turns around, but on his way out the door the proprietor grabs him by the sleeve, and asks in a threatening tone how he could ignore commercial etiquette like that. Chun-t'ae felt like shoving the man for his outrageous behavior and escaping. But this thought annoyed him, so he took out three hundred *wŏn*, tossed it at the man, and left.

Outside Chun-t'ae surveyed the sidewalk. The woman couldn't be seen. He asked himself what he would have done if he had seen her. Would he have thanked her? But he did not consider these questions seriously.

Only after boarding the bus did he realize the woman had taken his wrapping cloth.

After dropping Ŭn-hŭi in front of her house in Tonam-dong, Min-gu took the taxi to the end of the Chŏngnŭng bus line. Pyŏn was waiting for him.

As usual, Pyŏn was wearing a neat suit. His freshly barbered hair was parted to the left and smoothed back with hair oil. In general shamans tended not to keep themselves spruced up, but this Pyŏn was unusual. Moreover, his longish, slender eyes and full lips were pretty features for a man. He said he was thirty-two, but his beard hadn't really formed. Only his pale complexion was like that of other shamans.

"I'm afraid I've kept you waiting," said Min-gu.

Pyŏn displayed the traces of a smile. The two of them set off toward Chŏngnŭng, Pyŏn leading the way.

Before long they turned left along a stream. The water that

flowed over the large rocks covering the streambed was comparatively clean for Seoul. They crossed a bridge and walked for a while through a residential area, and then Pyŏn stopped in front of a house on the right. Adorned with white tile, the house was not large but looked cozy. Min-gu had assumed this was the house of the person wanting to sell the *ch'angbu* costume, but the nameplate was Pyŏn's. Although he knew Pyŏn's house was in Chŏngnŭng, he had never seen it.

Upon entering the yard, Min-gu noticed that sunflowers were planted along the wall around the house. The stems were thick and the flowers luxuriant, as if the plants had been fertilized and well cultivated. They brightened the whole yard.

Inside, Min-gu felt again that everything was bursting into sight before him. Curtains the color of sunflowers had been drawn over the walls of the room. Min-gu recalled what Pyŏn had told him. When he was twenty-one he had had a long illness during which he dreamed that the sun had surged over him and then changed into a sunflower whose seeds were implanted throughout his chest. After being called by the spirits to be a shaman he would use sunflower seeds as aids in telling people's fortunes, and although his prices were twice those of other shamans, people were drawn to him because his prognostications were accurate. Even so, he accepted clients only from daybreak until noon.

"Is this where you tell fortunes?"

Pyŏn gave a slight nod along with a smile that displayed the bluish tinge of his upper gum.

"You still haven't found someone who does the Hamgyŏng *ogu kut*?"[8] said Pyŏn in his usual calm voice.

"I sure haven't. I've been waiting for you to introduce me to one."

"I've found one."

"Really? Where does she live?" Min-gu asked enthusiastically.

[8]*Kut:* a ritual ceremony addressed to the spirits by one or more shamans. In the *ogu kut* shamans console the soul of a dead person and pray for its safe passage to the afterlife.

"In Oryu-dong. But she's been sick in bed for quite some time. She's an old woman, over seventy. If she gets a little better I'll let you know."

"That old, huh? I hope she won't pass away."

Min-gu, who had been recording the *ogu kut* of southern Korea, had not yet been able to record the distinctive ceremony of Hamgyŏng Province.

Pyŏn took a pack of cigarettes from his pocket and placed it before Min-gu. This was something he did for his guests, though he himself didn't smoke. The promise Min-gu had made to Ŭn-hŭi weighed heavily on him, but he took one of the cigarettes. Pyŏn gave him a light.

"Are you planning to have the owner of the *ch'angbu* costume come over?"

Pyŏn didn't answer immediately. Then, "Wait a minute, if you would."

Min-gu had smoked half the cigarette when Pyŏn's young maid brought in a tray containing a bottle of whiskey, two glasses with ice, and a dish of peanuts and jerky. The bottle—Johnny Walker Black Label—had yet to be opened.

Min-gu felt guilty. There was no reason for him to receive such hospitality, for Pyŏn had already gone to great lengths on his behalf. But when Min-gu said he did not feel quite right about receiving this kind of treatment, Pyŏn asked him not to worry—the liquor was merely a substitute for tea. Unscrewing the cap, he poured some whiskey in the glass in front of Min-gu and then a little in his own glass.

Min-gu had met Pyŏn over tea in a tearoom, but had never drunk with him before.

Pyŏn was one of those who are easily affected by liquor. His eyelids had reddened before he finished even the small amount in his glass, and before long his pale cheeks had turned pink. Pyŏn felt his cheeks with his palms. To Min-gu they looked hot.

"Please forgive me. I can't hold my liquor very well." Excusing himself, he got up and forged his way through the curtains into the next room. The curtains returned to their original position, swinging slightly. The sunflowers were various shades of bright and dark. Observing the curtains carefully, Min-gu found that even after they stopped swinging they did not become one color. Instead, they changed into various colors because of the sunlight shining through the glass window of the main door.

Perhaps five minutes had passed when the curtains rustled and were pulled apart. Min-gu was startled. It was Pyŏn, wearing the *ch'angbu* costume over traditional women's clothing and quilted socks. The sleeves of the costume were of multicolored silk, and the rest of it, which extended to just above the knee, was of green silk and separated front and rear and at the sides so as to make four pleats. There was a yellowish tinge to all of it, making it appear a very old piece of clothing.

Thrusting out his chest in a show of dignity, Pyŏn takes a step to the side, then a step back, all the while spreading and closing a fan with a flourish. He intones a shamanistic chant and, exclaiming *Ŏlsshiguna!* begins to dance.

Women generally look charming when they dress up as men, but there is usually something repulsive about men in women's clothing. This was not the case with Pyŏn, however. The clothing suited him perfectly. His dancing was smooth and soft, and his body and clothing became one slowly swaying whole.

The swaying dance changed into a dance of sudden, nimble leaps. At first they were about a foot high, then half again as high. So lightly did Pyŏn jump and land that one could not be sure whether his feet in their white quilted socks had touched the floor before he again leaped up lightly—his was not at all like a human form. The four pleats of the *ch'angbu* costume resembled the fluttering wings of a large butterfly.

As Pyŏn leaped higher and higher, his eyes gleamed as if he was possessed and the reddish alcoholic tinge in his face was replaced with white. Suddenly his leaps stopped, and, turning one revolution to the left, as shamans do when they finish a dance, he threw himself in Min-gu's lap and moaned that he needed a man.

Min-gu doubted his ears, overwhelmed by this unexpected action. And even though Pyŏn's voice was somewhat gentle for a man, in this instance Min-gu heard a voice just like a woman's.

Pyŏn said again, imploring Min-gu, that he truly needed a man—he couldn't stand it—and rubbed his chest against Min-gu's lap.

Min-gu had no idea what to say or do.

The children on the playground of the tent school go their separate ways, foregoing their usual playing as if the gathering of winter firewood has been too much for them. Sŏp-i too sets off for home, together with P'yŏng-i. The back of Sŏp-i's neck itches and prickles and he scratches it, projecting his fingernails like claws. He has caught an itch from a pine caterpillar while going up and down a pine tree to collect dead branches.

Sŏp-i notices somebody running up behind him, and there is a slap on his shoulder from the sixth grader Kŏl-i.

"Gonna watch television tonight? Count me in, huh?"

Sŏp-i shakes his head.

"How come?"

"I can't. My sister's sick."

When she was healthy his sister would help their mother by selling flowers out of a basket. Now and then she would slip Sŏp-i a ten-*wŏn* coin that would pay for Kŏl-i and him to watch television.

"Can't you sneak something out?"

Unit 609, in the middle of the row houses, was a comic-book shop by day and a place to watch television at night. The entrance fee was five *wŏn*, but an aluminum bowl or a pair of tongs for handling charcoal briquettes were also accepted.

"Batman's on tonight, ya know."

Gee, that's right, thinks Sŏp-i. He wonders what he can bring out of the house. P'yŏng-i, following along next to him,

says "If you get caught stealin' somethin' you'll get a scoldin'.'"
"Get lost, asshole." Kŏl-i gives P'yŏng-i a rap on the head
with his fist, then says to Sŏp-i, "How come this little runt's
always hangin' around you? He makes me wanna puke." No
one knew why P'yŏng-i tagged along with Sŏp-i. Their homes
were not near, nor did their parents know each other. It was
just that P'yŏng-i followed Sŏp-i whenever he saw him. And
today, when they went to gather wood, he had picked up the
dead branches that Sŏp-i had cut and sent down. Sŏp-i didn't
dislike P'yŏng-i, but upon hearing Kŏl-i, he told himself it
wouldn't do for him, a fourth grader, to be playing with a first
grader, and he picked up his pace.

Kŏl-i shouted from behind, "I'll swing by your place a little
later. Got it? Huh?"

Unable to catch up with Sŏp-i, P'yŏng-i heads straight for the
neighborhood's public toilet and goes in. Taking a pencil out
of his shabby cloth schoolbag, he begins drawing pictures on
the wall, as he has done before. Actually, he is thickening lines
that have already been drawn. The pictures resemble an arm
with a tightly clenched fist and an open bearded mouth that
seems about to swallow the fist. Again and again P'yŏng-i re-
draws the lines.

Not until the tip of the pencil becomes so blunt that he can't
draw does P'yŏng-i leave. A cat crouching at a corner of the
building and taking in the receding sun catches his eye. It is an
old black stray with white dots.

P'yŏng-i puts down his schoolbag and tiptoes toward the cat.
The cat remains where it is, hunching its back. P'yŏng-i, ready
to catch it, sticks out a hand. The cat lifts up a paw as if to cuff
him. P'yŏng-i starts. "Heyyy." In an instant he grabs the cat
around the waist. With a yowl the cat fixes P'yŏng-i with its
yellow eyes. P'yŏng-i did not want to just let it go. He goes
back in and throws the cat toward one of the holes. But
P'yŏng-i's arms aren't strong, and the cat, having guessed his
intent, doesn't fall in but clings to P'yŏng-i and then jumps

down nimbly and escapes. P'yŏng-i's wrist shows traces of the cat's claws. Speckles of blood form. Though his face is about to break apart in tears, P'yŏng-i endures and remains dry-eyed.

"I tell ya, I'd get more satisfaction out of a spoon o' cold rice than this here butt," complains Chŏnju Auntie, Kŏl-i's mother. Having scooped the evening rice out of a pot, she has stepped out of the kitchen and taken a cigarette butt from the waistband of her *ch'ima*.[9]

The woman next door catches this and responds with a laugh, "Whadja do with that one—stop in mid taste?"

"If my old man hadn't o' died, I'da never picked up this damn' habit in the first place." Chŏnju Auntie exhales with a whoosh.

"Ya cured your sore heart with cigarettes!"

"Ahh, nothin' better for an achin' heart. Once I got the taste of it, why, first thing that comes to mind when I wake up is a cigarette—yup. To tell the truth, worryin' about bein' outa cigarettes comes before worryin' about bein' outa rice."

"The Tobacco Monopoly Office is gonna give you a prize."

Kŏl-i returns.

Bringing out the bowls of rice, Chŏnju Auntie sits across from Kŏl-i. While working her spoon she says, "Is it too damn' much trouble to stuff a few spoonfuls o' rice into that yap o' yours?" Kŏl-i has dropped some grains of rice.

Kŏl-i is absorbed in wondering whether Sŏp-i will come over with some item that will get them into the comic-book shop. Although he suggested that they go watch "Batman," he is more interested in the adult shows and soap operas that appear after this cartoon program for children.

But that day some unexpected luck came Kŏl-i's way. Around the time they are finishing dinner Old Pak comes in.

---

[9]*Ch'ima:* a traditional Korean skirt with a high, pleated waist tied by a strip of cloth. The word can also be used for other types of skirts, but Chŏnju Auntie wears the traditional variety.

A carpenter who works downtown, Pak comes every Saturday and spends the night. But this week he is four days early. At Pak's appearance a smile fills Chŏnju Auntie's face, but for Kŏl-i too this is a fortuitous event.

Pak gives Kŏl-i forty *wŏn* to buy a *toe* of *makkŏlli* [10] as usual, but this time ten instead of five *wŏn* for watching television. Kŏl-i runs to a tavern carrying a one-*toe* bottle with *makkŏlli* sediment on the bottom. But rather than a *toe* he buys only thirty-five *wŏn* worth. After leaving the tavern Kŏl-i walks with measured steps, all the while glancing furtively about. He reaches the town water-pump and, looking about even more carefully, works the pump and makes up the difference. Then with a corner of his shirt he wipes off the moisture on the bottle. Kŏl-i is excited. Tonight he can go watch television without owing anything to Sŏp-i.

Sŏp-i has been fidgeting. He can't ask for the television fee from his bedridden sister, nor can he sneak out with something. Although he leaves his book open and reads the same lines several times, they don't register at all.

Batman, with his skeleton face and the black cape from shoulder to foot. All he has to do is open his arms, and the cape becomes bat wings. Batman, flying like a jet. Sŏp-i wonders if he'll have another thrilling adventure tonight and rescue the good guys.

Thinking that the show has probably started, Sŏp-i becomes more anxious. For a while he studies his mother, asleep from fatigue next to his sister, and then he creeps toward her feet, lifts the mattress, and takes ten *wŏn* out of her purse. It is the first time he has done this, and his heart throbs. But he can't help obtaining a queer pleasure from the ten-*wŏn* coin tucked in his pocket.

[10]*Makkŏlli:* a milky, weak rice wine. A *toe* is a unit of liquid and dry measure equaling 1.8 liters, or 3.8 pints.

Chapter 2

Sŏng-ho cuts some wild chrysanthemums, eulalia, and other wildflowers blooming in a grassy area midway up a hill in the public cemetery. *Ch'usŏk*[1] was about ten days away, but Sŏng-ho could occasionally see people who had come ahead of time to do some weeding. Here and there funerals were in progress. As Sŏng-ho comes round the spur of the hill toward Mrs. Hong's grave, he wonders if Tae-shik might come. Tae-shik was a three-year-old when Sŏng-ho first saw him. At that time Sŏng-ho was a high school student, not yet twenty. Mrs. Hong, the wife of the minister at the church he attended, was thirty-one. During his refugee life in Pusan Sŏng-ho had gone diving off a wharf in the middle of the night for tinned goods that had fallen overboard from the Yankee ships, and had brought them to this family. Tae-shik had jumped up and down in excitement. When Tae-shik was a little older and had completely forgotten the face of his father, Pastor Chŏng,[2] who had disappeared during the war, he had sometimes pestered his mother to call Sŏng-ho daddy. But Sŏng-ho was never more than someone who had long tried wholeheartedly to assist Tae-shik and Mrs. Hong—until an unexpected incident took place. From the viewpoint of others, a motive for suicide can be so incredible as to be ridiculous. Here it was only the sight of Mrs. Hong and a friend of her husband riding by together in

---

[1]*Ch'usŏk:* A major Korean holiday, occurring on the full-moon day of the eighth month of the lunar calendar, during which many people return to their hometowns and, together with relatives, conduct ceremonies at the graves of their ancestors.
[2]Tae-shik is the son of Pastor Chŏng and Mrs. Hong. Korean women retain their maiden name after marriage.

an automobile in broad daylight. After waiting until eleven at night for Mrs. Hong to return, Sŏng-ho went out and bought some sleeping pills. Until that night he had never slept at her house. People's capacity for speculation is limitless. Even though she has a bad heart she's running around with a man until all hours, Sŏng-ho had thought. He took the sleeping pills just as the midnight curfew siren was sounding. He woke up in the hospital. Mrs. Hong and her husband's friend had been delayed by the breakdown of their car while looking for a certain person in the outskirts of the city. Someone had said that this person might know the whereabouts of Pastor Chŏng. After that, the relationship between Sŏng-ho and Mrs. Hong changed. Keeping their weather eye open toward those around them, they eventually had to dispose of a four-month-old fetus. They never talked about the bloody lump, as if they had pledged not to. But amid this silence, Sŏng-ho came to feel guilty about the discarded fetus and the growing Tae-shik. This was Sŏng-ho's primary motive for entering divinity school.

There was no one at Mrs. Hong's tomb. Because Tae-shik had gone in the army, he couldn't have come even if he had wanted, without a special pass.

Sŏng-ho placed the cut flowers in front of the grave. Today is your birthday. So today we're having another outing.

He touched the small tombstone. It was warm in the sunlight. But that was all the warmth there was, and soon the coldness in the stone penetrated his palm. Sŏng-ho withdrew his hand and sat next to the grave. In the distance, away from the field below the steep hill on which he sat, the upstream curves of the Han River shone white, and far beyond it the ridge of Namhan Mountain was tinged with violet. This was the scene he looked upon whenever he paid his monthly visit to this place where Mrs. Hong had been buried in the spring. Suddenly he heard a voice from the bottom of the hill. "Don't let that cow go in the field!" There was no sight of the person or animal—only the voice distinct in the clear air.

You didn't like it bright like this, did you? thought Sŏng-ho.

Mrs. Hong had had chronic heart disease. Following the abortion she suffered a relapse, and after a spell in the hospital she went to the sanitarium at Sosa to recuperate. But the illness grew worse, and after two years in the sanitarium she returned to Seoul for a long stay in the hospital. The doctors gave up on her, and during the three months between her discharge and her death she disliked any kind of light. She drew a thick curtain across every door through which light might slip, and would sit beneath a black umbrella. At night she turned on dim lights, but even in this gloom she could easily read small handwriting. Her hearing, smell, and taste were equally sensitive. People had to be very careful in opening and closing the door. If in handling the dishes in the kitchen the maid made a slight noise it would alarm her. Spicy food was unacceptable, and if a little more salt was added to a dish she would notice it, though others could not. From the smell of Sŏng-ho's clothes when he entered the room she would correctly guess when the weather was going to be foul. Occasionally she would tell Sŏng-ho that he had been sitting next to a smoker on the bus.

When she breathed her last, Sŏng-ho was next to her. Having also become accustomed to the darkness, he was able to detect her glance when she looked up at him. For a long time they looked at each other. Sŏng-ho thought he had better call the doctor. Immediately sensing this, she had stopped him with her eyes. The eyes were saying something: We're going to be forgiven, we're going to be forgiven. At last her eyes came to rest. Sŏng-ho closed them. He did not cry. Over and over he said "We're going to be forgiven." It was not his voice alone but their voices combined. Not knowing, the maid came in with dinner. It had not seemed long, but an hour had passed since her death. Sŏng-ho got up and went to the post office. There he telegramed Tae-shik, who had entered the army. After leaving the post office he let his feet take him down a darkening street. Only then did his tears flow freely. His grief was mixed with gratitude that their relationship was unknown to the world, and with relief at being delivered from worldly surveillance.

We're going to be forgiven. Sŏng-ho repeated this toward the grave, as if meditating. When you met your fate you left behind this unspoken conversation—we're going to be forgiven. But in fact, through your long-lasting anguish and the bitter suffering you saddled yourself with at Sosa, you had already brought about forgiveness, not just for you but also for me. Today is your birthday. Let's imagine we're on an outing, looking out at the river and the mountain ridge beyond.

Again the voice from below: "Where's the owner of that cow!" Again neither man nor animal appeared—there was only the voice, plainly audible. Even a sound like that we can relax and listen to, thought Sŏng-ho.

A man, the legs of his workpants rolled up, came walking along the crest of a rise near Sŏng-ho. He was carrying a sickle, and asked if he ought to tidy up the grave. Great, thought Sŏng-ho. He decided to have it done.

The man trims and weeds the grass on the grave. The smell of the grass floated all around. Let's take in this smell too, for all it's worth.

Min-gu has finished his class and come to his office. As soon as he sits down he has the urge to smoke. But he endures, realizing he is not carrying around cigarettes. Leaning his head against the back of the chair, he looks out the window.

The sky was higher and much bluer, and the transparent air had become invigorating. The evergreens and the deciduous trees, their leaves as yet undyed by the colors of autumn, were a fresh green.

Here and there students were sitting on benches under the trees and chatting, or reading books, or going around campus in groups. The women students were especially conspicuous, and their clothing attracted Min-gu's attention. The various colors—crimson, yellow, orange, violet—seemed to be outrunning their season. Min-gu was unconsciously dressing the male students in this clothing, something he had done repeatedly upon meeting men and women on the street after the incident at Pyŏn's the day before.

When Pyŏn, wearing the *ch'angbu* costume atop women's clothing, had finished dancing and thrown himself in Min-gu's lap, appealing to him that he needed a man, Min-gu could only feel embarrassed. Leaning his chest on Min-gu's knees, Pyŏn kept his eyes softly closed, as if expecting something. His breathing was uneven, and his pale face had again turned crimson. Min-gu ignored him, and finally Pyŏn stood up gently and disappeared into the next room. Realizing this was his chance, Min-gu rose. While he was putting on his shoes Pyŏn reappeared in the traditional women's clothing and hastened to give him the *ch'angbu* costume roughly wrapped in paper. When Min-gu asked about the price, Pyŏn shook his head. Min-gu studied his face. It showed no anger. Some of the crimson color remained. Min-gu recalled a male shaman in Map'o whom Pyŏn had directed him to and who said he sometimes became a woman.

The day Min-gu went to Map'o to visit him, this shaman was performing an exorcism. A rooster, tied so it couldn't move, had been put atop a small table. The shaman placed a piece of paper with the birthday and name of the patient under the left wing and a piece of paper with four Chinese characters meaning "transfer this disease to another" under the other wing. Then a woman in her forties—the wife of the sick man—fed the rooster with rice she had brought. The rice grains, the number of which equaled the patient's age, had previously been placed in his mouth and coated with saliva. After opening the bird's beak and feeding it this rice, the shaman sat in front of the table and, while shaking a bell, murmured something for a time. He then recited an incantation: "General, please remove the evil spirit that has entered the body of so-and-so born in such-and-such a place on such-and-such a date, and look after him." While reciting the spell he blinked unceasingly. Min-gu guessed that shamans did this in order to concentrate. As soon as he had finished the spell the shaman grabbed the rooster with both hands, swung it around in the air several times, and gave it to the woman, ordering her to take it to some mountain to the east and bury it.

After the woman left, Min-gu asked the shaman, "If someone digs the rooster up and eats it, what will happen?"

"If someone wants to dig it up and eat it, that's fine. But it's full of disease, and that'll be passed on."

Min-gu asked if that was really so, and the shaman replied instantly that there was no question about it. In this way, shamanism tries to solve everything not by itself but by reliance on something else.

Min-gu then asked a taboo question: "When you exorcise an illness, what's the cure rate, roughly?"

"Unless they need an operation I can cure them all." Min-gu hadn't expected this clear-cut assertion. The shaman added, "But there are some exorcists who kill people because they don't know they need an appendectomy or some other operation. Because of that bunch our prestige is slipping."

Min-gu quickly proceeded to the main issue: "When did the spirit enter you?" He had visited the shaman that day in order to learn about this process.

"When I was seventeen I had this chronic disease." One of the common ways in which a spirit enters shamans is through an illness that cannot be diagnosed. Could this chronic illness be a trial that is sustained for the sake of receiving the spirit? Min-gu wondered.

"You couldn't stand the taste of food. All you could take in was water, right?"

"Hey, you know all about this. I can remember how many kettles of water I had every day."

One day while he was lying down, there was whispering in his ear. Someone was telling him to go outside wearing white clothing. But no sooner did he do as he was told than insects crawled into his clothing, rats massed around, and dogs ran up to him. All tore into him and finally, out of the blue, dung and urine were showered down on him. There was nothing for him to do but remove his clothes and soak them. But nowhere was there a stain. Of course there could not really have been all those insects, rats, and dogs around his house. But several times thereafter this calamity was repeated: whenever he lay down someone would whisper in his ear to go outside wearing white clothes. The people in the neighborhood, guessing that he was about to be possessed, but that an evil spirit was interfering, told him to undergo a *naerim kut*.[3] Unable to bear up any longer, he assented. At the climax of the ceremony a white horse galloped over to him, its mouth gaping, and gulped him down. It was completely dark, and the horse's intestines made his whole body feel sticky. But strangely enough, he was neither suffocating nor displeased. At that time, what did he see above him but a general, wearing a helmet and suit of armor and carrying a great sword, climbing high on the back of the horse. He then jumped up and ran out shouting "I'm a general!"

"Who was the general whose spirit you received?"

"General Ch'oe Yŏng."[4]

"So it was that very spirit of General Ch'oe Yŏng that enabled you to tell fortunes?"

"Not only that..."

"Not only that?" Min-gu wished to leave no gaps in this account. Noticing the shaman was hesitating as if he had started to say something unnecessary, Min-gu made it plain that his object in visiting was purely a matter of scholarly investigation.

Sometimes the general visited him in the middle of the night, he said. Min-gu had guessed as much. It was the very same general, wearing helmet and armor and carrying a great

[3] *Naerim kut:* a *kut* in which possessing spirits are invited to descend into a shaman candidate.
[4] Ch'oe Yŏng: Koryŏ dynasty general, killed in the rebellion that led to the foundation (in 1392) of the Chosŏn (Yi) dynasty.

sword, that he had seen when the spirit entered him. Then the shaman would become a woman. Wearing a green *chŏgori* [5] with a scarlet twelve-*p'ok ch'ima*,[6] he felt he was an incomparably pretty young woman. The shaman said that on such occasions he would welcome the general with a large table of various foods he had prepared, and then they would sleep together.

Looking anew at his pockmarked face, flat nose, and protruding lips, Min-gu thought the shaman must have been riddled with feelings of inferiority.

"Did your body also become that of a woman?"

"Sure. My chest and everything else."

He then said, half in complaint, that in the beginning the general would visit him once or twice a month—three or four times if the visits were frequent. But for the past several years it was once every three or four months, or in some cases no more than once every six months.

Min-gu asked the shaman how old he was.

"Thirty-nine."

"Do you have children?"

"One son and three daughters."

"And even now do you act the same way when the general visits?" Min-gu had been wondering about this.

For a moment the shaman had a faraway look in his eyes.

"There's no difference at all. I'm just like a young woman wearing a green *chŏgori* and a bright red twelve-*p'ok ch'ima*. We sleep together, and after that I have a lucky streak. People line up to have their fortunes read."

Min-gu compares this shaman and Pyŏn. Isn't it that Pyŏn, like the Map'o shaman, maintains a gloomy inferiority complex and because of that is possessed by the sun god, the opposite

---

[5]*Chŏgori:* a traditional Korean jacket, with baggy sleeves, a V neck, and a white collar, worn by men and women.

[6]*P'ok:* an inexact measure of length; a twelve-*p'ok ch'ima* is a *ch'ima* of unsurpassed width.

of darkness, and wants to become a woman? What could this inferiority complex be, really? Min-gu also wondered whether he had shamed Pyŏn. I'll have to see him before long. Since he didn't take any money for the *ch'angbu* costume I'd better make it up to him with something else.

Min-gu gets up and leaves his office. As he is emerging from the campus he overhears two students behind him talking about something that occupies almost everyone's mind these days—the miner trapped in a shaft 125 meters underground at Kubong Mine.

"Think they'll get him out today?"

"He's been trapped more than fifteen days, hasn't he?"

"Sixteen. Have to give the guy credit—he's a fighter."

This miner, Yang Ch'ang-sŏn, had fought cold and hunger with superhuman strength. Unable to stand his hunger and thirst, he had sucked at rice straw, the bark of the rough timbers, and, worst of all, the rubber packing in the pipes and the starch in his clothing. He had drunk from a water tank to which arsenic had been added. He had endured the cold by hugging a hundred-watt light bulb to his chest.

"As long as he's down there he ought to pull himself along for another five days, and then it'll be a new record—twenty days. Whaddya think?"

"Hey asshole, you think you got a license to talk bullshit just because you're not down there in his shoes? If he was like you, he would've kissed the world goodbye a long time ago."

Their voices were tinged with a delight that could not be hidden. To Min-gu even the second student's remark about a new record of twenty days came from their desire to take pride in human endurance and strength.

Min-gu's joyful expectation upon reading about the miner in the morning paper comes back. Today is a lucky day, he thinks. I'd better enjoy it while I can.

In this happy mood he saw a movie and had dinner with Ŭn-hŭi and then returned to his apartment, where at nine-thirty he heard a news bulletin that the miner had been rescued. The great excitement of the radio announcer, who called the rescue a paean to the triumph of humanity over death, was not particularly exaggerated, he felt.

Min-gu took a cigarette from the drawer of the table and lit it. Now that he thinks about it, he too is excited. The strength of humanity—bravo! He inhales deeply on the cigarette. He breathes out. Again he inhales deeply. He notices the photograph on the table. He blows smoke toward it. As the shroud of smoke spreads, a subtle smile forms on the lips of the woman directly before him. It is the expression of one who is aware of how beautiful she is and who is confident in everything. I'm smoking, Ŭn-hŭi—sorry about that. Min-gu again exhales in her direction.

The gate rattles, and Chun-t'ae hears their elderly maid undoing the bolt. The door of the room opens and his wife, Ch'ang-ae, steps in.

"Sir, do you know who I met in Seoul today?"

Ch'ang-ae had stayed out the previous night and was late this evening. Chun-t'ae could see she was intoxicated. He maintained the upright posture in which he had been writing out the manuscript of a translation. He took on this work now and then when it was available, in order to have pocket money.

"Sir, no matter how busy you are, please listen to what I have to say."

There were more "Sirs" than you could shake a stick at. As before marriage, this was how she addressed Chun-t'ae when she was in a good mood.

"Sir, I met Su-jŏng, Su-jŏng." This was the high school friend of Ch'ang-ae's who used to drop in at Chun-t'ae's boardinghouse with her. "She came to Seoul for a visit. She said she's still living in Mokp'o and she has three kids—can you believe it? She's so happy, she said. Sir, how does that make you feel? Su-jŏng liked you, and she looks happy—don't you have any reaction to that?"

"You must be tired. How about getting some sleep?"

"Okay. I'll go to bed. I guess it's a bother to have someone next to you while you're working, isn't it? Just one more thing. I may be starting a business with someone." She nimbly undresses and, sitting across from the bureau, removes her makeup. After brushing her hair she spreads out the sleeping pad and lies down, saying, "Don't wake me up later on." Then she turns the other way.

'Wake me up'? Who's going to wake you up? Chun-t'ae thinks. It had been over three months since they had stopped having relations. She had been commuting to Seoul, saying she ought to find some work, and that night too she had returned late. She showed no reaction as she lay beneath Chun-t'ae, winding her arms around his neck as if it were a formality. Her eyes, unmoving, had opened toward the darkness. Sweeping his hand over her chest had given her pleasure in the past, but this time she kept staring into the dark, displaying no emotion. Caressing her chest more firmly made no difference. Suddenly Chun-t'ae understood. In a flash, sentiment and passion disappeared from his body. He removed himself from his wife. For a while she remained as she was, not saying anything, and then he heard her turn away. He heard what seemed to be a sob, and then she fell silent again. After that Chun-t'ae made no more demands on his wife.

Chun-t'ae heard her snoring, as she usually did after returning from a night out. This had been the pattern for a while now.

Thinking that he too had better get some sleep, Chun-t'ae turned out the light and, taking care not to wake her, quickly went to bed.

Around noon two days later Ch'ang-ae rushed back to Seoul. Her mother had been injured in an automobile accident.

Chapter 3

Chun-t'ae had come to Seoul to attend Min-gu's engagement ceremony, but first he visited his in-laws in Ch'ŏngjin-dong. He did not often do this, but having learned of his mother-in-law's injury, he felt compelled to go.

His mother-in-law was flat on her back, unable to move. When Chun-t'ae asked how she felt, her face twisted and she cried out "*ayu, ayu*" again and again. Old people sometimes make a hue and cry over nothing, but agony was inscribed on his mother-in-law's round, fleshy face.

"It's fortunate it wasn't worse than this," said Chun-t'ae.

"It could have been really terrible," said Ch'ang-ae's sister-in-law. "They said that if the injury had been any more serious, they'd have had to operate." She explains the injury. The X rays show a crack in her right hipbone. There is no point in hospitalizing her, and the injury isn't severe enough to require a cast, so the only possible prescription was for her to lie down for a month or so. "She can't stretch her right leg," she says to Chun-t'ae.

Chun-t'ae noticed the quilt was turned up slightly, as if his mother-in-law's right knee was flexed.

"How can I stay like this, day in and day out, for a month? I'm hurting all over. Ohhh, it's my fate."

While she is saying this the quilt moves. She immediately grimaces and cries "*ŏgu, ŏgu*." It seemed to Chun-t'ae that her leg was trying to bend by itself.

Ch'ang-ae's sister-in-law quickly stuck her hands under the quilt and massaged the woman's legs. "You can turn over on your left side after about five days—try to be patient until then."

"I might as well be dead, having to put the family to such trouble."

Ch'ang-ae's sister-in-law, if not the other family members, must surely have gone to great pains, Chun-t'ae thought. Since the older woman couldn't turn on her side, she was forced not only to spoon-feed her but to remove her urine and feces as well.

The sliding door is whisked open and Chun-t'ae's six-year-old nephew appears. As soon as he walks in, he swiftly takes an apple out of the fruit basket Chun-t'ae has brought.

"You! Hadn't you better put that back?" his mother scolds him. "And aren't you going to say hello to your uncle? A little later we'll peel one for grandmother, and then you can have some."

"Let him eat it," Chun-t'ae's mother-in-law says. Then she turns her head and looks at Chun-t'ae. "You'd better go. The boy's aunt[1] came yesterday, but I told her to go back down right away. The leg's not going to get better just because she's here." And after a pause she murmured, as if to herself, "I wish you two would hurry up and have some kids."

Chun-t'ae remains silent. The previous night Ch'ang-ae hadn't returned to Suwŏn. And while going into his mother-in-law's room he had seen that she wasn't there. Looks like my hunch is on the mark, he thought. She might have gone out for a while, since the injury was not severe enough to require her constant attendance, but Chun-t'ae's intuition told him she had not spent the night there. Chun-t'ae betrays no emotion to his mother-in-law, who seems ignorant of Ch'ang-ae's activities, and instead changes the subject.

"How's my big brother's business these days?" Ch'ang-ae's father had passed away and her only brother managed a small variety shop in one of the market areas.

---

[1] The boy's aunt: a reference to Ch'ang-ae. In Korean society adults are often referred to not by their given name but by their relationship to some child.

His mother-in-law remained silent for a while, pretending she hadn't heard. Then she asked "Have you been able to raise some money? Seems like the boy's aunt has found a place to spend it in a hurry. Now you tell me where the money is in this family. The two of you must be in a sorry state if you have to ask me for what you need. It's even more frustrating for me when I can't give it."

This is something Chun-t'ae knows nothing about. But it is not surprising that Ch'ang-ae asked her mother for some money. She is very much a spendthrift, but her expenditures have become even more extravagant now that she is going to Seoul more frequently. At first Chun-t'ae had tried to pay attention to what she was doing. But soon he wasn't interfering at all. He now believed that a husband and wife should not try to control each other. Chun-t'ae knows that his own parents were like this. His father's neglect of the family had caused its breakup, and his mother had had no way to prevent it. He was young at the time, and found out about this only later. Nevertheless, Chun-t'ae didn't think that he could prevent his wife's indulgences. As long as we're a couple, let's just live together as long as we can, he thought. He considered it fortunate that, contrary to his mother-in-law's wishes, they had not had children.

Chun-t'ae left soon after. He had planned to ask Ch'ang-ae to go with him to Min-gu's engagement ceremony, but her absence at her mother's had made this impossible.

It was Saturday afternoon, and the streets were packed. One walked bumping shoulders with others. Chun-t'ae didn't meet one face he knew among the throng. But coincidences do happen, he thought. It's a one-in-a-million chance, but what if I ran into my wife? On top of that, what if she were walking arm in arm with some man? Fine, no problem. I'd rather see her like that, face to face. Then I'd have an opportunity to wind things up with her. But soon he was feeling wretched hoping for such an expedient.

A middle-aged man with a hunting rifle over his shoulder

comes toward Chun-t'ae. He wears a hunting outfit from head to foot—hat, clothing, leather boots. As he passed, the stock of the rifle bumped Chun-t'ae's shoulder. In his mind he takes aim at the gunstock. He pulls the trigger. Missed. Once more he pulls the trigger. Missed. I was the number one shot when I was in the army, he thinks, and pulls the trigger again. Missed. This time he doesn't aim. Even so, he misses. No matter how well he pulls the trigger, the target is not distinct.

Passersby look at Chun-t'ae out of the corner of their eye. Not until then does he realize he is smiling. He looks up. The sky has been demarcated into pieces of blue by the buildings.

Chun-t'ae crosses Chongno, goes south to Ch'ŏnggyech'ŏn, and turns east. Auto-supply stores and shops dealing in electrical equipment came into view. Chun-t'ae goes into one of the electrical-equipment shops. Kŭn-yŏng was there. He is a middle school classmate whom Chun-t'ae occasionally drops in on when he comes up to Seoul.

Kŭn-yŏng greets him with a smile. "What's up with you today? Familiar faces are showing up one after another."

Chun-t'ae parks himself in a chair. "Noggin frozen already? Is that why you're wearing the arctic cap?"

The shopboy turns away, stifling a laugh.

Kŭn-yŏng is wearing a winter cap made of yarn. Though thirty-six, he is bald as a billiard ball.

"I got drunk the night before last and bumped it on the edge of a wall," Kŭn-yŏng replies indifferently.

"Now you won't have so much of your face to wash. That'll be convenient."

"Oh cut it out. The injury's no big deal. I'm doing this to protect my precious head. Wanna hear how precious it is?" A few days ago, he explains, he was awakened by thirst in the middle of the night and drank some of the water he kept beside the bed. He tried to go back to sleep, but his head felt cooler than usual. Something was wrong. He looked toward the door, which he knew he had locked. Sure enough, it had been opened. With a yell he drove the thief away.

"So this skull o' mine is more valuable than a head of gold. Whaddya think?"

"How about calling it the diamond head instead—since it's so brilliant."

Again the shopboy suppresses a laugh. He goes to the other side of the shop and pretends to arrange the goods.

Kŭn-yŏng is unperturbed. "Yeah, I guess we could do that," he readily retorts. "A little while ago P'il-jae dropped by. Hadn't seen him in a long time. No kidding."

"Aha, old Dogmeat?"

"Yeah."

As his nickname suggested, this friend would routinely act in unusual ways. Once during physical-education class they were playing soccer and everyone thought he would make a back pass, but instead he shot toward his own goal. Then one day he was dozing in class and the teacher said to him, "Tell me what I just said." He sprang to his feet, stood completely still, and rattled off "You said 'Tell me what I just said'" in a loud voice.

"Yeah, it's been ages since I've seen that guy. Wasn't long after he graduated that he moved away from Suwŏn somewhere, right?"

"He said he's running an orchard near Ich'ŏn now."

"He's one of those guys who can accomplish whatever they put their mind to."

"He said to come on down with you some time. It's really been rough for him. Every year he's been clearing his land little by little and making an orchard out of it. Say, what are you up to today anyway, all decked out?"

Chun-t'ae, who usually wore a jumper when he came up to Seoul, was wearing a suit and necktie today.

"Remember my friend Min-gu, the one who got out of the army the same time I did? He's getting engaged today."

"The one who's studying shamans or something?"

"Yep."

"P'il-jae says he still isn't married," said Kŭn-yŏng. "If I'd taken a wife a little later on, I'd've made the right choice—at least as good as yours, you know?"

"Whether you do it early or late it's all the same."

Startled, Kŭn-yŏng looks over at Chun-t'ae. This calm, weighty tone of voice was quite different from Chun-t'ae's previous bantering.

A man stops in front of the store and Kŭn-yŏng gets up from his stool. The man did not appear to be a customer. Their conversation was hushed, but Chun-t'ae heard Kŭn-yŏng ask if it would be all right if he went later.

"If you've got to go somewhere, go ahead." Chun-t'ae stood up.

"I've got some merchandise to bring in."

"Go ahead and do it."

"But you haven't been here for a while—too bad. How about dropping by a little later? P'il-jae said he'd be back after taking care of some business, and then we can go have a snort of something. And while we're at it, we can disinfect this wound in my precious head."

Good idea, Chun-t'ae thought. But he didn't know what would happen after the engagement ceremony, so he couldn't promise to return.

Chun-t'ae left the shop and walked leisurely down the next block of Ch'ŏnggyech'ŏn. It was still too early for the engagement ceremony.

He crossed the street at a crosswalk, and soon the second-hand bookstores appeared. He thought about the cloth in which he had wrapped the books he had sold, and he walked toward the stores. He was wondering if the woman who had bought his books and unthinkingly taken the cloth might have returned it. It was not something he especially regretted losing. But then it was always good for wrapping up the things he carried around with him, like bundles of manuscript and the books he'd been translating. Of course I need it, he thought.

The second-hand bookstores all looked the same. He found the one where he had sold the books, and as he had thought, the wrapping cloth had been brought back. It had been squeezed into a nook under the end of a bookshelf in the back of the shop. The owner hands it to him. The cloth was wrapped in paper and a rubber band. After wadding it in his pocket, Chun-t'ae leaves the shop. Now the transaction with that woman is finished, he thinks. But he feels a sense of regret. Although he has obtained the cloth that he came here to find, he feels that something is missing. He lit a cigarette.

Before he has walked very far a man coming toward him asks for a light. But Chun-t'ae had not inhaled enough on his cigarette, and it was dying out. He took several puffs and, having brought the cigarette back to life, offered it to the man. The transfer completed, the man walks away after a brief nod. Chun-t'ae says to himself: The man who got a light from me and left. A passerby I wouldn't know even if we brushed against each other on the street again. And if so, a nobody. What's the difference between him and the woman who bought my books?

The engagement ceremony was over in a short time. The ceremony was simple, and the reception did not take long because no liquor was served. On Min-gu's side the only guests were his older brother, who had come up from the countryside, two college classmates, and Chun-t'ae. Everyone else was a guest on Ŭn-hŭi's side—her parents and relatives, executives at her father's company, and the minister and elders of the church.

Unwilling to part with his friends just yet, Min-gu asked them to wait at a nearby tearoom while he and Ŭn-hŭi had some photographs taken to commemorate their engagement. As they headed toward the car they found a man standing in their way. It was Pyŏn, neatly dressed in a suit, as always. Perhaps because of the fluorescent street lights, his attractive face looked paler than usual.

"How did you...?" Min-gu was startled to see him. True, two days before, he had met Pyŏn at the Uju Tearoom and bought him a pair of shoes in appreciation for the gift of the *ch'angbu* costume. And he had said something about meeting again after the engagement ceremony. But he had never expected Pyŏn to show up like this.

"Congratulations." Bending slightly at the waist, Pyŏn extended his hand.

"Thank you." Min-gu grasped Pyŏn's hand. It wasn't the first time he had shaken hands with him, but today Pyŏn's hand felt especially full and warm.

Pyŏn passed him a long box wrapped in paper, saying it was just a small gift.

Expressing his thanks and proposing that they meet again, Min-gu got in the car.

As soon as the car begins to move, Ŭn-hŭi asks who it was.

"Oh, someone I'm studying folklore with," Min-gu answered. He was not overly stretching the truth, he thought.

"He looks like a woman."

Could that be? This odd question settled into Min-gu's mind. That incident at Pyŏn's had been no trivial matter, and now the sensation of the hand he had just shaken was revived. Could it be Pyŏn is a transvestite? Min-gu couldn't help having a new interest in him.

Ŭn-hŭi plucks the present from Min-gu and opens the wrapping paper. It was a burgundy-colored wool necktie.

"Wow. It's really nice," Ŭn-hŭi says, trying out the tie on Min-gu's chest.

When Min-gu and Ŭn-hŭi arrive at the tearoom Min-gu's brother and friends all have a teacup in front of them except for one of the classmates, who gulps down a highball and snaps "I'm telling you, I was really craving a drink at the reception."

"Actually Western liquor should be drunk after a meal," the other classmate shoots back.

"That's a Western custom," said Highball. "We Koreans like drinking on an empty stomach, 'cause that's the only time the liquor really hits you." Then to Sŏng-ho, "And you Mister Preacher, perhaps you drank a lot back then?"

Sŏng-ho merely smiles.

"Nothing in the Bible that says you can't drink, is there?"

"But it says not to get drunk, right?" Sŏng-ho responds.

"You know, the first miracle Jesus performed was making wine out of water, wasn't it? Think about it: Jesus must've liked his wine a whole lot. It's clear to me he was pretty drunk the day he performed that miracle. Otherwise, how could he have told his mother, 'O woman, what have you to do with me?' It's not just a two-bit boozer who talks like that."

Ŭn-hŭi places a hand over her mouth. Clearly she thought Highball had gone too far.

Sŏng-ho, still smiling at Highball, says "People who have been drinking sometimes pick that phrase out of the Bible and joke about it. As if Jesus was telling his mother that he denied their mother–child relationship. But this is a matter of us Koreans not translating the Bible accurately. If you look at the most recent English version of the Bible, you'll find that there was some feasting going on at a house, and they ran out of wine. When Jesus' mother told Jesus there was no wine left, what Jesus had to say was this: 'Mother, what you are concerned about has nothing to do with me. My hour has not yet come.'"

"Uh-oh, I ran out of liquor and it looks like there's no one who has anything to do with that," Highball says, rattling the ice in his empty glass. "Is that because my time has not yet come?"

Everyone laughs, and Min-gu calls a waitress and orders another highball.

Highball begins some more silliness: "Now Mister Preacher, you haven't gotten a woman yet—d'you intend to stick to celibacy for the rest of your life like a Catholic priest?"

"I'm not quite up to that…"

"Our friend Min-gu just had his engagement ceremony, but I'm already the father of two kids."

"Quite a job you've undertaken, yes sir."

"It's quite a job all right, but from now on it'll be a pain in the neck," Highball says with studied gravity.

Wanting to change the topic, Ŭn-hŭi asks Chun-t'ae "Why didn't your wife come?"

"Her mother's ill, and so..."

"Is she in a great deal of pain?"

"Well, not too bad."

"Several days ago we saw your wife at a distance, in Wŏn-nam-dong."

"Oh really?" Chun-t'ae replies noncommittally. He lights a cigarette.

"Women's skirts are getting short these days, aren't they?" Highball breaks in, as if suggesting that Ŭn-hŭi converse with him too. "Is there any difference between that kind of exhibitionism and women showing off their vigor? Men get swelled heads just because their muscles are a little stronger, but in the end, you know, they lose out to women. Here's what a doctor said: When people don't eat in order to cure a stomach disorder, after just three days the men are practically crawling and shivering when they go to the toilet—they don't care how they look. But after a week the women are still keeping themselves up—several times a day they'll sit at their dresser and fix up their faces."

"But what if it were Yang Ch'ang-sŏn, the miner who was recently rescued?" It was Min-gu rather than Ŭn-hŭi who seized on Highball's words.

"He's an exception. But if he were a woman, who knows— she would've come out alive without everyone making such a big deal over her."

"In any event, being trapped underground for half a month and coming out alive is something we all ought to celebrate, and not just him," says Min-gu. "But there's one thing that bothers me—I don't like what he said after he was rescued. Now get this—he wasn't going in the tunnel again. That's not the way it should be. He should have said he was ready to go in again."

"I'm not so sure about that," Chun-t'ae said, inhaling slowly on a cigarette. "I think it was an honest thing to say. He'd be out of his mind if he said he was going back in—it'd be pure recklessness. What in the world would he want to go back in the tunnel for? To die?"

"But risking your life to be brave—isn't that something to be proud about? You can't expect progress where there's no daring."

"That's not the point. I can't imagine anyone expecting that man to go back in the tunnel unless they were curious about how much longer he could survive if he got trapped in there again."

"Anyway, he's a hero now—come on," said Min-gu.

"A hero? You mean someone made into a fake hero?" replied Chun-t'ae.

"A fake hero?"

"Frankly speaking, the mining company wasn't exactly in a hurry to rescue him. In fact, they may have wanted him dead then and there, because then they would've had to pay his family only three hundred thousand *wŏn* at most, plus the funeral fee. But didn't they end up spending something like nine million on the rescue? There was nothing else they could do, because of all the attention they got. The bottom line is that the company bought his life for nine million *wŏn*. But if we look a little more closely, it wasn't just one person's life they bought—it was the lives of all the miners. And here's why: the company is saying in effect that from now on they'll guarantee the lives of all the miners like this, and psychologically it's to their advantage to do that. If you look at it like that, then nine million *wŏn* is really a cheap price to pay."

Min-gu reaches out and pulls Chun-t'ae's pack of cigarettes toward him. Ŭn-hŭi gives his foot a kick. Min-gu turns the pack over a couple of times on the table and pushes it back, as if he had no intention of smoking. He then says, puffing out his chest, "The way I look at it, when a human looks death in the eye and wins, it's amazing."

"Amazing or not, it's time to wake up the mining companies so that they'll do everything they can to keep up the tunnels.

That's got to be done right now."

"If he hadn't had telephone contact with the people outside he might not've come out alive," said the other classmate, "no matter how well he was hanging on. Once telephone contact was established, it gave him the hope that he'd be rescued. That's why he survived. Otherwise he probably would've given up the ghost a long time ago.

"That's an important point," said Sŏng-ho. "The strength that hope gives us is beyond description."

"The reason he was able to establish telephone contact with the surface," said Highball as he put the new drink to his lips, "is that he had the scientific know-how and skill to reconnect that telephone line that had been cut off."

"But people can have hope without relying on scientific know-how or skill," said Sŏng-ho.

"Are you saying, Mister Preacher, that hope is possible if we believe in God?"

Sŏng-ho smiled.

"Didn't Nietzsche say that God is dead?"

"He's dead to those who think he's dead, and alive to those who think he's alive. In the final analysis it's not God who's dead," said Sŏng-ho.

"In my view," Chun-t'ae responded, "we've accepted this idea that God is dead but we don't have a true feeling for what that means." He slowly stubbed out his cigarette in the ashtray. "If we say that God is dead, isn't that based on the premise that he was alive until then? But for us, the god that Nietzsche talks about has never been alive. So it's natural that we're ignorant about this saying that God is dead, right? Even though there are some intellectuals who talk as if this Western saying meant something to them…"

Sŏng-ho and Chun-t'ae looked squarely at each other; both had earnest expressions.

"Like I said a little while ago, God enjoys serving people only where they want him," said Sŏng-ho. "And it's a fact that today there are people in our country who want him. Accordingly, we have to realize beyond a shadow of a doubt that God exists for us in the present too."

"That's still only a concept—it hasn't become part of our lives, has it?"

"I believe that there *are* people who have accepted God as part of their life. How many isn't important."

"But if you take a look at those people, it's not the word of God they accept—isn't it merely some practical benefit? In other words, a God who grants their desires, or sends them to Heaven, or forgives them if only they repent for all the sins they've committed."

"I feel the same way," Min-gu broke in. "It seems like there're a lot of people who go to church because they're expecting something practical rather than trying to understand the true meaning of what the Bible teaches us. It's just like expecting something from a shaman, you know?"

"And people like you are right in there among them," Highball says to Min-gu with a wink. He gestures subtly toward Ŭn-hŭi with his chin, implying that she is the reason that Min-gu goes to church.

Min-gu gives Highball a look that says, "Why you rascal!" and his large mouth opens in a smile. "Never mind. I'm different."

For a while now Ŭn-hŭi, whether uninterested in the subject or finding it unpleasant, has been breaking matchsticks, her eyes downcast.

Sŏng-ho quietly addresses Chun-t'ae and Min-gu. "I can't say there's no such tendency. It depends on the believer."

"The way I look at it, that kind of religion doesn't seem to be rooted in our spirit," said Chun-t'ae. "In other words, it's a religion that can't seem to keep clear of our nomad mentality."

"But religion changes people, and some day true religion will become rooted in them," said Sŏng-ho.

"You think so?"

Once more the eyes of the two men met. After a moment they stopped looking at each other, as if by silent agreement.

He sure looks like he's battling something, thinks Sŏng-ho.

He wished they could meet by themselves and talk it over. But Chun-t'ae did not look like one who would easily unburden himself. Instead, he would probably clam up more tightly no matter who reached out to him.

On the bus to Suwŏn, Chun-t'ae thought about this man Sŏng-ho. The address he made at the engagement ceremony had made an impression on him. Wasn't he hoping to convince us that in the future, when two people have formed a family, their happiness or sadness will not stop with them alone? That the happiness or sadness of the family that our parents form doesn't stop only with them, and that it's carried on with the family we form? Chun-t'ae understood that Sŏng-ho wasn't married yet, but he didn't get that feeling from what he had said. He wondered why. But in spite of the relationship between parents and their children, it has to stop when they become separate families. Ultimately they cannot and should not interfere with each other.

Chun-t'ae looked at the darkness outside the window. The darkness rejected the light coming from the bus, and the light rejected the darkness, as if each was insisting on its own standpoint. A yellow light appeared in the distance. He couldn't tell if it came from a dwelling or from some military checkpoint. Because of the light, the surrounding darkness appeared more dense. The light retreated and then faded from sight. But the darkness, thickened by the light he had seen, remained for some time.

The next morning Chun-t'ae gathered up the book he was translating together with some manuscript paper and prepared to go to the library at the college of agriculture. Ch'ang-ae had not returned, and so he could have spent that Sunday working all day quietly at home, but there was something he had to look up in the big dictionary at the library.

Wanting to bundle up the things he was taking with him, he spread out the wrapping cloth that he had brought home the day before. Two pieces of notepaper fell out. He picked them up and read them.

I've been humiliated several times in the past—it was hard to put up with. Now, once again, a new humiliation confronts me. No, I've already been flung into that humiliation. What should I do? Just face up to it.

The moment he read the first line Chun-t'ae flushed. The writing and contents were surely his. But had he really scribbled something like this and stuck it in the pages of a book? He looked at the next page.

Without realizing it I brought home this wrapping cloth along with the other things. I hope you'll forgive me. Also, this piece of paper wasn't part of the deal, so I'm sending it back to you. If you ever have to refer to any of these books you sold me, I'll always be ready to lend them to you.

The name Nam Chi-yŏn and a telephone number had been jotted at the bottom.

Because of his carelessness Chun-t'ae felt as embarrassed as if strangers had been looking at his privates. True, he had been exposed, but even so, she wouldn't know what this writing meant. Nevertheless, these lines had made him appear childish, and he was angry. He crumpled up the pieces of notepaper. He was going to throw them in the wastebasket but ended up throwing away only his own. The other one he put in his desk drawer, crumpled as it was. For a moment he stood there. Suddenly the darkness seen from the bus the previous night came near. It was the darkness that had become thicker because of the light. It was the darkness that had remained long in his eyes.

Chapter 4

There were not many passengers on the bus that stopped in front of Sŏng-ho. Although Stone Village was the first stop on the line, many people went downtown in the morning and had to stand in line to get on. But there were few passengers in the afternoon, so the buses frequently waited for them. Sŏng-ho got on the bus behind an elderly man. There were plenty of empty seats.

To Sŏng-ho's left a man who was getting on in years held up a land-survey map, as if he was on his way to examine some real estate. He said to his companion, "We came back last time through Ch'ang-dong, but on our way there it's okay if we take this road." Then, looking out the window, he said, "Take a look at those houses lined up over there. They produce a chain reaction at night." Sensing that his companion didn't understand, he went on. "They don't look bad from the outside, but the way they're partitioned into units is awful. The blocks in the partitions aren't solid, and the partitions don't go all the way up to the ceiling. So naturally the people in one unit can't help hearing what's going on next door. At night they start getting it on in one unit, and in the next one they hear it and so they can't just sit there..." Not until then did his companion understand. Stifling a laugh, he said, "They'll probably have babies all in a bunch, just like a ship's crew."

Fortunately, Sŏng-ho thought, he appeared to be the only one close enough to hear them. But unlike these two men beside him, he could not simply laugh at this story and then forget about it. First of all, he couldn't help thinking about Myŏng-suk.

Although Myŏng-suk was up and about now, she seemed to

have developed a more serious illness. As pale as her face was and as gaunt as she had become, she not only did kitchen work but also the laundry, unlike someone who had spent several days in bed. But she had been acting strangely. She would act rationally for a while and then suddenly rush outside, grab onto people, and pester them. She said to one person, "You're trying to figure out a way to get out of paying for that thing you bought, aren't you?" To a woman she said, "I know you stole a handful of anchovies from the grocery store yesterday." In this way she would blather at people and embarrass them. In the village it was whispered that Myŏng-suk had lost her mind.

Perhaps the structure of those houses also had a big influence on Myŏng-suk's failure to recover completely, thought Sŏng-ho. Once again he became gloomy.

The bus arrived downtown and Sŏng-ho got off at Shinmunno.

Having set out toward the office of the Council of Elders, Sŏng-ho stepped into the street in order to avoid some water that was gushing from a hose onto the sidewalk. It was being pumped out of the foundation of a new building. The muddy water made a *k'wal k'wal* sound as it was spewed from the maw of the hose.

Sŏng-ho noticed a man dressed like a day laborer. He immediately steps back up to a place on the sidewalk where less water is flowing. The man has rolled up his pants and is washing his shins with the muddy water gushing from the hose. He straightens up and then, his eyes meeting Sŏng-ho's, bends over again as if he hasn't seen him and begins rubbing his shins. An empty A-frame[1] hung from his back.

Sŏng-ho decides to wait until the man, P'yŏng-i's father, has stepped back from the hose. P'yŏng-i's father came to Stone Village as a flood victim and is one of the faithful at the church. Except when the weather is foul, he comes downtown every day to earn money with his A-frame. In the evening he entrusts the A-frame to someone he knows and goes home on the bus.

[1]A-frame: an apparatus used by laborers and farmers for carrying loads.

He also works on Sunday, and attends only the evening service at the church. Usually he remained bent over from the pastoral prayer through the closing hymn. At first Sŏng-ho thought that P'yŏng-i's father was offering a long prayer by himself, but eventually he realized that he was sound asleep.

P'yŏng-i's father continues to rub and wash his shins and arms with the muddy water. The earthworm-like veins protruding from his calves wriggle whenever his fingers pass across them.

Sŏng-ho finally addresses him. "P'yŏng-i's father, it's me."

P'yŏng-i's father now has to stand up. He gives Sŏng-ho a distorted smile.

"Please stop washing and come over here."

P'yŏng-i's father approaches, shaking his feet to empty the water from his *komusin*.[2] While walking away with Sŏng-ho, his head toward the ground, he suddenly says, "Preacher, I've heard that God made us in his own image."

"Yes?" Sŏng-ho said, looking at him.

"I'm so ashamed I can't stand it. If God looks down and sees that his image is the likes of me, won't that make him awfully depressed?"

Sŏng-ho doesn't have a good quick reply. He recalls a conversation he had with a minister in divinity school. Humans must take consolation from thinking about people who are more unfortunate than themselves, the minister had said. But was this genuine consolation? Sŏng-ho had asked. When we have good fortune we must be thankful, and when we are miserable we must think of people who are more miserable, the minister had answered. Sŏng-ho had asked another question: Can human beings obtain only that kind of sad consolation? Yes, was the answer, and therefore there is no other way except reliance upon God. Not wishing to console P'yŏng-i's father with this dialogue from days gone by, Sŏng-ho managed

[2]*Komusin:* rather long, narrow, dugout-shaped traditional Korean rubber shoes.

to come up with another answer.

"If God looked down and saw my appearance, maybe he would frown even more," he said.

"What? Preacher, how could that be?"

"No kidding. It's true."

A stationery store caught Sŏng-ho's eye. He had been looking for it awhile. After asking P'yŏng-i's father to wait, he went inside and bought some pencils and a notebook for P'yŏng-i.

The meetings of the Council of Elders normally took time, but today they dragged on longer than Sŏng-ho had expected.

The topic under discussion was whether or not to unite the Presbyterian churches. There were two organizations in the country with exactly the same title—the Presbyterian Church of Jesus. Popularly, they were known as the unification group and the integration group. The unification group managed the General Theological Seminary, and the integration group controlled the College of Theology. The unification group professed to hold to the doctrines and creeds of the Bible just as they were. On the other hand, the integration group professed an interest in the realistic adaptation and practical application of biblical doctrines.

Sŏng-ho, who was unaware of such differences and similarities, had graduated from the divinity school managed by the unification group. Mrs. Hong's husband, Pastor Chŏng, had also belonged to the unification group. During his years at the school, Sŏng-ho focused entirely on atoning for his sins. So, it was natural that he became a clergyman of the unification group without thinking twice about it. Even after finding out that the friction between the two groups was not something trivial, he emphasized his own beliefs more than adhering to the beliefs of a particular group.

At the meeting that day the two organizations kept the seeds of discord to themselves, and although some individuals argued forcefully that the two groups remain divided as at present, the end of the debate saw agreement in the direction of unification.

The other clergymen of the unification group concluded that interpretations of the Bible might differ slightly, but since dissolution of the Presbyterian church into two conflicting groups would be a deviation from the fundamental teachings of Christ, it would be better if the two groups united. Sŏng-ho had a great deal of influence in this. Early in the refugee period during the Korean War he had organized a boy's service corps. Crossing over to Kŏje Island with them, he had accommodated himself in several ways to the leading ministers there, and now they were supporting his proposals. Actually these well-known ministers had evoked disappointment and resentment in Sŏng-ho at Kŏje Island. For they had flung themselves at the foodstuffs and relief goods more than the common people had. But Sŏng-ho understood that circumstances could bring anyone to do this.

By the time the meeting ended, Sŏng-ho was more than two hours late for the appointment he had made with Chi-yŏn over a pay phone.

It is five or six years now that Sŏng-ho has known Chi-yŏn. He first met her at the hospital. She had been admitted, suffering from caries, in the ward occupied by Mrs. Hong. Perhaps because of the unusual circumstances under which they occupied this ward, they were eventually able to converse intimately. Even after being discharged, Chi-yŏn would come to the hospital to visit Mrs. Hong. Sŏng-ho vaguely suspected that Chi-yŏn was the only person who might have known about his relationship with Mrs. Hong. He had wondered anxiously how much she knew. Mrs. Hong could not have spoken to her about it, nor had Sŏng-ho himself disclosed it. Chi-yŏn, moreover, had had no occasion to bring up this topic. But for some reason Sŏng-ho felt she had gotten wind of their affair. Paradoxically, the more anxious he became about Chi-yŏn, the more he felt he had to see her. Perhaps he wanted to sound her out. But at some point—he was not sure when—he had ceased being concerned about whether Chi-yŏn knew their secret and had come instead to feel more relaxed with her than he did with anybody else.

While waiting for Sŏng-ho, Chi-yŏn played with her dogs in the yard. Her house, located in Changch'ung-dong, had a lawn of some two hundred *p'yŏng*³—unusually spacious for a house downtown. Chi-yŏn was a dog lover. At home her favorite pastime, the more so since her recovery from caries, was playing with the dogs in the yard. They were not established breeds, but she was raising three of them.

The dogs bayed even before Sŏng-ho pressed the buzzer. The one called Nero runs over and claws the metal of the front gate. A mongrel that contained some shepherd blood, Nero was the most ferocious dog Sŏng-ho had ever seen.

Chi-yŏn asks Sŏng-ho to wait. Not until she has grabbed Nero by the collar and dragged him to his cage does she open the gate. Nero continues to bay frantically after being locked up.

"He knows me a little by now—can't he have mercy on me?"

"A few days ago he bit one of my nephews, even though the boy comes here quite often."

"Could be he's got a few screws loose."

"There you go again. I told you not to be finding fault with the dog. His good points outweigh the bad ones."

Chi-yŏn leads Sŏng-ho to a bench beneath a tree and sits. Sŏng-ho stands in front of her. Most of the discoloration on the bridge of her nose seems to have disappeared.

"You're looking well. Maybe it's because these good dogs have been entertaining you?"

"Oh stop teasing me and sit down. I like dogs no matter what you say."

"No good news to tell me?" Sŏng-ho asks as he sits down next to her.

"Good news?" Chi-yŏn tilts her head to the side and looks slightly up at Sŏng-ho.

"No wedding bells off in the distance?..."

³*P'yŏng:* a unit of area equaling about four square yards.

"Come on, if I had some news like that you'd certainly be the first to know."

"Well, instead of wedding bells I'll have to make do with coffee again. Brewed by you, of course."

"All right. Let's go inside."

Nowhere else has he drunk coffee as good as the fragrant coffee Chi-yŏn brews—its richness and taste are just right. He has tried to make coffee at home, following the method he learned from Chi-yŏn, but no matter how he tries, it doesn't turn out well. Perhaps it followed that with coffee, as with food, a taste is imparted by the one who prepares it. All Sŏng-ho has to do is step into Chi-yŏn's room, and he can dispense with formality and face saving. And today too, harried by the church meeting and languid in body and soul, he buries himself in the sofa.

As usual, the room is bare. There was a record player and a wardrobe, and on the wall to Sŏng-ho's right a photograph of the Giacometti sculpture *City Square* framed in unfinished, unstained wood. It is a composition in which five figures, their arms, legs, and trunk all long and thin like chopsticks, walk toward the middle. The figures in the square seem to brush past each other, even while congregating in the same place. They seem to lack a means of communicating with one another. Whenever Sŏng-ho sees this photograph, it reminds him of a black-and-white print of Grünewald's *Crucifixion*. He had seen several other versions of Jesus nailed to the cross, but none had given him such an intense feeling of pity. The face of Jesus, his head slanting below one of his shoulders and streaming blood from the wounds of the crown of thorns; the distortion of the palms and feet with the huge nails driven in them; the chest protruding as if the weight of all his agony had concentrated there—all of his bitter suffering in this world seemed to be compressed in this picture. His was the image of a person barely sustaining himself, one who appeared an inch away from succumbing to his suffering. A memory of the beautiful image of the resurrected Jesus stood out in Sŏng-ho's mind, and for some reason he could not erase it from the image of Jesus steeped in agony and suffering.

There was a bookcase on the wall to his left. Like the wardrobe and record player, it was not meant to embellish the room. New books and old had been randomly inserted in the shelves. Reminding himself that on the way home he had better drop by a bookstore and purchase a few books on Korean customs, Sŏng-ho rises and walks to the bookcase. There are more books here now, he thinks. His eyes, tracing the title of one book and then another, come to a stop. Wait a minute—what's the story with these books? Inserted in the bookcase side by side were several volumes all in the same field. He takes them in his hands.

Chi-yŏn came in carrying a tray with two coffee cups and enough boiling water for two servings. She always joins Sŏng-ho in a cup when he visits.

A book in hand, Sŏng-ho returns to the sofa and takes a sip of his coffee.

"First time I've seen a book like this here. Since when have you been interested in agriculture?"

"How did you manage to track that one down? I have to confess, it's all Greek to me."

"But there're more of 'em too."

"I suddenly felt like buying them, so I did. Dirt cheap."

"Even though they're cheap, how can you buy books that you can't read? They're not exactly cultural assets."

Chi-yŏn told him the story. She generally told Sŏng-ho about her affairs, no matter what they were, without hiding anything—even the dates she had with men and a relationship with a young man that had extended from high school through college. She told him that the man who had come to the second-hand bookstore to sell the books looked very much at loose ends, that he appeared to need money urgently, and that her desire to quickly dispel the awkward look on his face had led her to rush out without even leaving the wrapping cloth. She had gone again to the bookstore that day to drop it off. When she went back later she found that the man had returned for it.

But Chi-yŏn didn't tell Sŏng-ho about the piece of paper stuck between the pages of one of the books. She didn't wish to touch the private life of others, or to discuss the note. She didn't know why.

Of course, Sŏng-ho had no way of knowing that Chi-yŏn was talking about the same man he had met at Min-gu's engagement ceremony.

Chi-yŏn suddenly regretted not telling Sŏng-ho about the piece of paper, so she changed the subject.

"I'm attending church. You had some influence on me after all."

"That's big news." Sŏng-ho smoothly took up the new topic.

"The minister of the church looks pretty good. His preaching seems to make a lot of sense."

"That's great."

"But you know that ecstatic praying by the whole congregation at the end of the sermon? Is it really necessary?"

"Well, some churches do it and some don't," said Sŏng-ho.

"Do you do it at your church?"

"Nope."

"I think it disturbs the solemn atmosphere of prayer. They're crying and at the same time waving their head and their hands...but then when the bell rings telling them to stop, they stop right where they are. In that case, how could you really say they were deeply absorbed in prayer?" asked Chi-yŏn.

"So you kept your eyes open during the prayer and watched all this—is that it?" Sŏng-ho smiles. "There are verses in the Bible that say go into a dark room, close the door, and pray in secrecy. And there are verses that say supplicate Jehovah, calling his name out loud. So I think either way is okay—it depends on what each person wants. Judging from your personality, I'd say that you prefer quiet prayer. But I think you'll soon be able to pray by yourself as quietly as you want no matter how noisy the other people are."

As always, Chi-yŏn feels peaceful with Sŏng-ho. Her feelings toward him are clearly not those of a woman for a man.

"Is that possible? I don't think my faith will ever reach that level," Chi-yŏn says as she walks over to the record player. "Say, you know what? It's pear season. We ought to go to the orchards in T'aenŭng and eat some pears, like we did last year."

"That's right. Pear season! Yes, let's make a point of going."

"When they're just ripe I'll let you know."

After Sŏng-ho left, Chi-yŏn started playing with the dogs again. The evening temperature is agreeable and Nero's movements become lively, as if his vigor has been replenished. After running over to Chi-yŏn, who is half bent-over, and making a circuit around her almost close enough to brush her, he stretches out his forefeet in front of her and extends his muzzle over them. Lying there, he observes her movements. Chi-yŏn signals the dog to come running again, and he immediately makes another tight circle around her, as before.

The dog named Hamlet is standing three or four meters away. Chi-yŏn beckons him to do the same thing Nero did. Not moving, Hamlet stares at Chi-yŏn as if he has been on the lookout for her. There was no dog more difficult for Chi-yŏn to tame than Hamlet. Having taken great pains to select a bitch to receive Nero's seed before he was too old, Chi-yŏn bred them, and among the resulting puppies Hamlet was the most attractive male. Nero's ears were pointed and Hamlet's drooped slightly at the ends, but otherwise the two dogs looked identical. Hamlet had never been obedient. Even when grown he would not stay beside Chi-yŏn but instead would linger hesitantly at a distance. The only hand whose touch he would allow was that of the maid who fed him, but Chi-yŏn didn't want to tame him by giving him food. At the same time, she always maintained her interest in him. At some point he'll become friendly, she thought.

When Hamlet failed to respond to Chi-yŏn's gesture the dog named Elizabeth, opposite him and a short distance from Chi-yŏn, approached her with her head swaying, as if this were her chance. Elizabeth was a hybrid pointer that Chi-yŏn's father had obtained from a friend. This dog has no sense of shame. She employs flattery and coquettishness, reading people's faces. Whenever Chi-yŏn is out of sorts she never comes near until she has detected an opportunity, and then she is upon her. Now too she intends to gain Chi-yŏn's attention in place of Hamlet, but just before she gets to Chi-yŏn Nero comes running over and collides with her, pushing her away. Elizabeth topples over. Nero was very jealous. He cannot sit still when other dogs are approaching Chi-yŏn. As if guarding someone in a basketball game, he prevents other dogs from getting near her. And it was the same when Chi-yŏn favored the other dogs. So she would have to cage up Nero, particularly when she had to look after Hamlet and Elizabeth. But even while in the cage Nero would sink his teeth into the wire netting and growl. It was the same when Chi-yŏn was with people. The nephew Nero had bitten was a frequent visitor whose face the dog knew well. Chi-yŏn suspected that the bite was the result of her showing the child extra attention. And as for his flying off the handle upon seeing Sŏng-ho—something that has been going on for several years now—doesn't this come from a similar attitude? But this wasn't a characteristic Chi-yŏn could dislike. When she looked at Nero's behavior as an animal's expression of its strong affection for her, which was different from the way humans expressed themselves, she couldn't help becoming attached to this mongrel who lacked the training that some well-known breeds received.

Having pushed Elizabeth over, Nero comes to Chi-yŏn and clings to her. Saying "No—you shouldn't do that," Chi-yŏn cuffs him on the back of the head. Nero abruptly rolls over on his back and while exposing his stomach whimpers, *k'ŭng k'ŭng.* Lying on his back and exposing his belly is a dog's way of expressing his best mood, but in this case Nero's actions are half an expression of regret and half the winsome behavior of a spoiled child. Chi-yŏn pokes Nero's stomach. This is her way of scolding Nero, telling him not to do that sort of thing again, but gradually the poking changes to tickling. Pawing the air with all four feet, Nero moves his head from side to side and groans with pleasure. Chi-yŏn too enjoys this. It's a good thing I didn't tell Sŏng-ho about that piece of paper, she thinks. No doubt about it. Chi-yŏn pokes Nero's belly again and again. Nero deflects Chi-yŏn's hand with his feet, and at length, snapping his teeth together, he pretends he is about to bite her. Now it is Chi-yŏn who avoids Nero, moving her hand here and there so that he cannot bite her. But then she is caught. The dog takes her hand firmly between his jaws, releases it, captures it again, and releases it, but never leaving a mark. Every time he releases her, Chi-yŏn gives a cry of delight and once again moves her hand here and there to avoid him.

Chun-t'ae stops beside the road in front of a zelkova tree whose shadows are gradually becoming thin, as he usually does on his way home.

This tree, perhaps hundreds of years old, had been struck by lightning one summer when Chun-t'ae was an eighth grader. About half of its bark was removed, and many of its branches were broken. The leaves on the rest of the tree withered. He thought it was dead. That year, though, the buds came out again. And it still survives, upright, its injury kept to one side. Chun-t'ae had been amazed by its tenacious vitality. Looking at the lofty bearing of this zelkova standing against the evening sky, Chun-t'ae feels a certain weariness. Could it be his tired body? Lighting a cigarette and placing it in his mouth, he goes on his way.

Ch'ang-ae was home, having once again returned after an absence of several days. The elderly maid came in with the table she had set for them.

The couple finish dinner without a word. Carrying a bowl of broth containing scorched leavings from the bottom of the rice pot, Chun-t'ae goes to his desk. He picks up the evening newspaper, and beneath it he finds several postcards. Chun-t'ae puts down the paper and picks up the postcards. The scenes are of Pŏpju Temple at Songni Mountain. Chun-t'ae had also gone there last summer. The colors in the photographs were lurid and unnatural, but certain aspects of the photographs made Chun-t'ae feel that he was seeing them for the first time. How different the same scene can be, depending on the angle of the lens, he thought.

Ch'ang-ae, listening to music on a transistor radio, turns the volume down. "Sir," she calls him with a serious voice.

Chun-t'ae lifted his eyes from the postcards.

"For a while now somebody's been asking me to open up a dressmaking shop with her, and I'm trying to make up my mind. I'm not completely ignorant about that sort of thing"— she had majored in applied fine arts in college. "What it comes down to," she continues, "is the money I have to put into it. So even though I have a mind to do it, I've been putting it off..."

And? thinks Chun-t'ae. While waiting for her next words, he picks up the newspaper.

"What would you think if I used this house as security for a loan? It's not doing us any good just sitting here. It's better if we make use of it, isn't it? And we've got a lender too, just when we needed her."

Fixing his eyes on the newspaper, Chun-t'ae says, "Can you guess how much money you can borrow if you pawn the house?" The house was completely run-down, although it occupied a large lot.

"We won't know that until we put it on the market. The person who said she'd supply the money will give it special consideration, or so she said. If I'm still short of money there's nothing else I can do but contribute a one-third share."

Looks like she'll even get rid of the house, Chun-t'ae thought. At the same time, curiously, Chun-t'ae was undisturbed, and he nodded to his wife to do as she wished. It was a humble dwelling, but it was the one real compensation he had received for the hardships he had undergone for a long time before marriage. Even so, he had no strong attachment to it.

Chun-t'ae and Ch'ang-ae had established their relationship one night toward the end of February four years before. It was a cold night that signaled how much longer it still would be before spring. It was nearing midnight. Chun-t'ae was lying in bed reading when unexpectedly someone arrived. It was Ch'ang-ae. In a gasping voice, as if she had rushed all the way over, she asked Chun-t'ae if she could stay there just for the night. All Chun-t'ae could give her was one end of his only quilt. Without hesitation Ch'ang-ae removed her coat and hung it up. Then she sat down, burying her feet under the thin sleeping pad. For a while she looked out of breath, but then she slipped under the pad, still wearing her clothes. Chun-t'ae decided to stay awake through the night and read a book. Some time later Ch'ang-ae, whom Chun-t'ae thought was asleep, asked if he had heard from Su-jŏng? Su-jŏng was a high school classmate of Ch'ang-ae and the younger sister of a friend of Chun-t'ae who was now working at the crop testing station in Mokp'o. Even after Ch'ang-ae moved to Seoul she would occasionally come to Suwŏn and the two of them would go see Chun-t'ae at his boardinghouse, as they used to do when they were in high school. The previous autumn Su-jŏng had accompanied her brother to Mokp'o and not long after, Chun-t'ae had heard from him that she had gotten married. Sir, you know Su-jŏng liked you, didn't you? Ch'ang-ae asked. Since Chun-t'ae was intent on his book, Ch'ang-ae merely prattled on: Your blunt appearance was charming, and so I kind of liked you myself. Aren't you wondering why I came late at night like this? You haven't asked one question—ah, that's your charming point all right. Now why do I have this urge to talk to someone who doesn't ask anything. Today was graduation day, and this evening we had a party. There were five couples, and one of the boys has a studio, so we went there and really did it up right—singing, dancing, eating, drinking—and just when I was feeling on top of the world my partner whispers in my ear, Let's go to some quiet place, just the two of us. Of course we've had a couple of dates, and I knew what he meant by a quiet place, so I said great, and the two of us sneaked out and caught a taxi. When we arrived at the hotel, this guy gets out first, but I stay in the taxi. He looks at me funny, and I shut the taxi door. I told him to wait and that I'd come back after I'd gotten ahold of myself. I said to the driver I'd give him a big tip and I came here. Since the car door was shut tight, maybe the guy didn't hear what I was saying. Ch'ang-ae broke into a laugh, as if she had enjoyed this. Shortly thereafter Chun-t'ae married her and bought this house with some money he had been scraping together. But Chun-t'ae wasn't regretting the loss of his life-style. Perhaps, he thought, everything is going its course.

Chun-t'ae opened the desk drawer. As he was looking for the deed to the house, a crumpled piece of paper came into sight. His hand comes to a stop, and he stares at the name and telephone number written on the paper. It is his contact with the woman who readily bought his books. The deed was underneath everything else. He takes it out and hands it to his wife.

"I think I'll have to have a copy of your *ingam chŭngmyŏng*[4] too." Ch'ang-ae's voice had become unusually firm.

"I'll do it tomorrow."

That night Ch'ang-ae, slightly removed from her sleeping husband, lay in the darkness, her eyes wide open. How could the two of us reach this point? Could it be my fault? All my fault? Maybe it looks that way on the surface. But I can't stand his indifference toward me. I really can't stand it. How could my husband be that indifferent? Before our marriage I thought it was charming. But now it's too much. I'm getting more suffocated every day. Why can't he put his foot down and take charge of our relationship sometimes? How many times have I done these crazy things just to wake him up? Maybe I'm still doing it. But he only pretends not to know, or else he thinks differently from me. It's the same with those postcards he was

---

[4]*Ingam chŭngmyŏng:* a certificate, kept in the local administrative offices, of the impression of the *tojang* (personal seal) that a person uses for all official purposes.

looking at. He didn't say anything—just looked them over as if he was looking at some scenery. If he'd asked who I'd gone to Songni Mountain with, I'd have answered frankly that I went with Mr. Kang, the painter—just the two of us. And if he had gotten angry and made a scene maybe I would have rushed to his arms again. But he was cool—didn't say anything at all. Even though we don't have the relationship of a married couple, it's only natural to ask who gave you these, where did they come from, when did you go there and who with. But my husband ignores this. Could he be doing this on purpose? Or maybe he's got no feelings. What's more, even when I say I'm going to pawn the house and go into debt, he agrees just like that. For a while now I've been telling him I'd better earn some money, so it must have come as no surprise to him when I said I was going to join someone in a business. But when it gets to the point where I'm actually rummaging for the deed to the house, shouldn't he say something from a husband's point of view? Like hold on now, let's be careful about all this. Even though we're man and wife, we're strangers. We're as unfamiliar with each other as strangers could be. It's too much. I don't know whether it's painful for him, but it sure is for me. It'd be good for both of us to escape from this situation as soon as possible. Since he's already taken out the deed, let's pawn the house and open up the shop. For the time being, we'll be virtually separated. As soon as I raise the money to pay off this debt on the house, let's wind up this life with him. It's an insult to scrape along like this for nothing. It'd be an insult to anyone. Somehow I've got to wind up this life. Ch'ang-ae repeated this to herself as she stared wide-eyed into the darkness.

Chapter 5

People were passing incessantly along the path between the lawns of Tŏksu Palace. Four in the afternoon is an in-between time of day, but the palace grounds were full of people on this cloudy Saturday.

A student wearing a college badge sticks the earplug from a transistor radio in his ear and passes by the bench where Chun-t'ae sits. He does not seem to be concentrating on what he is hearing.

The giggling of women bursts forth from the palace buildings. The laughter dies down and then rises, again and again.

Lighting a cigarette, Chun-t'ae looks toward the entrance to the palace grounds. She'll probably show up about now, he thinks.

Today Chun-t'ae had delivered the manuscript of his translation to a magazine publisher. He and the editor had gone out for a hot drink. Afterwards he had considered going to the Uju Tearoom but had come instead to nearby Tŏksu Palace. As soon as he stepped through the entrance a vermilion public telephone caught his eye. He had been balking at passing on his thanks to Chi-yŏn, and only now did he decide to do so. How he had tried to suppress this thought. On the phone, though, Chi-yŏn calmly replied that she would come to the palace, which she hadn't visited for several years.

"I'm really sorry about the other day. A taxi came by just then, and I caught it and went home. It wasn't until I untied the wrapping cloth that I realized I had taken it along too. I often do silly things like that." Chi-yŏn lowered her face slightly.

"Oh that could happen to anybody," Chun-t'ae said, remembering that he had discovered the loss of the cloth only after getting on the bus.

"Right after that I took another taxi back to the bookstore, but you weren't there. So the only thing I could do was leave it there. The next day, though, I was looking through one of the books and that piece of paper turned up inside. So I went back to the bookstore once more. You still hadn't gone back for the wrapping cloth, and I thought to myself that everything had worked out well after all, but...after that I dropped by the store two more times. When I heard that you'd come for the cloth, I felt so relieved."

"It was nothing to lose sleep over." Chun-t'ae meant not just the cloth but the whole incident, including the piece of paper.

"At any rate, I should return things that don't belong to me."

"Very cut and dried." Right after saying this Chun-t'ae feels that a trace of cynicism has entered his voice.

The momentary sparkle in Chi-yŏn's eyes disappeared immediately. Why that tone of voice? she wonders. It's not connected with returning the cloth. Maybe it's a defense mechanism—his way of telling me not to bring up the contents of that notepaper. Well, I'm certainly not going to cross-examine him about it, but that's not to say I'm not curious about what it means.

"Who is it that's involved with agriculture, one of your brothers?"

"No..."

"Well then, you yourself?"

"No..."

Then? Chun-t'ae inquires with his eyes.

"People don't always buy books that they need right then and there."

"True, but those books don't make very good ornaments. When you come right down to it, you bought them out of sympathy, right?"

"That's not it either."

"Then was it vanity? I appreciate your buying them, but..."
Again a taste of sarcasm entered his speech.

Chi-yŏn remained silent. From his point of view, I guess that
makes sense. But there wasn't anything unreasonable about my
wanting to buy those books. So what's wrong?

They had come to a pond. It struck them as unclean. Pieces
of wastepaper floated beside fronds of water lilies and the
cloudy sky had seemed to sink onto the pond's dull surface. A
school of red carp were coalescing and then disappearing
beneath the fronds.

Leaving the pond, they walked further into the palace
grounds on the path between the lawns.

A couple of third or fourth graders are running around on the
grass. One child, who is ahead by about a foot, is bent way over
at the waist. The other child chases him with his body upright.
The distance between them does not narrow or widen. After a
while, the child in front falls down, as if on purpose. The other
child falls on top of him. They turn into a lump and roll over.

Chun-t'ae and Chi-yŏn reach the fountain, from which no
water is spurting. A young woman is posing in front of it while
a middle-aged man focuses a camera.

As Chun-t'ae was wondering which way to go, Chi-yŏn
suggested going in the museum. They lacked something to talk
about, and a desire to escape this awkward situation may have
been at work deep within her mind.

Not even thirty minutes remained before the museum was to
close. Everyone was coming out and nobody was entering. But
Chun-t'ae followed her, more because he had nothing else in
mind than because Chi-yŏn, who had taken the time to come
all the way here, had suggested it.

Chi-yŏn is amazed at the stone ax, the elaborately polished
stone knife, and similar items among the Stone Age relics displayed in Room 1. Looking at the pattern of a combware pot,
she asks Chun-t'ae how people can put something like that on
the ground and use it. It looks like a crock, but because the
bottom protrudes there is no way it can be set down straight.

Chun-t'ae answered that because the people of that time lived by moving along rivers, they set the pots in the sand beside them. The pots could then be easily used, and so were fashioned in that manner. Chi-yŏn realizes all the more that almost all of the things that have come down to us from antiquity as art objects were manufactured more as practical necessities than as responses to an aesthetic impulse. She felt reluctant to leave these objects, for they seemed to contain the sagacious and devoted touch of those who made them.

Looming directly before them in Room 2 is an imitation gold crown from the Silla kingdom. But earthenware was emphasized here too. Chi-yŏn comes to an earthenware dish. At the bottom of it was an intaglio engraving of a fish. Absolutely exquisite, Chi-yŏn thought. Once again she was amazed that an item of practical use could yet remain so beautiful.

They were on their way to Room 3 when they heard a commotion from inside. A guard came out dragging a woman in a *ch'ima* and *chŏgori*. She appeared to be approaching forty. Her face is ashen and she is pleading with the guard as she attempts to struggle free.

"Chip off just a little of it. Please. That's all I need to save my child. Won't you help me?"

Without replying, the guard hauls the woman past Chun-t'ae and Chi-yŏn and out the building.

From what the people behind them were saying, the woman had been caught trying to remove some lacquer from a coffin: How could she say she'd cure an illness with that? Good lord! Well, she said the child couldn't turn himself over, and he's more than two years old, and if she boils a bit of lacquer from the coffin for a long time and feeds it to him, he'll get better. Even so, something in a museum...

Upon entering Room 3 Chi-yŏn goes to the coffin. Chun-t'ae comes up beside her. It was a huge wooden affair, long and wide and immensely high. Several people together might have had difficulty moving the massive thing, and they wondered whether there had really been a person big enough to fill it. The coffin was coated with a thick crimson lacquer, which looked even thicker in the places where it had cracked and come off. Only one end of the lid remained, and lacquer could also be seen inside. According to the label, the coffin was from the Nangnang period.[1]

They walked up to Room 4 on the second floor, and while they were looking around at the white celadon from the Yi dynasty and the green celadon from the Koryŏ dynasty the closing bell rang.

Outside, Chun-t'ae and Chi-yŏn went to the rest area in back of the museum. Beach canopies have been set up and beverages are for sale.

Chi-yŏn orders some juice and drinks it. Then she asks, "If she boils some lacquer from the coffin and feeds it to the child, will he really get better?"

"How could it cure anything? It's hard to come by, and I'm sure that's why we end up with a folk belief like this. It sounds like the kid has polio, so what's the use of boiling something like that and feeding it to him?"

"No matter what kind of superstition it is, I pity the mother. She was going to steal it for the sake of the child..."

"Blind love, isn't it?"

"Don't you think that's good?"

Chun-t'ae lights a cigarette and says nothing.

"What's going to happen to her? Do you think they'll hand her over to the police?" asks Chi-yŏn.

"Hard to say."

"I've been thinking about this," Chi-yŏn said, putting her elbows on the round table. "You remember that famous millionaire who bought a national treasure so cheaply, knowing full well it had been stolen, and then sneaked off to Japan and sold it? And then there's that well-known industrialist who was

---

[1]Nangnang (Chinese, Lorang): an administrative district established by Han dynasty China in 108 B.C. in the northwest part of the Korean peninsula; overthrown by the Koguryŏ tribes in A.D. 313.

running a large-scale smuggling operation from Japan. It seemed like they both got hardly any punishment at all. But the women who go around peddling various foreign goods get everything confiscated. The same thing happens with those kids who sell gum. Can you believe it?"

Chun-t'ae drew on his cigarette.

"You know, that kid's mother, no matter how superstitious she acted, she wasn't afraid to do something like that to save her handicapped child. It's worth forgiving her this time. Better to warn her so she understands."

Smiling, Chun-t'ae says, "You have a great deal of empathy." There was again a touch of sarcasm in his voice, but his smile had no hidden meaning. Chi-yŏn couldn't help smiling as well.

For the first time Chun-t'ae looked directly at Chi-yŏn. The brown pupils of her double-lidded eyes looked deep, as if shrouded in a thin mist. The discoloration spreading along the bridge of her nose, the end of which was slightly sharp, gave her the appearance of mischievousness and somehow upset the balance of her longish face. Her long neck was exposed above her black sweater with its tiny, narrowly spaced buttons.

Keeping his eyes on her face, Chun-t'ae asked, "Did you read that article in the paper some time ago? In Vietnam they shot some big businessman for smuggling."

The pupils of Chi-yŏn's eyes shone through the mist.

"They even showed a photo of it."

"Yes, I remember," said Chi-yŏn. "But it was so frightening I couldn't look at it close up. Even when I go to the movies I shut my eyes tight whenever someone dies or there's a horrible scene."

"The photo was fuzzy, so you couldn't see it clearly. It was a man with his hands tied behind his back. He'd been shot, and his head had sunk forward on his chest That's all I could recognize. While looking at that photo I thought of something. Ultimately people don't die in vain. That's because there's something for us to learn from the death of innocent people and something for us to learn from the death of guilty people.

Even though the nature of death is different in those two cases."

Chi-yŏn was also looking at Chun-t'ae—his forehead with the couple of deep furrows engraved in them, his eyes with their shining pupils but the whites tinged with a tired crimson, his fleshless chin, the neck with its prominent bones.

They get up from their table, and as they are walking back toward the main entrance Chi-yŏn quietly asks, "Do you have some free time tomorrow? It's Sunday."

Chun-t'ae winces, searching for an answer, and Chi-yŏn hastens to ask, "Do you like to watch sports?"

"Well, I never used to play a particular sport, but I don't have anything against watching." His voice seemed to be floating, he thought.

They decided to meet at two in the afternoon the next day. The place would be Seoul Stadium, but since neither of them knew a tearoom in that vicinity they agreed to meet at the first one they saw on the left after turning left off of Ŭlchiro near the stadium.

They leave the palace grounds. Before parting, Chi-yŏn looks up at Chun-t'ae and says with a giggle, "I still don't know your name."

Hmm, is that so? Chun-t'ae thinks. He replies in a formal tone, telling Chi-yŏn his name, workplace, and occupation.

That night Chi-yŏn had a dream. She was by herself on a mountain, and a huge forest fire broke out on all sides and came toward her. The soaring flames, kindled by sparks shooting up, spread without end. In an instant the flames had reached her. But she wasn't frightened. The sparks began to touch her clothing, but they ended up turning to ash. More sparks shot toward her. But whenever they touched her they turned completely to ash. Suddenly Chi-yŏn was driving a truck. She was wearing a blue denim jacket and pants and white sneakers. The sneakers were the ones she used for tennis in high school. The truck was going over a pass now. She was blazing a path where there was not even a human footprint.

The truck clattered and tilted on the bumpy ground. But Chi-yŏn continued to drive, as if nothing was bothering her. She is on her way to pick up some farm produce, but she doesn't know where. She crosses the pass, and some recently cleared land opens up before her. She continued to drive. At the end of all the cleared land was a gully. In the bed of fine sand at the bottom of it, a small amount of clear water had collected. A huge crucian carp was lying there. It was a very attractive fish. Its bluish scales had an iridescent glitter. Gasping for water, the fish pleads to Chi-yŏn, Could you move me to a place with a lot of water? Chi-yŏn doesn't answer. Again and again the fish begs her: Please, move me to a place with a lot of water. Without saying anything Chi-yŏn continues to drive along. Although she sits in the driver's seat, she knows the wheels of the vehicle have run over the fish, crushing its middle. She also knows that blood flowing from the crushed fish has filled the gully completely. But she doesn't think of this as cruel or outrageous. She drives further. She feels refreshed. Ahead, though, is another gully across the road. Like the previous gully, not much water remained in it. A huge crucian carp was also lying there. The fish is slender, its flesh having worn away. Its scales are blackish; they have lost their luster, and only the eyes sparkle. Chi-yŏn guesses this fish too will ask her to move it to a place with a lot of water. But the fish is not even gasping. After waiting for the fish to say something, Chi-yŏn sets the truck in motion again. I'm sure this one has been crushed by the wheels too. But although blood flows from the fish, it remains as it is without being flattened. Its blackish scales have lost their luster and only its eyes sparkle. Good lord! Chi-yŏn wakes up instantly.

In the public toilet in Stone Village a man in his fifties is writing an advertisement on the wall in black ink. He is about to draw the last stroke of the word *inn*. The letters are of different sizes and the thickness of the strokes is uneven, for the proprietor of the inn hasn't hired a sign painter but is doing the work himself.

Above, an advertisement for an eating house had already been written. The writing of the dishes that are offered—*karak kuksu* and *nambi kuksu*[2]—is disorganized, as if it too has been written by the owner. And rain has washed over the letters, leaving them all muddled.

A glance at these advertisements would lead one to believe that the public toilet itself is the inn and eatery. The fact that no arrow marks have been drawn in the advertisements would reinforce such an impression. But then there is no way of drawing arrows. The eating spot is at the far end of the block and the inn at the near corner, both at an angle impossible to indicate with an arrow.

The man who has written both these advertisements steps back a pace or two and looks at the letters as if appreciating them, then turns and walks away.

About this time, Old Pak is waking up from his nap at Chŏnju Auntie's.

"Wow—out like a light, and in the middle of the day...and your eyes are all swollen," said Chŏnju Auntie. She had been sitting beside him all along.

Still lying there, Pak yawns, spreads both arms, and stretches. With an outstretched arm he slaps Chŏnju Auntie on the bottom and says, "Boy, I guess I slept for a while—didn't have to worry about anything either. That's why it's great to be home."

Pak had come home the previous evening and still has not left for the woodworking shop.

Sensing that Pak is looking for a cigarette, Chŏnju Auntie takes one out of a pack and lights it, and after drawing deeply on it a couple of times she exhales and puts it between his lips.

"The house doesn't belong to us anymore now that we've sold it," says Chŏnju Auntie.

[2] These are long wheat-vermicelli noodles that have been boiled. *Karak kuksu* is served in a bowl, *nambi kuksu* in a shallow saucepan.

"But it's ours as long as we stay here."

"I want to move to the new house we bought right away. This lousy area's no good for bringin' up kids."

"There's only nine days left—since we're moving on the thirtieth."

"How about them? They gonna move out for sure that day?"

"You bet. We got the rest of the money from this end, and when we pay the rest of the money at that end, the house is as good as ours."

"I hope we don't have to do a lot of fixing up over there."

"How many times do I have to tell you? We'll be better off as soon as we get there. They were up to their ears in debt and that's why they sold it. Otherwise we never would've ended up with it. No way, no sir."

Pak had told her that there was a good house for sale in Pulgwang-dong, and from the day they decided to buy it—Pak adding his 100,000 *wŏn* to the 68,000 *wŏn* they would get for their house—Chŏnju Auntie's heart swelled in anticipation. Since it was Pulgwang-dong, it would be nothing like this out-of-the-way area, and since there was room in the new house to set up a woodworking shop, they could live together all day long. Previously Pak could visit no more than once a week because he worked at night.

Pak puts out the cigarette, holding it between the ends of his fingernails, and after slapping her again on the bottom he grabs her arm with the same hand and pulls her toward him.

Pretending to shake free, Chŏnju Auntie lowers her voice and says, "You must be crazy—it's broad daylight. Kŏl-i 'll be coming for lunch any minute now."

"I gave him some money and let him go out, so he can play around and buy what he wants to eat."

Chŏnju Auntie points with her chin to the wall next to them.

"So what? We can get even with them now." Pak keeps hauling on her arm.

"Easy, easy. My clothes're gonna get wrinkled," she says, her voice dying out. Giving Pak a sharp sidelong glance, she removes her *ch'ima.*

As he has planned with Chi-yŏn, Chun-t'ae turns off of Ŭlchiro toward Seoul Stadium and goes up the stairs to the first tearoom on the left. It was on the second floor, above a variety store. It immediately struck Chun-t'ae as disarrayed—perhaps because it served primarily the intermittent flow of passengers through the suburban-bus terminal next door.

Chi-yŏn, who had arrived first and was sitting at a window facing the main street, rose halfway to let Chun-t'ae know she was there.

They both ordered tea, as if tacitly understanding that the coffee didn't taste good in a tearoom such as this.

After the waitress has turned around and left, Chi-yŏn says, "I saw you get off the bus."

The bus stop in front of the stadium appeared through the dust-covered window. It seemed to Chun-t'ae that he would have been unable to distinguish who was who among the people pacing back and forth there, no matter how well he might have known them.

"I've got excellent eyesight—twenty-twenty," said Chi-yŏn with a smile.

"Those aren't normal eyes." Chun-t'ae joined her in smiling.

Chi-yŏn observes Chun-t'ae's smile. There's something out of tune about that bright smile, she thinks. She watched the way Chun-t'ae carried himself as he got off the bus just before, and even from her higher vantage point she seemed to detect something discordant about him. She remembered that she was able to pick him out of the crowd instantly because of this air of discordance—his tallness, his slightly hunched shoulders and back. Could this be what draws my gaze and attention? Is this the reason I bought his books almost on impulse?

The tea wasn't very good, so after a couple of sips they left the tearoom and crossed the street, heading toward the stadium.

An industrial league game was under way in the baseball

stadium, and there appeared to be a meet going on in the track-and-field stadium as well.

"We're in luck—it's a clear day," said Chi-yŏn. "Which one would you like to watch?"

"Anything's fine with me."

"How about tennis?"

Chun-t'ae had watched basketball, soccer, and baseball before, but had never seen a tennis match.

The tennis stadium was between the other two stadiums. In one of the middle courts a women's doubles match was in progress. Only a few spectators were in the stands.

"Tennis doesn't have the speed and thrills of basketball and other sports, so it loses more spectators every year." This was partly an excuse and partly a way for Chi-yŏn to say that the number of spectators didn't matter.

In tennis everything characteristically looks white, but in the pellucid air of that day the players' uniforms, hats, socks, and tennis shoes, plus the lines and balls, appeared even whiter. Listen to the sound of the ball, Chi-yŏn says to Chun-t'ae, whose eyes are transfixed by the white color. The *p'ŏng p'ŏng* that comes to him now is hollower than the sound from the public courts that he used to walk by, apparently because this court, surrounded by the stands, is recessed like a swimming pool. Among the few spectators, there were cheers or applause only when the player at the net hit a smash or poached on a return. Apart from that, the quiet surroundings made the sound of the ball ring even louder.

Chun-t'ae, watching the ball crisscross the net, rests his eyes on Chi-yŏn's face. In this half profile her face is most beautiful, he thinks. Chun-t'ae shifts his eyes to the spectators. His mouth wears a spontaneous smile, as if he has thought of something.

Chi-yŏn stares at Chun-t'ae as if to ask what the matter is.

Chun-t'ae turns his head to the left and then to the right several times.

Chi-yŏn also smiles. "We're bound to exercise our necks

nonstop watching tennis."

A set ended.

"Miss Nam, were you a tennis player at one time?"

"I just played because I enjoyed it. I probably would've played more if I hadn't had caries."

Chun-t'ae has the strange notion that the discoloration on the bridge of her nose might have appeared when she had caries.

"You know, for several months I was laid up in a cast, and when I didn't have anything to do I'd pass the time imagining the white ball against the blue sky making a *t'aeng t'aeng* sound as it passed back and forth in front of my eyes. Sometimes I was the umpire and announced the score, and sometimes I was a player in a match."

Chun-t'ae's smile remains.

"It wasn't just a coincidence that I started liking tennis."

Chi-yŏn had had an unusual experience when she was young. Just after Liberation, when she was seven, she had heard the grownups saying that everything was going to disappear in ashes. Not until she grew up did she learn that they had been talking about the atomic bombs dropped on Japan. At the time, young Chi-yŏn, knowing nothing about this, asked her mother if her friend living next door was going to disappear too. She worried more about her friend than about her mom and dad. Her mother said yes. Everything turned gloomy. Actually, it was afterwards that all had seemed gloomy—at the time she may only have been thinking about how awful her friend's disappearance would be. But it was while fleeing south during the Korean War that she truly felt that all was gloomy before her. The moment she saw the shapeless village that had been destroyed by roaring planes passing over, something like a black curtain came down over her eyes and she ended up plopping herself down where she was.

"I think I've had weak nerves from the beginning. One day right after we'd returned to Seoul, school was over and I was leaving the schoolyard when I heard this clear *t'aeng t'aeng* sound. It made me feel really good. It was the sound of a tennis

ball. But it didn't compare to the *p'ŏng p'ŏng* sound here. This
court has everything." Down on the court the next set had
begun. "I used to be in the art club as an extracurricular activ-
ity, but I moved over to the tennis club. I thought that as long
as I could see and hear that white ball, there wouldn't be any
more gloomy fear."

"A pacifist!"

Although Chi-yŏn's eyes seemed to say, There's that tone of
voice again, they quickly took on a hue of composure deep
within, as if she had accepted Chun-t'ae's words and smoothed
their rough edges.

Cheering and applause came from the crowd. One of the net
players had made a beautiful smash.

"What position did you play, Miss Nam, net or backcourt?"

"Backcourt. It was okay. Everyone says playing the net is so
much of an offensive position, but the backcourt is important
too—for defense. For example, if the backcourt player makes a
bad shot, then her partner up front gets caught..."

"Well, that means tennis isn't just a matter of whiteness and
peace."

"It's a game. But if you compare it with other sports, it's
nothing. So not many people watch it. It doesn't look like you
enjoy it either. No speed and no thrills, I guess," she said
quietly with a smile.

Sŏng-ho had no idea why Min-gu had suggested going
downtown in Elder Han's automobile. He asked several times,
but Min-gu, his large mouth breaking into a broad smile,
merely repeated that Sŏng-ho would find out when he got
there. They arrived downtown and got out of the car in front
of a pharmaceutical company. While going up to the second
floor, Sŏng-ho remembered Min-gu telling him that Elder Han
owned a pharmaceutical company. Ah, this is it, he thought,
but he still couldn't understand why Min-gu had fetched him
here.

When they enter the president's office Elder Han is talking

with someone. After asking his visitor to stop by later, he receives Sŏng-ho. At the engagement ceremony Sŏng-ho had found that a smile never left Elder Han's face and that his voice was gentle. And now too Elder Han's face was filled with a smile. As he shook hands with Sŏng-ho, he said in a soft tone that he appreciated Sŏng-ho's efforts at the ceremony. His unaffected manner soon softened Sŏng-ho's reserve.

The three men sat down and exchanged small talk while drinking the tea that an office girl had brought them. Finally Elder Han broached the matter at hand. Could Sŏng-ho transfer to Elder Han's church? The church was being expanded to two stories, and another clergyman was needed. The invitation was completely unexpected, and Sŏng-ho felt too grateful to speak. To become a clergyman in a large church in the center of the city is everybody's hope. Sŏng-ho knows, of course, that there have been more than a few instances in which people campaigned behind the scenes for such a position. Sŏng-ho told Elder Han that he would be forever thankful, but he didn't care to leave his church. Min-gu's big eyes blinked and his face reddened. He had earnestly asked this favor of Elder Han, his future father-in-law, and having received his consent had arranged all of this without saying anything to Sŏng-ho, in order to surprise him. And now Sŏng-ho's unanticipated reply had left him agitated. But Sŏng-ho, though deeply grateful to Min-gu and aware that he had put him in a difficult position, couldn't change his mind. Elder Han's smile never vanished, and in his gentle voice he asked Sŏng-ho to take his time and think it over, for the matter wasn't that urgent.

"How come you turned it down?" Min-gu asked as soon as they left Elder Han's office. Displeasure was written on his face.

"I'm planning on staying where I am until they don't want me anymore," Sŏng-ho said quietly.

"When's that? A thousand years from now? You're nuts! You think the people at that church'll let go of someone like you? You've got to screw up your courage and make a decision."

Min-gu gave no sign that he would acquiesce.

But Sŏng-ho, observing that even his present church was more than he could handle, remained convinced that he should do the best he could in the circumstances allotted him.

"All right," said Min-gu. "If you really feel that way, let's forget about it for the time being. Actually you might be right—who knows. But even if you aren't, maybe it's better if everyone lives their own life. Anyway, let's go to my place and order out for lunch or something. And while we're at it you can take a look at what I've been collecting these days." He led Sŏng-ho to his apartment.

The most recent additions to Min-gu's collection were two paintings. Each was on a piece of silk two *cha*[3] wide by three *cha* long. Both had been stained by moisture, and their colors had faded.

After relating how he had stolen the paintings from a shrine on Kanghwa Island Min-gu said, "This one's the *sambul chesŏk,* the three highest gods that shamans worship."

In the foreground of the picture were two figures, and behind them a third. The body of each was propped up on a lotus frond. All three wore the same dull yellow peaked hood and Buddhist robe. Each had a black rosary around his neck. The strange thing was, the right lapel was scarlet and the left one blue. The clouds painted in the upper part of the picture showed that the three of them lived in the sky.

"Originally these were the gods of the shamans, and later, because of Buddhist influence, the lotus blossoms and rosaries were added. Now this one here," said Min-gu, referring to the second painting, "is the *sŏ-nang* god."

A full-length figure had been painted, and behind him a horse. The figure wore white *paji*[4] and *chŏgori,* an indigo-blue

---

[3]*Cha:* see Part 3, chapter 3, note 2.
[4]*Paji:* traditional Korean trousers, having baggy legs and tied at the waist and ankles with strips of cloth; modern trousers are also called *paji*.

k'waeja,[5] and a copper-colored helmet. His straw sandals were indigo blue. His right hand held a bridle and his left a whip. The horse was copper-colored.

"The *sŏ-nang* god is a spirit who wards off calamities that come from outside the village. He also serves as a guide for travelers. And that's why the horse was drawn. Back in the old days was there any other means of transportation besides the horse? Interesting, huh?"

"But aren't the villagers near that shrine going to raise cain wondering who stole the paintings?" Sŏng-ho pointed out. He thought Min-gu's fervor in collecting materials on shamanism had gone too far.

"I don't think so. Instead of wondering who stole them, they'll think their devotion was insufficient, and so the gods moved to a different location. They'll paint new ones and hang 'em in the shrine."

"That makes it easy for you." While the execution of the paintings was artless, in places their naiveté drew Sŏng-ho's eye. "What kind of people do paintings like this?"

"You know, when shamans put up portraits in their house, they're generally printed ones that they buy. But these are different. In the past it seems that this kind of painting was done by a group of shamans who painted well, but I heard that lately the shamans have been going to temples and asking a monk to do it. I think this is one respect in which shamanism and Buddhism have come together. Here's something you might be interested in. If you look at Yuk Tang's[6] *Theories of Pulham Culture*, you'll find that Tan-gun[7] is the Sino-Korean pronunciation of the Mongolian word *tang-gul*. Now if you look at *tang-*

---

[5]*K'waeja:* a knee-length vest secured around the chest. Originally worn in combat, it is now worn primarily by children, along with the traditional *pok-gŏn* hat, on holidays.

[6]Yuk Tang: pen name of Ch'oe Nam-sŏn (1890–1957), historian, writer, and primary author of the Korean Declaration of Independence (March 1, 1919).

[7]Tan-gun: mythical founder of the Korean people (2333 B.C.–?).

gul as *tan-gol,* then this indicates that Tan-gun was nothing less than a shaman. Because even now if you go south, you'll see that they call shamans *tan-gol* there. That offers some proof that Tan-gun was a *tan-gol*—in other words a shaman. So my hunch isn't necessarily wrong. You know how in the *Samguk Yusa*[8] it's recorded that Kojumong was the son of Tan-gun? Now judging from the dates, how could this be the case? But if we interpret the word *Tan-gun* as 'shaman,' then there's nothing strange about it at all. The *Samguk Yusa* also says that Pak Hyŏkkŏse's[9] son King Namhae was given the title of *ch'ach'aung* or *chach'ung,* and it interprets these words as 'shaman.' In other words, they mean a male shaman. Therefore, if we look at the ancient system of inheritance, it's not wrong, is it, to say that Pak Hyŏkkŏse was also a shaman? These days the shamans aren't able to govern others—instead there's a tendency to disregard them. But originally I don't think it was like that. Since they were prophetic and clairvoyant and cured chronic illnesses, they must have seemed awesome and mysterious to the people back then. So it's obvious that they became chiefs of the others. And at the beginning of the Yi dynasty, people honored shamans by referring to them as *teacher* rather than *shaman.*" Min-gu's tone of voice was that of a lecturer who had warmed up to his topic. "Nowadays the students have a great interest in shamans too. Some time ago a student where I teach made a point of looking me up, and what he had to say was really unusual. He said he'd found out that people definitely have a soul and he pointed out that not everything fortune-tellers say is superstition. He looked so serious that I asked him how he'd found that out, and he said that his friend's death had given him the opportunity..."

The two of them were old friends from the same town who had been classmates throughout high school. The student's

---

[8]*Samguk Yusa* (Memorabilia of the Three Kingdoms): a miscellany of poems, tales of early Korean history, Buddhist fables, and more, collected ca. 1279 by the Zen monk Iryŏn (1206–1289).

[9]Pak Hyŏkkŏse: mythical founder of the Silla kingdom (57 B.C.–A.D. 906).

friend had appeared in a dream. He had the feeling that he was about to fall off a towering cliff. The student was terrified and called out to his friend to wait. He woke up as he was climbing up the cliff to restrain him. Then, while he was wondering if something had happened to his friend, the news came that he had died.

"…When I asked him whether the death had been a suicide he said no way—his friend just wasn't the sort to kill himself.…"

Sŏng-ho nodded.

Every year during the rainy season the bridge over the stream in front of their village was washed away. Unable to stand by any longer, the friend had begun bringing back large rocks from the mountain with which he intended to build a permanent bridge. Then one day he had lost his step and fallen into a pond at the foot of the mountain and drowned. But no matter how they tried they couldn't recover the body. So they consulted a fortune-teller, who said that not until the student himself went to the pond would they be able to find it. The student went to the village and, as the fortune-teller had directed, stood on the bank of the pond and called his friend three times, and sure enough the body came to the surface, right in front of him.

"…At first the student was reluctant to follow the fortune-teller's instructions, because he considered them all a bunch of superstitions, but he went ahead after he saw how grief-stricken the parents were when they couldn't find the body. But the way things turned out made him think about a lot of things. Of course some people might feel it was a coincidence—the decomposed body happened to rise to the surface at the time he was calling his friend's name—but he couldn't think of it only in those terms. He believed his friend wanted to display his dead body to him. I didn't expect this, and when I asked what made him think like that, he said his friend told him once that his one fear in life was not death but rather losing his zest for doing things. Now he said he believed that his friend's soul had called out to him in order to make him remember those words. You see, he was getting tired of working his way through school, and just when he was wondering whether to give up his studies his friend had died. He felt that this incident was surely the essence of friendship."

"The essence of friendship?" Sŏng-ho said, ruminating over this tale. "So his interpretation was that this dead boy's soul had called him to his corpse in order to remind him of something. It's a beautiful story whether it's true or not."

"But what's been attracting my interest is the prediction of that fortune-teller. It was on the mark. Suppose we look at it this way: it was autumn and all the mugginess was gone, and in the cold water the body decomposed slowly, and so the body happened to become buoyant when the student called out his friend's name from the bank. It's nothing but a coincidence. But what is this thing we call coincidence? There are all sorts of weird accidents and coincidences. Let's pretend we're gods looking down on what humans call accident or coincidence. From that standpoint wouldn't it look like something inevitable? And what if we look at these inevitabilities as being revealed to shamans and fortune-tellers, who then make their predictions?"

"It's an interesting thought, but..."

"But making and receiving revelations isn't Christianity, and therefore it just won't do. Isn't that it?" said Min-gu in an insinuating tone.

Sŏng-ho pondered this for a while and then spoke.

"From the beginning—or to borrow your expression, from the time of Tan-gun, that's okay—we Koreans seem to have accepted all kinds of gods without thinking twice about it. Even those who have religion are always going back and forth between Christianity and shamanism. And if we substitute Buddhism for Christianity, it's exactly the same. If they go this way they've got Christianity, that way and they've got shamanism. I'll tell you a story from church. Just recently a deaconess came to me for a prayer because her grandson had gotten sick. Now get this—I heard that the same night, she called a shaman and an exorcism was performed. What she had in mind all along was to obtain whatever efficacy she could from the two of them. You understand? This kind of thing goes on all the time."

"Anyway, is it true that people get some kind of consolation from shamanism?"

"Perhaps they receive temporary consolation, but shamanism is always creating new anxieties. And along with that, people are always coming out with excuses and pretexts. It's a big headache. Well, enough of that. About your fiancee's family— they don't say anything about what you're doing?"

"Like what? I'm doing literary research. What can they say?"

During his next trip to Seoul Chun-t'ae thought about meeting Chi-yŏn again, but when it actually came to telephoning her he wavered. Isn't it okay to meet her like this? He had to feel decisive before doing so, but his decisiveness had been overtaken by a vague longing to see her. He couldn't define his feelings. Deciding he would rather not meet her, he ended up going back down to Suwŏn as soon as he had taken care of his business. At the same time, he felt he was missing something.

Chun-t'ae still had these mixed feelings the day he received a postcard at work from Chi-yŏn. It read simply: How about going to the orchards in T'aenŭng to eat some pears?

Chapter 6

Students from an agricultural high school in the countryside nearby had come on a field trip to the agricultural testing station. Chun-t'ae was standing behind them listening to a newly appointed researcher talk about an artificially hybrid sweet potato.

The researcher proceeds with his systematic, detailed explanation.

In the first week or so of April you plant a morning glory seed in a pot thirty centimeters across and forty-five centimeters deep. Take good care of it. Then, in the first week or so of June, graft a sweet potato bud that has four or five leaves onto the bottom of the morning glory. You do this by taking a razor blade and cutting off the stem beneath the sprouts on the morning glory and making a one-centimeter wedge-shaped cut in it. Then sharpen the sweet potato bud so it makes a good fit, and insert it in the cut. Wrap the joint with cotton, fasten it with straw, and then prop it up. The researcher accompanied his explanation with a series of pictures on the blackboard. After grafting it like this, give it tap water every day so that it won't dry out, and set it in a cool, dry place for about a week. After the skin of the morning glory stem and the skin of the sweet potato bud have healed, the bud will grow just fine by absorbing moisture from the morning glory's roots. We can tell if the graft has been successful if the withered potato bud gradually comes back to life and starts to thrive.

"...Students, think of this as a marriage between a withered old bachelor sweet potato and a pretty young lady morning glory."

The students laughed.

Though he admired this young researcher, who looked so composed, Chun-t'ae did not laugh along with the students. What if the joining of humans were as simple as that of plants? he wondered.

Starting the tenth day after grafting, the researcher continued, expose it to sunlight every day for nine to ten hours and then leave it in a dark room for fourteen to fifteen hours. This is because the sweet potato is an annual plant that goes through the summer solstice and blooms as soon as autumn arrives, and when provided with the proper surroundings it blooms quickly. Cultivate it like this, and within the first ten days of August the sweet potato will produce a flower stalk at the joint where the leaves are hanging from the stem. At first there are only one or two flower buds, but the stalk will develop, little by little, and eventually you have twenty or thirty flowers hanging from that joint. The flowers start blooming on a full-scale basis in September.

"So even a sweet potato blooms?" asked a student. It was a natural, worthwhile question to ask, thought Chun-t'ae.

"As you know, originally the sweet potato transferred nutrients from the vine, where they are manufactured, to the part of the plant that is under the soil, and stores them in the roots. In other words, it's the roots that contain the facilities for storage. Therefore, it's difficult for the sweet potato to bloom. But if there's an overmanufacture of nutrients and some are left over after storage, then in some cases it blooms—for example, in tropical areas. But it's difficult in our country's climate. So if we're going to cross-breed a plant, it has to bloom. But because the sweet potato doesn't ordinarily bloom we exchange its roots for those of the morning glory. Because the morning glory's roots have no facilities for storing nutrients, if we graft a sweet potato bud onto a morning glory plant, then it's natural that the sweet potato will produce flower buds using the excess nutrients stored in the above-ground part of the morning glory."

Chun-t'ae tilted his head back and looked up at the sky. What if Ch'ang-ae and I had a child? But if having a child is the only

way to keep us together, then it's not a solution to the fundamental problem, and in that case it would be better not to have
one.

The researcher proceeds with his explanation of the
techniques of grafting. The flower of the sweet potato has the
appearance of the lavender flower of the morning glory, and is
characterized by five stamens. Pierce the side of the flower bud
and remove all of the stamens. The next morning apply pollen
from the stamens of the sweet potato plant in question to the
head of its pistil. This completes the grafting. The researcher
displays a pot in which he had finished this cross-breeding process several days earlier.

"Needless to say, after doing the cross-breeding it's necessary to enclose the plant in a wax-paper envelope so that pollen
from other flowers can't float in. Fifty days after the cross-
breeding a pod five millimeters across will mature where the
flowers blossomed. There are three to five seeds inside.
They're umber in color and triangular. They're like miniature
morning glory seeds. If you make a small scar in the husk of
these seeds and then sow them, then next spring the buds will
come out just like sweet potato buds."

Chun-t'ae knew all of this, but this time the word *scar*
weighed in his mind. For sure, Ch'ang-ae and I both wear
scars. Scars that we have clothed each other in.

"Why do you make a scar in the seed?" another student
asked.

"That's so it can absorb moisture easily."

Right. It shouldn't be a scar that leaves only an ugly mark.
From these rotten, ugly scars we should make new flesh come
forth. Then what about Ch'ang-ae and I?

There are no sprouts on the sweet potato bud, the researcher
went on, but the variety we obtain from cross-breeding has
roots and its buds have sprouts. If we cut off a bud from each
variety and look at it, we can't distinguish between them. But
if we plant one of these hybrid buds in a field, the root can
thicken instead of branching out. Then that year we'll harvest

a huge sweet potato. We store this sweet potato and then stick it in a greenhouse the following spring and grow more buds. We plant these buds in the field and test their productivity. In this fashion we plant an artificially cross-bred seed just once, and because starting the next year we plant the buds just like we plant a regular sweet potato, we can make this improved variety succeed after a comparatively few years, as long as the nutrients continue to propagate without altering the characteristics of the plant.

"It won't work if you directly cross-breed the sweet potato flower and the morning glory flower?" came another question.

"No, it can't be done. The part that produces the nutrients—namely, the flesh of the two plants—we can do a good job of grafting. But it's not possible to cross-breed through the flowers. Likewise, there's no mixing of cows and horses."

In the end, is the relationship between Ch'ang-ae and I like that of a morning glory flower and a sweet potato flower?

The researcher finished by explaining the characteristics and uses of the *Suwŏn 147, yusim, ch'ŏnmi,* and other varieties of sweet potato being promoted among the farmers of Korea.

At home that evening, Chun-t'ae sinks into a light and relaxing mood, as if he has returned to the boardinghouse life of his past. After opening up the dressmaking shop Ch'ang-ae continued to return home once every several days. But this morning she went to Seoul early, saying business was so hectic that from now on she wouldn't be able to drop by more than once a week. It was a guarantee that from now on he would be living a solitary life for a week at a time.

What's this light-hearted feeling all about? It's not that I've felt restricted living with her. We've tried as much as we could not to restrain each other. Still, even after getting married, wasn't there a subtle yearning in my unconscious for the boardinghouse life of the old days? Didn't that make me appear indifferent to her? Didn't it change her? If that's the case, then it's more my fault than hers. But what's the use of trying to blame someone at this point? From now on we'll try to start new lives. She does what she wants, I do what I want.

Chun-t'ae goes to his desk and sits down. It is an object he has spent a long time with, an object that has stayed by him—much more so than his wife. The stains and even the flaws on the surface of the desk were things that were relevant only to him; the ink stain created some time ago when he had propped up a nearly empty ink bottle with its lid on its back edge and then put a fountain pen in it, the burn mark made when he stayed up all night reading a book and dropped a cigarette while dozing, and so on.

Chun-t'ae looks around the room from a fresh perspective. The mirror on the bureau is reflecting the lamplight. He covers the bureau with the spread for the quilt. He lays out his bed on the floor, putting cigarettes and ashtray near the head, along with several magazines from the bookshelves. These days there's no suitable material to translate, so he hasn't taken on any translation work.

He gets in bed and stretches. He picks up a magazine. Looking at it while lying supine, looking at it while lying prone—he can do whichever he wishes. And he doesn't have to listen to Ch'ang-ae's snoring.

Ash from the cigarette between Chun-t'ae's fingers falls on the leaves of the magazine he is reading as he lies on his stomach. Chun-t'ae takes his eyes from the magazine, applies saliva to the tip of the index finger of his other hand, and brings it to the ash. This too is something he hasn't done in ages. With extreme care he sticks the ash to his moistened fingertip. Then he silently moves his finger toward the ashtray. But midway the ash falls and scatters in a cloud. Perhaps because he hadn't done this for a long time, he didn't stick the ash firmly enough to his fingertip. He stamps the scattered ash with his thumb so that it sticks, and then flicks it off in the ashtray. With one breath he dissipates the rest of the powdered ash. Dirtying the floor of the room this way used to be an everyday occurrence before marriage.

Chun-t'ae's eyes stop in space on their way back to the magazine. Tomorrow is Saturday. The day that Chi-yŏn suggested going to the pear orchards. She probably considered my work situation in choosing Saturday afternoon. Let's do it. There's no need to attach a deep meaning to meeting her. Why don't I just meet her when I can, without us burdening each other?

PART **II**

Chapter 1

Only after wandering for a while was Ŭn-hŭi able to find Ch'ang-ae's dressmaking shop. The directions Chun-t'ae had given her were vague. Ŭn-hŭi had met Chi-yŏn and Chun-t'ae at the pear orchards in T'aenŭng and had inquired about Ch'ang-ae. When Chun-t'ae said she had opened a dressmaking store Ŭn-hŭi had asked where it was. Chun-t'ae, replying as if this was none of his concern, had said something about it being next to the hospital attached to Usŏk College, in Myŏngnyun-dong. Moreover, he didn't even know the name of the store. Ŭn-hŭi was amazed. How could he be like that? When she got there she found that the store was some distance from the hospital, at the entrance to a large side street. The name of the store was Eve.

Three middle-aged women were sitting in a sofa inside the shop. One of them told Ŭn-hŭi that Ch'ang-ae had gone out on business. She said it was about time for her to return, and asked Ŭn-hŭi to take a seat. She sat down in a new armchair with spongy cushions.

In the show window hang two kinds of cloth, and on the shelves of patterned wood on one wall are several rolls of cloth all in order. It's the salon style that's becoming popular these days, Ŭn-hŭi thinks. There appeared to be a tailoring room on the second floor, judging from the stairs that led up from a recess deep inside the store.

Ŭn-hŭi turned to two oil paintings hanging between photographs of fashion models. They were abstract paintings whose content she couldn't guess, but she could tell from their predominantly crimson color and sticky texture that the same artist had painted them. They had been signed KANG. The paintings seemed to brighten the inside of the shop.

Taking little notice of Ŭn-hŭi, the women continued their random conversation.

Men are hard to understand, Ŭn-hŭi thinks again. Since he doesn't know the location or the name of his wife's store, it's clear that he hasn't come here even once. And he's going around with other women in the outskirts of town. This Nam Chi-yŏn—what kind of woman could she be anyway? What's her relationship with Chun-t'ae? Min-gu said he'd never seen her before either. She seems to know Sŏng-ho pretty well, but there's nothing strange about that because Sŏng-ho's a preacher and knows quite a few people. The only thing I can't figure out is why Chun-t'ae's going around with her. Chi-yŏn had worn a hiking hat with a big brim, a dark, ash-colored sweater, light gray slacks, and tennis shoes—the complete outfit for a picnic. This was too much of a contrast with Ŭn-hŭi, who had come in high heels and clothing she would wear in the city. She didn't realize that in order to get to the orchards they had to walk in from T'aenŭng and cross several slopes. If she had known this, she too would have dressed for an outing, and so she was displeased with Min-gu, who hadn't prepared her. He's got this bad habit of not being attentive, and then kind of jumping into things.

The middle-aged women break out in laughter. Ŭn-hŭi, who hasn't been paying attention, wonders why. She returns to the pursuit of this woman Chi-yŏn. She doesn't look healthy with all that discoloration on the bridge of her nose, but she appears firm. As soon as they had entered the orchard a dog started barking its head off. It was tied up a short distance from the watchman's hut. It was a gigantic shepherd. It came running out barking furiously until its leash tightened. It looked like the leash would break any second and the dog would run over to them. Ŭn-hŭi was frightened and clung to Min-gu as they walked along. Min-gu asked the owner of the orchard if the dog was dangerous. The owner admonished the dog, and just when they thought it had quieted it started barking again. Ŭn-hŭi was the first to enter the watchman's hut. Chi-yŏn, however, had slowly walked over to the dog by herself. The dog was ready to spring upon her, but the leash was too short and so it stood up on its hindlegs and barked. The owner told her to be cautious and not get close. Even so, Chi-yŏn didn't stop until she was almost within reach of the dog. The animal bared its long teeth and snarled, foaming at the mouth. It had all the energy it needed to bite her if she had moved just a little closer. But Chi-yŏn was unperturbed. For some reason the snarling of the rampaging dog gradually died out, and it looked in Chi-yŏn's direction. Chi-yŏn merely stood there. Finally the dog bowed its head slightly and its ears lay back. Chi-yŏn stood silently, as before. Little by little the dog's tail started wagging. Chi-yŏn extended her hand toward the dog. Observing Chi-yŏn's intentions, the dog crept near her. Chi-yŏn maintained the same posture. At last the dog lifted its neck and touched its nose to her hand, then started licking it. Chi-yŏn let the dog do as it wished, then removed her hand and patted the dog's head and scratched under its chin. The dog wagged its tail vigorously. Not until then did Chi-yŏn step back. As if hoping for more caressing, the dog tried to follow, whining. An extraordinarily daring woman, Ŭn-hŭi thought after seeing this.

The sudden darkening of the interior of the shop and the patter of raindrops told those inside that a downpour had begun. The woman who had greeted Ŭn-hŭi got up and looked inside and outside the store to see if there was anything to put away. The people on the sidewalk were scurrying to get out of the rain. The squall made the outside a blur.

Even after the shower stopped, it was some time before Ch'ang-ae returned. Upon seeing Ŭn-hŭi, her face lights up and she takes her hands. "Your visitor's been waiting quite a spell," the middle-aged woman tells Ch'ang-ae. After apologizing to Ŭn-hŭi, Ch'ang-ae introduces her to the woman—Mrs. O, one of the co-owners of the shop.

After giving Mrs. O the bundle she was carrying, Ch'ang-ae sits down opposite Ŭn-hŭi.

"You've gotten prettier."

"Oh come on. I don't have what it takes to be pretty." Ŭn-hŭi observes Ch'ang-ae. "Your face looks like it's gotten some sun."

"I've been doing some looking around—for this little business of ours—and not taking care of it." Ch'ang-ae sweeps a palm down her cheek.

"You're more attractive with a bit of color."

"Not any more. I've passed the age where a tan is attractive. By the way—I'm doing this backwards—congratulations on your engagement. And Mr. Song is well?"

"Yes, he is. And thank you."

"I'm really very sorry I couldn't attend the ceremony."

"Your mother was ill? That's what I heard from Mr. Ham. Has she recovered?"

"Yes, she's all right now. By the way, when will the wedding be?"

"We haven't picked a date yet."

"I'll be sure to go this time."

"Mrs. Chang, could you come here for a minute?" It was Mrs. O.

"I'll be right there," said Ch'ang-ae.

The olive-colored chamois coat that Ch'ang-ae had brought back in the bundle was displayed on the round table in front of Mrs. O and the two other women.

"Isn't it nice?" Ch'ang-ae said, going over to the table. "Sure enough. Nothing can beat chamois from Israel. Here, feel it. It's different—you can tell from its gentle touch." "I wish it were sepia," said the plump member of the middle-aged trio. "Oh no—sepia is too ordinary," said Ch'ang-ae. "Madame Ch'oe, if a refined woman like you doesn't wear it, then who can? Here, try it on and see if it becomes you. We won't be able to tell just by looking at it." Ch'ang-ae helped her on with the coat. She had not been mistaken—olive lent a taste of elegance to this woman's rust-colored skin. "What a fine color," says Mrs. O, as if impressed. "Yes indeed," chimes in the last of the middle-aged women. "The overall length and the sleeve length are a perfect fit. It couldn't be better even if it had been tailored." Mrs. Ch'oe inspected the appearance of the coat from various angles. "I wish it had a little more room." "These days a tight fit is the fashion, but if you insist I can let the buttons out a little." While measuring to see how much more room she can provide, Ch'ang-ae says in a low voice, "I heard it's only been worn a couple of times—it's just like new." Removing the coat, Ch'ang-ae goes to the nook in the wall and then up the stairs. In addition to serving the customers who came for tailor-made clothing, she has carved out a business in buying and reselling foreign-made clothing. Having come this far, she plans to have her own business in due time, come what may.

Presently Ch'ang-ae came down from the second floor and returned to Ŭn-hŭi. Ŭn-hŭi asked about having a suit tailored.

"Well, I appreciate your coming to our little out-of-the-way place... Now what kind of clothing? Town wear? For parties?" Ch'ang-ae sizes up Ŭn-hŭi's figure anew.

"Please pick out a decent one for me."

Ch'ang-ae leafs through a fashion magazine.

"How would this kind of outfit be? It's good for town wear, and for simple occasions it makes you look elegant if you don't wear the top."

"Not bad," said Ŭn-hŭi as she looked at the magazine. "But I'll leave it all up to you—just don't make it too loud."

There is no material at the shop now, but Ch'ang-ae says she will find some and cut it to size.

After measuring Ŭn-hŭi, Ch'ang-ae asked her to return three

days later and accepted partial payment for the clothing. She then led her to a tearoom cross the street. Actually, this had been Ŭn-hŭi's intention, and she followed willingly.

"I was really hot for that chamois coat," said Ŭn-hŭi.

"I'll bet. It's hard to find an item like that."

"Where did it come from?"

"I got it from a woman who lives with a foreigner in It'aewŏn. Sometimes I get hold of some brand-new stuff. If something good appears, would you like me to tell you?"

Ŭn-hŭi nods inattentively. Now that they were by themselves, she does not know where to begin.

Next to them was an aquarium. In it were several varieties of tropical fish, some staying in one place and silently pursing their mouth, others flitting through the water.

Still unable to begin, Ŭn-hŭi observes the playful scene.

"Do you like these aquariums, Miss Han?" asked Ch'ang-ae.

"We keep tropical fish at home, and I always enjoy taking the time to watch them swim."

"Is that so? I get frustrated when I see something like this. It's worse with birds. I don't have the heart to watch them fluttering around in their cages. I get uneasy."

The lower half of one of the walls of the tearoom had been plastered, and a nude woman embossed on it. It was a crude job, a typical tearoom decoration.

A first grade girl, if not a kindergartener, has become attached to the engraving and is tracing its lines with her fingertips. Two housewives in their thirties sit chatting in front of it. Having traced the breasts in the carving, the girl shakes one of the women by the shoulder and says "Mom, Mom, this is number eight, isn't it?" Again she follows the breasts of the engraving with her fingertips.

Ŭn-hŭi turns to Ch'ang-ae. "Isn't it inconvenient going back and forth to Suwŏn?" She is barely able to get these words out.

"That's why I don't go home more than once a week."

Ŭn-hŭi smoothly extends the conversation to household matters. "Well, what about the house?"

"We have an old housemaid. There's not a lot to do in the house anyway..."

"Since your family live in Seoul, you can probably stay..."

"No. I have a bedroom in the second floor of the shop."

"By the way, I've been wondering why you haven't had children yet," Ŭn-hŭi said, recalling her remark to Min-gu that Ch'ang-ae and Chun-t'ae could probably have an ideal baby.

Ch'ang-ae laughed softly. "I didn't intend it like that, but it just turned out that way." While saying this she entertained the thought that if they had actually had a child, they would not have reached their present situation. But she immediately changed her mind. No, even assuming there was a child, it would have been just the same.

"Poor Mr. Ham—he must be lonely. I mean, your going down there only once a week."

"It's already been several years since we got married, you know."

"Even so..."

"He's not one to put a lot of emphasis on family life, and I'm the same way."

Ŭn-hŭi did not comprehend. She kept her eyes on Ch'ang-ae's face.

"We're kind of a strange couple. We've arranged not to interfere with each other."

"That means you trust in each other that much?"

"No, it's not that. Maybe we don't want to injure each other's pride."

At this point Ŭn-hŭi decides it is time to come to the point. She strongly believes she has the duty to say this for the sake of their marriage.

"What if something unseen arose that could injure your pride?"

"What do you mean?"

"What if, you know, Mr. Ham and another woman..."

"Is there something like that going on?" There was no hint of surprise in her voice.

"I mean, if by chance that kind of thing happened." Ŭn-hŭi begins to tap the teacup on the table. It is she who becomes embarrassed by this unexpectedly lukewarm reaction.

"It's all right, even if it's for real," Ch'ang-ae said, smiling. "The truth is, if he becomes serious with a woman, it won't hurt my pride. The more of that precious feeling we have around us, the better, don't you think?"

Ŭn-hŭi is taken aback once more, this time by Ch'ang-ae's calm voice.

Chŏnju Auntie was caught in a shower. But it didn't occur to her to get out of the rain. She couldn't delay even an instant. Today was the day she and Old Pak had arranged to move to the new house he had bought in Pulgwang-dong. Noon had passed, however, and Pak, who had said he would come with a rented motorcycle, had not appeared. Upon arriving, the new owners of her Stone Village house had asked Chŏnju Auntie why it hadn't been emptied. Burning with worry, she went downtown to look for Pak. Maybe he had come down sick all of a sudden and couldn't move. Or maybe he had had an accident. But at the woodworking shop she was told that Pak had left ten days before. What's this all about? she thought. When he came around last Saturday night, just three days ago, he didn't say anything about that. She asked where he was working now, but they didn't know. Absent-mindedly she turned and left, but after walking for a while, it occurred to her that the people at the woodworking shop were hiding something. It was on her way back to the shop that she encountered the shower.

Her soaked clothing was of no concern to her. Her sole desire was to meet Pak as soon as possible. Upon returning to the shop she was informed that Pak had left two days before with all his tools, saying he was going down to his hometown because his wife had fallen ill. When she asked where his hometown was, they said it was something like Anyang or Ansŏng. To her knowledge, Pak was a native of Seoul and a widower. Thinking they were talking about somebody else, she described Pak to them; it was him all right. Chŏnju Auntie couldn't figure out what was what.

Bereft of her senses, Chŏnju Auntie returned home. She got off the bus and began walking. Her whole body drooped. Her shoes scuffed along, and her sodden *ch'ima* hung about her feet.

Behind her a truck approached, its horn sounding. Chŏnju Auntie moved slightly to the side, but not enough for the truck to pass. Sŏng-ho, on his way home from the office of the Council of Elders, where he had been ordained a minister, had been looking back at this. He ran up to Chŏnju Auntie, took her arm, and led her to the side of the road. Cursing at Chŏnju Auntie, the truck driver went by, raising a cloud of dust.

Sŏng-ho looked around. Brightened by the slanting sunlight of the approaching evening, the surroundings showed no trace of rain. The shower must've only covered downtown, he thought. It looks like she got caught in it.

The eyes that met Sŏng-ho's were vacant. He had not seen her on the bus but guessed they had gotten off together. Her shabby appearance and her expression were those of a lifeless soul.

They parted at the junction of the entrance to Stone Village and the lane to the hill where the church was located.

Chŏnju Auntie's pace became heavier. She didn't want to live. But she didn't want to die alone. She wanted to die with one other person. It struck her that perhaps the person she wanted to die with had been at home while she was struggling around downtown. Maybe he's loaded the motorcycle and is waiting for me. Suddenly her step quickens. Whether or not he had a wife was something to worry about later—her only wish now was for Pak to show up. If only that gentleman is there at home, then there's no need for anyone to die.

Pak wasn't to be seen, inside the house or out.

The man who had bought the house looked tired of waiting. Knitting his brow, he asked, "What's going on? We're going to have to move in before it gets dark."

Chŏnju Auntie collapsed in a heap on the floor of her room and for a moment stared blankly into space. With a great effort she opened her mouth.

"They aren't out of the other place yet. What can I do?"

"So the other place isn't empty. Then how long d'you plan on going on like this?"

"They say they'll clear out tomorra." She wanted to stay there just one day more, if nothing else. At this point there was no place for her to go, but she hadn't yet lost hope that Pak might appear by evening.

"At any rate, we'll have to move in today."

"Don't be so harsh."

"Now look here, Ma'am. What's this talk about being harsh. Am I wrong to move in on the day we're supposed to move in?"

"Didn't I give you this place cheap?"

"Huh, now that it's over and done with I hear all this non-sense. You don't remember that we gave you as much as you wanted for the middle installment?"

It was true. She could have gotten seventy thousand *wŏn* for the house, but ended up selling it for sixty-eight thousand on the condition that she get a seven-thousand-*wŏn* down payment and a middle installment of sixty thousand, with only a thousand *wŏn* remaining to be paid. It was Pak's idea. He had said that although they were selling somewhat cheaply, obtaining a large middle installment would help them acquire the new house.

"No matter how you look at it, I can't clear out today."

"Huh! You got some nerve."

"Nerve or whatever—you're telling me to go live on the street?"

"Can't you spend a night in a hotel or something? We've gotta do like the contract says."

"You think they're gonna put me up for free?" While saying this Chŏnju Auntie suddenly thought of something. She put some energy into her voice. "Don't you owe us another one thousand *wŏn*? Could you give me that?"

"The final payment? If I give that to you, then you'll go to a hotel here and now?"

"Uh-uh. I'm not going to any hotel today. Instead I'll clear out tomorra—for the life o' me. If you can't come up with a thousand, then gimme five hundred."

The new owner of the house thought it over. The shape she was in defied description. Her clothes were soaked, as if she had fallen into some water. Could she have had an argument with the people at the other place and gotten doused by them? Anyway, there's nothing to be gained from ruffling the feathers of a woman like this. Even if she doesn't clear out the next day, just to aggravate me, it's not my job to throw her out. No need to injure her feelings on account of a measly five hundred *wŏn*. He told Chŏnju Auntie that tomorrow she had to leave the house whether or not the other place had been vacated, and after obtaining her promise he gave her the money. He leaves the room and, looking toward the kitchen, thinks he's done well in hanging the rice pot over the cooking range, as his wife had asked. Having at least set up the rice pot first, he considered them to be partway into the new house, even though they hadn't completed moving in that day. This was because this was the last day of August by the lunar calendar, and there would be no *son*[1] wandering around. *Son* are a bad omen, for no matter what direction they inhabit, *yŏkkwi*[2] follow them around. People who believe in *son* consider dates and directions not only in moving but in obtaining puppies and kittens and even hammering a nail in a room.

"Don't light a charcoal briquette tonight. I've given the range a new coat of cement," said the new owner gently.

A gloomy reply came from the room: "Don't worry."

Good! I finally tricked it. You're a goner, kitten! Without

---

[1] *Son:* wandering evil spirits, thought to inhabit each of the four quadrants of the compass in turn on certain days of the month.

[2] *Yŏkkwi:* spirits that carry highly contagious diseases.

much effort Kŏl-i grabbed the stray cat crouching beside the public toilet. I'm not gonna just let you go. Kŏl-i was out of sorts. Again today there was no reply to his message. He and the girl he'd held hands with at the comic-book shop with the television set had agreed to correspond by writing messages on the wall of the public toilet. It was two days ago that he had written suggesting they meet in the evening on the hill in back. Not only had she not responded thus far, but yesterday and the day before she hadn't appeared at the comic-book shop. Yesterday and today he had gone several times to hang around her neighborhood. He was constantly in and out of the toilet, with no intention of leaving a load, but there was not a word for him. Kŏl-i fretted. This was the day for his family to move downtown.

Kŏl-i stands holding the cat, wondering how he will torment the damned thing. Sŏp-i appears, P'yŏng-i at his side. They are on their way home from the tent school, tattered cloth schoolbags in hand.

"Haven't you moved yet?" Sŏp-i asks, drawing close.

"We can't go until the motorcycle comes for our stuff."

"How'dja catch that cat?"

"I caught one too once!" P'yŏng-i proudly uttered before Kŏl-i had a chance to reply.

"Hey kid! Why don't you get lost?" Not until then did a plan for the cat come to Kŏl-i's mind. "Hey Sŏp-a,[3] go get some cord from your house."

"Cord?" Sŏp-i hesitates for an instant. "Oh yeah, we'll tie it up like a dog and play with it—it'll be fun." Sŏp-i ran home, P'yŏng-i following.

With both hands Kŏl-i grips the cat firmly by the waist. The cat meows, wriggling its feet. Ya little bastard, beg all ya want—it's no use. Who's gonna letcha go?

Sŏp-i and P'yŏng-i return with the cord. They have left their

---

[3] The suffix -a (or -ya), attached to a name, is used when close friends or family members address each other or when people address animals.

bags behind.

Taking the cord, Kŏl-i walks ahead of the others. He is not thinking about tying up the cat.

"Where we goin'?" says Sŏp-i.

Kŏl-i walks on without a word. The others will soon know.

P'yŏng-i more than Sŏp-i wondered where Kŏl-i was going and what he intended to do. Guess I better go as far as they do and find out. He feels lucky that Kŏl-i isn't telling him to go away.

Reaching the foot of an oak tree midway up the hill, Kŏl-i tells Sŏp-i to hold the cat. He then lashes the cord around its neck. The cat projects the claws of its forefeet and tries to scratch Kŏl-i. Kŏl-i shouts at Sŏp-i to hold onto its feet. Sŏp-i groups the feet together and holds them, two to a hand. But with the squirming cat exposing its sharp teeth and about to bite, Sŏp-i almost loses it. Kŏl-i pulls the cord that is wound around the cat's neck and yells again at Sŏp-i, "Can't you hold on to that thing, asshole? Do it right!" Strangled by the cord, the cat darts its crimson tongue in and out, hacking.

Kŏl-i hangs the other end of the cord over a branch that is within reach. The cat's legs wriggle in space, causing the cord above it to shake and then swing back and forth. Kŏl-i, holding the other end of the cord, moves away so that the cat can't touch him; Sŏp-i retreats further. P'yŏng-i, who had taken several steps back when Sŏp-i almost lost the cat, moves back once more, behind Sŏp-i.

Kŏl-i's intention had been to tie the other end of the cord to a branch, but because of the cat's movements he could do nothing else but just hold onto it. The cat was trying to crawl up the cord, hooking onto it with its forefeet and drawing up its hindlegs. Alternately letting out the cord and jerking it back, Kŏl-i shakes the cat's forefeet off of it. A blue flame lights up in the cat's eyes. It seems greater in circumference than its eyeballs. Again the cat hooks onto the cord with its forefeet, and this time it starts trying to bite through it. Kŏl-i shakes the cord and throws it off. This contest is repeated several times.

The speed of the cat's attempts to grasp the cord gradually slows, and after a while its forefeet merely scrape off the cord without catching hold of it. The strength with which it draws up its hindlegs likewise fades, and eventually there are only limp movements of its waist. Its tail stretches out stiffly, and its body becomes much longer than normal. The blue flame in its eyes flares more strongly and turns crimson. As Kŏl-i stares at the cat a feverish gleam comes from his eyes. His grip on the cord tightens even more, and he grits his teeth.

Not until the cat shows no further signs of attempting to claw onto the cord does Kŏl-i tie the other end of it to a branch. After observing the cat for a while, Kŏl-i turns around as if to say that's that. Sŏp-i follows Kŏl-i without speaking, and P'yŏng-i, far removed, brings up the rear. Frightened by the cat suspended from the tree, P'yŏng-i hastens past Kŏl-i, all the while looking back at the hill. At times the cat hanging there seems to twitch, at times it seems motionless. "Isn't the cat gonna die if we leave it like that?" P'yŏng-i blurts out.

"You don't know shit, kid," says Kŏl-i, exasperated. "What're you hangin' around for?" Kŏl-i gives him a rap on the crown.

P'yŏng-i curls up, his hands covering his crown, and then breaks into a run.

Kŏl-i thought of something, and shouted to P'yŏng-i far ahead. "Hey kid, if you don't want me to call ya 'kid' any more, then how about untyin' that damn' cat tonight and bringin' it to me?"

P'yŏng-i kept running.

Sŏp-i wanted to run away too. What was he going to do if Kŏl-i said the same thing to him? Instantly Sŏp-i was panic-stricken.

But what Kŏl-i had to say to Sŏp-i was completely different.

"You know a place called Pulgwang-dong?"

Sŏp-i shook his head.

"That's the neighborhood we're movin' to. It's different from this dogshit neighborhood."

But Kŏl-i had never been to this area called Pulgwang-dong.

And he wasn't pleased about having to live with Old Pak. He picked up a rock from the road and heaved it toward the sky with all his might. Actually it wasn't as if he never had any fun here, he thinks.

After changing her clothes, Chŏnju Auntie goes out and with the five hundred *wŏn* buys a half *toe* of newly harvested rice, a half *kŭn*[4] of beef, a pack of cigarettes, and, with the rest of the money, a couple of vegetables.

She rinsed the rice and placed it on the coal-briquette stove, marinated the beef, and kneaded the vegetables with seasonings, all the while lighting up a cigarette whenever she had a free moment. Her usual method had been to extinguish the cigarette halfway down and save the butt, but now she smoked it all the way down. The woman next door said she'd never seen her enjoy a cigarette so much. Chŏnju Auntie managed a smile and replied, Is that so?

She scoops out a separate bowl of rice and sets aside some grilled beef and a portion of each of the vegetables. That way she can feed Pak if he comes late.

Kŏl-i, sitting in front of the dinner table, is in the dark. He had understood his mother when she said they were moving the next day, but why, he wonders, could she be preparing such a nice meal this evening? It's hard to see a table like this even on a holiday or a birthday. The freshly harvested rice, unmixed with other grains, was no sooner scooped into his mouth than it was on its way to his stomach. And there was even grilled beef and vegetables. Kŏl-i kept on wolfing down the food.

"Hey, not so fast. Take your time."

Although he tried to eat slowly, aware of his mother's concern, the movement of his spoon had quickened again before he knew it. The food was tasty, but there was another reason too. I've gotta get to the television place early. That girl might

---

[4]*Kŭn*: a unit of weight equaling 0.6 kilogram or 1.3 pounds.

be waiting there. For admission he had some money left over from what he had obtained the previous evening by interrupting the couples who had come to the hill in back.

Kŏl-i had emptied his rice bowl and was about to stand up when his mother said "Hey, wouldja please stay in tonight?" Although her voice was not loud, there was a strength in it that he couldn't oppose.

Chŏnju Auntie had her own reason. If Pak were to step in, wouldn't she have to send out Kŏl-i for some liquor? Chŏnju Auntie finishes her meal deliberately, then goes outside and does the dishes, taking her time there as well.

Kŏl-i becomes anxious. I've gotta sneak out somehow. Even so, it's obvious that lightning will strike if he disobeys his mother and leaves. If Pak would just show up, and if he could only be set free—but Pak hasn't arrived yet, and it looks like he's not coming this evening. Kŏl-i lays out his bed and gets in. His plan is to get her to go to bed early, like himself, and then sneak out while she is sleeping. But when his mother comes in after finishing the dishes, she sits, one knee up, smoking cigarettes, without going to bed.

Chŏnju Auntie smokes three cigarettes in a row, lost in thought. Suddenly, sweeping the bottom of her skirt into her lap, she turns toward Kŏl-i.

"Hey kid, you cold?"

"Yeah, a little." Though he wasn't very cold, Kŏl-i said this in order to get his mother into bed quickly.

As if she has forgotten something, Chŏnju Auntie springs to her feet and goes outside, her motion stirring the air. She returns shortly, carrying the coal-briquette stove. This was the stove she had lit after the new owner had hung up his rice pot and asked Chŏnju Auntie not to set a fire in the cooking range.

"There's gonna be trouble with that gas smell," said Kŏl-i in alarm.

Even though Kŏl-i used the Seoul dialect when he was outside, his Chŏlla Province dialect appeared when he was alone with his mother.

"It's okay—it's almost burned up." She then turned off the light and got into bed.

Kŏl-i lay silently, waiting for his mother to fall asleep. Since the television programs hadn't ended yet, he could go a little late. The later programs were more fun. If that girl had come to watch television, she wouldn't be leaving right away.

Even while lying down Chŏnju Auntie continued to smoke. Pak's not gonna come after all. And tomorra I've gotta give over the house, don't I? I'm just sick and tired o' scrapin' along. I don't wanna leave Kŏl-i behind to become a beggar. She sucked on her cigarettes with a sense of urgency.

The darkness around the stove lightens. Whenever Kŏl-i's mother inhales on a cigarette the area around her nose and eyes is highlighted. Her eyes are wide open. She's not gonna close her eyes and fall asleep until she puts out that cigarette. Kŏl-i thinks about the girl. At the television place they turn off the lights to create the mood of a theater. From time to time short squeaks would come from the girls. It was the boys, up to no good. But that girl remained silent even when Kŏl-i held her hand. If I see her tonight I'll hold her hand a little tighter.

Chŏnju Auntie feels the room spinning before her eyes, as if she has smoked too much. Her hearing becomes fuzzy. I've gotta stop smoking. A sound is entering the fuzziness of her ears. It is a faraway sound. It appears to be someone calling out to her. She'd better get up and open the door, she thinks, and put the stove outside. However, the sound disappears. Everything becomes dark. After that she doesn't even realize it is dark.

Kŏl-i sees that his mother's cigarette has gone out. Mother has finally gone to sleep! Kŏl-i gets up and goes out. But he realizes that his body merely lies there in the room. He enters the television place. He isn't even aware that his body just lies in the room. The light has gone out in the television place. The television too is off. The room seems to be filled with television viewers; it seems to be empty. His hand gropes out. The girl's hand isn't there. His hand is not there either. Nothing is there.

P'yŏng-i slipped out of his bed. His father, who still goes downtown and packs an A-frame, was already snoring, and his mother too had fallen asleep. P'yŏng-i slips on his pants and shirt, which he had placed behind his head, and tiptoes out.

Most of the houses were dark, and outside it was pitch black, though a few families had kept their lights on. P'yŏng-i walked out along a path between the dark houses, his heart palpitating.

The lights were out in Sŏp-i's house too. P'yŏng-i suppresses the urge to call Sŏp-i outside. He knows that Sŏp-i's sister has suffered a relapse and that their mother is always ready to break into tears these days. Sŏp-i's eyes are suffused with tears when he sees his mother crying, and when P'yŏng-i witnesses this, tears almost fall from his own eyes. Even with the lights out, Sŏp-i and his mother, who has been going out to sell flowers, might be crying. But this is not the reason he suppresses the urge to call Sŏp-i outside. His mission tonight is something he must carry out alone.

P'yŏng-i stops for a moment where the dwellings come to an end. He wants to turn on his heels. But something prevented him—Kŏl-i's voice saying "Get lost, kid." If he turns around now, he will forever be treated with contempt as a kid. He clenches his fists and steps forward.

Since he has taken this path several times, he can get there straightaway in spite of the darkness. But at the foot of the hill P'yŏng-i hesitates again. The trees and rocks, which appeared darker in the gloom, frightened him. They resembled the outlines of wild animals. Scaredy-cat, scaredy-cat. Uh-uh, I'm not a scaredy-cat! No, I'm not! He begins to ascend the hill. Though not short of breath, he pants. The amplified sound of the leaves trodden underneath and the rolling rocks struck by his feet make his hair bristle. His breathing becomes more labored.

At last it comes into view, stretched out in the gloom. It looks much longer now than it did in daylight. It appears to be moving, a little at a time. P'yŏng-i cautiously approaches. He looks intently at the cat, just dangling there lifeless. The flame that had shown in its eyeballs was gone.

P'yŏng-i didn't know where to begin. The branches were high, and he couldn't untie the upper end of the cord, even on tiptoes. Nor could he climb the tree and crawl out the branch. The branch is too thin for that. To untie the cord from the cat's neck would mean touching the cat, and he was afraid of that. There was no other way but to break the cord between the branch and the cat's neck. He tries grabbing the rope in the middle and pulling it down. It doesn't break. Though he tugs with all his might, the cord doesn't give; the only result is a sore palm. It occurred to him that the cat had hooked onto the cord with its forefeet and bitten into it. P'yŏng-i starts to worry the cord with his teeth. As the line shakes, the carcass of the cat bumps against him. Horrified, P'yŏng-i continues to chew on the cord. Finally the cord breaks and the cat's body plunks to the ground.

As soon as he grabs the line that is tied around the cat's neck P'yŏng-i is off down the hill, away from that place. P'yŏng-i rushes on, dragging the cat along the ground, feeling that the thing is chasing him. Though he almost falls, his feet having caught on tree stumps and the jagged edges of rocks, he speeds along, grasping the cord even more firmly. Though his energy is being exhausted and his pace is gradually slowing, he continues to run even after descending the hill to the flat area below and entering the village.

Upon reaching the house he shouts, not pausing even a second to catch his breath.

"Kŏl-a!"

There is no reply from the darkened room.

"Kŏl-a! It's me! Come on out for a minute!"

Yet all is silent within the room.

"Come take a look! I brought the cat! The cat!"

As before, there is no sign of life from the room.

P'yŏng-i becomes desperate. Grabbing the ring of the door, he tugs if open. In the dark room, lit only by the reddish glow from the coal-briquette stove, the reclining forms of Kŏl-i and his mother could be faintly discerned. P'yŏng-i was disheartened. Wondering how they could be sleeping so soundly, he raised his voice and shouted again.

"Hey Kŏl-a! Get up so you can see the cat! Darn it all!"

Religious counseling was one of Sŏng-ho's occasional duties, and the people who came to see him for this purpose would usually outline their family circumstances to him. Not infrequently people would come and appeal to him to cure an illness. Sŏng-ho would also relieve psychological disorders through consolatory words and prayers.

And there were those who came to ask questions. Inasmuch as almighty God had to know that Adam and Eve would partake of the fruit of the tree of knowledge, why did he create it? And inasmuch as God would never allow lightning to strike his holy shrine the church building, why do we install lightning rods on the roofs of churches? Though irrelevant, the questions were not scornful. In response Sŏng-ho would emphasize that God's administration was not something with which humans should be concerned. Humans should do what they can do by themselves and not depend only on God. Though Sŏng-ho was not sure how well his questioners understood this explanation, he would realize afresh that humans should do what was within their capacity as humans to do. To what extent am I doing the work I should do as a human? he wondered.

Of the couple whom Sŏng-ho now confronted, only the thirtyish woman was a churchgoer. Twice previously she had sought out Sŏng-ho for counseling. On the first visit she had come whimpering to Sŏng-ho. What could she do about her husband's tyranny? she appealed. Her husband was a drunken brute with no job, and a gambler to boot. He took from her the few coppers she earned from her tiny store, and at the slightest remark he would beat her. Sŏng-ho, who could see the purplish bruise on her left temple, had told her to try to remain silent no matter what her husband did. The second time, the woman said her husband was as violent as before.

Whenever she remained silent, as Sŏng-ho had suggested, he would harass her by saying, "Now that you're a *yesujaengi* I don't sound like a human any more?" This would be followed by a demand for money and another thrashing. Although her face showed no marks, her manner was uneasy, as if she had been beaten in places not visible. Sŏng-ho had told her again not to resist and to try to put up with it. This was the couple who had come today.

"Rev'rend, he says he's decided to come to church," the woman said, her face too enlivened to hide her joy.

"I appreciate that," Sŏng-ho said to the man. "You've made a difficult decision."

"Now he can live in the bosom of God too," the woman said, looking at her husband with admiration.

The man lowered his eyes, avoiding Sŏng-ho's gaze. His bloodshot eyes revealed to Sŏng-ho that he had overindulged and stayed up all night gambling. His trip to the church appeared to be taking a toll on him. It took him some time tc become comfortable.

The three of them concluded a short worship, and as the couple were leaving, the man scooped up some well water and gulped it down. Sŏng-ho accompanied them to the main gate.

On their way down the hill the man looked back to make sure Sŏng-ho had gone inside, and then said to his wife, "I got to go downtown."

"What for?" said the woman, an inquisitive gleam in her eyes.

"Uh, this fellow I know—his father's celebrating his sixtieth birthday. You'd better give me a little money. I can't go empty-handed, can I?" His cajoling was accompanied by gestures of servility.

"What about the Wednesday worship service that begins tonight?"

"I'll be back by then."

"Honest? You can't violate an oath before God now."

"I know."

"Better not come home drunk."

"Oh, who d'you think I am? Don't worry and just gimme a little money. Five hundred *wŏn* or so..."

"Now wait a minute, you. Five hundred *wŏn*? In the shape we're in? What are you talkin' about?"

"I agreed to believe in Jesus like you said, so hadn't you oughta go along with what I say too? Gimme five hundred, and that way I won't have to bother you for pocket money."

That afternoon, just when Sŏng-ho had finished preparing the sermons he would deliver during the Wednesday worship service, Deaconess Cho came rushing in. She told him that Myŏng-suk's family was holding a *kut* designed to infuse Myŏng-suk with the spirit of a shaman.

"It's been going on since this morning, and I just found out about it. Gracious!"

Infusing Myŏng-suk with the spirit of a shaman! Sŏng-ho followed the deaconess out. He wasn't sure what he should do when they arrived at the site of the *kut*.

"Last night there was another case of a mother and son almost dying of gas poisoning. Goodness, what a state the neighborhood is in..." On their way down the hill Deaconess Cho reported what had happened. "The kid's friend came looking for him in the middle of the night, and it's a darn good thing he did. If it'd happened any later, they'd be at heaven's gate by now. This woman falls head over heels for some good-for-nothing—and she's old enough to know better—and ends up kissing that little shack of hers goodbye. It seems the new owner was plastering over the firepit, and she couldn't light a fire there. But does that mean she had to bring that coal-briquette stove in her room? Was she afraid of freezing to death? I guess if you're far enough gone, then nothing registers. People said she must've been out of her mind. They say she went downtown, and when she came back she'd lost her senses. She must have gone to look for that guy or else raise some money. The people in the neighborhood say she might as well have died instead of getting better. What's the use of recovering when you don't have a penny to your name? Actually, they're not sure yet whether she's going to recover. We'll have to wait another day to find out. They took her in the middle of the night to one of those clinics where they treat you for free. That's what I heard."

Sŏng-ho now realized that the woman Deaconess Cho was talking about was the woman he had seen the day before. That woman dragging herself along as if she wasn't even aware her clothing had been drenched by the rain. He had watched her, though just for a short time, and could see she was in agony. However, he hadn't helped her, not even a little. According to Deaconess Cho, people thought the woman had brought the stove into her room because of the cold. But Sŏng-ho believed her intentions were different—there was no other way to interpret it. For she was about to take not only her life but that of her child. Sŏng-ho had no way of knowing whether she had already planned this when he saw her on the street, or whether she had made the decision later. In any event, Sŏng-ho had not known about it. Only one thing was clear to him: the woman had been brooding over something. Why hadn't he tried to lessen her agony, whether or not this would have helped her? No, I didn't even try to find out what was troubling her. Was it because she wasn't a believer? Is a clergyman always supposed to deal with believers and no one else? Sŏng-ho was besieged with regret that he had neglected this question.

Myŏng-suk's mother was unable to resist the suggestion of the neighborhood women to hold a *naerim kut*. Myŏng-suk's illness had dragged on without improvement, and it appeared her life would be endangered if there were no change. Her mother had decided to hold a *kut* so that she could at least say she had done everything possible for her daughter.

At one side of a room, rice cake, fruit, a pig's head, and other offerings had been placed on the *kut* table. A short distance from it the table for the divinities had been set with nine small bowls, three rows of three each. Amid the beating of an hourglass drum and the playing of a fiddle, the head shaman chanted a ritual song, waving a fan with one hand and shaking the *pang-ul* with the other.

As the various *kŏri*[5] proceeded—the *kŏri* for expelling impurity from the site of the *kut;* the *kŏri* in which the *kamang* spirit enters the shaman and speaks through her; the *kŏri* for the mountain spirits; the *kŏri* for *chesŏk,* the great heavenly spirit; the *kŏri* for the martial spirit; and the *kŏri* for ancestors—Myŏng-suk sat up in bed as the shamans instructed. Her entire body trembled, and her eyes closed. Her colorless face convulsed again and again. And between her twitching lips murmurs leaked out. God...Father... Tears squeezed out from between her dark eyelids and flowed down her cheeks. Next to her was her mother, curled up in a ball and soundlessly shedding tears with her.

As soon as the ancestor *kŏri* was finished, the head shaman stood Myŏng-suk up and began clothing her in a shaman's costume. They were about to begin the initiation. Though Myŏng-suk resists, twisting her body, the shamans force her into a blue *ch'ima,* red *ch'ima, k'waeja,* blue *ch'ŏllik,*[6] red *ch'ŏllik,* and other clothing. Myŏng-suk's body, swollen by the clothing, appears to have become shorter and broader. Moreover, the slits beneath the shoulders of the blue and red *ch'ŏllik,* where her arms come out, make the empty sleeves seem rather like long wings suspended behind her. In comparison, Myŏng-suk's arms appear thin and short. Her fingertips are trembling ever so slightly.

The head shaman places her fan in one of Myŏng-suk's

---

[5] *Kŏri:* one of the sections or stages of a *kut.* There are usually twelve *kŏri* in a *kut,* each having its own function and paraphernalia.

[6] *Ch'ŏllik:* A traditional warrior's outfit consisting of a high neck, bulky sleeves, and a skirt with a pleated waist. Higher-ranking warriors wore the blue *ch'ŏllik,* lower-ranking warriors the red one.

hands and the *pang-ul* in the other. Then she takes the fiddle from an assistant shaman and, alternately playing the instrument and chanting, begins walking in circles around Myŏng-suk. Myŏng-suk looks pained. Her face is distorted and she exhales forcefully, softly biting her lower lip as if in defiance.

The head shaman accelerates her fiddle playing and chants more quickly. Suddenly Myŏng-suk has a faint convulsion and her hands and feet begin moving. The movement changes into a dance. The spirit is about to enter her. Myŏng-suk's body moves in a lively dance, following the sound of the fiddle. Although she is enveloped in several layers of thick clothing, she does not appear to be weighed down. She dances for a while to the same rhythm, and then her movements quicken as the rhythm of the drum and fiddle becomes faster. Her body was not a body anymore. It seemed to have dissolved in the air; now there was only movement. And the various layers of clothing were not clothing anymore. Her clothing and body harmonized, as if the fluttering articles of clothing had become a part of her body and her body had turned into clothing. Everything had dissolved into one movement.

Intoxicated with the dancing, Myŏng-suk is led by the head shaman to the table for the divinities. Without hesitation she reaches out and picks up one of the nine bowls arranged there. The head shaman receives the bowl from her, removes the plain white paper covering it, and looks inside. It contains sesame seeds. She shouts that the mountain spirit has descended into Myŏng-suk. If she had taken the bowl containing rice grain, it would have been *chesŏk*, the great heavenly spirit; if she had picked the bowl of red beans, then it would have been the guardian spirit of the village; if soybeans, then the martial spirit who protects the family; buckwheat, the earth spirit; water, the ocean spirit; money, the divine general; chaff, a goblin; and ash, the spirit that expels impurities.

The playing of the drum and fiddle intensifies again, and Myŏng-suk dances to their rhythm. The suffering that colored her sweat-soaked face has faded, and her visage is now suffused

with geniality. Suddenly she breaks her silence, and a gleam
darts from her eyes.

I am the spirit of the shrine of the famous mountain,
I am the spirit of the shrine of the people here...

"Do you know who I am?" she shouts. "I'm the spirit of Sam-
gak Mountain." At the same time, she squats abruptly.

There is murmuring from the spectators, who have been gazing at Myŏng-suk's movements, their faces straining with fear.
Several women among them, knowing that divination is most
efficacious following a *naerim kut,* place one or two hundred
wŏn in front of Myŏng-suk and ask her to tell their fortune.

For a time Myŏng-suk shakes the *pang-ul* and blinks. Then
she speaks to a middle-aged woman:

You are suffering a time of distress
So you will set the rice stalks afire
And now you will pick up the broken grains...

The spectators voiced their admiration as soon as these
words dropped from Myŏng-suk's lips. "How can I avoid this
catastrophe?" the middle-aged woman implored Myŏng-suk,
rubbing her hands. Her face had lost its color. Myŏng-suk
resumed shaking the *pang-ul.*

I pray, I pray
O spirit, I pray
Rid forty-year-old Mr. Yi's family
Of the malicious gossip that has befallen them...

At this moment Sŏng-ho made his way through the spectators toward Myŏng-suk.

The instant she saw Sŏng-ho, Myŏng-suk cleaved the air with
a shout: "Get out of here, Jesus ghost!"

The surroundings became silent. Sŏng-ho watched Myŏng-
suk calmly.

The area around Myŏng-suk's mouth lost its color and
twitched, and the *pang-ul* and fan dropped from her hands.

Myŏng-suk retreated to a corner of the room, squatting and squirming as if she were being driven by something. She huddled there and, exposing the whites of her eyes, stole glances at Sŏng-ho.

Sŏng-ho silently approached her. With an eerie shriek, Myŏng-suk fell on her side. The corners of her mouth were foamy, and her eyes were closed. A look of outrage appeared on the faces of the shamans, and among the spectators there were murmurs that Myŏng-suk had become the way she was because of the *yesujaengi*.

Bending over Myŏng-suk, Sŏng-ho remonstrated with her. "Myŏng-suk, open your eyes." Instantly her eyes were wide open. "And take off those clothes." Myŏng-suk gladly rose and removed all of the shaman costume. Then, clasping Sŏng-ho's hand, she began crying. "I've done wrong—please forgive me," she said amidst the tears. "My sickness is all better now." After a while she fell into a deep sleep, as if she had forgotten all her anxieties. Naturally, the *kŏri* that were to have followed in this *naerim kut* could not be performed, and Sŏng-ho incurred the displeasure of the shamans and the people gathered there.

The next day, Myŏng-suk began taking in food as she had before falling ill. She said she had acted and spoken unconsciously during her possession by the spirit the day before. And she had no idea how she had been able to respond to Sŏng-ho.

Myŏng-suk's mind and body seemed to have recovered completely. But within three days, symptoms of a severe illness appeared.

First, she stopped talking. Her eyes alternately became sunken and unfocused and then widened in a glare as if she were staring at something, and the corners of her mouth would turn up in an idiotic grin. She would not initiate conversation and would not respond appropriately to questions. She developed a strange habit: she would skillfully pull out her hair, one hair at a time, but only from the crown of her head. There was no sign of discomfort when she did this. When her mother or Sŏp-i told her to stop, she would desist for a while, but then the hair pulling would resume. Eventually, she would pull her hair out in spite of their prohibition, pretending she didn't hear them.

Sŏng-ho's daily visitations had no effect, and occasionally he couldn't help hearing through the cement-block wall some critical remarks from the P'yŏng-an Province woman next door. "What does that *yesujaengi* think he's doing, messing around and driving innocent people crazy?" Finally, Myŏng-suk's mother again called on a shaman to perform a *kut*, but this time there was no result. In the end Myŏng-suk, a bald spot as big as the lid of a small bowl on the crown of her head, was moved to a mental hospital.

Sŏng-ho felt snarled up. Clergymen have been curing people's diseases since Christianity entered this land. This had become the great strength of missionary work. And during the reign of the Silla king Mich'u a monk named Ado was almost put to death for propagating Buddhism. But because he alone had been able to cure the princess's illness, he had received permission to spread his faith. Needless to say, healing the human body is not the ultimate responsibility of the clergyman. But in any event, there was no help he could offer Myŏng-suk, whose illness had surely arisen from her oversensitive nerves or from mental instability. Sŏng-ho was very much aggravated. Hadn't he been too neglectful before the *naerim kut*, simply performing his customary visitations? Why couldn't he have served her with a little more of the love that comes from sincerity? The more Sŏng-ho thought, the more he took to heart his immaturity as a human being and his insufficiency as a clergyman.

Chapter 2

Min-gu stepped out of the agricultural testing station with Chun-t'ae, who was on his way home. He had not waited long.

"Now that winter's just around the corner, I guess you won't have very much work around here."

"Not really. There's still plenty of work to do for autumn. Did you have some business to take care of down here?"

"Yeah, but it looks like I made the trip in vain."

Hearing from Pyŏn that a *kut* was to be performed by a *chakdu* shaman,[1] Min-gu had come with Pyŏn to Suwŏn, but the trip had proved fruitless. The shaman had suddenly taken sick, and the *kut* was postponed indefinitely.

In the end, Min-gu felt as if he had come to Suwŏn for an outing with Pyŏn. Indeed, Pyŏn seemed more inclined in this direction. On the bus ride to Suwŏn, he had kept his knee close to Min-gu's and rubbed shoulders with him. Such actions didn't seem the inevitable result of the shaking of the bus. Min-gu patiently pretended to ignore them.

While getting off the bus Pyŏn had dusted off the front of Min-gu's suit jacket, though there were no smudges on it. But Min-gu, pretending there was a smudge, himself repeated the action, and then took a cigarette from his pocket and put it in his mouth. Darn good thing I brought cigarettes at a time like this, he felt. Even so, Min-gu was not as disgusted or intolerant with Pyŏn as he had been the time before. Unable to see this *chakdu kut,* the two of them had gone to a tearoom, and in the course of their conversation Pyŏn had taken every opportunity

---

[1] *Chakdu* shaman: a shaman who walks barefoot on a sharp *chakdu* (a large knife used to cut straw) as a sign of divine assistance.

to lean toward Min-gu. For some time now, whenever they met at a place such as a tearoom Pyŏn would not fail to sit next to Min-gu even if there was a seat across from him.

When Min-gu said he had to meet a friend and would return to Seoul later, Pyŏn indicated that he had plenty of time and wouldn't mind waiting so that they could return together. But saying that it would be quite late by the time his meeting ended, Min-gu sent Pyŏn off first.

When it came time to part Pyŏn said "Just a moment" and gently straightened Min-gu's necktie. Not knowing whether it was actually slanted, Min-gu allowed Pyŏn to do as he wished. Min-gu was slightly embarrassed. The necktie was the one Pyŏn had given him at his engagement ceremony. He wondered whether he had selected it knowing he was meeting Pyŏn. Enough of that, thought Min-gu. What kind of person could Pyŏn be, really?

As Min-gu and Chun-t'ae walk toward the city, a boy on the bank of a field far ahead of them is looking up at the sky and shouting "...I'll give you a hen, so turn round and round..." An eagle is gliding through the sky, tracing circles. "...I'll give you a rooster, so turn round and round..." While appearing to remain in the same position, tracing circles, the eagle moved behind the college of agriculture and disappeared.

"Just what I thought—Suwŏn's a real utopia," said Min-gu.

"How's that?"

"It's obvious—just look at the eagles floating around."

"You mean this is the countryside. But it's the same if you go a little ways outside of Seoul."

"When I see eagles it reminds me of the Yakut people in eastern Siberia. You know, these Yakut people worship the eagle."

"Here we go again," said Chun-t'ae with a smile.

"They believe that the greatest shamans are sent by eagles. So when an eagle appears at someone's house, the head of the house has a duty to raise it. If there's no meat he has to slaughter a calf and feed it to the bird. In eastern Siberia, generally speaking, when an eagle seeks out a human habitation it's forecasting its own death, and so they feed it like this until it dies. Afterwards they feel it should have a proper burial. And this doesn't mean digging a hole for it in the ground—they make a platform in a tree and enshrine it there. If they don't do this, all hell breaks loose. And here's something else you'll get a kick out of..."

"Hey, give me a break. My ears are getting worn out."

"No more talk about superstition—is that what you're telling me?" Min-gu said, as if dissatisfied. "Even among folk beliefs there are many things that have scientific validity—did you know that? To give you an example, when people in our country have a baby they hang a straw omen on their door, right? This isn't something we attribute just to superstition. It keeps people outside the family away from the weakened mother and the vulnerable infant. Now that's really hygienic, you know? The *kut* is just an extreme case of this. We can view it as a means of psychoanalytic cure, can't we? And how are you going to explain the more fabulous elements of folk beliefs in the West, with its scientifically advanced civilization? If a black cat..."

"The problem is," said Chun-t'ae, again cutting Min-gu off, "when we compare the superstitions of our country with those of Westerners, before we consider which side is more superstitious we'd better ask which side adapts more readily to them and makes them part of their life."

"You know, though, the gods are especially good at attaching themselves to Koreans. Why do you think that is?"

"Well, let's see...maybe it comes from our lack of stability. In other words, perhaps it's because our people didn't discard their nomadic mentality while they were drifting down from the north. Has there ever been a time when Koreans have truly been politically or mentally stable while they've inhabited this peninsula? Of course I'm not saying that other peoples settled down in one spot right from the beginning. But there's no country like ours that was continually invaded by alien powers and ruled by people who lacked broad, everlasting autonomy. And even the Silla unification[2]—it's the same thing. It wasn't our power that unified the peninsula but rather our borrowing of the Tang Empire's power that did it. Silla got involved when the Tang Empire was getting rid of Koguryŏ, which was threatening its borders. Anyway, we have to remember that this business of foreign soldiers honorably setting foot on our soil started with Silla, and the lack of sovereignty that is frequently talked about these days dates from that time. So here we are, a people who live on, having lost our stability—this is the basis of our life. And I say this knowing I'm a part of that." Chun-t'ae's voice became slightly louder. "Consider this and you'll be able to understand. In the early 1800s there was a beggars' guild in our country. They divided Seoul among themselves into several districts. As if they were collecting taxes on land or houses that they owned, you know. Ridiculous! I can't help looking at things like this as the result of our gypsy mentality. And this mentality has lingered right up to the present. We still can't seem to shake it off."

"Speaking of guilds," said Min-gu, "a guild for shamans existed before that beggars' guild. You know the Chaeinch'ŏng, which existed from the late eighteenth century to the early twentieth century? It was a guild for shamans, but it also included wicker workers, *kisaeng*,[3] and itinerant performers. The restrictions on them were enormous. If one shaman infringed upon another's territory, she forfeited the income. If she did it again, she was fined twice the amount of her income. A third time, and she was expelled from the bureau. Even now, depending on the region, each shaman is in charge of her own territory and keeps other shamans from infringing. And it's

[2]Silla unification: the series of wars through which the Silla kingdom assumed control of most of the Korean peninsula in the seventh and early eighth centuries.

[3]*Kisaeng*: professional female entertainers trained in song, dance, poetry, and other arts; they performed primarily at drinking parties and anniversary celebrations.

not just the shamans—the residents of that area also want it that way."

"The sad history of a nomadic people, isn't it?"

"Let's not look at it so negatively. Koreans have some good points too. They're good-natured people, and they're good-hearted."

"Now that kind of thinking is dangerous. In fact Koreans aren't like that, but they're caught up in all this talk about being good-natured and good-hearted and so they think that's just what they are. We don't need that kind of delusion. You know how cruel factionalism was not so long ago, not to mention back in the old days. Killing off a political opponent, and his son and grandson for good measure. Killing people by tearing them limb from limb. And how about the Korean War? Another thing—even if we're a good-natured and good-hearted people, what's so virtuous about that? We passively accept suppression by others, yet why have we had to support the shameless bunch who cling to those in power now and then, using the pretext that the Korean people—good-natured and good-hearted subjects that they are—will forgive them? We have to know how to be furious when it's time to be furious."

"Even so, the fact that we worship the bright sun is a sign of optimism, isn't it?"

"That's just another adverse reaction to a gloomy and frustrating life. You can see this from the fact that we're always ready to say 'I'm so tired I could die,' 'I'm so happy I could die.'"

"That's just not true. There're no people like our ancestors. Far from dying, they were especially concerned with creating. It seems to me that the word *ha-nŭl*[4] originally came from *han-al*.[5] Our ancestors saw the sky as a huge egg that shone forth and sent down rain so that all creatures might grow. This is probably why there are a lot of legends in our country about

[4]*Ha-nŭl:* "sky."
[5]*Han-al:* "big egg."

people being born from eggs. The egg represents the mother's body giving birth to life. A while back I took a three-day weekend and went east to the coast, and I found there's still some phallic worship there. This is precisely the kind of proof that our people worshiped reproduction—in other words, creation."

After making several inquiries, Min-gu had located a seaside village called Shinnam, about one hundred *ri* from Samch'ŏk on the way to P'ohang. He had gone to a cape that stretched out to sea. There he found no shrines as such but only a platform of stones. Upon ascending a stairway to the platform, he discovered a huge Chinese juniper serving as a shrine tree. A cluster of phalli carved from wood hung there, like dried corvina fish suspended from a line of plaited straw. Against the backdrop of the waves tossed up by the ocean, the cluster of hanging phalli didn't appear at all obscene. The villagers said that in the first third of January by the lunar calendar, the whole village would hold a large ceremony; smaller ceremonies were frequently observed by individual villagers. On each such occasion, phalli were hung from the tree. Only by holding this kind of phallic worship would they catch many fish and avoid accidents while at sea. The phalli were slim and straight, about an inch thick and six or seven inches long. According to the villagers, they were made that way now because the ones shaped just like a penis, which were made as recently as a few years before, made the viewer somewhat uncomfortable. Looking around the circumference of the stone platform, Min-gu had discovered two old phalli in a chink among the stones. Although one had virtually rotted away, only its bare outline remaining, and the other was slightly rotten, worm-eaten, and split along the grain, the glans penis and the narrower part of the shaft above it were obvious. He stuck both in his bag and left.

"I'll show them to you sometime. They're extremely precious items."

"Then why don't you go set up a shrine to them? If we're

going to increase agricultural production, we've got to develop agricultural techniques, and if we're going to harvest more marine products, we've got to develop fishing techniques. You think making a penis and holding a worship service for it is going to work?"

"In any event, it's clear that our ancestors wanted to reproduce and create."

"Look, the weaker and more unstable we are, the more we desire to reproduce ourselves. And the only reason for that is so we won't cut off the family line. That's another inevitable legacy of our nomad mentality."

"So we fall into this nomad mentality or whatever you call it—then what the hell can we do about it?"

"Beats me. But first we'll have to stop this empty beautification of ourselves and start becoming thoroughly aware of the present. Aware of the fact that we've been nomads! No matter who we are. Okay, let's go over there and wet our whistle."

"I thought you'd quit smoking. What's the occasion?" Chunt'ae asks, obtaining a light from Min-gu's cigarette.

"Yeah, I quit for a while. Couldn't handle it, though." Min-gu refrains from smoking in Ŭn-hŭi's presence, however.

They drank *soju,*[6] with grilled intestine for a snack. Min-gu, a little tipsy, abruptly says, "Hey, you're too free and easy."

Chun-t'ae looks at Min-gu, trying to determine from his eyes what he's talking about.

"I mean, how can you not know where your woman is and what she's doing?"

"What's this all about?"

"According to Ŭn-hŭi, because of your directions she had to wander all over the place before she could find the dress shop."

"Is that so?"

"Listen to yourself. Have you figured out where it is by now?"

---

[6]*Soju:* a low-grade ginlike liquor.

"Am I supposed to know?"

"Yessir, everything under the sun is just fine with you."

"Listen my man, if you're so interested in women, then why aren't you hanging around a beauty shop?"

"Hey guy, is that all you can say? Don't you think you should at least know where your wife works?"

"Sorry about that."

"Nothing to apologize to me about... Is it true she only comes home once a week?"

Chun-t'ae confirmed this. "These days it's once every couple of weeks," he added.

"And that's okay?"

"What's wrong with that?"

Min-gu, about to take a drink, put down his glass. "I just can't figure out what makes you two tick," he said, parroting what Ŭn-hŭi had said to him.

"Well, we can manage." Even while saying this Chun-t'ae realized that a third party would have trouble understanding the two of them. But it wasn't just him and Ch'ang-ae. Weren't there many married couples whom other people would have a hard time understanding? Sure, wasn't that the way couples were?

"You're the man, so why don't you commute down here from Seoul?"

"Well, I'll have to look into that..."

"I guess that means I better not interfere in the married life of others. Okay, I'll be discreet. But be careful."

"About what?"

"Listen to you. I'm talking about that woman."

"That woman?"

"You know—the one who was with you at the pear orchard."

"You mean Miss Nam? What about her?"

"Seeing her these days?" Min-gu leaned forward and then, some grease from the intestine shooting up in his face, jerked his head back.

"If we have occasion to meet, then we meet."

"Like I said, be careful. She's not your normal woman. There's more there than meets the eye—something daring about her. So be careful. No need to stir up rumors." She's not your normal woman, so he'd better be careful—this too was something Min-gu had heard from Ŭn-hŭi.

"Uh-huh. And so?" Chun-t'ae replied inattentively with a smile.

Chun-t'ae was supposed to see Chi-yŏn the next day.

Chapter 3

For several days now Hamlet had not been letting Chi-yŏn near him. It had started after he received a rabies inoculation. Nero and Elizabeth, held by Chi-yŏn, were docile as they received the shot, but not Hamlet. The maid covered his head with a sack and the veterinarian's aide tied him to a tree; not until then did the aide give him the shot. What the hell kind of dog was this, he had grumbled. Chi-yŏn felt awkward, but to her, Hamlet was not hateful. Perhaps it was natural for him to have become more reluctant to let her come near him since receiving the shot, she thought. She had tried to understand this as his way of reproaching her for standing by and watching the maid and the veterinarian's aide hold and inflict pain on him. In any event, the signs of distrust in his expression and behavior had become more obvious. And this was the dog that had touched her with the end of his nose the day of that downpour.

After the downpour Chi-yŏn looked out the window. Her eyes were drawn to a Chinese juniper. Multicolored beads of water were hanging from the tree. This kind of phenomenon did not appear either in the Chinese juniper next to it or in the other broadleaf trees. The beads were not hanging everywhere on the tree but were limited to the side facing the northwest and to an area about the height of a person. From Chi-yŏn's south-facing second-floor room, the beads could be seen to the right and below. The brilliance of these yellow, crimson, and blue beads of water, which were formed from water droplets and the angle of the sunbeams this autumn afternoon, seemed so miraculous to Chi-yŏn that she wasn't able to move her eyes from them. The beads were roundish, slightly oval, somewhat more than oval, and various other shapes. The moment they fell they turned into colorless drops of water. Some of the beads that remained hanging from the tree also turned to colorless drops of water, depending on the movement of the sun's rays. The reverse also occurred, and new beads of water formed. Chi-yŏn went out on the lawn and sat down on the bench on some old newspaper; the beads of water now appeared more transparent and brilliant. Nero, who had gone inside the kennel to escape the shower, comes and stands in front of Chi-yŏn. The other two dogs are looking toward Chi-yŏn, Elizabeth from slightly further away and Hamlet from in front of the kennel. Chi-yŏn stroked Nero's head. The dog's damp body reeked. But Chi-yŏn doesn't mind the smell. One by one the beads of water lose their shape and vanish. Wasn't the very last one to disappear a yellow one? she thinks. Suddenly she turned her head, sensing something touching the back of the bench. Hamlet has propped his forelegs there. Happy, but momentarily bewildered, Chi-yŏn extends her hand, but the dog quickly retreats. Purposefully, Chi-yŏn turns back to the front, tenses her body, and tries to remain still. Soon there was again the sound of something touching the back of the bench. Chi-yŏn didn't budge. Something is touching her back. She knows it is Hamlet's nose. She remains quiet. But Hamlet's nose doesn't touch her again. Chi-yŏn sensed he was still taking precautions. Even so, she was delighted that he had come that close—it could have been worse.

Now too Chi-yŏn is sitting on the bench waiting for Hamlet to approach. He alone has been released from the kennel. He is observing Chi-yŏn from about a foot away. Their eyes meet. Chi-yŏn wants to melt his distrust with her gaze. But Hamlet doesn't come even one step closer. It's something that will take more time. Nero and Elizabeth are scratching at the chicken wire with their forefeet and whining. But today there is no time for Chi-yŏn to play with them. It's time for her to meet Chun-t'ae. Rising from the bench, Chi-yŏn smiles to herself, thinking how she sometimes compares Chun-t'ae to Hamlet, who is somehow out of balance.

Chun-t'ae gave her a feeling that she hadn't had with any other man. It was a unique looseness, and it drew her with a strange force. This looseness, which seemed to come from the imbalance she perceived in his body and his mind, made her feel comfortable with him. This enabled her to see Chun-t'ae without burden, and perhaps that was why she was happy when they met.

Chi-yŏn easily poured herself out to Chun-t'ae, but it wasn't quite the same as her candid, almost confessional conversations with Sŏng-ho. Once, at the end of a conversation about a long-time boyfriend from high school whom she didn't see anymore, she said to Chun-t'ae, "I've run into him a couple of times since then. He went to a technical college, and now he's working as an engineer for some company. He says he won't get married before I do."

"You mean you can still find someone who's pure of heart?" Chun-t'ae shot back in jest. "Compared with him, you're too cruel."

"Me? How come?"

"While he was having a tough time of it in the army, you couldn't be patient, and so you had a change of heart."

"Good grief, you haven't been listening very carefully. It's not fair to call it a change of heart."

"Well, then, his face must have changed. The bright face he always had, as if he had just gotten out of the bathtub, right?"

"That's not it either. It's true his face was kind of tanned, but it was clear and clean like in the old days. Something else made me decide. I still believe a long tour in the army doesn't give a person any spiritual development—not even a little. We'd spend time together, but our conversation wouldn't have any focus. It didn't used to be like that. For example, whenever he'd start to say something he'd keep coming out with 'Frankly speaking, frankly speaking'...I mean, it wasn't necessary to say that. He really disappointed me. Do you understand?"

"Seems like you prefer not speaking frankly to speaking frankly." As usual Chun-t'ae responded to Chi-yŏn's remarks with a touch of irony.

"If you want to look at it that way, it's true. But you should realize that you speak even less frankly."

"Is that right? For example?"

"You haven't said anything about your past."

"What's the relationship between that and not speaking frankly? Okay, now I get it. You're talking about what I scribbled on that piece of paper. Well, there's nothing special about it. When I thought about it later, I was kind of ashamed of it, but that's all."

Chun-t'ae and Chi-yŏn felt almost the same way about seeing each other, though Chun-t'ae was more cool. Some time ago he had heard Ch'ang-ae say, You can't love anybody—you only know how to love yourself. Perhaps he had lost the passion that would throw him headlong into love. And perhaps that was why he could laugh off what Min-gu had said about Chi-yŏn. For in Chun-t'ae's mind, meeting Chi-yŏn was not much different from returning to his boardinghouse life and meeting a like-minded friend.

It was possible, however, for this congenial, free and easy mood to be broken. This is what happened evenings of the days Ch'ang-ae dropped in at their house. Even so, he could tolerate her coming, spending the night, and leaving. She was merely a vagabond who stayed for the night and departed. Of course this was nothing but a disguise to impress the gossipy that the two of them were still a couple. The disguise will continue until they part for good, and each of them knows this.

The day before, Ch'ang-ae had arrived late at night. Again she was intoxicated.

She told the old housemaid that she wouldn't eat dinner and asked her to bring some water for washing up. Chun-t'ae was leafing through a book, waiting for Ch'ang-ae to finish washing and go to bed. Suddenly he heard the sound of retching. Ch'ang-ae was vomiting, her head thrust into the washbasin.

Chun-t'ae wondered whether she had drunk too much and gotten sick from mixing her liquor. Ch'ang-ae had placed her finger in her mouth to make herself vomit. Chun-t'ae went over and propped up her forehead with one hand while with the other he rubbed her back. He did this from habit. Ch'ang-ae showed no reaction. Giving herself up to him like this was also habitual.

There was not much solid matter in what she threw up, but there was a great deal of liquid. Mixed in among the sour stench was the reek of liquor.

After rinsing her mouth with clean water brought by the maid, Ch'ang-ae spreads out the bedding and slips beneath the quilt, not bothering to tidy up her face. She becomes still. Thinking she was sure to snore if she went to sleep now, she said "Aren't you sick and tired of this?" Her voice was quite subdued. Her tone made Chun-t'ae realize that he was indeed sick and tired of her. She spoke again. "Hadn't we better escape from this situation?"

Chun-t'ae felt he had been outdone. These were words that had been forming in his own mind. He opened his mouth, as if this would confirm what he had been thinking.

"Not a bad idea."

"It doesn't look that complicated."

"Mmm."

Chun-t'ae had feared that he would have to undergo various crises, large and small, before the two of them separated. But when he heard her say it wasn't complicated, it occurred to him that this might well be the case.

"I've been thinking. There's no need for us to shuffle off the blame on each other. Instead, we'd better share the responsibility."

Her tone was subdued, as before, but perhaps because of her vomiting the signs of tipsiness in her voice had vanished.

Chun-t'ae agreed. A debate over who was right and who was wrong could not rebuild what had broken down. The two of them were like the bank of a reservoir, and the hole in it that at first would only admit sand was now so big that it couldn't be plugged. All the water had leaked out and the reservoir was dry. Or perhaps the hole had always been there and water had never collected. But this kind of speculation about their marriage, though they might have dredged it up, would not have been helpful. Instead, it could have developed into useless sentimentality. At this juncture sentimentality was taboo.

"I could find some time tomorrow," said Chun-t'ae.

"How about if we do it like this?" After a short pause, Ch'ang-ae continued. "You know that we borrowed three hundred thousand *wŏn* on this house. Now my colleague Mrs. O promised she would get her *kye*[1] money before too long, and the first thing she'll do is pay off the loan for us and get the deed back. We'll set the date for the day the deed comes back."

"Instead of that I think we ought to sell the house and pay off the loan ourselves."

"What are we going to do if we sell the house?"

"The house is no big deal."

Having sold the house and payed off her debt, he would not object to entering a boardinghouse for real, he thought.

They said nothing more. Chun-t'ae felt this was the first time in their married life that they had talked calmly and openly without injuring each other. Only now, when they were separating? he wondered.

Chun-t'ae turned off the light so that she could fall asleep right away, and then he too got in bed. Tonight he wouldn't mind if she snored. However, he was the first to be enveloped in sleep; it was so deep he didn't know whether she snored or not.

"When you pass in front of a vehicle like this one, do you feel

---

[1] *Kye:* an informal cooperative association of neighbors or relatives in which each member contributes a certain amount of money at certain intervals (usually every month), the sum then being used by each member in turn.

it's more dangerous with a driver or without one?" asked Chi-
yŏn. She and Chun-t'ae were walking around a truck that was
blocking their path.

"Dangerous? You mean the danger of getting hit by it?"

"I guess that's what I mean."

"Well, then, I think it's more dangerous if there's a driver,"
Chun-t'ae said, burying his hands deeper in his raincoat.

"Not me. Sometimes I'm more scared of an empty vehicle
because I wonder what would happen if it started rolling. But
a driver couldn't possibly let the thing get out of control,
right?"

"But have you ever seen an empty car get into an accident?"

"An accident? That's a different matter...Which would you
feel was safer—if no one was in control of the universe, or if
someone was in control?"

"That's quite a jump. Let me state your conclusion—you're
saying we should have a god, right? Which church do you go
to?"

"A church in Changch'ung-dong."

"Is it a devout congregation?"

"Is there a congregation that's not devout?"

"What I mean is do they wave their hands and make noise
when they pray?"

"When they pray aloud by themselves, yes."

It also happened when the minister prayed for the sick, she
explained. Halleluiahs and clapping would surge forth like a
huge wave. At the end of one such prayer, the minister asked
those who had recovered from an illness to confess their faith.
A woman stood up and said that for several years she had felt
stuffed up and hadn't been able to breathe right, but that she
had gotten better just then and felt some relief. An elderly man
whose knees had tingled and ached walked as far as the pulpit
to show that the problem had cleared up. Whenever someone
confessed his faith by saying he had recovered from a sickness
the other believers shouted halleluiah or clapped, and held
their hands aloft and waved them around.

"But when devoutness is overdone it becomes fanaticism, and then we've got a problem, don't we?" said Chun-t'ae. "I was looking at this magazine a while back. It was really something. There was an article about a revival that's held outside of Inch'ŏn. There are over three thousand people, and when they sing a hymn in a fast tempo—some of them are keeping time with drums and bugles—they nearly go crazy. The majority are women, and the article says it's common for old women in their seventies right down to children a little over ten to clap and dance. The minister holds up a red cross and leads them like a cheerleader. Then the believers move their heads and hands and bodies every which way, screaming all the while. The magazine had this scene showing them glassy-eyed and waving their hands around while this yelling is going on. It's like they're possessed. The reporter asked a twenty-year-old woman why she was dancing. She said she didn't know—it just happened. It must have been God directing her, she said. But the best part was what the minister told the reporter. He said some people called him a heretic, but he just believed in the Bible and did as it said. The world was filled with crazy people—crazy about money, crazy about politics. But if he was going to be crazy about something he might as well be crazy about Jesus. The more ministers there are like this, the more the church will prosper. What do you think?"

"I really don't know."

Chi-yŏn was slightly embarrassed that a conversation she had started innocently had reached this point.

"Me neither," said Chun-t'ae. "But there's one thing I can clearly say. That minister's motive for being crazy about Jesus is very simple. Since other people are crazy in their worldly desires or mad for power, he's going to be crazy about Jesus. Okay, since that's his prerogative, it's of no concern to me. But a minister with a motive like that for being crazy about Jesus makes all his followers crazy like him, and that's the issue. So my question is, what's the relation between this kind of thing and the spirit of Christianity?"

"And so..." Chi-yŏn paused briefly, taking in what Chun-t'ae had said. "Are you denying the beliefs of Korean Christians?"

"Maybe so. Perhaps Koreans can't grasp religion in its true meaning."

"Even so, you seem to have a great deal of interest in Christianity."

"Back in middle school and high school there was a time when I went to church constantly. And I never failed to attend the prayer service at dawn."

"And now?"

"Not any more."

"Why is that?"

"Because I realized that my religious beliefs were only for the weak."

"That's too much for me to understand."

"In short, there's a belief that since we can't have a good life in this world we should try to go to heaven, which we can't do until after we die. And there's a belief that we should try to gain consolation or whatnot from the proverb that it's easier for a camel to pass through the eye of a needle than for a rich man to enter the kingdom of heaven. It's because of things like this. The sermons of the minister also called for beliefs like these. I tried switching churches, but it was all the same. So how about your beliefs? Have you reached the stage where you dance and move your head and hands around in the air?"

"Do I look like that kind of believer?" Chi-yŏn said with a chuckle.

"Yes, and then some."

"And what makes you think so?"

"Obviously because you said you felt it was more dangerous to walk past an empty truck."

Chi-yŏn laughed again.

"In that case, maybe I'll try to become a believer like that."

That night an invisible rain was falling. It was a misty, dense drizzle. The asphalt had become damp and glossy before either of them knew it. The various colors of the neon lights shining from the shops on both sides of the street were dissolving on its surface like dyes in water. It was a soft and warm night, atypical of autumn.

A child standing in the middle of the sidewalk was hawking oil-paper umbrellas to passersby.

Neither Chun-t'ae, who was hatless, nor Chi-yŏn, who wore a scarf, felt the need for an umbrella.

From Ŭlchiro they turned onto Samillo, and then entered Ch'ungmuro. Before they had walked very far on that street, Chi-yŏn spoke to Chun-t'ae in an undertone.

"Do you know that woman?"

Chun-t'ae slowed down.

"She looked over here and then turned her face away. I have a hunch she knows you."

Chun-t'ae turned and looked back.

"It's the woman over there with the man in the beret."

It was Ch'ang-ae. They too hadn't put up an umbrella.

"Yes, I know her." Chun-t'ae turned to the front again. "It's my wife."

Chi-yŏn was dumfounded. Stopping almost instantly, she said, "But didn't she see you and then pass on by as if she didn't know you?"

Chun-t'ae thought he probably would have done the same if he had seen them first.

"I can understand—it depends on the circumstances."

"She's really something. She probably thought the proper thing to do was to pretend she didn't know you since you were with a woman she didn't know."

"No. She doesn't get concerned over things like that. And there's no need for you to get concerned either," Chun-t'ae said coolly.

Chun-t'ae had wanted to confirm that Ch'ang-ae was meeting another man. But he had also hoped he would not have a confrontation like this, for he felt it would be an insult to witness the scene. But having done so he did not feel unusual. Once more he wanted to apply his stamp to the vermilion inkpad and then clearly imprint his seal on their divorce paper, which might as well have been stamped already.

"Let's have another hot drink," said Chi-yŏn. They had been walking for a while without talking.

Her feminine intuition had told her to say this. Chun-t'ae hadn't gone into detail about his wife and Chi-yŏn hadn't presssed the matter, but she could guess what his marriage was like. Rather than leaving him in his present state she wanted to spend as much time with him as possible.

A tearoom caught their eye and they went in.

At first they said nothing. But for Chi-yŏn their silence was not burdensome. They merely tasted the tea placed in front of them, and finally it went cold.

Thinking that quite some time must have passed, Chun-t'ae opened his mouth as if to continue what they had been talking about.

"This humiliation I'd been thinking about proved to be nothing after I finally experienced it."

Chi-yŏn too was ready to resume their conversation. "That's very fortunate."

"I think I've just realized that the period before a direct confrontation is worse than the event itself," Chun-t'ae continued slowly. "After all, this humiliation is merely something I've brought on myself, because I'm indecisive."

"It looks like the tearoom's about to close already."

A youth in his undershirt had pushed the empty chairs to one side and was cleaning the room. Chun-t'ae and Chi-yŏn discovered they were the only customers.

Outside the misty drizzle was much denser than before, more like thick fog than rain.

Chi-yŏn hailed a taxi. She got in first.

"Where to?" asked the driver.

"Just go for now," said Chi-yŏn. Though she felt she had to stay longer with Chun-t'ae, she felt awkward that she hadn't decided where to instruct the driver to go.

"I can't go very far," the driver said rather bluntly.

"Why is that? There's still a lot of time before curfew."

"As you can see, this is just the weather for an accident. I'd like to get back to the garage a little early."

Just as Chi-yŏn decided that they had better go somewhere nearby, the driver stopped in front of a hotel. His guess had far outdistanced hers.

Chun-t'ae and Chi-yŏn looked at each other with a laugh of amazement as they got out of the taxi. Chi-yŏn entered the hotel first, asking herself what there was to shrink from since they had a different object in going there.

A bellboy guided them to a Western-style room.

Judging from the furniture in the room, it was probably a class 2 hotel. They sat down opposite each other in two armchairs, and just as they were about to give another wan smile there was a knock. This time a girl came in. She lit the kerosene stove and then asked if they would be staying overnight. Chun-t'ae replied that they would be leaving in about an hour. The girl turned and was about to leave when Chun-t'ae asked her to bring them some beer.

When the beer arrived Chun-t'ae poured a glass for Chi-yŏn and then himself. Without any formalities Chun-t'ae brought his glass to his lips. It was his way of telling Chi-yŏn to drink if she wanted and if not, to leave it at that.

Chi-yŏn raised her glass and took a swallow. It was not the first time she had tasted beer.

Sitting astride a bar stool, Ch'ang-ae occasionally brought her wine glass to her mouth and moistened the tip of her tongue. She was drinking more carefully than ever before.

Mr. Kang sat next to her, a short distance away. His style of drinking was to wrap his hands about his cocktail glass, swirl the drink around and around, and then throw it down.

Ch'ang-ae quietly observed Mr. Kang. Exhaustion was written all over his face. Some time before, he had been asked to take over the scene painting at a movie company, and now he seemed weary from that, Ch'ang-ae thought.

"You look even more done in today," she said.

"Mmm."

"Haven't they finished shooting that movie yet?"

"I'm handling another movie now at a different studio."

"Well, then, don't drink a lot."

Instead of replying, Mr. Kang closed his mouth and stretched out the corners—his way of asking her to leave him alone. Ch'ang-ae liked this childlike expression.

Ch'ang-ae had been keeping something within her, but what she brought up now was different.

"On the way here, you know, we passed my husband going the other way. I guess it was a mistake not to act as if I knew him. I could have introduced you to him."

"That's in bad taste." Mr. Kang tossed down more of his drink.

"You think so?"

"You said you were going down to Suwŏn this evening, didn't you?"

"Well, I was thinking about it..."

Mr. Kang swirled his drink around and around.

"But I've decided not to," Ch'ang-ae concluded.

Mr. Kang filled his pipe and put it in his mouth.

Suddenly Ch'ang-ae feels nauseated. She quickly leaves her stool and goes to the washroom. She vomits a little of the wine she has drunk, plus a sourish fluid. And she had been moderate in her drinking today, she thought. Though nothing more came up, her retching continued. As the doctor had said, it was an infallible sign of the loss of appetite that comes from pregnancy. And wasn't it because of this physiological change that she had vomited when she went down to Suwŏn that time? Her period, always punctual, hadn't arrived for two months, and now there was this occasional retching, which had started three or four days ago. So that morning she had gone to the hospital, where she had discovered that she was indeed pregnant. An indescribable joy briefly filled her chest, but soon a feeling of dread shrouded her entire body. It wasn't merely the dread of being pregnant by a man other than Chun-t'ae. There was also the question of Mr. Kang's reaction. It would be fine if he was happy, but if not, what then? This apprehension was the reason Ch'ang-ae had kept this news to herself a short time before. And now too, amidst her retching, she was possessed by this thought. Other thoughts intruded. Why should I be bound to his reaction? Can't I handle things my own way? But at this point such thoughts were useless.

Chun-t'ae slowly filled his glass and drank the beer by himself. After a while he looked up at Chi-yŏn.

"I just thought of something one of my college professors told me. He said that people shouldn't resolve to die in order to die. Instead they should resolve to die in order to live, and then go on living. But it's not the easiest thing in the world either to resolve to die in order to die, and then go ahead and do it."

Although Chi-yŏn's eyes received Chun-t'ae's squarely, Chun-t'ae looked away. Then he continued.

"When I was fourteen I graduated from elementary school and took the entrance exam for middle school."

He passed the examination, obtaining the second highest score. Then on the day of the entrance ceremonies for the new students at the middle school it rained. The rain had started the previous evening and was now heavy. After obtaining an oil-paper umbrella from the pharmacy where he worked as an errand boy, Chun-t'ae dashed off to school. His sneakers were in bad shape because of the mire. The soles were worn out, and the muddy water came in through a hole and covered his feet. The ceremony was being held in the auditorium. The children who came first formed an orderly line. When Chun-t'ae entered the auditorium his black cotton socks left messy prints on the wooden floor. He felt ashamed of himself.

"But that wasn't the worst of it." Chun-t'ae drank some beer to moisten his throat. "I tried to squeeze in among the kids, you know, but this teacher came over, class list in hand, and dragged me out of the line. He told me I couldn't participate in the ceremony because I hadn't paid my entrance fee. Can you believe it? I wanted to die. So I made up my mind to do it. And—"

Just then the telephone rang. Chi-yŏn went over to the nightstand and picked up the receiver. After a pause she said she understood, and in that case they would spend the night there. She then gave the person at the other end her home telephone number and asked to be connected with her family. Finally she asked for a plate of fruit to be sent up. She spoke calmly, as if she had prepared what she would say.

Chun-t'ae looked at his watch and saw that it was eleven fifteen. He took out a cigarette and lit it. A short while later the telephone rang again. Chi-yŏn immediately picked it up. She said she was sleeping at a friend's house, and she hoped they wouldn't worry. After hanging up, Chi-yŏn returned to her chair. Though she had spoken calmly on the telephone, her face was flushed.

The girl came with a tray of apples and pears and set it on the table in front of them. Chun-t'ae ordered two more bottles of beer. Chi-yŏn asked him which fruit he would like. He replied that he wasn't in the mood for either of them at the moment. Chi-yŏn peeled an apple and ate it. As before, Chun-t'ae slowly poured himself a glass of the beer that had just arrived and drank it.

Even after Chi-yŏn had finished the apple, Chun-t'ae did not resume his story. There was no need to hurry, Chi-yŏn thought.

After gazing for a while at the glass he was holding, Chun-t'ae began speaking again with difficulty.

"Now that I'm telling you this I feel kind of awkward. But as long as I've started, I'll finish. I wish I could've sunk right into the ground or else died. No kidding. So I made up my mind to die and I found my way to West Lake. My plan was to drown there."

He had a reason for wanting to drown in West Lake. The winter of the year he turned six, he guessed it was, his mother had taken him there deep in the night. He still remembered how he had shivered from the cold as he stood beside her, and how she had gripped his hand so tightly he couldn't stand it. The six-year-old boy had no way of knowing why his mother had brought him there on a cold winter night. But at fourteen Chun-t'ae was able to fathom his mother's heart back then. She had wanted to drown with him. At that time, Chun-t'ae's father frequently left the house and didn't return at night. His mother would sit by herself in a corner of the room and weep. She began to wish she could die together with Chun-t'ae. However, the two of them did not die that night, and Chun-t'ae did not know why. Perhaps it was because the lake was covered with ice and they couldn't throw themselves in. Then again his mother may have had a change of heart. The thing that remained imprinted in the mind of the fourteen-year-old boy was that West Lake was the spot where his mother had come to die. Better go there and drown, he thought. Having been driven from the entrance ceremony, Chun-t'ae went to the lake. The rain was pouring down, and the wind was rippling the water. Facing the pouring rain, he shouted again and again to himself "Drown! Drown!" But in the end he could not throw himself in.

"Maybe I was afraid of the riffles on the water and the rain streaming down on it. Anyway, I can't tell you how ashamed I felt. Do you know what I mean? And this—" Chun-t'ae lifted his eyes from his glass and looked at Chi-yŏn.

"Why, you look kind of pale. Is something wrong?"

Chi-yŏn shook her head. "I'm all right."

Her face had turned ashen. She was shivering from an unbearable chill that had set in a short time before. It was not because of the beer. The glass that Chun-t'ae had originally filled for her was still about half full. Chun-t'ae had not urged the beer upon her, and Chi-yŏn herself had not cared to drink more. The misty drizzle they had encountered had soaked through to her shoulders, and this was the result. And the kerosene stove had still not removed the chill from the room.

"If you don't feel good, why not lie down?" said Chun-t'ae in a subdued voice.

In fact, Chi-yŏn wished only to lie down and pull the quilt over her face, but she resisted.

"I'm all right. Go ahead and finish what you were saying."

Chun-t'ae was nine. His mother and father had already gone their separate ways and Chun-t'ae had been taken in by a family that peddled bean curd. Hawking bean curd on a wooden tray, Chun-t'ae would go in the yard of houses whose front gate was open. From within one of the rooms would come a voice saying they didn't want any, and a door would open, not to close until Chun-t'ae was completely out the gate. At first he thought the people were opening their doors to tell him they weren't buying. But this was not the case. Some families opened their door, and rather than leaving their shoes outside they took them in.

"What a humiliation for a child. But when I think about it now, it's nothing to be bothered about...Wait a minute, you're even whiter now."

The way they looked at each other now was different. When Chun-t'ae had begun his story he had avoided Chi-yŏn's gaze, but then Chi-yŏn had gradually averted her eyes from Chun-t'ae's and now was resting them on the table. Chi-yŏn reflected. As Chun-t'ae had said, perhaps that incident was nothing to worry about now. Nevertheless, she was sorry that she was causing him to dwell on such painful experiences. I wanted to spend time with him, but surely not for the sake of that. After all, I lied to my family for the first time in my life tonight.

"You don't look well at all. Why don't you lie down?"

Chi-yŏn wavered for a moment and then stood up.

"All right."

Sensing her hesitation as she went over to the bed, Chun-t'ae said, "You can turn off the light."

After doing this, Chi-yŏn got in bed. She didn't want her reclining form to be exposed by the light. Again she heard Chun-t'ae's voice.

"You don't have to turn it on."

Chi-yŏn looked toward him. Although at first she couldn't see anything distinctly in the darkness, Chun-t'ae's silhouette was revealed by the electric light filtering through the blinds from outside. He was sitting in the same posture. His form became inscribed in her mind. A shudder went down her spine, and she drew the quilt to her chin.

Ch'ang-ae clutched Mr. Kang's arm. Before, she had done this to keep herself steady when intoxicated, but today she was propping up Mr. Kang. Although the hard-drinking Mr. Kang had consumed a fair amount, he did not lose his footing.

Ch'ang-ae looked at the asphalt dyed with the colors of the neon lights.

"Wouldn't you like to try painting those colors over there?"

The water-soaked colors were spread out in various tints.

Mr. Kang moved along without a word. Ever since he had started in at the movie company, he had refrained from talking about painting.

Suddenly the various colors before Ch'ang-ae's eyes composed themselves into a river that appeared to be flowing backward. The current was quite strong. A man was swimming along, following the flow of the water. Endlessly and ardently he swam...

Ch'ang-ae stopped in front of a fruit vendor who was tidying up some fruit spread out on a wooden tray.

The aging vendor, dressed in rain gear, brings her hands to a halt. "It's first-class stuff."

Ch'ang-ae examined the fruit in their plastic covering.

"How about this banana? It's just ripe, and nice and fresh."

Shaking her head, Ch'ang-ae pointed to some tangerines.

"Those are navels. They came from overseas."

"I meant those tangerines over there. Could I have a look at them?"

"You can't eat those. They're sour," Mr. Kang said curtly.

"You're right. They're a little sour. Please try these navels."

"Why not just show me those tangerines without all the talk?"

The vendor produced some of the tangerines, and Ch'ang-ae randomly picked out two and bought them.

Even after arriving at the hotel they sometimes dropped in at, Ch'ang-ae had to go directly to the bathroom. Unable to endure her queasiness, she threw up a bit more of the bitter fluid.

When she came out of the bathroom, Mr. Kang was lying across the middle of the bed, his legs dangling from the side. When the two of them were all alone in the hotel room, Mr. Kang would quickly seek Ch'ang-ae's lips, unbutton her blouse, pull down her stockings, and unhook her bra—but not today. He was exhausted.

The river reappeared, along with the figure of the swimming man, but Ch'ang-ae erases this scene and peels a tangerine and eats it. It did not taste very sour. Ch'ang-ae takes a piece of tangerine and sticks it in Mr. Kang's mouth. Not even trying to eat it, he contorts his face and attempts to spit it out. Ch'ang-ae takes the piece of tangerine in her lips and again pushes it inside his mouth. Mr. Kang tries to move his head aside. Ch'ang-ae's mouth chases the tangerine and with her tongue she drives it into Mr. Kang's mouth. If you're tired, just sleep tonight, she whispers. Mr. Kang gently bites the piece of tangerine along with Ch'ang-ae's tongue and, still lying down, hurriedly begins to remove her clothes.

When Chi-yŏn opened her eyes the room was as dark as before. Her chill had disappeared, and she felt refreshed. Instinctively she looked toward Chun-t'ae. His silhouette was projected by the light from outside filtering in through the blinds. He was leaning back in the armchair, as if he had fallen asleep.

Without a sound, Chi-yŏn got out of bed and walked past Chun-t'ae to the bathroom. She opened and closed the bathroom door silently.

When she came out a short time later she lost her bearings. The blinds had been lifted high, and the room had brightened. The misty drizzle had cleared during the night, and the early-morning sunbeams outside the windows dazzled her eyes. She heard a church bell not far away.

Chun-t'ae was standing in the middle of the room.

"How are you feeling? I noticed you had a nice sleep."

"Not bad at all." Seeing his bloodshot eyes, she added, "Looks like I'm the only one who slept comfortably...sorry."

Chun-t'ae slowly shook his head. The two of them looked at each other and smiled, neither knowing who did so first. It was a natural smile, not like the awkward smiles of the previous evening.

Chun-t'ae approached Chi-yŏn. She stood where she was, not avoiding him, and their mouths met.

After parting with Chi-yŏn, Chun-t'ae went for a long walk. The chilly air grazing his face was exhilarating.

Chun-t'ae felt as if something sleeping deep within him had been awakened. Never before had he experienced the seemingly groundless ecstasy that now flowed steadfastly into his chest, leaving no chink unfilled. He shouldn't let this ecstasy escape, he thought. All of a sudden his breathing became heavy and a surge of coughing swept through him. In order to control his breathing and settle his coughing, he stood silently where he was and tried to keep warm. But his breathing did not stabilize. He could inhale, but exhaling was difficult. Meanwhile, his coughing continued without interruption. His breathing became even more labored. Unable to bear it, he half squatted. Still the coughing went on, and from his throat came the rattle of blocked-up phlegm.

When the spasm finally cleared and Chun-t'ae was able to recover his breath, his entire body was wet with perspiration.

He remained crouching until he had regained his strength.

Early though it was, he sought out Min-gu's apartment.

Wiping his freshly washed face with a towel, Min-gu opened the door for Chun-t'ae.

"I was wondering if you were still asleep..."

"No way. I might not look like it, but I get by on diligence. It's my number one asset. But what's this look on your face? You look like you're scared of something."

Chun-t'ae was noncommittal.

"The wind's pretty cold. I guess that's why."

"Must be something urgent that brings you up here practically at daybreak."

"Could I have a cup of coffee?"

"Sure. I was thinking of having some myself. I was just about to boil some water."

Min-gu goes into the kitchen.

Chun-t'ae picked up a spread-open copy of the morning paper that Min-gu had been looking at.

Min-gu returned, saying, "It might be a little strong. I always like my coffee strong in the morning."

Chun-t'ae, however, drank it without sugar.

Min-gu felt something was unusual, but pried no further. This was not the time to ask, he thought. The sight of Chun-t'ae looking at the newspaper gave him an idea.

"Say, you know my friend Sŏng-ho? He's a minister now, you know..."

Min-gu gets up, takes a page from a newspaper out of a table drawer, and unfolds it in front of Chun-t'ae.

"That's some essay he's published there."

It was *The Christian Weekly*. Above the title—"Korean Customs and Christianity"—there was a photograph of him.

"To make a long story short, he's concluded that Christianity has gone too far with our customs. He gives several examples, but I'll mention just two—ceremonial occasions such as ancestor worship and funerals. He says these can't be regarded as superstition. According to him, we perform funeral rites and ancestor worship out of reverence toward our ancestors rather than to obtain salvation. Of course, amending the cumbersome formalities of funeral rites or ancestor worship according to one's circumstances is a different question. He guesses that the idea of regarding funeral rites or ancestor worship as superstition could have started with the first Western missionaries, who saw us as an uncivilized people. He says the Korean consciousness is different from that of Westerners, and so they shouldn't disregard our native customs. Therefore, we'd better set things straight right now. Yes sir, that's the right way to look at it. But I'll bet he has a tough time arguing this position of his."

Looking inattentively at the photograph of Sŏng-ho, Chun-t'ae listened casually to Min-gu. He was thinking about his recent fit of coughing.. What in the world could have brought it about?

"Oh—I forgot. The other day I saw him and he mentioned your name."

"How so?"

"Nothing special. He asked how you were and said he'd like to see you sometime."

Only then did Chun-t'ae look carefully at Sŏng-ho in the newspaper. It was an ordinary frontal view, but the print was not good and the definition poor. Nevertheless, some hidden aspect of Sŏng-ho, not visible there in the photograph, gave Chun-t'ae the feeling that he was meeting him face to face. This Sŏng-ho had made Chun-t'ae feel very close to him. Chun-t'ae too wished to see Sŏng-ho when he had the opportunity. He felt they would have much to talk about.

Chapter 4

Again Sŏng-ho noticed the faint shadow flit across the dingy, fading wallpaper. It was the light coming through the window and reflecting off of Elder Ch'oe's rimless spectacles.

"Our family used to get along by serving the spirits too, ahem." Elder Ch'oe was talking about how in Stone Village the shamans and fortune-tellers were increasing more than the church members. "And we really went overboard."

"I didn't realize that," said Sŏng-ho.

Knowing only that Elder Ch'oe's grandfather was the founder of the church and that both his father and his grandfather had been elders, Sŏng-ho couldn't help being surprised at Elder Ch'oe's remarks.

"What do you reckon made our grandfather do away with the spirits and come around to believing in Jesus? Ahem." This habit of ending each utterance with an "Ahem," which wasn't because of phlegm in his throat, was even more pronounced today. "It wasn't a matter of being attracted to the truth of Christianity from the beginning. He hinted at that privately when he was alive, ahem, but the real reason was that believing in Christ was less expensive than serving the spirits."

"Ah, I see."

"In spring and autumn he'd choose a good date for a shaman to hold a *kut*, and in early January and July seventh by the lunar calendar he'd never fail to devote himself in prayer to the spirits, ahem. And that's not all. Whenever anything came up, he'd have an exorcism or try to mollify the spirits by offering up a meal. As a matter of fact, he wore out the threshold of the shaman's house, ahem. Today a *kut* would require tens of thousands of *wŏn*, and a prayer session in early January or July seventh would take about forty-five hundred *wŏn*, ahem. And he'd be able to save even more than that, since he'd have to give up drinking and smoking if he started believing in Christ, ahem."

"At any rate, your grandfather was a splendid man. It took a great deal of courage to make a decision like that."

"It would be nice if you could mention something like that in one of your sermons. But don't say it's about our family."

Sŏng-ho had been thinking about this. It would be worthwhile to awaken the people to how expensive shamans and fortune-tellers are for those having a hard time. Since it takes time for true faith to develop, the first thing to do is to get people to come to church.

"By the way, Pastor, ahem, what do you think about renaming? You don't think it's superstitious, do you? What I mean is altering one's name, ahem."

"Altering one's name? Whose name are you speaking of?"

"My name. Isn't there a lot of name changing in the Bible? Ahem."

"What did you change it to?"

"Yŏng-hŭng—'Yŏng' meaning 'eternal' and 'Hŭng' meaning 'to rise.' An old man who's good at making names gave it to me. He said the name I've had till now, Ch'un-shik—'Ch'un' meaning 'the spring season' and 'Shik' meaning 'plant'—was all right when I was young, ahem, but it's not so good now that I'm old. Changing my name to Ch'un-shik is just like Jacob changing his name to Israel, and Simon to Peter, ahem. Unlike Abraham and Sarah, I changed my whole name and not just part of it."

Sŏng-ho had forgotten what he had intended to say.

"Yesterday I went to the district office and found my new name on our family register, ahem. That's why I'm telling you this."

Elder Ch'oe hadn't come to visit Sŏng-ho to consult with him on ways to lead the faithful, but for something else.

A strong distaste began to seep through Sŏng-ho. If there's

a need to alter one's name, then it's justifiable to do so. There's no need to drag in the Bible. But Elder Ch'oe's name change didn't sit right with him. Elder Ch'oe was sixty-two. He owned a considerable amount of land in the neighborhood, and he had a large textile company in the city that he managed through a son. Enjoying the good life at his age and yet saying it could be a little better if he altered his name—maybe it was just willfulness. But Sŏng-ho felt that a shadow of meanness bred of greed lurked in Elder Ch'oe's name change. It's safe to say that the more property one has, the more avaricious one becomes, he thought. Sŏng-ho looked right into Elder Ch'oe's face. The expression in his eyes was shielded by the lenses of his spectacles. Even though Elder Ch'oe wanted him to inform the congregation of his name change during the worship service, he would not do it, he decided.

In a short while Elder Ch'oe got up. The shadow on the dingy wallpaper moved to and fro. "I guess we'll have to do over the wallpaper before it gets really cold, ahem." These words contained equal measures of concern and triteness.

"Oh well, we can get by," replied Sŏng-ho. "Before we do that we'll probably have to put a new roof on the sanctuary. If not this year, next spring."

"Can't we make do by giving it another coat of paint and flattening out those bumps and hollows?"

"Well, some rain might be leaking through, too."

"That won't do. If it leaks, the whole building'll be damaged. We'll have to climb up there and fix up the places where it's coming through. Like people say, a stitch in time saves nine." Elder Ch'oe then muttered, "The money we get from the Council of Elders isn't enough to cover a rat's tail, ahem, and even that's getting smaller every year. Brother."

After Elder Ch'oe left, Sŏng-ho left for the mental hospital to see Myŏng-suk.

When he had first gone to see her, less than a week after her admission, her condition was much better. As soon as she saw him she smiled brightly and thanked him. She had even stopped pulling her hair out. Sŏng-ho was very satisfied to see this surprisingly quick improvement. When he was leaving, Myŏng-suk begged him to take her home, saying she was all better. Sŏng-ho then took her to the head doctor and hinted at this. But the doctor shook his head. Myŏng-suk abruptly challenged him, saying she had always been healthy and had never gotten ill. "All right, all right," the doctor said, and with a gentle expression nodded and asked her to wait outside. He then told Sŏng-ho that Myŏng-suk's attitude and speech they'd just witnessed were symptoms of disease. The people who are recovered from illness, he said, are those who realize that they were not normal in the past. The patients are the ones who maintain that they were perfectly healthy all along. The doctor had elaborated: If Sŏng-ho were to take Myŏng-suk out of the hospital, he would by no means stand in their way and force her to stay. But Sŏng-ho had to keep one thing in mind: many people had been discharged after showing a slight improvement, only to take a turn for the worse and be readmitted. There were several patients like that in the hospital, among them one who had been admitted five years before, when the doctor had first come to the hospital. Over and over he would be discharged, suffer a relapse, be readmitted, be discharged, have another setback, be admitted again, and now there was no hope at all of curing him. To be discharged and admitted like this was possible only because the patient was from a wealthy family. Self-possessed though the doctor was, it was his final words that stuck in Sŏng-ho's mind: Myŏng-suk was being hospitalized and treated free of charge. If he had her discharged too hastily and she had a relapse, it would be a big problem to have her readmitted. While Sŏng-ho was escorting Myŏng-suk to her ward on the second floor, she pressed him to take her home. Sŏng-ho could only urge her to bear up for the time being.

If she badgers me again today to take her home, Sŏng-ho thought, I'll have to do a good job of reasoning with her until the doctor says it's all right to release her. He went up to her second-floor ward and pressed the buzzer beside the entrance. He heard the door being unlocked, and a nurse peeped out. Sŏng-ho gave her Myŏng-suk's name. Asking him to wait for a moment, she closed the door. Sŏng-ho heard the lock being fastened. Apparently the wards were always locked while the patients' rooms within were left open. Presently he heard the door being unlocked again. The same nurse asked him to see the head doctor, on the floor below. No doubt she had spoken with him over the intercom.

The head doctor was alone in a laboratory. He asked Sŏng-ho to take a seat.

"It's better if she doesn't have visitors. Her mother came just now, but she had to leave without seeing her."

It was not what Sŏng-ho had expected to hear.

"What happened?"

"She's in a very excitable state. She hasn't settled down since the last time you came. But since yesterday she's been somewhat improved. Sometimes they can handle the shock of having visitors, but it depends on the patient."

Sŏng-ho was reminded of how he felt when he saw the resignation in Myŏng-suk's eyes and her look of resentment toward him when she reentered the ward the last time.

"Has she been pulling out her hair again?"

"No, she hasn't."

"What reason did she give you for doing that?"

"She said the kids at the Sunday school tell her do it."

"The kids at the Sunday school?"

"Yes. We have patients like that now. There was one who was always hearing voices, and once when the nurse wasn't watching, she chewed off her fingers and swallowed them. When we asked her why, she said her brother had spoken right into her ear and told her to eat her own flesh and not just that of others. We call this kind of thing partial suicide."

"What's your opinion: is there any chance she'll get better?" Sŏng-ho knew he was being hasty, but he couldn't help asking.

"Strictly speaking," began the head doctor in the same self-possessed tone, "there's no complete cure for a mental disorder. If a patient can just get along in society without too much trouble, then we discharge him. In reality, though, curing a mental illness involves many ups and downs, so there's no need to be pessimistic because of a slight deterioration. If only there are no symptoms of regression in the patient from now on...by regression I mean returning to a childlike state. It seems the most comfortable time for people must be when they're inside the womb—even though they remain still, they're provided with nutrients. The next most comfortable state is probably infancy: if they cry they're breast-fed, and if they urinate or defecate, their diapers are changed. When people become severely mentally ill, their character disintegrates and they regress to infancy. Just eating, sleeping, excretion. In the end they relieve themselves anywhere and smear their faces with excrement—a complete regression."

If I could just see Myŏng-suk's face before leaving, Sŏng-ho thought. "It wouldn't be possible to have a quick look at her?"

"The rule is to keep any visitor, no matter who, out of the patient's room. And it wouldn't be much fun even if you looked inside."

With a heavy heart Sŏng-ho got up from his chair.

"Well, then, when *would* be a good time to see her?"

"Hard to say. Why don't you call before coming — in ten days or so?"

Sŏng-ho returned home in low spirits to find a letter inside his door. His mail was always delivered this way, whether he was home or not.

It was from the Council of Elders. The typewritten contents were simple and brief, like the writing in a telegram. They instructed Sŏng-ho to come to the office of the council the following Thursday at two o'clock. The letter seemed like an order, perhaps because it ended with the words "We hope you will come without fail." Moreover, he couldn't help feeling there was a long story behind the letter's abbreviated contents, which offered no hint of the business at hand. The following

Thursday was still a ways off; the council probably presumed that since he lived in the outskirts the mail might be a couple of days late, and so they'd allowed ample time for the letter to get to him.

"I heard you were at a bakeshop in Myŏng-dong today," said Ch'ang-ae during a lull in her conversation with Mr. Kang.

"Oh?" Looking slightly embarrassed, Mr. Kang briefly paused as he was filling his pipe.

Ch'ang-ae was surprised by this. Her partner Mrs. O had told her of seeing Mr. Kang there, but she hadn't been hinting that he had had a date with someone. In the first place, Mrs. O didn't know about Ch'ang-ae's relationship with Mr. Kang, assuming only that they were friends because she had graduated from art school and he was a painter. In mentioning Mr. Kang she had merely lamented that because of her poor memory it had taken her a moment to recognize him as the man who had hung two of his paintings in the shop. Ch'ang-ae had thus brought up this matter lightly, but Mr. Kang's unexpected reaction made her question him in detail.

"Who were you with at the bakeshop?"

"What are you talking about?"

"Who was the girl with the long hair?"

"Ah, that one."

"What does she do?"

"She's a college kid who wants to be a star."

This was more or less what Ch'ang-ae had anticipated.

"How long have you known her?"

"About a month or so."

"Do you see her often?"

"Occasionally."

Then something Ch'ang-ae had not even thought of leapt from her mouth. "And at the same time you've been keeping it a secret?"

Immediately she realized she'd made a mistake, but it was too late. How could I've said something like that? Just like a fool with no pride.

"A secret? What're you talking about? Don't be foolish."

"All right. Let's not talk about being foolish anymore."

She made an impetuous decision. She would have an abortion without informing Mr. Kang. That way she could reimburse herself for having wounded her pride because of her senseless jealousy.

When Ch'ang-ae returned from the hospital the next day she told Mrs. O she was suffering from overwork, and went up to her second-floor bedroom and lay down. A corner of her heart had been emptied, but she was filling it with the thought that she was now free. She would not be placing any burden on Mr. Kang but would be freeing him as well. Love is not dependence on another, nor is it another's dependence on me, she thought. As soon as she received the money she'd asked Mrs. O to lend her, and had handed it over to Chun-t'ae, she would no longer be bound to anyone.

There was a knock, and one of the seamstresses quietly entered. Of the girls who worked in the shop, she was the one most attached to Ch'ang-ae.

"Are you very sick, Auntie?" she asked carefully, the huge eyes in her roundish face opening wide.

"No, just a little."

"Have you been crying, Auntie?"

"No. Why should I be crying?"

Wondering why the girl was talking like this, Ch'ang-ae turned away and closed her eyes.

"I'll tell you a funny story that'll make you forget about the pain."

The girl sat astride a corner of the bed.

"Auntie, pick a number from one to ten, your favorite number."

"Nine."

"Aha. You'll probably have nine children."

Ch'ang-ae tried to smile, but she only felt that her facial muscles were being distorted.

"Okay, now pick your favorite number from eleven to one hundred."

"Ninety-nine."

"Aha. You'll be ninety-nine percent successful when you fall in love, Auntie. I'll bet you're happy with that. Ninety-nine percent is just the same as one hundred percent, right? I said twenty."

You're too much, thought Ch'ang-ae. My eyes are getting heavy. She hoped she would go to sleep just as she was. And she felt sleep would come.

"Now Auntie, pretend it's night. The lights are out, rice is burning on the stove, a baby is crying in the room, and the doorbell rings. What would you do first?"

"The lights, the rice..."

"And the baby and the bell?"

"The bell, and then the baby..."

The girl giggled.

"Auntie, the lights stand for sex, rice is vitality, the bell means getting along with people, and the baby means motherhood." She counted them off on her fingers with delight.

A faint wave of sleepiness swept over Ch'ang-ae's entire body, and she allowed herself to be wrapped in its several layers.

"Now here's another one. Imagine these scenes: a high mountain covered with white snow, a broad, open field filled with cosmos, a blue lake with carp jumping to their hearts' content. Okay?"

"Huh?"

"Which one of them do you..."

From this point on, Ch'ang-ae couldn't hear the girl distinctly. She was wearing a student's uniform. A stiffly starched white collar had just been pressed and inserted in it. For some strange reason, she became nervous. With thumb and forefinger she pinched the collar on this side and that, deliberately making wrinkles in it. Not until then did she relax. A new notebook was in front of her. Again she felt nervous. She let a drop of ink fall on the clean paper. Only then did she feel comfortable. She was about to jot something in the notebook when someone interrupted.

"No fever."

Mrs. O was feeling her forehead.

"Try to drink this."

It was a can of pineapple juice. Saying she would drink it later, Ch'ang-ae thought about her dream. What was she about to write in the notebook?

"You've worn yourself down, that's what. And worrying about money... You just get a good rest."

Mrs. O went downstairs.

What Ch'ang-ae had been about to write in the notebook was an "X." When she was in fifth grade, her teacher had put up a catch phrase in their classroom: "One good deed every day." On the days the students had done a good deed they were to enter a circle in their diary with a red pencil; otherwise they were to draw an "X." Although the teacher rarely punished the students, she was thorough in having them put the phrase into practice, and she mercilessly punished children who falsely entered a circle. The students who entered the most circles were the class monitor and Ch'ang-ae. Not surprisingly, competition arose between them. In order not to lose, Ch'ang-ae searched enthusiastically for ways to earn a circle. On her way to and from school she would escort to the police box children who had lost their way home and offer support to old people as they walked along the street. In school she would patrol the classrooms of the four lower grades, stopping children from fighting and consoling them, and search for lost belongings. But then she realized something was strange. She was hoping for an increase in the number of crying children who had lost their way and old people who had fallen in the street. Likewise she was hoping that the children in the four lower grades would fight more and that students would continue to lose their school supplies. This was repulsive to her youthful spirit, and from that point on she gave herself nothing but "X" marks. That was what she was about to do now. But suddenly, a red circle as large as a bean appeared. The circle moved about instead of staying in one place. It moved incessantly, like a living thing. Horizontally and vertically it scurried away from her and then toward her. Looking at it carefully, she discovered it was not a circle but a drop of crimson blood. It rushed around her body. She stripped herself naked. As if possessing a will, the drop of blood sped here and there, almost touching her nude body but always keeping a slight distance. She wished the drop of blood would touch her and leave a stain. She then tried to move toward it, but her body didn't budge. She wanted to grab the drop, but her hands refused to obey. She became impatient.

She awakened to hear the soft tapping of the sewing machine in the workroom. There was a slight ache in her abdomen. She took some of the pain pills she had been given at the hospital and longed for more sleep.

People who are making an important decision can sometimes get subtle guidance from something trivial, and this was the case with Chun-t'ae. An insignificant chat at work enabled him to establish a course of action.

A colleague had told a story about a rat in his house. A room with the usual heated floor had been built where a kitchen had been, and a new kitchen built beside it. A rat had since been chewing at the paper covering the ceiling of the room. Nothing like this had ever happened before. It appeared to be the work of a single rat. The rat would gnaw tiny holes in one place and then move to another, as if to hide when light came through. So Chun-t'ae's colleague made a hole one foot square in the middle of the ceiling so light would shine in. But the rat didn't disappear. Instead it kept making holes in the untouched paper. Then, the previous day, ten days after Chun-t'ae's colleague made the hole in the middle of the ceiling, a rat fell through it. Completely emaciated, it was a warped and dried-up thing, unable to walk properly. His wife identified it as the rat that had inhabited the old kitchen. Out of all the rats in the house, a second colleague asked, how did she know it was the one that used to be in the kitchen? It was obvious: it was the old rat with half of its tail cut off that she had gotten used to seeing there; she had never seen it in the new kitchen. How could the rat have gotten to look like death warmed over and fallen from the ceiling? someone else asked. Who knows? replied the first colleague. I sure don't. Still another colleague said, What's so strange about that? I'll bet there was nothing for it to eat, so it started nibbling at the paste in the paper of the new room. That's how it happened.

The story ended up being interpreted like that. But it didn't fade from Chun-t'ae's mind. To him it was quite possible that it wasn't a lack of food in the new kitchen that had made the old rat gnaw at the paper of the ceiling. But why would the rat have been reduced to a twisted, shriveled skeleton in the ceiling of the new room? And why wouldn't it have dared to come around to the new kitchen, whether there was food there or not? At that point a thought grabbed him. The rat hadn't gone to the ceiling of the new room to eat the paste there. It had wanted to enter the former kitchen. It believed that if it returned to the old kitchen there would be something there for it to eat. So, wanting to enter the old kitchen, it had begun gnawing holes in the ceiling paper, but with people below, it had not been able to descend. Finally, nearly starved, it had had no choice but to jump down.

My imagination may have run wild, thought Chun-t'ae. But that wasn't the question. What was important was that such thoughts had helped him find a clue to his future.

On his way home from work on Saturday, Chun-t'ae dropped by several real estate brokers whom he had asked to sell his house. The brokers harped on the fact that no houses were being bought or sold these days, and that if Chun-t'ae wanted to lease, it might be the tenant who would come out ahead. But Chun-t'ae's house was not for rent; after having the brokers lower the price, he asked them again to be sure to sell it. Before Chun-t'ae heard the story of the rat, he had considered resuming his boardinghouse life in Suwŏn once the house was sold. No such thoughts surfaced now.

The way home was downhill. The road was newly cut and had not yet been blacktopped. Nor had the roadsides been filled with houses.

In the distance Chun-t'ae could see a boy riding a bicycle up the hill toward him. He had lifted his bottom from the seat and was pedaling vigorously, leaning first to one side and then to the other. The boy and the bicycle had become united in a vigorous rhythm.

Just before the bicycle reached Chun-t'ae, its handle bars lurched toward the middle of the road as if the wheels had caught on some rocks. The moment Chun-t'ae noticed this, both the youth and the bicycle sprang up in the air. They had been hit from behind by a car. The boy fell onto the road, but he appeared unhurt and was not bleeding. Even so, he was quivering all over, and this gave him a look of death. In contrast, the bicycle, its front wheel spinning briskly at an angle to the ground, appeared to be alive. As onlookers gathered, the driver of the car hoisted the boy over his shoulder, put him in the car, and drove away. Even then the bicycle wheel didn't stop moving.

Chun-t'ae smiled bitterly in spite of himself. It was difficult for him to believe that the boy who had moved so tautly just before the accident was now this deathlike creature. Human will had done nothing to bring about this sudden change. The bitter smile remained. If Chi-yŏn had viewed this scene, what would she say? That the accident was God's way of telling us that human life is ephemeral, of making humans realize the impermanence of the present world and the eternity of the future? But isn't God, if he does exist, something ephemeral? Chun-t'ae wondered. Because he created ephemeral humanity in his own image?

At the bottom of the hill, Chun-t'ae entered a building that opened out onto the road. It was a shooting range. Though he had seen its sign several times in passing, this was the first time he had gone inside. He paid fifty *wŏn* to a girl sitting at a table and received a target and an envelope containing ten bullets. Circles had been drawn on the target along with their corresponding scores: 10 for the bull's-eye and 9, 8, and 7 for the circles outside it.

Two steps led up to the entrance of the shooting gallery. Inside, the area along a wooden beam about one meter off the floor had been screened off into ten or more compartments. Four or five were occupied by shooters.

Chun-t'ae entered an empty compartment and picked up the rifle lying on the beam. It was a bit lighter than an M-1 and slightly heavier than a carbine. While he was attempting to load it a middle-aged man came over and explained in an obliging way how to pump air into it, how to load it, and what position to take when firing. Chun-t'ae remained silent, as if he had never touched a rifle before. By turning the pinwheel attached to one of the partitioning screens, the man sent the target to the wall opposite them, no more than ten meters away.

Chun-t'ae takes aim and pulls the trigger. There's no recoil at all; only the thud of the bullet embedding itself in the target. Chun-t'ae can't tell where the bullet lodged. The man, who had been keeping an eye on Chun-t'ae from the side, turns the pinwheel so the target comes out slightly from the wall. The place where the bullet hit is exposed by a fluorescent light attached to the wall. It is an 8. The man praises Chun-t'ae, saying that it's superb shooting for a first try. Chun-t'ae turns the pinwheel and returns the target to the wall. He shoots again. He removes the target from the wall by himself and sees that it's another 8. What's going on here? he asks himself. I was the top marksman in my army unit, and this target's only a hop, skip, and a jump away. Maybe because I haven't held a rifle for a while? His third shot was at the border between 8 and 9. The fourth was another 8, and the fifth was a 9 near the 8 zone.

Chun-t'ae stopped shooting and lit a cigarette. It seemed to him that his failure to hit the center was due more to his state of mind than to being out of practice. His relationship with Chi-yŏn kept clinging to his mind. He couldn't identify the groundless ecstasy that had awakened deep inside him as he walked away from the hotel by himself. Nor could he understand that spasm that had surprised him. It was an entirely new experience.

Chun-t'ae loaded the rifle again, sighted carefully, and pulled the trigger. Another 8. The man, who had gone to advise another shooter, approached Chun-t'ae, who had kept the cigarette in his mouth while shooting, and asked him to hold off on the smoking.

The next shot was not where he wanted it either. In the end, wouldn't I only be leaving Chi-yŏn with scars? The next round was similar. The least I can do is lessen those scars. For the first time in his relationships with others, Chun-t'ae was trying to be careful. But no, whatever happens, I'll see her as long as I can. The next time he shot, he stared at the target after pulling the trigger. The bullet had bored right into the center. The remaining bullet was also a 10.

Dusk was settling in every direction. Chun-t'ae felt that even the air had just the right weight as he sat calm and composed in one of the rooms of his house.

Chun-t'ae remained sitting silently where he was. Just before turning on the light, he would sometimes devote a few minutes to forgetting how weary he was. It was a short interval, but before he knew it the darkness had thickened.

He got up and turned on the light. After selecting a volume from the bookshelf, he sat down again on the warm part of the floor.

Chapter 5

For two or three days the people in the house across the street have been constructing a garden. Four men, two in front and two behind, are transporting huge stones for the garden by suspending them from poles. Bending at the waist, they cry "Heave ho" and straighten up. But the stone remains unmoved, perhaps because they haven't coordinated their actions, and the men remove their shoulders from the poles. The pair in front switch with the pair in back. This time when they straighten up they advance the stone the length of a foot-print, whereupon one of them totters. The other three also stumble and all end up removing themselves from the poles. Although sometimes they can't even straighten up when shouldering the weight and are unable to advance more than one or two paces when they do, they continue their attempts. The stone is moved little by little. Observing this spectacle, Chi-yŏn doesn't even think to change the record.

Straw Basket Valley, where P'il-jae lives, is just across a ridge from one of the national highways. As the name suggests, it is surrounded on three sides by modest hills and opens into a plain. A hamlet of twenty households sits on the plain, and skirting one of the hills to the side are the five hundred trees of P'il-jae's orchard.

A house stood in front of the entrance to the orchard. In its wide yard four or five people were sitting around mounds of apples and sorting them. Chun-t'ae asked if someone named P'il-jae owned the orchard, and the youngest among them said he did. When he asked if P'il-jae was in the house, the youth pointed to what appeared to be a storehouse at the end of the yard and asked him to look there.

The building was locked, so Chun-t'ae went around to the back. He found a man in shabby work clothes, a cap pulled down over his forehead. Although P'il-jae had undergone a substantial transfiguration in the last decade, his features— the high, protruding cheekbones and the eyes that were too small for his face—remained the same. He was so engrossed in his work he didn't seem to notice he had a visitor. Chun-t'ae remained where he was, taking in the sight. P'il-jae was doing something with a hawk.

Two poles about four or five meters apart have been connected with an iron chain. The hawk, perched on the tip of one of the poles, is bound to the chain by a long cord tied around its ankle. P'il-jae nimbly tosses into the air a dead chicken he had been concealing behind him. As if it can't wait for the chicken to fall to the earth, the hawk, its eyes darting here and there, swiftly descends and with one set of claws hooked in the chicken's back and the other in its head begins pecking at its pate. A bell tied to its tail tinkles. In one swift motion, P'il-jae takes the hawk from the chicken and places it on his left wrist. He is wearing a glove on that hand and a thick wristlet above it. The hawk pecks at the glove and wristlet, angered at being deprived of its food. P'il-jae has prepared for this: he feeds the hawk something the size of a jujube and then returns it to its perch, looking at it all the while. Presently the hawk regurgitates what it has eaten. P'il-jae catches it in his palm.

P'il-jae turns to Chun-t'ae. "Did you get a good look? It's probably the first time you've seen a hawk being trained." His tone suggested that although he didn't know who had come, he had kept silent so that the visitor could observe.

"Hey you, someone you haven't seen in a dog's age comes from a long way off and all you can do is train a hawk?" said Chun-t'ae as he approached.

P'il-jae shook hands with Chun-t'ae, using his ungloved hand. "It really has been a dog's age. And you haven't changed at all."

P'il-jae's palm felt rough and his fingers knotty.

"Where's Kŭn-yŏng?" P'il-jae asked.

"He seems pretty well tied up with his shop."

"The son of a bitch has gotten more mercenary. I've heard about you from him. Okay, let's go."

"Just a minute. Do you mind if I touch the hawk?"

"Of course not."

Chun-t'ae extended his hand and attempted to pat its back. The hawk's light chrome-yellow eyes darted back and forth.

"You can't do it like that. You have to pat it here." P'il-jae stroked the bird from beneath its beak to its breast. "If you stroke its back it becomes docile, and that's no good. You have to stroke its throat like this."

"By the way, what was that stuff it threw up?"

P'il-jae showed Chun-t'ae what he was holding in his gloved hand.

"Meat."

It wasn't just meat.

"Why feed it meat wrapped in chicken feathers—is that what you're wondering?" asked P'il-jae, seeing that Chun-t'ae had become skeptical. "I do it so it'll throw it up in its original condition."

"You make it throw up?"

"This hawk preys on pheasants, but not for people, for itself. When it catches one, I take it away. So, in order to make it hunt pheasant I have to make it hungry, see?"

"Well then, why can't you just starve it?"

"You don't understand. You've got to get hawks to think they can eat anything they hunt. It's a kind of con job."

"Even so, you can't just let them starve, can you?"

"That's right. But on the other hand, if you fatten them up, they won't obey you."

"This one looks pretty big, but you're training it. Is it still young?"

"Yeah. It's what they call a falcon. Since they hunt pheasants from the beginning, they'll chase them into a brier patch or wherever, they don't care. They're good hunters."

"Exactly how long have you been playing with this hawk, sir?"

"Life would be miserable if all I did was fumble around in the orchard, you know?"

P'il-jae took off the glove and wristlet and threw them and the dead chicken on top of a box of apples beside the door.

Behind them the bell tinkled as the hawk changed position.

"When can you start using it for hunting?"

"After another month or so of training."

P'il-jae called toward the people who were sorting apples in the yard. "Auntie, could you make some rice and kill a chicken? But before you do that, get us something to drink."

A middle-aged woman dusted off her hands and stood up.

The orchard was well managed, and the signs of nurturing were evident. Even now, in order to straighten the branches, P'il-jae had had them propped up with poles or tied down with rope. Such earnest efforts had been made with each of the fruit trees.

"Some of these trees look older than the others." Although he had not been able to tell from a distance, up close Chun-t'ae noticed the disparity in the ages of the apple and pear trees.

"Right. It's because I planted them in several different stages over the ten years I've been cultivating them."

"Boy, it must have taken a hell of a lot of work to come up with all this. The trees all look healthy."

"Yeah, but you can bet there've been a few problems."

"I guess you'll be rewarded for your labor from now on — your harvest'll increase every year."

"In principle that's how it works, but..."

The two of them came up to a fruit tree beside the path they were following through the orchard. P'il-jae scrutinized the surroundings. Compared with the other fruit trees, this one was short and lifeless. Chun-t'ae asked what the problem was.

"This was the first tree we planted. It's in pretty sad shape." P'il-jae passed his fingertips over the scars on its branches.

"You wouldn't believe the bugs. They were swarming all over it. It got sick and stunted and turned out miserable."

"Don't you have to weed out trees like that right away?"

"Of course. If fruit trees don't do well, the thing to do is dispose of them early."

Chun-t'ae cast P'il-jae a look that said, "Well then, what about this one?" Chun-t'ae thought it strange that someone with P'il-jae's turn of mind would just keep this tree.

"Isn't this a case of the proverbial child who looks cuter for being handicapped?"

"No. The only reason I keep it is to use it for testing."

"What if your sentimental nonsense allows the disease to move to another tree?"

"If that happens, it happens. What do I care if a few more trees die?"

P'il-jae's tone gave Chun-t'ae the feeling that even though he had put his heart into the orchard, if something didn't work out as he had expected he would leave it at that.

P'il-jae's large, simple room of four or five *p'yŏng* contained only a steel cabinet, which served as a closet for bedding and clothing, and a desk of similar design. There was no other furniture or decoration.

Chun-t'ae had heard through Kŭn-yŏng that P'il-jae was still single. Although he associated the life of a bachelor with his own boardinghouse life of the past, the two were different in that P'il-jae, according to Kŭn-yŏng would keep his eyes on the straight and narrow until he arrived at his objective.

The middle-aged woman brought in a small table on which she had placed some wine together with apples, pears, kimchi, and some sliced vegetables that had been preserved in soy sauce.

P'il-jae asked the woman to cook the head of the chicken and give it to the hawk. Then he turned to Chun-t'ae.

"Now that you've come to this little orchard of ours, you'll have to try some fruit, but first let's have a drink. This is something I make."

It was apple wine. Although it tasted a bit acidic, it had a slight apple fragrance. It appeared to be tolerably strong.

"I bet if I drank this stuff without knowing what it was, I'd be trying to find my legs after a while, right?"

"It leaves you feeling nice and clean, so relax. I wish that son of a bitch Kŭn-yŏng had come too.... If he keeps on growing bald like that, I'll bet he won't have a hair left before too long."

"That guy's a real success story. And so are you."

"Oh cut it out. I'm just what I appear to be. What you see is what you get."

"But it's not easy to make something out of nothing."

"Hey, come on now. That's enough." P'il-jae straightened his arm and passed his glass to Chun-t'ae. Then, lowering his voice, he said, "I'd say that whatever I've gained, I've learned from working with the hawk."

"You're back to that hawk again?"

"I'd like to have you watch that hawk hunt, but unfortunately it's not old enough. And it still needs some more training."

"Hawk, hawk, hawk. The way you talk, it must be really good at hunting."

"Whether it catches a lot of pheasants or not isn't the point. The lesson to be learned is in the act of hunting. A learned man like you will never understand. It's different from something like fishing. You catch fish with a fishing rod, right? It's the same with a rifle and hunting. An inanimate object like a gun becomes an intermediary, and that's what kills the animal. But in falconry it's one animal, the hawk, that kills another animal, the pheasant."

"What's so new about that?"

"Just listen. Now take the relationship between fishing, fish, and a human and the relationship between a rifle, an animal, and a human. Each is fundamentally different from the relationship between a hawk, a pheasant, and a human."

"Is that your philosophy?"

"Did you know that in the old days most of the kings and their ministers enjoyed falconry and that families with money had their sons learn it?"

"So?"

"The standard line is that they did it to foster a masculine disposition in a boy. Of course, there's an element of that in falconry, but the fundamental objective lies somewhere else, you know. In a word..." P'il-jae glanced casually across at Chun-t'ae and said slowly, "they learned the principle of governing others."

Chun-t'ae smiled, wondering what outlandish tale this friend who had exhibited such strange speech and behavior since middle school would come up with.

"Don't laugh. In falconry, you give the hawk the minimum and take away the maximum—that's the principle. See?"

"Some principle."

"Just listen. If the hawk has a full belly it'll end up leaving its master. That happened to me. It was the first one I had, and I put my heart into raising it. When I took it out to hunt pheasant, I noticed too late that it had caught one, and by the time I ran over, it had already eaten into its back. That damned hawk took one look at me and just flew off and perched way up in a tree. It wiped off its beak on a branch and then whoosh— off it went into the sky, and that was that. That must have been what the rulers learned from hawks, that it was no good for their subjects to have full bellies. But feeding the hawk nothing at all is no good either, and likewise the rulers couldn't starve their subjects and still benefit from them. You saw how I fed the hawk some chicken wrapped in feathers. Even though the rulers deceived their subjects, it was only by making them think from time to time that they wouldn't starve them that they got them to work in order to fill their stomachs. The result was that the subjects ended up having things taken away from them."

"It's just like you to come up with an analogy like that," said Chun-t'ae. "Here, take this glass."

"If you compare humans and hawks," continued P'il-jae, "the human is the ruler and the hawk the subject. And with hawks and pheasants, the ruler is the hawk and the subject the pheasant, right? There's something interesting, though, between the hawk and the pheasant. I observed it myself last autumn. I thought the hawk would ride the back of the pheasant, but it hopped down and looked like it didn't know what to do. There was a reason for that. When a hawk swoops down on a pheasant, the pheasant usually gives up. It's like it realizes it's done for. But this one flapped its wings and hit the hawk. I don't know whether it became violent in spite of itself or whether it was a last-ditch stand. But one smack of the pheasant's wings took care of any more thoughts of swooping down on it, and all the hawk could do was sit there puzzled until the pheasant flew off somewhere. After that the hawk turned into an idiot that couldn't catch a pheasant at all. So hawks can be fierce and get scared at the same time. See? Interesting, isn't it? I think we can see this same characteristic in rulers."

"Well then, are you going to try again with the falcon you're training now? To see if it'll turn into another idiot when a pheasant hits it with its wings?"

P'il-jae emptied his glass without a word.

The two of them finished their meal, and while they were lighting cigarettes the youth who had directed Chun-t'ae to P'il-jae came in and gave P'il-jae some money, saying it was for some nursery trees that had been sold.

"You raise nursery trees too?" asked Chun-t'ae.

"Yeah, a few."

Chun-t'ae thought the time was right to talk about what had brought him to see P'il-jae.

"What are the land prices like around here?"

"Why?"

"I've been wondering if it wouldn't be possible, you know, to settle down in this area. And maybe start an orchard like yours..."

"Looks like you've put away some money over the years."

"Why would I want to come to a place like this if I had lots of money?" Chun-t'ae was calculating how much retirement pay he would receive when the time came for him to leave his job. "I wouldn't mind starting out with less money than you did."

"No way. A gentleman with a degree in agriculture, and you don't know squat about this. A little while ago you told me that from now on I'd be rewarded for my ten years of hardship. But you're wrong. What can I do with five hundred trees? Common sense says that in autumn, when pears and apples come pouring off the trees, you put only a limited amount on the market. Then you store a lot to tide you over the winter, and sell them dearly. Now how can you manage that with a small-scale orchard? It's no different with any other business. If you try to do something on a small scale, you end up like a hawk that's caught a pheasant. You think you've caught it and then some big outfit comes along and takes it away. It's going to be even worse in the future. However..." P'il-jae crushed out his cigarette in a huge wooden ashtray. "The reason I can still make ends meet with this small-scale orchard is the cheap price of labor. In other words, exploitation. You know those people sorting apples out there in the yard? The men get a hundred and fifty *wŏn* a day, the women a hundred. How can anybody call that a wage? Wages are going to rise—they have to. And when they do, the wings'll flap and knock over the small-scale orchards. What can I do if something like that happens? Really, though, I don't think a hawk like me'll get hit by the pheasant's wings—if you get what I mean."

Chun-t'ae had to give up his idea of settling down nearby. But since he had no other plans, his only course now was to devote some thought to what he'd better do.

When it was time for Chun-t'ae to leave, P'il-jae told him to come by with Kŭn-yŏng during the winter. Thinking they would probably be able to go hawking by then, Chun-t'ae said he would try. But he knew the odds were slim that he would ever return.

In Seoul he'd caught the bus at its starting point and found a seat. But now the bus was packed and he had to squeeze in

among the people standing up. Holding on to the overhead rail
as the bus bumped along, Chun-t'ae was steeped in confusion,
as if possessed by something. He felt almost as if his going to
see P'il-jae had been only an opportunity to hear a story about
a hawk. If I judge myself in terms of his theory, he thought,
what am I, a pheasant or a hawk? If I'm a hawk, what kind of
hawk? If I'm a pheasant, what kind of pheasant? Chun-t'ae
found himself envying P'il-jae's striking decisiveness.

"35-year-old shaman. Hand movements while reciting chants
are unique," Min-gu recorded in a notebook. As soon as church
had ended, Min-gu had told Ŭn-hŭi that he had to meet a
hometown friend of his. He had then carried out his original
plan of going to see a shaman, and returned home. Often shamans blink their eyes continuously, or move their head around
more than they need to, but this one was different. "Continuous drumming with one hand on the chest of clients can be
considered one of the obvious characteristics peculiar to shamans."

It has become an established theory that the word *shaman*
originated in the Manchu word *saman*, whose root, *sam*, can be
seen in the Manchu word *samarambi* and the Mongolian word
samoromoy, both meaning to be excited and beat vigorously. In
addition, the Manchu *samdambi* means dancing, and the Mongolian *samagu* refers to one who is excited. Consequently, *shaman* means drumming and jumping here and there in a state of
excitement. It is no wonder, then, that shamans lose themselves in dancing while beating their hourglass drum and clapping their cymbals.

"This shaman's power of clairvoyance is extraordinary," Min-
gu wrote. Today, as before, he had visited a shaman under the
pretext of having his fortune read. Nobody had recommended
this shaman, and he was visiting her for the first time. He
reasoned that the best way to get some stories from her would
be to act like a client. This shaman, however, after reciting
chants while tapping Min-gu's chest, had suddenly declared

that he had not really come to have his fortune read. Min-gu had confessed, adding that the shaman was very good at reading people's minds, whereupon she poured out her story to him. "Whenever her husband meets another woman, she asks him if he met a woman of such and such an appearance at a certain time. Her guess is always on the mark. When I asked if her husband had played around before, she said he was a great womanizer. And as if it wasn't enough to be heartbroken, she had also fallen ill. She struggled with her dissatisfaction with her husband, and finally she was convinced she had become a shaman. Her tapping clients on the chest as she reads their fortune can be seen as an expression of her unconscious desire to give her husband a beating."

Some time before, Min-gu had met a woman who had been squeezed by poverty and become a shaman. When reading fortunes she would take the money left by clients and make circles with her trembling hand around a bowl of cold water, calling out to the money god, "Just as this money circulates throughout our country, please examine this person's situation and tell me about it." As Min-gu was recalling this, the telephone rang. It was Pyŏn. Min-gu had not heard from him for a while. Saying he had something to discuss, Pyŏn asked if he could come right away to the Uju Tearoom.

Upon arriving Min-gu took a seat across from Pyŏn, who then subtly moved next to him.

"My face looks haggard, doesn't it?" Pyŏn asked.

Indeed, his face did look a little thin to Min-gu.

"Is anything wrong with you?"

"No." Stroking his cheek, Pyŏn said, "I look very haggard, don't I?"

"Well, just a little…Have you been to the countryside?"

"No, I've been in Seoul all along."

"But you haven't gotten in touch with me. You must have been very busy."

"I guess it's a major project for you to contact me first." Pyŏn looked intently at Min-gu, as if Min-gu were someone he had been hoping to see for a long time. "I made up my mind not to see you until I'd arranged the Hamgyŏng *ogu kut*. I guess I was worrying about that business and got worn out." Pyŏn grinned, disclosing his bluish upper gum, and then covered his mouth with the back of his hand.

Min-gu thought the gesture made Pyŏn look feminine. "So you arranged it?" he asked.

"That's why I asked you to come here."

"You mean the old woman consented?" Min-gu's voice was a bit unsteady.

"Yes. Anyway, you're too much."

"How so?"

"How so? In other matters you don't think of me at all, but when there's some mention of that old woman..." Pyŏn glowered at Min-gu.

"So, when can we meet her?"

"I just now got her consent. Any time is fine. It's up to you."

"I really appreciate it."

"You don't have to say that."

"The best bet would be to meet as soon as possible, before the old lady changes her mind..."

"That makes sense."

"Well then, what about tomorrow... But wait a minute, that's no good—I've got a class late tomorrow morning. How about going to see her the day after tomorrow, in the morning, after my classes are over?"

"She said we can't meet at her place. So I decided to bring her to my house."

"I'm really sorry I'm putting you to all this trouble."

"I told you not to mention it."

Min-gu placed his hand atop Pyŏn's, which was lying on his knee. Pyŏn turned his hand over so his palm rested against Min-gu's. The two of them remained like that for a moment. It's nothing more than an expression of friendship, Min-gu thought. But he couldn't fathom what kind of friendship it was, or how his counterpart accepted it.

When Min-gu returned to his apartment he was surprised to find Ŭn-hŭi there.

"Have you been waiting long?" Min-gu asked, casually removing his coat and hanging it up.

"Where have you been?" Ŭn-hŭi scowled fiercely at him.

"Didn't I tell you a little while ago? I said I was meeting a friend from back home."

"You shouldn't play tricks with me."

"Play tricks? Who's—"

"By the way, how much longer do I have to go in and out of your apartment like this? I don't feel comfortable."

"You don't feel comfortable?" Min-gu stole a glance at her.

"Aren't people giving me strange looks?"

"Who cares what others think?"

"I won't be thought of as a common girl."

"What kind of talk is that?"

"You ask because you don't know?"

"Well, like I said, who cares what other people think?"

"I've decided to stop making these frequent visits until we get married." Uň-hŭi took the key to Min-gu's apartment from her handbag and placed it on the table. "Okay, so long. Don't forget to be on time when we meet."

"I don't know what this is all about. Stay just a little longer."

Ŭn-hŭi shook her head and walked toward the door. Without knowing why, Min-gu grabbed her shoulder. Turning her around, he placed his mouth on hers without the slightest hesitation. Saying "Oh, that cigarette smell," Ŭn-hŭi pushed him away. The force of freeing herself from his arms made her tumble onto her back. Giving her no respite, Min-gu threw himself on her and held her down. Although this behavior puzzled him, Min-gu felt a vague need to break down Ŭn-hŭi's self-righteousness and obstinacy. Ŭn-hŭi said, "Don't," thinking she should appear to be standing firm at a time like this and produce her usual smile, which was neither subtle nor overdone. But this remained only a thought, and, unable to do as she wanted, she strained to assert herself. "You shouldn't treat me like a common girl. I didn't expect this kind of thing. And you know what day it is? It's Sunday, Sunday..." Even so, her resistance gradually abated as Min-gu's hands reached the skin beneath her clothing.

Chapter 6

Chi-yŏn paused before the blank telegram form in front of her. She was about to wire Sŏng-ho to drop by her house, and was wondering how to phrase the message. She hadn't realized selecting a phrase could be so difficult. It wouldn't do to say "Drop by quickly," "...tomorrow," or "...soon," as it would give the impression that an accident had occurred, and would alarm him. And she shrank from saying "It's been a while, I'd like to see you," since that would misrepresent her true feelings. Finally, she merely wrote "Hope you drop by sometime— Chi-yŏn." When she handed the form to the post office clerk and paid the fee, she felt she had completed a major undertaking.

As Mr. Kang stepped through the door, a couple of paces ahead of Ch'ang-ae, several people approached him and shook his hand, asking why he was late. The party had already begun. The occasion was a preview of a movie whose sets Mr. Kang had designed.

Upwards of thirty people were moving about in the modest-sized room, sipping drinks or picking up snacks from a table. Several actors and actresses whom Ch'ang-ae had seen in photographs caught her eye as they mixed with one another.

Following Mr. Kang to a table where cocktails were being served, Ch'ang-ae could feel the gaze of others, and she wondered whether she should have come. She looked intently at Mr. Kang. He didn't appear especially concerned.

"Mr. Kang..." A young woman with short hair came up beside them. After giving Ch'ang-ae a curt nod with her thin chin, she shot a hard look up at Mr. Kang and said, "How come you're late? You didn't even see the preview."

"I had some business to look after."

"The settings were very, very good."

Mr. Kang and Ch'ang-ae took glasses of beer from a waiter.

"This time give me beer instead of cola," said the young woman to the waiter. Her voice was well modulated. Taking the glass of beer, she toasted Mr. Kang, clinking her glass to his, but then merely touched it to her lips. Saying "I think I'll make an exit," she walked lightly, as if performing a dance step, toward a group of women. The women sent Mr. Kang a greeting with their eyes.

Shouldn't he go over and mingle with the ladies? Ch'ang-ae wonders. That would surely be in keeping with the spirit of the party. If he does, then what about me? Again Ch'ang-ae felt awkward. It would be unseemly to slip out first. Besides, she'd been brought especially by Mr. Kang.

Before coming they had gone to a park, at Ch'ang-ae's suggestion. The park was on a hill, at the bottom of which only two people could be seen. An older man was sitting on a shabby wooden bench that needed paint, taking in the thin sunlight, and a youth was exercising with iron dumbbells in a secluded spot. Mr. Kang and Ch'ang-ae had found a quiet place in some woods halfway up the hill. A bird agilely threaded its way among the trees and then soared into the sky. They looked up, and their eyes were dazzled by the expanse of clear sky among the branches. Ch'ang-ae plopped down on the dry clumps of grass. "Oh, it's too much for me." She had selected this hilly park in order to find a quiet spot, but her condition was still delicate from the abortion, and the walk up the hill had proved to be quite beyond her capacity. Mr. Kang had snorted in amusement, gently pushing up the front of his beret. "You're the one who suggested coming here," he had said, "and it's too much for you. This makes me feel like I'm hiking. It'd be a good place to come in spring or summer." Pressing some tobacco into his pipe, his eyes panned the surroundings...

—— I'm working on this scenario where the hero and

heroine get to know each other in an unusual way, a young man in a navy blue leather jacket next to Ch'ang-ae said to a man beside him while picking up chicken giblets on a skewer. It's always a headache deciding how the hero and heroine are going to meet.

Showing little interest, the fellow next to him sampled his drink.

—— It's simple: they get involved with each other through a coin. The heroine stops by a movie theater on her way home from Seoul Station. She's just seen one of her friends off and she feels empty. Autumn days like we're having now might be good. She could wear just simple clothing and carry a little pocketbook. When she enters the theater, she finds the movie has already started. She takes a seat. She's absorbed in the movie for a while, and then suddenly realizes she's been snapping her pocketbook open and shut. It's a habit of hers.

—— It's obvious what'll happen next, the fellow next to him said.

—— Just listen, will you? She quickly closes the pocketbook and to her dismay a coin falls out and goes rolling away. But she keeps watching the screen—she doesn't want to be bothered by searching under the seat for something so trivial. However, someone nearby softly strikes a match and looks under the seats. Even in the darkness she can see that it's a young man.

—— Now there's a recipe for a soap opera.

—— Keep listening. Here's where it gets interesting. After the match has gone out he lights another one. "It's all right, don't bother," the woman whispers, but the young man just goes on searching. "How much was it?" he asks her. "Probably ten *wŏn*," she answers. She remembers getting that much in change when she got off the bus. "If it's that big I should have seen it," says the young man. He stops looking for the coin and as he's about to sit down there's a scraping sound under his shoe. "Ah, there it is," he says, and he gives it to her. As soon as she takes it she covers her mouth with both hands to stifle her laughter. "What's the matter?" he asks. "It wasn't ten *wŏn*," she says in a shrinking voice. "It was only one *wŏn*." What do you think?

—— Now I've got it, said a third man with long sideburns before the other could reply. She's a woman who messes around with several men.

—— What are you talking about? the first young man said, raising his voice.

—— A woman who has a habit of opening and closing her pocketbook is short on virtue.

—— Whose theory is that? Is it based on your own experience?

—— If she keeps on opening and closing her pocketbook, she'll drop her rouge, she'll drop her keys, and if she gets something going with a new man each time...

I had an operation, Ch'ang-ae had said to Mr. Kang as he sucked away at his pipe. She had wanted to say this with a free mind, and thought this was the time to do it. She would probably start having sex with him again as soon as she recovered, which would mean becoming tied to him again. She wanted to tell him about the operation first and had chosen the hillside park for that purpose. With a look of disbelief, Mr. Kang had removed the pipe from his mouth. Don't you know what I mean by an operation? Ch'ang-ae had asked, steadying her quivering voice. Only then did Mr. Kang say anything. Operation? He had gazed at Ch'ang-ae in surprise. Mmm, she had replied. An abortion. When? A few days ago. So that's why you're pale. After looking briefly at Ch'ang-ae's face, Mr. Kang had turned away and again just smoked his pipe. Even if I'd asked your advice, you couldn't have made up my mind for me, so I went through with it myself, Ch'ang-ae had said. Well done, Mr. Kang had answered, exhaling a long stream of smoke. What, my deciding to do it by myself? I mean getting rid of it. Why? It'd probably be a miserable baby. Really? Now that I think of it, I made a mistake not giving birth to it. Mr. Kang had turned back to Ch'ang-ae and stared at her. His face showed that he didn't know her true motive. Suddenly Ch'ang-ae couldn't help bursting out in laughter...

A woman erupted in laughter.

—— Since then I've detested men who eat sausage, said a woman who looked like the heroine of the movie that had just been previewed.

—— Is that so. From now on I'd better be careful what I eat in front of women I like, said a young man who seemed to be a newspaper reporter. He had squeezed in among the group before they realized it. He then asked the woman what her interests were.

—— Oh, driving around the outskirts of town by myself.

—— Do you do that very often?

—— Three or four times a week.

—— I'd like to ride a horse, interrupted the young woman with short hair. Now that I've graduated from mountains I wish I could ride a horse. Even in a tearoom, I feel good when I'm sitting in a tall chair or at a high table.

—— You instinctively wish you could make up for your lack of height, is that it?

—— We're not talking about height. We're talking about interests...

...Ch'ang-ae couldn't control herself whenever she burst into laughter. One day during the summer, she had taken Mr. Kang to the country house of some friends. She had not notified the couple, and it turned out they had gone to Seoul. After resting in the yard, Ch'ang-ae asked the caretaker for a fishing rod and a can of worms and went down to the river. It was a branch of the Han River upstream from Seoul. The wind, stronger than Ch'ang-ae had expected, was making the river choppy. Not a fisherman could be seen. Put a worm on the hook for me, said Ch'ang-ae. Doesn't look like you'll catch anything, replied Mr. Kang as he slowly impaled a worm on the hook. Because of the wind Ch'ang-ae was able to make a straight cast only after sweeping the rod to the front and back several times. Even if I don't catch any fish I'll keep trying, she thinks; it's been a long time since I've been fishing. Ch'ang-ae looks at Mr. Kang. He appears bored. Ch'ang-ae instantly drops the fishing rod and begins removing her clothes. She had worn a swimsuit in case she went swimming. What are you going to do, with the wind blowing like this? asks the bewildered Mr. Kang as he smokes his pipe. I'd better wake up those creatures, says Ch'ang-ae. She enters the water and at first gestures as if to drive the fish along. When the water reaches her thighs she begins to swim. Peering into the water where the line from the rod had dropped, she asks, Where did those creatures go? and swims out into the river. A dusty wind rose from the beach on the opposite side. In the middle of the river Ch'ang-ae turns and comes back. The water's really warm, she says while coming out, but she's panting and shivering. Mr. Kang looks at her as if he doesn't understand. You can take in the rod now, says Ch'ang-ae. All the fish swam away because they saw a big fish and got scared. While saying this she began laughing uncontrollably. Her laughter at the river had gushed forth freely, but now at the park it was interrupted by choking. Sensing something, Mr. Kang had moved closer to her and put an arm around her waist. The trembling against his arm was different from trembling caused by laughter. Tapping the bowl of his pipe and placing it in his pocket, Mr. Kang had looked gently at Ch'ang-ae. Are you crying? No. Ch'ang-ae had shaken her head and continued to laugh. Objects near and far became muddled in her sight, so she closed her eyes tightly and then opened them. The moisture had vanished and the objects had reclaimed their shapes, when unexpectedly something mottled entered her field of vision. Thinking there was still some moisture left, she had rubbed her eyes. Then she had stopped laughing. From the slope to the right, a woman's breasts were looking up at her. The woman's body was small and her face thin. Wearing a *chŏgori*, a baggy pair of men's work trousers, and *komusin* on her bare feet and holding an iron rake in one hand, she was gazing stupidly at Ch'ang-ae. Her trousers were falling down, and the front gusset of her *chŏgori* had come undone, exposing the dark red areolae of her breasts. It was these unusually large and dark areolae that had caught Ch'ang-ae's eyes. The breasts were huge, and out of proportion with the rest of the woman's body. They drooped slightly, covering her entire chest. Moreover, they were not empty and wrinkled but fully rounded. The woman had maintained the same posture, unaware her chest was exposed. Ch'ang-ae had averted her eyes, and her entire body had shuddered once. Let's go down, she had said. Mr. Kang had gotten up without a word. It was at the bottom of the hill that he had mentioned the party.

"I'm really glad you came, even though you're late." The young woman with short hair came over to Mr. Kang again. "You haven't seen the movie yet, but that cave setting sure is impressive. The wet wall of the cave and the moss on it are so realistic. And the inside of the cave looks so, so deep—it's marvelous."

Without replying, Mr. Kang said, "When did you start liking a high chair and table? I remember when you used to pick out only the tearooms with low, soft chairs."

"Yes, but that was then, and now is now. There have to be changes, right?"

One of the other women called out, and the young woman with short hair, gesturing in response, excused herself and left, stepping lightly as before.

"Isn't that the girl?" Ch'ang-ae asked Mr. Kang.

"What girl?"

"You know, the girl you meet from time to time, the one who wants to be an actress. She's the one, isn't she?"

"How did you find out?"

Ch'ang-ae smiled. Her hunch was on the mark. She'd heard from Mrs. O that the young woman's hair was long, but after meeting her at the party she'd guessed she had cut her hair short since then. It's probably one of the ways she enjoys change, Ch'ang-ae thought.

"What's her name?"

"Miss Chŏn..."

"Say, Mr. Kang..." A man in a checked homespun jacket and a pink shirt without a tie approached. He was holding a glass of *chŏngjong*[1] and looked slightly intoxicated. For some time now he had been catching Ch'ang-ae's eye. "Now that I've seen that cave in the movie, I was wondering, you know, if you couldn't come up with a set for me. I'd like to use deep-sea fish to express the love between men and women. First you'd probably have to make a set showing the pitch darkness in the bottom of the sea where the sun and the moon don't shine. Then I'd like you to have the deep-sea fish enter and focus on their love life. The fish are *sera* or something like that. I've got a photo I'll show you. The female is a meter long but the male's just barely ten centimeters. That got me interested in them, but it's their love life that's unique. When a passable female appears, the little male bravely dashes up and mates with it, clinging to it like a leech and not leaving. You got it? That's the way they begin their love life, but what's more interesting, as time passes, the skin of the two becomes the same and even their blood vessels become connected. Isn't it magnificent?" Then he whispers in Mr. Kang's ear: "Another beauty you've got there. How long's it been? That fish I was talking about hasn't got anything on you."

"There's another type of deep-sea fish," Mr. Kang countered in a tone full of hidden meaning, "and all it does is open and close its maw in the pitch darkness, waiting for something edible to go in. It does this day and night, and so its head becomes enormous but its body gets awfully small. No matter how it works its jaws it doesn't seem like anything edible will go in. Just because the head is huge doesn't mean the brain is also well developed—it's just that there's a huge mouth in the head. See?"

Ch'ang-ae had been feeling listless all over for a short time. Telling Mr. Kang she was going to sit down for a moment, she went toward a chair at one side of the room.

[1]*Chŏngjong:* a refined rice wine, similar to sake.

She leaned back in the sturdy wooden chair and closed her eyes. Thoughts surfaced in her mind and she had the urge to deal with them and yet avoid them. Then, hearing a familiar voice among the hum of conversation, she opened her eyes. Miss Chŏn had returned to Mr. Kang and was talking about something. She couldn't hear the whole conversation, but she understood that Miss Chŏn had been instructed by a movie director to cut her hair short and that she might appear in a film. Miss Chŏn gazed intently at Mr. Kang while speaking, her head with its thin, sleek chin lifted at an angle. She looks prettier from here than she does up close, though she's more or less frivolous, thought Ch'ang-ae. Miss Chŏn did not look once at Ch'ang-ae. Strangely, though, Ch'ang-ae felt no jealousy. Instead, she wished Mr. Kang would be a little more friendly and not act older than his age.

Ch'ang-ae closed her eyes, and again the urge to deal with the previous thoughts and to avoid them crisscrossed her mind. When she tried to avoid them, she would tune in to the hubbub of the room. Sundry words—for the most part disconnected fragments of sentences—reached her ears: The carnation's always there in her room, maybe that's why she puts a lot of milk in her coffee...We manipulate words as much as we can, but there's no disguising our feelings. You know, feelings...The premiere was in Seoul, but the theater was like a no-man's land—just flies buzzing around. But out in the countryside...When I go walking with that sweet young thing she tells me to keep my eyes straight ahead—no checking out the other ladies...You don't feel you're on a boat unless it's moving up and down on the waves...Even he can't help being on the skids...

In addition to being exhausted, Ch'ang-ae was bored. She opened her eyes. Standing in front of Mr. Kang, Miss Chŏn was laughing, her eyes wide open. Now she was gently rubbing the corners of her eyes with her fingertips. She seemed to be trying to get rid of any wrinkles her laughter may have formed. It was an artful ploy, but Ch'ang-ae didn't find it distasteful.

After all, she thought, wrinkles don't come just from distress, they can come from laughter too. At the park on the hill the wrinkles at the corners of her own eyes had probably increased and deepened. One of the previous thoughts surfaced again. Why on earth had her sudden burst of laughter at the park been garnished with sobbing? He had said their child would have been pitiful. But even while wondering how he could talk like that, she realized how miserable she was at not being able to deny it. She felt awkward. Wasn't it my imagination that had made the breasts of that woman at the park seem so large? Unknown to Ch'ang-ae, worry was gathering in her chest. There was a hardness within her breasts that didn't soften, and her nipples were stiff, as if she were having her period. These symptoms had continued after the abortion. She thought her mind and body would be cleansed when they disappeared.

Here comes Mr. Kang. Perhaps he'll say let's go. Ch'ang-ae got up. She made up her mind to go down to Suwŏn as soon as they left. It was one of the thoughts that had been spinning in a corner of her mind.

Darkness was descending as Chi-yŏn walked leisurely toward the bus stop, a paper bag in one hand. Inside the bag were a record and two books she had bought that day.

As she walked past the street lights, which stood at intervals along the street, she was seized by an illusion. Why am I staggering along like this? I'm stumbling all over the place. This is dangerous. She stopped abruptly. A woman, her hands stuck in the pockets of her raincoat, was tottering across the street toward the sidewalk where Chi-yŏn was walking. A car sped by, narrowly missing her.

The woman had barely reached the sidewalk when with a great lurch she fell over. She floundered about, her hands still inside the raincoat. Chi-yŏn ran over and helped the woman up. The smell of liquor hit her. Chi-yŏn discovered the woman was about her age. Fortunately, her ashen face showed no sign of injury except for a trace of blood on her lower lip.

The woman got up heavily and slowly shook her head. Only then did she remove her hands from the raincoat. She gestured as if to clean off the dirt that had stained her clothing. Actually she was staving off Chi-yŏn, who was merely propping her up. She continued doing this until Chi-yŏn retreated.

Chi-yŏn reached the bus stop and watched the woman recross the street. She was pawing the air, as if warning the cars speeding by. Though staggering along in the same dangerous manner as before, she reached the other side safely. But again she took a great shambling step and stumbled over. A man passing by helped her up. Again she brushed herself off in order to fend off the man, and without accepting any assistance she stumbled down an alley and disappeared. Forgetting even to catch the bus, Chi-yŏn watched the woman until she could no longer see her, unconsciously murmuring, "All right, that's the way."

"Sir," said Ch'ang-ae, as if from habit. Her eyes were wide open in the darkness. The sound of this appellation she used for Chun-t'ae revealed a mixture of emotions, though in the past it had only meant she was in a good mood. "When we go our separate ways I don't think there'll be a winner or a loser."

"That goes without saying."

"I guess I came to you on my own back then, and now I'm leaving on my own. I'm sorry, but there's nothing I can do."

"Anyway, I'm grateful you made the decision first."

They had agreed to begin the divorce proceedings the next morning. Although Ch'ang-ae had intended to repay the three hundred thousand *wŏn* she had obtained by mortgaging the house, she suggested that they first liquidate their marriage, which by now existed in name only, and Chun-t'ae had not objected.

"I only wish we'd brought it to an end earlier, when we saw things turning out this way."

"Now's a good time, too," said Chun-t'ae. "It's not early, but it's not too late either..."

"I'm very sorry I'm not leaving you with a good image of me."

"Same here."

"But if we were to drag on like this, it would be nothing but a mess for both of us."

"Yeah, you're right."

"You'll probably meet a better woman next time," said Ch'ang-ae. She sounded sincere.

"Well, I'm sure you'll meet a better man," said Chun-t'ae in the same straightforward tone.

"Now that I think of it, some time ago...it was the night when there was a misty drizzle, I'm sure of it. The woman you were walking with on Ch'ungmuro—do you still see her?"

"Uh-huh."

"From now on I hope you'll be careful not to make a woman bored. It's not good to be too disinterested toward her."

"I'll try."

"As I said before, you only know how to be loved. No, you're a person who doesn't know how to be loved and doesn't know how to love either." Ch'ang-ae laughed lightly. She could laugh like this now that everything was in the past.

Chun-t'ae laughed too. "Maybe I was born that way."

"You just love only yourself, right?"

"Really?" Chun-t'ae ruminated on what she had said. "No, I'm someone who doesn't even know how to love himself. But you tend to overdo it when it comes to love."

"That may be true too. But I don't regret it. Remember four years ago when I had that party on graduation night and left my date at the hotel and came over to see you? I really liked you then." Ch'ang-ae withdrew an arm from the quilt and extended it toward Chun-t'ae.

Even though he couldn't see in the darkness, Chun-t'ae knew what Ch'ang-ae wanted. It was the tacit understanding of two persons who had lived together for four years, happily or unhappily. Chun-t'ae also removed an arm from the quilt and extended it toward Ch'ang-ae. The two hands clasped, not too loosely, not too tightly.

"I don't regret that time," Ch'ang-ae repeated. "Because I was true to myself."

"It looks like I didn't accept it for what it was when you came. But in the end we're not a good match." Whether water had collected in the reservoir or not was secondary when the reservoir may not have been built in the first place, Chun-t'ae thought.

"I guess that's the way it was. That's probably why we never wanted to have a baby."

"And I don't want to have one in the future."

"Even if you meet someone better than me?"

"Uh-huh."

"Why's that?"

"Well...if you really want me to say it, it's so I won't bring someone else like me into this world."

"Anyway, I'm glad we don't have a child."

"Me too."

"But I'll probably want to have a baby in the future."

"Sure. Why not?"

To the end they remained composed, not carried away by emotion or sentiment. But while their discretion toward each other was laudable, they felt desolate. It was something they had to endure. For a while longer they held hands. Then, without knowing who acted first, they tightened their grip once and released their hands, as if saying farewell for the last time.

Although Chi-yŏn was very tired, sleep didn't come easily. When it finally did, she found herself in front of a tall white building. She and her surroundings seemed to be inside a vacuum. Everything was peaceful and quiet. No matter where she stood she could see no entrance to the building; all four sides consisted of windows set together. The windows glittered in the sunlight but behind the glass it was black as night. For a while she had been itching to go inside and turn on the lights.

Thinking she had to go in through the windows if not the doors, she approached the building and tried pushing and pulling on one of the windows. It was locked. She pushed and pulled on the next window, but the result was the same. She tried every window, even the ones near the top, but not a one opened. While she was fretting over what to do, a key vendor appeared from an alley. A full array of keys dangled from all over his body. But Chi-yŏn didn't hear the clinking of the keys, and there was nothing but silence in every direction. Probably because I'm in a vacuum, she thought. Even though I'm telling him I want to buy a key, I guess he doesn't hear me. While she stood there anxiously, the vendor brushed past her and suddenly all of the keys were clinging to her body. Great, she thought. She tried inserting the keys in a keyhole, but none of them fit. As before, all the windows that composed the tall white building were glittering in the sunlight while inside it was black as night. Itching to get in and turn on the lights, Chi-yŏn worked with the keys, but the windows remained tightly closed.

Chapter 7

"It's been quite a while, hasn't it?" asked Sŏng-ho as he followed Chi-yŏn up to her room on the second floor. "What made you send me a telegram?"

Because Sŏng-ho lived in an out-of-the-way area, Chi-yŏn's telegram had arrived only that morning. He had thought of dropping by two days later, on his way to the appointment with the Council of Elders, but decided he couldn't wait that long to respond to a telegram.

"Oh, nothing special. I just wanted to see you..."

Neither of them took this answer seriously. Nevertheless, Sŏng-ho sidestepped the issue rather than questioning her. "It's been a while since I've had some of your coffee," he said in a voice louder than necessary. He wanted to give her some time to compose herself.

Chi-yŏn turned on the record player and went downstairs.

Sŏng-ho looks around the room. As always, it gives him a feeling of security. He focuses on the photograph of Giacometti's sculpture *City Square* hanging on the wall to his right. He can't help thinking of Grünewald's *Jesus Nailed to the Cross*. Why is that? he wonders. In appearance the two works have nothing in common. But just as the latter doesn't stop only with the tedious suffering of Jesus nailed to the cross but contains in his body the loneliness of all the people in the world, so the former doesn't stop with just the loneliness evident in the failure of the people to encounter each other in the plaza but contains within them an immeasurable pain. Could that be what makes me associate one work with the other?

Now what could be going on with Chi-yŏn? It's obviously nothing ordinary.

Chi-yŏn came in carrying coffee cups and boiling water on a tray. "You take two sugars, right?" she asked as she put the cubes in his cup.

"You shouldn't have to ask."

Chi-yŏn put two cubes in her cup too.

"Which piano concerto is that?" Sŏng-ho threw out another topic that would help them relax. He stirred his coffee.

"It's Tchaikovsky's First."

"Maybe it's because I don't know much about music, but I seem to prefer violin to piano. How can I say—perhaps it sinks into my heart more, touches me more."

"That's true. But the piano reaches my whole body, not just my heart, and it affects me more broadly and deeply."

"Hmm, is that so." Thinking the conversation isn't going smoothly, Sŏng-ho slowly takes a couple of sips of his coffee. "As usual, your coffee's super. But what is it that makes me feel the chef is somehow different from before?"

"How's that?" The smile that formed around Chi-yŏn's mouth seemed slightly stiff.

"First of all, your face looks a little drawn."

"It's probably because I haven't been able to sleep well." She recalled the disturbing dream of the previous night.

"Did something happen to make you sleep badly?"

"Well, could you figure out a dream for me?"

"Figure out? You mean interpret?"

"There was this building, you know, with more windows than I could count, and no matter how hard I tried to open them, one by one, they wouldn't open." She couldn't express the dream in words, she felt.

"Is something getting you down these days?"

"Not really..." Chi-yŏn lowered her eyes. "Well, could you say something to my parents?"

Sŏng-ho sensed that Chi-yŏn was finally opening up.

"They've been telling me to get married," she continued.

"There you go. Looks like I'll finally get to hear those wedding bells."

"Please tell them not to talk to me about marriage." Chi-yŏn lifted her eyes and looked directly at Sŏng-ho. "No. Never mind. You don't have to."

"I can't tell what's what here." Sŏng-ho was about to ask jokingly if there was someone Chi-yŏn couldn't inform her parents about, but he stopped. The expression in her eyes blocked him. He tried to soften it with his own before it became too strong.

Chi-yŏn's eyes firmly resisted Sŏng-ho's, but then they dropped. Chi-yŏn remained still, not even thinking to turn the record. By and by she snapped up her head, as if straining to control herself. The discoloration on her ashen face was even more prominent. A creaky voice escaped from her drawn lips.

"You know the most wretched woman in the Bible?"

"The most wretched woman?"

"Wasn't there a woman who was stoned, and they dragged her in front of Jesus?"

A premonition flitted through Sŏng-ho's mind.

"Her body wasn't hit," continued Chi-yŏn, "but many of the rocks struck her head."

"What's the matter, Chi-yŏn?"

"Rocks have started to strike my heart too. I mean, I feel they're about to start hitting me now."

Sŏng-ho groaned without noticing. He himself had caused a woman to suffer that kind of stoning countless times. The bitterness he had tried to bury in oblivion came back to him.

"I won't avoid the rocks." Chi-yŏn's eyes reddened in an instant. "As long as the rocks keep coming I intend to get hit."

"Chi-yŏn, try to calm down and tell me about it. Who is it, anyway?"

"Reverend Yun, until now I've told you everything. You know that, don't you? But just this once…I don't want to tell you. Until I've solved it…" Chi-yŏn's breathing accelerated. "I need him. And I think he needs me."

"Now who is this person?"

Chi-yŏn turned her head toward the bookcase. It was a decisive action.

"He's the owner of those books up there. The ones on agriculture..."

So that was it. Sŏng-ho turned toward the bookcase, but he didn't look carefully for the books. There was no need to. At the same time, Sŏng-ho didn't feel very surprised or alarmed. The affair had already started the day Chi-yŏn told him why those books—so different from her usual tastes—were in her room.

"I've decided not to go to church." Chi-yŏn's parched lips trembled. "God couldn't need somebody like me. God—"

"Chi-yŏn!" Sŏng-ho's voice was strained.

"God isn't lonely. There are all sorts of people who worship him in a spirit of sacrifice, and somebody like me doesn't belong with them."

Chi-yŏn reeled like someone completely exhausted, but then with an effort she straightened up. Her eyes blazed red, like the last flames of a fire.

How did quiet, cheerful Chi-yŏn end up like this? Sŏng-ho wondered. He felt frustrated. Perhaps the path he had taken as a man was the same one being taken by Chi-yŏn as a woman. But he had become a minister because of a woman whereas Chi-yŏn was going to leave the church on account of a man; there was a significant difference, though it didn't look that way. Sŏng-ho had something to tell Chi-yŏn—the story of the ninety-nine sheep and the one that lost its way. But he doubted there was room in Chi-yŏn's mind for it now. He had been told the same story but had been unable to appreciate it because his heart had been saturated with an affair with a woman. Yet he couldn't just leave Chi-yŏn as she was. Instead of speaking, he looked at her and shook his head as forcefully as he could. Shaking his head had never been as weighty or difficult as now.

Sŏng-ho left and set out not toward the bus stop for Stone Village but in a different direction. He plodded along. He was going to visit Chun-t'ae, though he hadn't talked with Chi-yŏn about it. When he had gotten acquainted with Chun-t'ae at Min-gu's engagement ceremony, Chun-t'ae had struck him as one who was involved in a fierce struggle with something. Sŏng-ho had wanted to meet this man alone and chat with him, and now he was going to visit him. Though he didn't give the impression that he would readily unlock his heart, Sŏng-ho intended to confront him directly.

"I'm very sorry to interrupt you at work," said Sŏng-ho after greeting Chun-t'ae.

Realizing that Sŏng-ho wished to talk, Chun-t'ae said it was all right. He told a colleague he was going out, and the two of them left the agricultural testing station. Having left his desk in the morning to sign the divorce papers, Chun-t'ae knew he shouldn't be going out again, but he wanted to go somewhere else so that he could talk openly with Sŏng-ho.

There was no such place nearby. In the summer people visited West Lake, behind the testing station, and so a seasonal tearoom had been established there. But autumn had arrived, and now it was closed.

They took a bus downtown. On the way, they passed the time talking about Min-gu, whom they hadn't seen recently, and about the houses that would be standing in the rice paddies and dry fields in that area within a few years.

They got off the bus at the edge of the city and went to a tearoom.

After the waitress had taken their order Sŏng-ho said, "I'm really sorry I had to come without giving any notice. And you look kind of tired too."

"Do I?" Chun-t'ae stroked his chin. He didn't want to think about anything in particular, but he couldn't help reflecting that the divorce procedures wouldn't be very pleasant.

Sensing that he was about to saddle his weary-looking counterpart with another serious problem, Sŏng-ho wondered how to bring up the purpose of his visit. "Humans seem to have the habit of placing others within the boundaries of their own experiences," he finally began.

It was a thought that had crisscrossed his mind on his way down here. He couldn't help thinking that his involvement in the affair between Chi-yŏn and Chun-t'ae stemmed only from a judgment made from within the limits of his own experience.

"That's true in most cases," said Chun-t'ae. "I guess that makes it close to impossible to understand others." He lit a cigarette.

"What would you think if I told you I tried to kill myself once?" The question jumped from Sŏng-ho's mouth, surprising even him. But somehow it didn't seem that unnatural. The atmosphere that reigned over Chun-t'ae, sitting directly opposite him, seemed to have produced such a question.

"Did you really?" Chun-t'ae was not particularly alarmed at Sŏng-ho's question either.

"It's something that's known only by God and a woman who is no longer alive. And I hope it stays that way."

"I see." Chun-t'ae recalled that the remarks Sŏng-ho had made at Min-gu's engagement ceremony rang true—they were not what a single man would say. And, in Min-gu's apartment, while observing the photograph of Sŏng-ho that accompanied his essay "Korean Customs and Christianity" he had felt close to him because of some hidden agony unrelated to the contents of the essay.

"Because of a complete misunderstanding I almost did myself in. Only after I'd taken some poison did I realize how little I'd understood."

"I tried to kill myself once too," said Chun-t'ae. "in my early teens."

"I was a little older. I was past twenty by then."

Perhaps because they felt that they were accomplices, or that they understood each other, the two of them burst out laughing.

"I guess Christianity regards suicide as the gravest sin," said Chun-t'ae.

"I didn't have time to think about that then."

"And now?"

"Of course I think it's a sin."

"You're saying that humans shouldn't carelessly cut off the life God gave them?" A smile remained around Chun-t'ae's mouth, but it had turned cold. "I guess that's natural from the standpoint of Christianity. Being the handiwork of God, humans don't have the right to kill themselves. In other words, since God's the Creator, he's the only one who can live forever, and the only one who can kill himself, right? I've thought about this. After Judas sold out Jesus, he was so sorry for what he'd done that he committed suicide. From our point of view, he deserved to be forgiven because of that, but instead it's written that he committed an even greater sin. I decided that because Judas dared to imitate God by committing suicide—which only God could do—he excited God's anger. But later on I changed my mind: whatever sin we commit, perhaps God hopes we'll put up with the consequences until the end, no matter how painful. In that respect God can be harsh, because capital punishment can be more merciful for humans than a life sentence."

"God wants people to come back to him anytime they realize their mistakes. To that extent he's magnanimous."

"Is it really possible, though, for humans to kill themselves?" Chun-t'ae drew deeply on his cigarette. "Montesquieu said that suicide is an action humans take as a result of doting on themselves. But the way I look at it, the question of whether humans can ever be worth that much is secondary, because it's not possible, strictly speaking, to say that we kill ourselves—whether we take poison, hang ourselves, shoot ourselves, or jump off of something."

Sŏng-ho maintained a warm smile but remained silent.

"Just as dying in an accident, dying on the battlefield, dying from an illness are ways of being killed by something, we should look at suicide as death caused by something."

"Then what do you make of death from natural causes?" Sŏng-ho asked quietly. He no longer feared that Chun-t'ae would close his shell more firmly the more he approached him.

"It's the same. Right up to the present, humans have always tried to extend their life span. Although we say 'death from natural causes,' in the end we die eager to live some more. We don't will ourselves to be born and we die without wanting to, so isn't it a fact that we die from some cause? The upshot is that no matter how humans die, and no matter what name we attach to death, it has to have some cause. In that sense, Reverend Yun, you and I were almost killed in the name of suicide, but we were snatched away from it."

"That's interesting. So then what's the right way to be killed? In the name of suicide, or through natural causes?"

"I guess it depends on people and their circumstances," replied Chun-t'ae.

"Since we're no more than the handiwork of God, as you said, then hadn't we better follow the will of the Creator?"

"Speaking of the Creator, I'm not sure about other countries, but in Korea what we call the Creator isn't being received in the right manner."

"Is that what you think?"

"I remember talking about this before. We Koreans don't seem to have the temperament for accepting religious beliefs as they truly are."

"I'd like to know more about why you think that way."

"Somebody told me," began Chun-t'ae, "about a minister who danced in joy when following his son's coffin to the grave. And he was quite sane. The elders advised him to stop because others wouldn't think it proper. Can you imagine what the minister said? 'Since my child is leaving this troubled world and ascending to heaven and God's bosom, how can I not feel joyful?' This minister died being looked up to as even more of a miracle worker than he was when his son died. Is that Christianity?"

Sŏng-ho kept nodding at what Chun-t'ae was saying.

"In the Lord's Prayer, there's a frightening phrase," Chun-t'ae continued. "'Forgive us our trespasses as we forgive those who trespass against us.' In the Second World War, as you know, the Nazis massacred countless Jews. I heard that for some time after the war the Germans omitted that phrase when they said the Lord's Prayer. During the Korean War, we killed and were killed by those of the same blood. We went so far as to cut off men's privates and gouge out women's and hang them from tree limbs. They say that passing soldiers were aroused by the sight. And even today, after the war, you can hear people bullshitting about this, as if it were some kind of dirty joke. At the same time, we pray 'Forgive us our trespasses' with the same peace of mind with which we pray 'We forgive those who trespass against us.' How could religion spring up among such a people?"

"The closer people are, the more cruel they are to each other as enemies, or so I've heard."

"Anyway, don't you think that people have to know how to reflect upon themselves? As a whole, we Koreans are worse than Judas." Chun-t'ae lit another cigarette from the butt of the one he'd been smoking. "A friend of mine working in Kyŏngju told me he planted some roses near Ch'ŏmsŏngdae Observatory, and within a few days they'd all been dug up and taken away. And that the trees in Kyerim were so old they imported some new ones and planted them there. The same thing happened—within a year they'd all been dug up. How about that? And this is probably just a very small example. How can people like that, who don't know how to love the past or think about the future, be qualified to hope for eternal life?"

"Even so," said Sŏng-ho, "there was a time when Buddhism flourished in our country. You know, we have records that temples were scattered all over like stars and that pagodas were lined up like flocks of wild geese."

"Why would it have collapsed, then? It wasn't just because of the anti-Buddhist sentiment during Chosŏn. It was because the people didn't have the capacity to accept Buddhism with all their heart. What I mean is Buddhism was supposed to rise above power and material interest, but when we accepted it we held on to those kinds of things. After all, our people have a temperament that makes them strive only for relationships of immediate benefit and not for those with future prospects. On top of that we adulate those with power or wealth—and the Christian circles are no exception. After the 1945 liberation weren't there church-backed clergymen blindly seeking political power? There was no law preventing clergymen from becoming politicians. But the believers who supported them didn't judge them on their qualifications as politicians. Instead, the church, like other circles, had to put people up for office to get a better deal, and they did it only out of a desire to benefit themselves—isn't that the case?"

"Not all the believers supported those people," responded Sŏng-ho.

"But there wasn't a single person, was there, who tried to figure out whether that kind of support was right or wrong. It looks to me like this kind of thing still exists, though in a different form. People make up sects, skillfully taking advantage of the Korean tendency to worry only about practical benefits, and then say that they represent the advent of Christ and the millennial kingdom on earth, and that those who don't join them can't be saved and can't be a part of that kingdom. And all the time they're working behind the scenes to mobilize their believers and get them all hot and bothered about managing businesses. There's one sect operating a company that manufactures rifles, and they went so far as to hold an international hunting tournament in Korea so they could expand their marketing network. Even if they hadn't been so concerned about boosting their business, they'd still sing Hallelujah, not even caring that our wild animals are decreasing every year and their breeding stock is getting smaller. Can Christianity accepted in this manner be true religion?"

"That's heresy. The Bible has revealed to us that on Doomsday all sorts of phony individuals and groups will appear."

"I can buy that. But why would such heretics spread like wildfire, particularly in Korea? I really doubt if there's anything in the Bible that says such heresies will rage in our country. Here again, it probably proves that the Korean temperament is well endowed with the makings of that sort of behavior."

"Still, you can't deny that there have been a lot of martyrs since Christianity came to our country."

"They were probably victims rather than martyrs. Since way back such victims have emerged from all levels of society, and not just Christians. And they'll probably emerge in the future, too."

"It'll take time, but some day I believe Christianity will sink its roots in Korea and grow into a sound religion."

"You think so? You're very optimistic." Chun-t'ae's smile became colder and then disappeared.

For a while Sŏng-ho had sensed that something hot and passionate lay within Chun-t'ae's frosty smile. That passion harbored anger. It wasn't just the anger of one who denied something for the sake of denying it. It appeared to be the anger of one who couldn't help denying something in order to search for something affirmative.

Chun-t'ae felt he had been engaging in a lot of useless chitchat. He regretted dwelling on this irrelevant topic instead of establishing why Sŏng-ho had come. There must have been something else he wished to bring up.

"I guess you're here because of Miss Nam."

"Ah, yes." Sŏng-ho realized Chun-t'ae had probably guessed why he had come, but felt it was good he had brought up the matter first. "Miss Nam is really suffering now."

"And you're saying it's because of me?"

"For sure." Sŏng-ho paused briefly. "However, she doesn't know I'm here."

"I see. And you're saying that in light of your experience, I shouldn't make her suffering worse."

"You're taking the words out of my mouth." Having said this, Sŏng-ho suddenly felt distressed. Recalling his days with Mrs. Hong, he wondered if their suffering was really only a result of unhappiness.

"Okay. I get the point."

The conversation, which could have become complicated, had ended with one stroke, Chun-t'ae felt. The load on his mind seemed to have diminished. But, thought Chun-t'ae... But then he refrained from saying he was now divorced. He looked across at Sŏng-ho, who without relish was sipping his tea, which had become cold. My being divorced has nothing to do with Chi-yŏn, he thought. Though he told Sŏng-ho he understood he shouldn't increase her suffering, he decided he would have to take another look at his affair with her. For that was not something he could simply finish off with one stroke.

Min-gu had agreed to meet Pyŏn at his house, and on his way there his spirits soared with expectations of the unknown. He was going to observe the Hamgyŏng Province *ogu kut.* In preparation he had listened the previous night to the tape he had made of the shamanistic chants of the *ogu kut* practiced in the southern part of the country.

Along with the *shijun kut,* in which prayers are offered for an auspicious birth, the *ogu kut,* in which prayers are offered for the passage of a soul to a good place after death, constitutes one of the important ritual ceremonies of shamanism. The chants of the *ogu kut* are called *Parigongju* in the Seoul area, *Paridegi* or *Ogumullim* in Chŏlla Province, and *Piridegi* in Kyŏngsang Province. Although the phrases are somewhat different from one region to the next, the basic story and the theme are the same. Fed up with having produced only seven daughters, a noble family abandoned the youngest of them. The parents subsequently fell ill, and upon having their fortune examined they were told they would not recover until they drank medicinal water from the kingdom of Sŏch'ŏnsŏyŏk.[1] The six daughters, starting with the eldest, were asked in turn to obtain the water, but under one pretext or another, none of them went. Finally the youngest daughter obtained the medicinal water, suffering

[1]Sŏch'ŏnsŏyŏk: originally, a name for India.

all kinds of hardships to do so, and revived her parents, who had already died. Afterwards she went to the underworld, became a goddess, and took charge of guiding the souls of the dead to Paradise.[2]

In examining the chants from these three areas, one finds that those of the Chŏlla region are colored the least by Buddhism and those from the Seoul area are colored the most. An example is the following variations in the accounts of the abandoned youngest daughter: Chŏlla region—"She grew up on sunlight and dew at night"; Kyŏngsang region—"A pair of cranes descended from the sky; one spread one wing on the ground and with the other covered and protected the child, while the other crane raised her, bringing food in its beak"; Seoul region—"Buddha, leading three thousand followers, came down to view the world and, discovering Princess *Pari*, ordered Charitable Grandfather and Grandmother *Piri* to raise her." And her father is called "Great King Ogu" in the Chŏlla region, "the Great General of Ch'ŏnbyŏl Mountain" in the Kyŏngsang region, and "Great King *mama*"[3]—a title characteristic of the Chosŏn dynasty, since it was applied to actual rather than godlike persons—in the Seoul region. From this comparison it is obvious that the Chŏlla version of these chants is the earliest, the Kyŏngsang version represents the next stage of development, and the Seoul version a third stage.

How did this Hamgyŏng *ogu* ceremony I'm going to see come about? Min-gu wondered. He was filled with excitement.

The leaves of the sunflowers planted along the inside of the wall around Pyŏn's house had already died and curled up. Even the stems that had been thick and fresh were now lifeless and dusty and the once-enticing petals withered and unattractive. Only the fully ripened seeds protruding from the roundish

[2] A verse translation of this story appears in Kim Tongni, *Ulhwa the Shaman*, tr. Ahn Junghyo (Larchmont, N.Y.: Larchwood, 1979), pp. 192–207.
[3] *Mama:* an honorific suffix used with the titles of kings and their family members.

center remained. It would not be long before they could be picked.

⋅ Min-gu was guided inside by Pyŏn. He wavered momentarily, dazzled by the sunflowers on the curtain. They were particularly vivid and, together with the scarlet of a carpet he had not seen before, presented a striking contrast to the withered sunflowers outside.

As Min-gu's eyes adjusted, Pyŏn offered him a cigarette and struck a match for him, asking, "Doesn't this kind of color appeal to you?"

"Well, it's all right but..."

"I just don't like pale colors or anything else that's in between."

Pyŏn's young maid came in with ginseng tea. Min-gu could see that it had been made from ginseng roots rather than powder.

With a smile that barely exposed his bluish upper gum, Pyŏn said, "You can't imagine how I've waited—for this occasion, I mean."

"I really appreciate your efforts to—"

"Oh it's not that. I'm talking about meeting like this."

Pyŏn's hair was beautifully groomed and his suit tidy as usual.

Avoiding Pyŏn's gaze, Min-gu said "Where's the *halmŏni*?"[4]

"Please relax. I'm completely at your command."

"How about getting on with business?" Min-gu wanted to meet the old woman as soon as possible and listen to her chants.

"We don't have to rush. She's already here." Pyŏn closed his mouth tightly and then said, "There's a problem, though. I can't understand her very well."

"That Hamgyŏng dialect is really something, isn't it?"

"And you wouldn't believe how stubborn she is."

"Being an old lady, I guess she can't help it."

---

[4] *Halmŏni*: literally "grandmother," but often used in reference to an unrelated elderly woman.

"I've conned her into doing what you say, but..."

"Anyway, why don't we meet her?"

"Oh my, no interest in anything else. How about taking off your jacket?"

Looking askance at Min-gu like a woman would do, Pyŏn came behind him and removed his jacket. Keeping his own jacket on, he picked up the tape recorder and camera that Min-gu had brought.

Min-gu followed Pyŏn through the curtain-covered door to the next room. With a cabinet and dresser, it gave one the feeling of a main room. The old woman was lying on a reed mat on the heated part of the floor and smoking. Pyŏn cautiously helped her sit up.

The woman's smallish figure looked quite sturdy. She was in her seventies, but her hair wasn't very gray and her plump face was unwrinkled. Min-gu was relieved to see no sign of her lengthy illness.

But after taking the old woman's picture, Min-gu had to struggle to extract the chants of the Hamgyŏng *ogu kut* from her. There was her dialect—she said she had been born in Hamhŭng—but in addition, as Pyŏn had feared, her murmuring could not be deciphered. Moreover, her memory had diminished, causing her to invert the sequence of the chants so that Min-gu frequently had to begin taping all over again. This would invariably vex the old woman, and they would have to pacify her. And then, saying she was thirsty, she would rest while drinking some juice, and saying the next verses had not yet come to mind, she would smoke. Before an hour had passed, she had flopped down on her back, saying she was dizzy. She recited the chants in this position and then nodded off. They could do nothing but wait for her to wake up.

Min-gu hadn't expected them to progress smoothly, but he had no way of knowing it would take so much time. When dinner was brought in, the old woman had not even gotten to the part where the seventh princess had left to obtain the medicinal water.

Nevertheless, the day had not seemed all that grueling to Min-gu, since he had been able to discover some points of difference between the old woman's chants and those of the *ogu kut* performed in the southern part of Korea.

The chants of the *ogu kut* of Hamgyŏng Province were entitled "The Seven Princesses" or "The *Ogi* Exorcism." Their form, first of all, was unique. Whereas in the southern part of the country they were sung, in Hamgyŏng Province they comprised a mixture of song and speech with an additional dramatic element. At first Min-gu thought the old woman had changed a few of the chanted songs so that she would not have to go through the hard, drawn-out process of singing all the chants. But when he asked her to repeat the same passages, he found that the parts that were sung continued to be sung and the parts that were spoken continued to be spoken. And in the Hamgyŏng *kut* the father of the seven princesses is called "Excellency," and while the seventh princess was still inside her mother he disappeared somewhere and the mother alone became ill.

There wasn't much progress after dinner either. The old woman enumerated a mishmash of words, as if her mind had become more muddled. And even more frequently than during the day she would fall into the never-never land between sleep and wakefulness. Unable to stand by any longer, Pyŏn suggested that they continue the next morning, when the old woman's mind had cleared. Min-gu consented, as he had already decided he could no longer do a good job of collecting. His wristwatch showed it was almost nine.

Pyŏn and Min-gu returned to the room with the sunflower curtain and the scarlet carpet, and in no time a table with drinks and snacks had been set up.

"Take your time and relax," said Pyŏn. Sitting with his legs gathered to the side like a woman, he opened a new bottle of Johnny Walker, as he had done the time before.

Feeling exhaustion rush over him, Min-gu also wanted a drink, and he did not object when Pyŏn offered him one.

"I've learned a bit about drinking since last time," Pyŏn said, keeping a smile on his thickish lips as usual. "The glass you left behind that night—I finished it off, sip by sip."

Actually, Pyŏn had already had quite a lot to drink that day, and every time Min-gu lowered his glass from his lips, he offered him some *chogaegwi*[5] or dried meat.

Pyŏn emptied his second glass. "My face is red, isn't it?" He patted his cheeks with his fingertips and showed them to Min-gu. The color of his face couldn't be distinguished clearly, though, because it was tinted with the sunflower colors of the curtain and the scarlet of the carpet. "Not very attractive, is it?"

"Not very," Min-gu said, meaning that Pyŏn didn't appear to be intoxicated.

"My chest is on fire." Leaning forward, Pyŏn rested a hand on Min-gu's knee. His steamy breath tickled Min-gu's neck.

Min-gu took out a cigarette and put it in his mouth. He realized immediately that he had done this to defend himself. Pyŏn removed his hand and struck a match. Min-gu quickly drew several times on the cigarette.

"How would it be if I took up smoking, too?"

Min-gu was silent for a while and then said, "Hard to say."

"I'll do anything you say." The corners of Pyŏn's slanted eyes became liquid.

Min-gu abruptly looked at his wristwatch. "I guess it's about time I excused myself."

"It looks like you're afraid I can't hold my liquor." Pyŏn covered his smile with the back of his hand. "Didn't I say I'd learned something about drinking? A few drops like this aren't going to make me drunk. So stop worrying and have another glass."

"I've had enough. Well, today—"

"Now wait a minute. What's the rush?"

"It's late, and I'd better be going. I really owe you a lot for all you've done today."

---

[5] *Chogaegwi:* the adductor muscle of shellfish.

"No more of that. You know that your work is my work. I'll tell you what. Even though it might be a little inconvenient for you, why don't you spend the night here, and then we can get an early start tomorrow morning. Wouldn't you like to work with that *halmŏni* when she's just gotten up and her mind's all clear?"

"That's true, but...I'll go home, and then hurry back at daybreak."

"Well, like I said, you don't have to do that. Why not sleep here, if you don't mind the inconvenience?"

"It wouldn't be inconvenient for me, I'm just sorry—"

"There you go again." Pyŏn looked at Min-gu with his eyes aslant, and without waiting for an answer called the maid and had her prepare a bed and some drinking water for him.

It was almost midnight when Chun-t'ae returned home. It was rare for him to stay out late drinking by himself. The elderly maid had stayed up, and she asked Chun-t'ae if he hadn't better have some dinner, but he refused. Although he had drunk a lot, his mind was quite clear. He stood absently in the middle of the room. They had decided that Ch'ang-ae would take the wardrobe, cabinet, and dresser. Then he could truly feel he had returned to his boardinghouse life of the past, but he realized it would be nothing more than a facade. As he thought about this, Chi-yŏn's significance enlarged and established itself before him. It was certainly strange that he didn't feel at all burdened by this.

Chapter 8

Ch'ang-ae finally climbed out of the large tub at the public bathhouse. Staying in longer than usual may have been what made her feel so languid. While she was sitting beside the tub, enervated and limp, a middle-aged woman beside her said she would rub her back. Without giving Ch'ang-ae time to refuse, she took hold of her shoulder, turned her around, and began rubbing with a rolled-up towel. "How can your skin be so smooth and white, and it's silky too, even the dirty skin is white, and you must have had some children by now but how could you have such tight skin, my old man said my skin'd be good for making shoe soles out of..."

When Ch'ang-ae's turn came to rub the woman's back, the woman didn't rest her tongue for an instant. "Yeah, a little harder there, good, good, no, over there, a little higher, this time splash a little water on it, yeah over to the side, put some zip into those hands, oh that feels good..."

Barely freeing herself from the woman, Ch'ang-ae began to rub herself, starting with her chest and not, as she usually did, with her arms. At the same time she looked closely at her body in the mirror. The menstrual symptoms had disappeared—the bleeding had stopped and the tightening in her breasts had softened. Of course there was no reason the stretch marks of childbirth would have appeared on her stomach, and her waist had not thickened. But her breasts didn't look quite the same as before. She stopped rubbing away the dirty skin and held up her breasts. Clearly they were fuller than before, and the nipples seemed to have darkened. Ch'ang-ae rolled up the towel again and began rubbing away the dirty skin. This kind of change is nothing to worry about, she thought. Everything's starting all over.

Ch'ang-ae stepped out into the dressing room. She felt lighter in mind and body. Wearing only her underwear, she ran her fingers through her hair and began shaking it in order to dry it. A woman who had removed her clothes murmured to her, "The flowers are blooming." Only when Ch'ang-ae followed the woman's gaze did she comprehend: something red was coloring her panties. How can this be? It stopped completely, she said to herself. She had nothing with her to protect against this. She stopped drying her hair, dressed hurriedly, and left.

It was early morning, and some coolness remained in the air; Ch'ang-ae still felt gloomy. As she was walking along, a strange noise made her recoil. It was a feeble cry, and there was no doubt it was escaping from her body. She listened calmly.

There was an animal hospital on the street, and Ch'ang-ae dragged herself toward it. Through a window she could see a three-tiered wire hutch. In the top layer a black terrier pup sat yelping, its feet lifted against the mesh. Ch'ang-ae continued to listen to the pitiful crying coming from its little mouth as if it were escaping from her own body.

Min-gu was awakened by voices. The room had become bright. Thinking he had slept late, he looked at the wristwatch he had put near his head. It was past seven. If he were at home, he would have been up by now.

The voices came from the main gate. The maid was arguing with some of Pyŏn's clients, saying there would be no fortune-telling that day. Min-gu heard Pyŏn call to her to put something up on the gate. Probably a notice that Pyŏn was taking the day off, he thought.

Though it was past his usual time to get up and he had to get an early start with the old Hamgyŏng woman, he remained in bed a little longer. How in the world could that have happened last night? It was too vivid to have been a dream.

Min-gu had been awakened by a strange sensation in his genitals. When his head cleared he discovered that someone was sucking on him. He simply told me to sleep well and left—

could he have come back in without my realizing it? True, his revulsion toward Pyŏn for the way he had acted when he showed him the *ch'angbu* costume had gradually been replaced by curiosity. But once again something unexpected had happened—what was it all about? Before he knew it, his organ had been pushed unhindered into a deep, velvety cavity. It was certainly the inside of a woman, and it slowly began to wash over him in waves. Rising up from the waist, Min-gu fumbled toward his counterpart. He felt the other's face. He jerked back his hand and then extended it again, groping below the face. Just before reaching the naked chest, his hand was brushed away by the other's. Crotch spread open, the other had knelt astride Min-gu's thighs and was using one arm for support and the other to ward off Min-gu's hand. The hand moved quickly and forcefully, as if to defend something, repeatedly thwarting Min-gu's attempts to reach out. And all the while the waves continued, in various patterns. Although they sometimes ceased momentarily, there was merely a change in direction and they were generated anew. Min-gu's penis drifted and swayed this way and that from the motion of the waves. Min-gu wished he were a rock that the waves could not budge, but he was swept over and over by them. The waves gradually quickened and became rough. I'll become a rock, I'll become a rock, he thought, but then the strong, rough waves shattered him. He attempted to gather the broken pieces, but in the end he dissolved completely, and immediately a satisfaction devoid of regret surged throughout his body. It was a weird experience.

Thinking he couldn't just lie there, Min-gu got up and went to the bathroom. He returned to find his bedding folded up and a basin of water and dentifrice salts put out for him. He washed his face, and the maid quickly brought in a bowl of rice-and-pine-nut porridge on a tray. Min-gu ate the porridge, and when he had almost finished a cigarette Pyŏn entered. He said good morning, looking indirectly at Min-gu. His normally white face was tinged with red.

Min-gu still couldn't understand. As always, Pyŏn's hair had been finely groomed with hair oil in a fashionable style, and he was dressed in a neat man's suit, but his legs gathered to the side and his hands folded together atop his knees were surely the posture of a seated woman. What's going on here? Min-gu had had no answer all night, for Pyŏn had immediately sneaked away as soon as the incident was over.

"The *halmŏni* must be up by now," Min-gu said, shaking off his unsettling thoughts.

"About that," Pyŏn said, lowering his voice as if embarrassed, "she won't start until she's had breakfast. She says she just doesn't have any energy before eating."

Even after her breakfast tray had been removed the old woman didn't start for a while. The process of collecting her chants proved as annoying as it had the previous day. Although it was morning, her mind had not cleared. She smoked continuously, saying her mind wasn't working, and flopped on her back complaining of aches and pains. It was a repeat of the day before. Min-gu was on the point of exhaustion.

Noon was approaching when the old woman finished her chants. Min-gu was astonished by the results of his day and a half of research. How could the conclusion be like that? he wondered. All the main characters had ended up dying.

The seventh princess had obtained the medicinal water, but when she returned to her family, she discovered her mother's coffin being carried away. Pleading to the bearers to put it down, she scoops up a small gourdful of the water and puts it to her mother's lips, and the woman opens her eyes. Another gourdful of the water, and her decayed flesh is reinvigorated. After still another gourdful she gets up and walks. Hand in hand, mother and daughter return home.

What follows is the problem.

Inside the house the other six daughters were dividing up the household goods, ignoring their mother's funeral. It wasn't simply a matter of dividing the goods—each item was being broken into pieces and divided. There would have been no problem if they had been broken into exactly six pieces, but there were seven pieces, and the daughters are wrangling over the remaining piece, saying, "I'll take it—No, I'll take it." But when they see the seventh princess coming in with their mother, they go out to the kitchen and hide inside a large cooking pot. The virtuous seventh princess begs her mother to call her six older sisters back and divide the household goods among them. But her mother calls the daughters out and condemns them saying, "Yes, I'll give you some goods—the goods of the ten kings of Hades." Then and there the bodies of the six daughters swell up and they fall over dead. Overwhelmed by this, the seventh princess tells her mother she is going to sleep for a moment and lies down. Her mother agrees, saying she must be tired, and prepares some rice. But when she returns from the kitchen, the seventh princess doesn't get up, no matter how she tries to wake her. There is nothing else to do but bury her. The mother begins wailing day and night. Annoyed, the mountain god has an awe-inspiring old goddess go to the woman as she is on her way to the third memorial service for her daughter. She instructs her as follows: "Don't go, the seventh princess has dug her way out of the grave and become a fox. She's waiting to kill you. Don't go." If the mother had merely continued on to the grave, ignoring these words, she would have become a goddess. But she became scared; she thanks the awe-inspiring old goddess and gives her all the food in the wicker basket she is carrying on her head. In return, the goddess invites the mother of the seven princesses to attend a Buddhist mass for the dead, to be held at such and such a temple on such and such a date. Captivated only by the mention of the mass, the mother forgets the name of the temple and the date and wanders about, inquiring from one temple to another. Finally, she arrives at a certain temple and a monk asks her why she is wandering around. When she replies that she has come to attend a mass for the dead, the monk tells her it was concluded two days earlier. Not knowing what to do, the starving mother of the seven princesses goes behind the temple, where she sees a bucket of slop consisting of leftovers from the mass and the water used to rinse the rice. She shovels it into her mouth. Then, on her way home, she trips over a three-year-old stump and is killed by the fall. The next part of the chant was spoken rather than sung:

> After she died people said,
> The family of a filial daughter won't do well.
> The family of a filial son won't do well.
> A virtuous woman and a loyal retainer aren't good
>   for a family.
> So let's not hope for a virtuous woman or a loyal retainer.

Something very unusual happened at the end of the old woman's performance. Sensing that she wanted to stand up, Pyŏn and Min-gu helped her to her feet. Surprisingly, she began fluttering her arms and dancing. As if irritated by having merely sat there all the while, the old woman was light on her feet, despite her sluggish appearance. And her voice, unlike before, was higher and clearer.

> From long ago, long ago, there've been sacrifice days
>   from long ago.
> The soul of history has gone away.
> The soul of the seventh princess has gone away.

Finishing the song and dance simultaneously, the old woman feebly sat down in a heap and then flopped on her back, resuming her posture of a short time before.

This was the end of the Hamgyŏng Province *ogu kut*. Min-gu cajoled the old woman into repeating it several times, but the conclusion was always the same. Min-gu could not understand it. What is the function of an *ogu kut* with an ending like that? he asked himself.

The outlook of shamanism toward the universe, spirits, gods, and ancestor worship—the essence of all the chants in the *ogu kut*—is fundamentally different from those of Buddhism and

Christianity. In shamanism spirits inhabit all living things, including humans, and even inanimate objects. A tree becomes the guardian spirit of a village, a rock becomes the spirit of good fortune and makes people's wishes come true, the spirit of smallpox attaches itself to an article of clothing. Shamanism, moreover, considers the universe to be divided into Heaven, Earth, and Hades. The head deities dwell in Heaven, humans inhabit Earth, and humans who have died go to Hades, which is divided in turn into upper, middle, and lower levels. Those humans who have practiced virtue in their lifetime go to Paradise, the upper level; those who have committed vicious acts go to Hell, the lower level; and those in between go to the middle level. But even those humans who deserve to go to Hell can go to Paradise if an *ogu kut* is performed for them. And in shamanism, ancestor worship is a custom of economic exchange—while the adults retain their capacity to work they protect and raise their children, but when they become feeble with age and fall ill their grownup children repay them—along with the practice of filial piety, which is necessary even if the parents have not fulfilled their part of the bargain.

This general essence of shamanism, far from being reflected in the Hamgyŏng *ogu kut*, is utterly destroyed by its conclusion. Only the seventh princess is depicted attractively. Even her death, which seems like sleep, is depicted very beautifully, though tersely. But her asceticism, lovely to the point of pity, brings her to an ugly death rather than the salvation of any of her family. Moreover, families having filial sons and daughters and virtuous retainers are condemned to misfortune. We can conclude only that in several respects the chants of the Hamgyŏng *ogu kut* represent a stage of development more recent than those of the southern part of Korea.

What could be the cause of so much unconventionality? wondered Min-gu.

"Can it really be like this? How can it function..." Min-gu couldn't endure all his doubts.

"I'm not sure what to say." Pyŏn also wore an uneasy expression. "The ceremony is slightly different depending on the place, but still..."

"This one's pretty much opposite, isn't it?"

He couldn't understand it. All he could do was guess. Perhaps they were the same at first but changed as they came down through subsequent generations. But in that case, what could have caused the changes?

Even while he and Pyŏn were escorting the old woman home, Min-gu was full of questions. For a while he looked down as he walked along. Then he lifted his head. That's it! The haunting scene of the old woman singing and dancing stood out clearly in his mind, and he hit upon a slender clue. The decidedly light, fluttering movement of this old woman who looked so sluggish, and her clear, high-pitched singing, so unlike the beginning, lent the conclusion a tinge of resistance toward something.

From the beginning, Min-gu recalled, the Hamgyŏng area was different, topographically and historically, from other regions of Korea. Bordering a continent, it was subjected to frequent invasions. Furthermore, it was a place of exile during Chosŏn, a place where loyal retainers and filial sons, falsely accused, were banished. Confusion arose as to who was really a loyal retainer or filial son, and this could be reflected in the chants of the *ogu kut*, couldn't it? The filial son and daughter and the loyal retainer—in the face of death there's nothing different between them and the greedy. And in the face of death the good and bad are six of one, half a dozen of the other. "The soul of history has gone away," "The soul of the seventh princess has gone away"—couldn't this be the attainment of an equalizing process that relied on death? In any event, the recurring thought that he had collected these materials made Min-gu forget how exhausted he was.

"What was that?" Min-gu asked. He had not been paying attention to what Pyŏn was saying.

"Well, you're that absorbed in your thoughts, are you?" Pyŏn came up beside him.

"Yes, I guess I am..."

Pyŏn whispered to Min-gu, carefully reading his face. "I guess you won't have occasion to see me now. But would you? Would you?"

To Chun-t'ae, the sale of their house the very day after he and Ch'ang-ae had concluded their divorce was totally unexpected. It was as if the two events were two halves of a lottery ticket that matched perfectly. Chun-t'ae had learned from the elderly maid that while he was out attending to the divorce, the old man who was their realtor had brought someone over to look at the place. He had shrugged off this news, realizing that not everyone who looked at the house would be interested in buying it. But then the old man had visited Chun-t'ae at work the following day, and although he proposed lowering the asking price below the house's market value, Chun-t' ae ended up consenting. He was in no frame of mind to stick to his price, although he might have received more for the house if he had. Having concluded the divorce the day before, he considered the sale of the house trivial and didn't want to be bothered with it. Chun-t'ae stamped the contract the realtor had drawn up and handed it to him.

As soon as the realtor left, a colleague next to Chun-t'ae asked him if he had sold his house.

"Yeah."

"Why so sudden?"

"Oh, just because."

"You're going into a bigger house."

"No."

"Well then, are you moving to Seoul? You said your wife had set up a shop there."

Chun-t'ae smiled instead of answering.

"Seems like you didn't get a very good price."

"Why's that?"

"You look kind of gloomy, you know."

Although Chun-t'ae was not aware of how he looked, it was

clear that relief was not his only feeling. He didn't feel the lightheartedness that he had expected upon settling his affairs with Ch'ang-ae. Perhaps that's the way human relationships are, he thought. At any rate, now that I've come to the end of this chapter with Ch'ang-ae, only my problems are left.

Having concluded the Wednesday worship service and waited for all the believers to leave, Sŏng-ho extinguished the lights and followed a woman outside. It was the woman who had made her husband, a problem drinker and a gambler, come to church. Now she was asking Sŏng-ho to come to their house.

"Is something wrong?" Sŏng-ho asked.

"My husband's done come back, Rev'rend."

"Did he go somewhere?"

"You haven't heard this shameful story, Rev'rend; six days ago he scraped together all the money and clothin' in the house and took off."

Sŏng-ho recalled that her husband hadn't been in church the previous Sunday.

"I was just 'bout to head up to the church, and you'd never believe it, Rev'rend, someone came carryin' him home piggyback, lookin' 'bout like a corpse."

"Now hold on. Was he in an accident?"

"I wish. Then I wouldn't hate him so bad. He comes back sick, and he's 'bout to kick the bucket."

This was no exaggeration. With his sunken eyes, shaded by the light, and his hollow cheeks, he had the look of someone who was dying after a long, serious illness.

"Look, you. The Rev'rend's come," said the woman in a loud voice, leaning toward her husband's ear.

The man's eyes remained closed and he showed no reaction.

The woman seized her husband and shook him. "How could you come back lookin' like this? Everything you told me before was lies, wasn't it? You said you failed in every business you tried. You lied, didn't you?"

The husband remained still, his eyes closed.

"Try ownin' up to everything in front of the Rev'rend. What's the good of lyin' there like a log?"

Finally the man's eyes opened, with difficulty. They were like the scars of deep wounds that had healed only to be reopened. It was impossible to distinguish whom he was looking at.

"Rev'rend..." The man stuttered, his feeble voice caught in his throat. "I...been punished...by God." The scarlike eyes closed again.

"And somethin' else, you did the same old thing with that money, didn't you?" the woman hastened to inquire.

The husband's fleshless chin could scarcely be seen going up and down.

"You call yourself a human bein'? You're no better than an animal. You deserve to be punished. You deserve to die!"

The husband's expression remained the same. There was no sign of shame or regret. He seemed to have abandoned himself completely to whatever punishment might be handed down to him. He was not exercising a strong will but instead was yielding to the belief that he could not avoid succumbing to temptation. So humans can be this weak, Sŏng-ho thought. When this man and his wife had pledged to come to church together and become believers, he had thought it would be quite some time—how long he wasn't sure—before the man would come to church of his own accord. If it takes a while, then I'll just have to wait, he had told himself. But now the first order of business was for the man to recover.

Sŏng-ho tried to reason with the woman as she led him out. "It'd probably be better if you didn't treat him too harshly while he's sick."

"Rev'rend—" The woman momentarily cut herself off, as if unable to control her rage. "I can't forgive my husband."

"I know how annoying it is, but you should be patient and forgive him."

"No. I can't. You heard what he said, Rev'rend. He'd never drink or gamble again. He gave his word before God. Since he went back on his word he deserves to be punished. I've prayed to God with all my heart to beat him without mercy if he sinned again. And the prayer came true, Rev'rend. God won't forgive him. He deserves to be punished!"

But, thought Sŏng-ho, we can't condemn humans for mistakes they commit out of weakness. "Why God forgives or doesn't forgive is something we can't know. We can tell only that God's thoughts and magnanimity are not as intolerant as our own."

The woman held her body erect for a while, then suddenly covered her face with her hands and began sobbing.

Sŏng-ho's heart was heavy. I can't say I'm not responsible for the way these couples think these days, not to mention the other things. What a deviant belief: she thinks her husband's bad health from drinking or gambling is God's punishment, and that she achieved it through her prayers. Is this the best that can come of the beliefs I pour into them? Sŏng-ho stood with the woman in the darkness until her weeping had subsided.

The *t'aeng t'aeng* of the white tennis ball reverberates in the clear morning air. Chi-yŏn jumps back and forth lightly. During the past two or three days she hadn't completely regained peak form, but she feels less apologetic toward her opponent because her swing is smoother and her unforced errors noticeably fewer.

Listening to the distinct *t'aeng t'aeng* of the white ball in the clear air, Chi-yŏn thinks that with every flight the ball punches a hole in the sky. *P'ong p'ong*—one by one the holes are punched, and one by one they lighten up to reveal another bright space. Chi-yŏn sets her mind in the direction of that bright space. If I haven't heard from Mr. Ham by this Sunday, I'll go see him.

Chi-yŏn picks up a stray ball, tosses it high in the air, and makes a smooth serve.

Chapter 9

"If you have the time to wait for me here, then you ought to be able to go to my apartment, right?" Min-gu was sitting across from Ŭn-hŭi, who had arrived at the Uju Tearoom first.

"Didn't I tell you I wasn't going there anymore?" she retorted.

"Well then, now that we've got the chance, let's head outside the city for the day."

"Not me."

"We could go to Suwŏn or Inch'ŏn and have a quiet—"

"No more of your harebrained ideas." Ŭn-hŭi took an envelope out of her handbag and pushed it toward Min-gu. "Go on over to the Council of Elders' office. Take this along."

"The Council of Elders? What's this all about?" Min-gu looked concerned.

"It's my father's orders. He said you can see Reverend Yun if you go there, and to help him as much as you can."

"You mean Sŏng-ho?"

"That's right."

"What are you talking about? What's all this about helping him?"

"Your guess is as good as mine. Father said you'd find out when you get there. He said to give that letter to the head elder."

"Now really, what kind of riddle is this?"

"All I know is something's happened for sure, so you'd better go quickly. Before it's too late."

To get to the Council of Elders' office Sŏng-ho had to pass through a small reception room. As soon as the receptionist saw him she asked him to wait briefly and went into the office.

Thinking there might be another visitor, Sŏng-ho glanced at the clock on the wall. It was about ten to two.

Sŏng-ho sat in a hard chair and gazed out the window. A corner of the stone church took up one third of the window, and the roofs of houses in a middle-class residential area occupied the rest. In the hollow of the curved roof-tiles, which were more than half shaded, a dark fungus was growing and the stalks of dried weeds appeared here and there. The weather forecast had called for increasing cloudiness followed by rain, but the sky was still clear. Now how do you suppose Chi-yŏn's getting along? Sŏng-ho asked himself. I wonder if she's gotten hold of herself. She's pretty smart; she'll probably get squared away.

At the sound of a door opening and closing, Sŏng-ho looked back toward the entrance to the reception room. It was Pastor Chu, whom Sŏng-ho had long known. He was carrying a brief-case under his arm. Although Sŏng-ho felt their eyes had met, Chu went straight into the office. With those thick eyeglasses he must have a tough time making people out, Sŏng-ho decided.

Shortly the door to the office opened and the receptionist came out. She asked Sŏng-ho to go in and then disappeared.

Three ministers were sitting at a table deep inside the room. Sŏng-ho had known all of them since the time he had led his boys' service corps to Kŏje Island as a Korean War refugee. They had each adopted a different posture. In the middle, Pastor Shin, head of the Council of Elders, was looking at some papers before him. To his right Pastor Chu was blowing dust off the table, almost touching it with his thick eyeglasses. To his left Pastor Pae was staring up into space. Their postures suggested some kind of tension. Sŏng-ho recalled how Pastor Chu had passed right by him in the reception room, appearing to avert his face, and it was now obvious that something had isolated him from the three ministers. He couldn't bring himself to greet them, as he had intended.

"Please sit there," said Pastor Shin as he lifted his eyes from the papers. His voice seemed rather hard to Sŏng-ho.

Feeling alienated, Sŏng-ho sat down. Then, asking them in his P'yŏng-an Province dialect to bow their heads, Pastor Shin began to pray. He beseeched God that everything from then on be a matter of his will and not that of humans, and be directed by him and not humans, from the beginning to the end.

Sŏng-ho's chest throbbed. His summons by the council was obviously no trivial matter.

Finishing the prayer, Pastor Shin looked immediately at Sŏng-ho. "Today's meeting will not be at all pleasant but since it is an affair of God's and not ours, we hope we can exchange questions and answers with no secrets held back."

Although Sŏng-ho realized where he stood, he had no way of knowing why.

"I'll question you first," said Pastor Shin. After a short pause, he began. "Did you write the essay 'Korean Customs and Christianity,' published in *The Christian Weekly*?"

So that's it, thought Sŏng-ho. His heart calmed. "Yes."

"What was your intention in writing this essay?"

"I wanted to try to arrange my thoughts as a clergyman."

"You say you wanted to try to arrange your thoughts; what thoughts did you arrange?"

"I should've done it a long time ago. What I wanted to do was to fix the limits of Christianity in regard to our country's customs. In other words, I wanted to say that as long as no conflict of doctrine is involved, Christianity shouldn't overly interfere with our customs."

"Then you're saying that performing ancestral ceremonies doesn't violate the rules of Christianity?" Although Pastor Shin would sometimes speak in P'yŏng-an Province dialect, he used Seoul dialect much more now than when Sŏng-ho had met him on Kŏje Island.

"That's correct."

"How can that be? Doesn't it contradict our doctrine on serving idols and superstition?"

"Through those ceremonies people cherish their ancestors. It's not a matter of worshiping spirits."

"Ah, I see. So preparing a table and bowing before it and then preparing a meal and asking the soul of a dead person to come and partake isn't a case of serving idols and superstitions?"

"I think we ought to look at that as a form of reverence. Food is the most precious thing in a poor country such as ours, so perhaps that's why we prepare it for our ancestors."

"Ever since Christianity entered our country it has banned the ancestral ceremony, and now you intend to turn things upside down. Isn't that an act of heresy?"

"I mentioned in my essay—"

"Who is it?" Pastor Shin said, raising his voice as he looked behind Sŏng-ho.

Sŏng-ho had not noticed anyone entering the office.

"We're in the middle of a meeting, so please leave," ordered Pastor Shin.

Someone walked past Sŏng-ho toward the three ministers. Sŏng-ho absently looked up at the visitor and was taken aback. What's Min-gu doing here? What's he got to do with all this? Min-gu held out a white envelope to the ministers. Pastor Shin opened the sealed envelope, read the contents, and then passed the note to the other two ministers. Looking perplexed, the three of them discussed what to say, and then Pastor Shin motioned to Min-gu to take a seat.

Min-gu turned around, and on his way past Sŏng-ho he twitched his hairy eyebrows and smiled at him. Here I am, he seemed to be saying.

Sŏng-ho didn't know what was what. I guess Min-gu came to listen in—he even brought a letter of introduction, he thought. Although Sŏng-ho had been notified several days before to come here, he had had no idea what was at hand. Even if I'd known it was something more serious than this, I wouldn't have done anything to prevent it, he told himself.

"Continue your story, Pastor Yun."

"When Western missionaries first came to our country, they misinterpreted the ancestral ceremony as a religious ritual and banned it. But I believe it's not too late to set straight the things that need straightening out."

"Even if I went along with you this far and agreed that the ancestral ceremony isn't a superstitious act, would it be a good thing to confuse our believers, who up to now have been taught that it's taboo?"

"There may be some temporary confusion, but shouldn't we correct what ought to be corrected? I read in a book that there was a Western minister who used to go to his wife's grave morning and evening. In the morning he'd say, 'Did you sleep well last night, honey? The kids and I did.' And in the evening, 'Honey, the kids had a good time again today. Sleep well.' Like that. Before inquiring into whether or not this constitutes the worship of idols or superstitions, shouldn't we look at it as the expression by humans of a wonderful affection?"

"Let's stop this talk about others and get down to our own problems," Pastor Shin snapped.

Min-gu spoke up from behind Sŏng-ho. "May I offer my thoughts on the subject? The fact is, in Christianity itself there's a shamanistic element that is not unimportant, and it's been there since the birth of Jesus. Take the example of the three *paksa*[1] from the east."

The three ministers simultaneously furrowed their brows.

"These *paksa* followed the stars to Bethlehem," Min-gu continued. "In other words, they were shamans who were good at astrology. And I believe these three shamans are highly applauded in Christianity."

"They weren't shamans," said Pastor Shin, "They were *paksa*."

"When we translate the term into Korean," said Min-gu, "*paksa* is how it comes out. But how could there have been *paksa* in astronomy at that time? In all likelihood it was astrology that they were well versed in. In English the term is *wise man*. And there's something else. Only after Jesus had grown

---

[1] *Paksa:* (a) learned person; (b) holder of a Ph.D. degree.

up and spent forty days fasting and praying in the wilderness did he perform some miracles. There are also examples of ministers fasting and praying and then receiving the Holy Spirit and having their diseases cured. And shamans have long-lasting diseases in which they take in hardly any food. Only then does a spirit descend into them, and then they're able to prophesy and cure illnesses. So Christianity and shamanism have something in common. And then there's Santa Claus on Christmas Eve, and on top of that, some people paint eggs all kinds of colors at Easter. Now if that isn't a shamanistic practice, then what is? I mean, there's a notion that the resurrection of Jesus is like a chick being hatched from an egg."

Dazed, the three ministers fixed their eyes on Min-gu.

Whenever Min-gu began talking about shamanism, he became worked up like this. "And then the pictures of Jesus. I've often seen believers who appear to be bowing and praying in front of a portrait of him, and I've seen quite a few people who believe that the Jesus in the portrait will listen directly to their prayers. What's more, you can often see a picture of the young Samuel kneeling and folding his hands in prayer stuck on the dashboard of taxis, but if you ask the driver whether he's a Christian the answer's usually no. The fact is, it's young Samuel in the picture rather than the driver who's doing the praying to Christ, but it's the driver who takes consolation in the fact that he won't get into any accidents. I think this is a phenomenon that can't even be seen in a country that's made Christianity its state religion."

"Is there something bad about that?" asked Pastor Shin.

"I'm not talking about whether it's good or bad. I'm only saying it's interesting that the picture of Samuel functions as a charm."

"The picture of Samuel isn't a charm or an idol. It's different from portraits of evil spirits," said Pastor Shin in a tone of displeasure.

"But what we need to understand is that the picture of Samuel is becoming the same as a portrait of a shaman. I can see the day when portraits of Christ will have Korean instead of Western features. Already the holy Virgin Mary has been changed into something Korean, hasn't she?"

"For us Christians, the pictures of Jesus we have at present are sufficient."

"But the portraits of Jesus we have aren't photos of him. They were drawn by Westerners from their imagination. We don't know how Jesus looked in reality. As you know, in Greek portraits Christ is depicted as a shepherd, and depending on the area he's sometimes rendered as a black. I don't see any reason why he shouldn't have our face and our clothing from now on. Then his portraits'll give us a more friendly feeling toward him—just like the portraits of shamans do. And—"

With an "Ahem," Pastor Shin stopped Min-gu. He looked at the other ministers. The three of them put their heads together and conferred in low voices, and then Pastor Shin said to Min-gu, "In regard to what you've said, it's all right if you have something to add to our discussion of matters relating to Pastor Yun, but we'd like you to confine yourself within those limits."

For a while now Sŏng-ho had been in the dark. He didn't know why Min-gu had come. At first he had thought Min-gu was an auditor, but here he was defending him. It was incomprehensible. He didn't know whether Min-gu was acting freely or not. And it wasn't pleasant at all. He wished he could take care of his affairs by himself.

But Min-gu didn't remain still.

"I read Pastor Yun's essay when it was published, but since it can stand on its own I have nothing to contribute to it. The way I see it, the only thing remaining is for the Council of Elders to decide whether or not to put his suggestions into practice. So I'll add just one thing to what I've read. It's about the cross. Many believers think that the Holy Spirit dwells in the cross itself, and they believe that the sick can recover by touching and kissing it, and that people can deflect evil spirits by carrying it around with them or hanging it in their room. It's just like the shamanistic belief that certain implements have magical powers. I'm afraid I've annoyed you by carrying on about shamanism, but please think about this. Is there a difference between the cross and the implements of shamans? If we look into this, we can see that the cross is nothing more than the instrument used to punish Jesus. He was nailed to the cross only because Roman law required crucifixion. If it had been Jewish law, he would have been stoned to death. And if that had been the case, then stones would probably have to be hung in the church, inside and out, and people would have to go around with stones hanging from their necks. And if he had been hung, then it'd be a noose, or if he'd been beheaded, then a guillotine. I don't know what shape it'd be if he'd been drawn and quartered, the way we used to do in our country. Anyway, in my view, as I said just a minute ago, there's no difference between the belief that a holy spirit dwells in the cross and the shaman belief that certain implements have magical powers."

"You can't judge all believers by what some do."

"But I'm sure you'll find that such believers are gradually increasing. And if it keeps up, then who's to guarantee that the day won't come when people will worship shamans or even fortune-tellers, and hold *kut* and have their fortunes told in front of the cross and a portrait of Christ depicted like a Korean? The point that excites me is that between Korean Christianity and shamanism there's an indivisible—"

"All right, since we don't have much time," said Pastor Shin, cutting Min-gu off, "let's return to the matter at hand and question Pastor Yun. In your essay you wrote that the church should not interfere in the ancestral ceremony or in the practice of *saju*[2] and *kunghap*[3] before marriage. Do you really believe that?"

---

[2] *Saju:* the year, month, day, and time of one's birth.
[3] *Kunghap:* the analysis of a man and woman's *saju* according to the five cosmic elements of metal, wood, water, fire, and earth, to determine if they would be a good match in marriage.

"Let's suppose that the church banned these practices. Then it would also have to consider it superstitious and unacceptable when the bride bows and offers gifts to her parents-in-law and people throw jujubes into her lap hoping she will have many offspring. And the same thing with a child's first birthday, when people place things like a skein of thread or books or pencils or money on a table to see which one the child picks up. But the more regulating the church does—you can't do this, you can't do that—naturally the greater the rate of violations. And then people will easily become accustomed to violating regulations that as believers they really shouldn't violate. Suppose Korea were flooded with all sorts of laws that you don't see in other countries—we couldn't abide by all of them, and finally we'd discover that we'd become immune to them and weren't even abiding by the ones we absolutely had to. In the end, the more prohibitions are enacted, the more likely the believers' sense of guilt will waste away. Rather than enacting prohibitions, we should help our believers to take an interest in how they can nurture goodness and combat evil through true faith in Christianity."

"In other words, Pastor Yun, you have no intention of revising even one phrase of your essay. All right, then, I understand."

With this, Sŏng-ho thought, the inquiry of the ecclesiastical court was finished. Pastor Shin, however, took some papers from the bottom of the pile before him, put them on top, and cleared his voice. "With this next matter I hope we can also have questions and answers without any secrets. As you know, this session is superintended by God and not people."

Sŏng-ho immediately perceived that everything so far had been a preliminary and that they were now coming to the main issue.

"When did you first meet Pastor Chŏng?"

"Did you say Pastor Chŏng?"

"Pastor Chŏng, who was kidnapped to the North during the war."

At the mention of Pastor Chŏng, Sŏng-ho's heart quickened and then began to thump wildly. "Pastor Chŏng was the minister of the church I attended during high school," he replied.

"Were you close to him?"

"It was more that I respected him and he regarded me with affection."

"Did you frequently call at his house?"

"I used to drop by after the worship service. He taught me many things. It was probably through his influence that I formed the boys' service corps and went to Kŏje Island during the refugee period."

"You said influence. What kind of influence?"

"He fostered a spirit of sacrifice in me."

"Did you go to Kŏje Island purely on behalf of the refugees?"

"Of course."

Pastor Shin closed his mouth slowly and tilted his head.

I didn't lie, thought Sŏng-ho. At that age, his spotless enthusiasm had been able to overcome the usual hardships of life. It was through this enthusiasm that Sŏng-ho, unwilling to go to Kŏje Island just by himself, had organized the service corps. He had set up tents for the refugees there, distributed food and other relief goods among them, cleaned up their surroundings, cared for the sick, and gone around to families with problems and taken care of them one by one. His two or three hours of catnaps a day—he certainly slept no more than that—were a continuation of this sacrifice. All his efforts were the result of his enthusiasm. And the three ministers before him, like the other refugees, were in several ways beneficiaries of his sacrifice. Sŏng-ho didn't even want to recall how he had assisted each of them in turn. Far from leaving these episodes in his memory, there were many he wished to forget. One of these three men had asked to have his family's ration increased, one had said their blanket was somewhat threadbare and asked to have it replaced with a new one, and one had made a frantic attempt to pick out relief goods slightly more valuable than the ones he had been allotted. Their actions were no better and perhaps somewhat worse than those of the other refugees, and they were outspoken and persistent in their demands for the privileges due them as clergymen. In truth, such actions were indecent to Sŏng-ho, who was not even twenty at the time. But as time passed he came to understand that since they were only human, they probably couldn't help themselves. And now here they were, having buried those actions inside their wrinkled faces. Of course there was no relation between their behavior then and their inquiry of him today. Nevertheless, he could never have suspected that they would doubt the purity of his motives then.

Pastor Shin resumed.

"Wasn't it perhaps a case of your going to Kŏje Island to visit Pastor Chŏng's wife?"

The chickens have come home to roost, thought Sŏng-ho. "Yes, that was also the case." It was the complete truth. But at the time, he had considered Mrs. Hong merely one of the refugees and had not strayed an inch from that position.

"You said yes when I asked if you went to Kŏje Island purely on behalf of the refugees, and you said yes when I asked if you had gone to see Pastor Chŏng's wife. Now where does the truth lie?"

"Both are true."

Again Pastor Shin paused briefly.

"Well then, did you also leave Kŏje Island for Pusan in order to find his wife?"

"That's correct. I couldn't tell by looking at her, but I found out later that her heart was bad. Because of her health, I tried to find her among the refugees in Pusan so I could help her."

There had been another reason, however, for Sŏng-ho's departure for Pusan. Because clergymen and their families had concentrated mainly on Kŏje Island, Sŏng-ho had waited a long time for her there, but even though he had wanted to continue asking around for her, he couldn't bear to witness the disgusting behavior of these clergymen any longer and had left the island.

Again Pastor Shin began to consult in whispers with the other two ministers. Pastor Chu on his right, brushing away dust on the table from time to time, and Pastor Pae on his left, looking up into space, had both listened intently to Sŏng-ho, and now their heads had converged with Pastor Shin's.

Sŏng-ho felt that sparks were jumping between him and the three ministers. It was all right if the sparks landed on him and burned him up, but he genuinely hoped they wouldn't extend as far as Mrs. Hong. Since he was sure to be reprimanded, he hoped the inquiry would end at this juncture.

The consultation continued, and then Sŏng-ho saw Pastor Shin pick up a notebook from the papers before him and pass it to Pastor Pae, who then handed it to him. It was a well-thumbed notebook.

"Have you seen this notebook before?" Pastor Shin asked reluctantly.

"No." Sŏng-ho looked down at the empty gray cover of the notebook with its dull yellow discolorations.

"Take a look through it."

Sŏng-ho opened the cover. His eyes were drawn immediately to the tiny handwriting. So the sparks have finally reached Mrs. Hong.

"Can you recognize the handwriting?"

"Yes." Feeling dizzy, Sŏng-ho closed his eyes.

"Now read over only the places marked in red pencil."

For an instant Sŏng-ho remained still, steadying himself. Jump in, jump in anywhere, even if it's fire. Nailing his eyes to the pages, he picked out the flickering letters.

The style was like that of a journal. In some places simple facts were noted, in others her feelings were elaborated. Buried in near oblivion and hidden among the leaves of the notebook, the affairs of seventeen and eighteen years ago had come back to life. The ardent joy of some days, the painful regret of others, sliced away at Sŏng-ho's heart.

Sŏng-ho wasn't aware of reading slowly or quickly. At some passages he couldn't endure his feelings of guilt and wished they would quickly pass, at others he would converse with Mrs. Hong and linger over the page.

After finishing, Sŏng-ho sat for a while with his head bowed. Mrs. Hong's suffering, to which his own could not be compared, wrung his entire body. He slowly lifted his head, as if he were lifting the weight of that agony. The three faces set in his direction had no relation whatever to that suffering.

"Have you finished?" asked Pastor Shin in a heavy voice, as if he were representing the owner of the notebook.

Sŏng-ho remained silent.

Pastor Pae closed the notebook and took it from Sŏng-ho.

"I believe the 'Y' that appears inside stands for your name," said Pastor Shin. "What do you think?"

"That's right."

"Then do you acknowledge that everything written here is fact?"

"Yes."

One question remained—Where had the notebook come from?—but Sŏng-ho stifled the urge to ask. Although Mrs. Hong hadn't been able to dispose of the notebook before passing away, who in hell could have dug up her past from the grave—a past that had already faded from people's memories—and exposed it? He flared up. But what's the use now of knowing who it was? Shouldn't I seize the notebook instead? Having seen the contents, Sŏng-ho thought the notebook properly belonged to him and Mrs. Hong. Now it was something outsiders were unjustifiably trampling as they wished. I've got to snatch it away, Sŏng-ho thought. But at that moment a revelation rushed into his chest. It was not that Mrs. Hong had been unable to dispose of the notebook before passing away. There was absolutely no reason for her, a woman of great circumspection in every matter, to be inattentive about such a thing. She deliberately passed it on, hoping it would catch someone's eye. Even though she had disclosed nothing during her lifetime, she was trying to inform others of her past after her death. By doing that she wanted to break herself to pieces. And she wanted me to, also. So I'd better do it. No matter how many pieces. And then I'll have to shape myself into some other form. Sŏng-ho realized then and there that the process he was undergoing today was a premise for the message he had received from Mrs. Hong's silence on her deathbed: we have been forgiven. God, I thanked you for protecting our affair, not disclosing it to the world. But that was a mistake. Now I thank you for giving me the strength to bear up to being broken into fragments and breaking myself to pieces.

"Whatever you have to say, say it," said Pastor Shin, as if this was his last act of mercy.

"There's nothing to say," said Sŏng-ho, a peaceful expression on his face for the first time that afternoon. "Only that I sincerely regret having caused the three of you so much anxiety. You won't have to trouble yourselves any more because of me." Sŏng-ho calmly got to his feet. "Though it's somewhat late for this, I'm resigning from church work as of today."

"I can't believe he harbored a past like that," Min-gu mumbled as he left Sŏng-ho.

As the two of them were walking out of the office of the Council of Elders Sŏng-ho had said to him, "You're wondering what was in the notebook, aren't you?" He had then related with comparative serenity the events that had brought about his downfall. "In short, I've been a coward all this time."

After giving up trying to find Mrs. Hong at the refugee camp on Kŏje Island, Sŏng-ho had learned that she was on Cheju Island and had decided to journey there any way he could. Because it was wartime, civilians couldn't travel on the boats, so he had gone as far as to plan to stow away. Luckily, though, he was able to notify Mrs. Hong through a soldier to come to Pusan in order to learn whether her kidnapped husband was dead or alive. It was all an expression of the spirit of genuine sacrifice and public service of his forgotten youth, as were the rented room and even the living expenses he provided her, through the kindness of his father. And then there was the time he had recovered the canned goods that had fallen overboard from one of the Yankee ships. To put her mind at ease he had told Mrs. Hong that he had been on the swimming team in middle school, but in fact he was a poor swimmer and a worse diver. But with no fear of dying, he had jumped recklessly into the cold night sea that shriveled his body, desiring wholeheartedly to make Mrs. Hong and her son Tae-shik happy. Young Sŏng-ho was satisfied with what he had done. And then that ridiculous misunderstanding that led to the overdose of sleeping pills. He was rather ashamed of that now, but at the same time the sense of shame made him feel somewhat polluted. That action was the epitome of purity. In plain words it was the result of jealousy, but at the time he had had no earthly concerns and wished only to disappear from the world. Mrs. Hong had recorded in her notebook then a mixture of horror and indescribable happiness. Some time later she wrote that she had hidden her Bible in a place where it would not catch her eye. They had become bound by a strong affection, undaunted by their difference in age. The next entry finally disclosed the thing that had terrified Sŏng-ho until now—the abortion of the four-month-old fetus. In this passage Mrs. Hong confessed that she was not sure they had done the right thing. But in the next entry she had written that they had not said even one word to each other about the abortion, but wouldn't it have been better to have given birth to the child? It wasn't that she wanted the child, but rather that people would have known, and she could therefore have avoided the hidden vexations that followed.

"It seems I missed my first opportunity to be brave," Sŏng-ho had said.

Min-gu had strained to listen, not saying a word.

Sŏng-ho had returned to Seoul with Mrs. Hong and obtained a house with the inheritance he had received from his father. His mother secretly sent him spending money. The house was registered under Tae-shik's name. At about that time Mrs. Hong's health deteriorated noticeably. If she stood for any length of time or walked even a short distance she would begin gasping and get dizzy. Sŏng-ho had her admitted to a hospital. A comprehensive examination revealed that she had progressive heart disease and that her nerves had been strained. She was subsequently released and readmitted to the hospital several times. Each time she would write in her journal that it was too painful knowing how burdensome her existence must have been to Sŏng-ho. At some point Sŏng-ho had begun to drink. Although he told her that it wasn't to forget things but to make them more vivid in his mind, he was in fact trying to escape the reality that confronted them. His sending her to Sosa to recuperate was something she had wanted, but Sŏng-ho couldn't rule out the possibility that he had done it in order to be away from her for a time. He wanted rest—mental and physical. Once a month he went down to Sosa. He had told himself it wouldn't be good for her health to visit more frequently. Why, Mrs. Hong had written, does he come only once a month, and why can't I tell him to come once a week? At the same time, she prayed that Sŏng-ho would leave her forever. If that happens, she wrote, I will endure it, whatever the price—no, I will try to endure it. In the middle of all this Sŏng-ho had another opportunity to be brave. More than a year after Mrs. Hong had gone to Sosa, Tae-shik entered college. Tae-shik was now older than Sŏng-ho was when he had first met Mrs. Hong. Sŏng-ho went to Sosa, and Mrs. Hong asked him how he would feel if she were to confide in Tae-shik, and no one else, about their affair.

"I couldn't agree," Sŏng-ho had told Min-gu. "When he was a kid he'd sometimes tell his mom 'Let's call him Daddy,' but I was afraid of him more than anyone else. So I let that opportunity slip away too. Who knows, things might have turned out differently if we'd told him. In the end, I'm the one who made her suffering worse. What I mean is, she had no chance of recovering, but I shortened her life. Entering the seminary didn't help her either. She couldn't put up with her distress, and she ended up tormenting herself. If you look in her journal, you'll see that she ate less and less. She went from three meals a day to two, and then from two to one. She wanted to make things harder for herself any way she could. I brought her back to Seoul and put her in the hospital. She was in for quite a spell, but it was useless. The doctors gave up on her, and when she got out of the hospital she'd already given up the ghost. She didn't want any light, any sound, any smells. She had thick curtains drawn all around the room—it was too dark for anyone else—and even then she sat under a black umbrella and wanted to plug up her ears and nose. I'm the one who made her like that. Why couldn't I have shown some courage in the first place? Why did I cling to face saving instead of being proud and letting everyone know about our relationship? If I'd done that we'd've been criticized by others for a while, but we wouldn't've made things as wretched for ourselves as they are today. And something else—when she passed away I wandered the streets with tears streaming down my face, but they were tears of relief rather than sorrow. That's how cowardly little Sŏng-ho was."

A smile of bitter scorn had risen on Sŏng-ho's lips.

Min-gu hadn't immediately offered consolation or encouragement. Instead he had asked, "What are you going to do from now on?"

"No plans as of now." Even so, Sŏng-ho hadn't appeared jittery or anxious.

Before leaving, Min-gu had explained that he too had been summoned to the Council of Elders. Sŏng-ho had nodded serenely.

Min-gu could have stopped at any of several bus stops, but he walked by them thinking about Sŏng-ho. It was amazing that Sŏng-ho had borne such great pain, he reiterated. But then why did Elder Han involve me in the inquiry? Min-gu could only conjecture that since Elder Han had known in advance of this affair, his power must extend even to the Council of Elders. Elder Han knew that Min-gu could be of no help to Sŏng-ho, for the matter of the essay in *The Christian Weekly* was secondary to that of the notebook. What, then, could have been his underlying motive? Perhaps he wanted to show me Sŏng-ho in this fix, since I was the one who recommended him and said what a fine man he was. At any rate, we'll find out before long what his reason was. But in the meantime I ought to watch my step. Seeing that the bus halting at the next stop was going his way, he ran over and boarded it.

PART III

Chapter 1

The pellets of snow sprinkling down seemed to have been sown all around rather than dropped from above. In the Taegwallyŏng region of Kang-wŏn Province winter was surely advancing several paces faster than elsewhere.

The snow really is different up high, thought Chun-t'ae as he looked out the window. Though the snowfall was sparse, it brightened the land in every direction as if momentarily halting the onset of dusk. The grains of snow hitting the ground bounced and rolled and gathered in hollows, giving them a singularly white appearance.

Chun-t'ae stepped outside the office with one of the other agricultural specialists, a man named Pak. The pellets hit their necks and rolled down their backs, chilling them. Though he realized less snow would come in if he held his head straight, Chun-t'ae kept his head slightly bowed and merely quickened his pace.

The man in the dimly lit guardroom put down his newspaper and rose to greet them. Past the guardroom and directly outside the front gate ran a national highway. On the other side of the highway ten-odd thatch-roof houses crouched in a line. Over the open hill stretching behind them were three farming

243

households, which couldn't be seen from the guardroom. One of them, occupied by a couple on the verge of old age, was where Chun-t'ae was boarding.

Chun-t'ae waited for Pak and the two of them entered one of the thatch-roof houses across the highway. As if resisting their will, the sliding door opened with a series of lurches. Serving the farmers scattered in the vicinity with foodstuffs and a variety of other goods, the shop was the only place in the village with panes of glass in its main door.

Chun-t'ae took down a bottle of *soju* from one of the shelves. The proprietor said that unless it's midwinter he doesn't keep *makkŏlli* because it may go bad. He then placed two glasses and kimchi in a space amidst the humble merchandise. As Pak had done several days before when he had treated, Chun-t'ae brought over a dried squid. Instead of asking the proprietor for this and that, the customers just take what they want themselves and tell him what they had when they pay up. The proprietor pushed a squat, earthen stove that he had been embracing with his legs towards them and then lit the kerosene lamp, raising and lowering the wick until it was burning at the lowest position possible. Finally he disappeared into the room at the back of the shop. Because it wasn't yet dark, the light thrown off by the lantern was sufficient.

"The snow's not that early this year," Pak said to Chun-t'ae, who was looking outside disinterestedly. "Some years it comes two weeks earlier than this."

"Sometimes it snows earlier than any other place, and I hear that when you get hit, you really get a lot of it. Seems to me I read an article last year about a heavy snowfall tying up everything for several days around here..."

"Yeah, the roads were blocked for about three days. That happens every so often."

"I'll bet there's quite a bit of damage from the snow."

"Well, avalanches are common. We didn't have many back when the trees were thick. But when the hillsides got stripped the way they are now, we had 'em pretty often. And then the floods in summer...I just don't know. Think about it. Caterpillars munch leaves, and human caterpillars chew up the trees, stumps and all—you can't even tell there was a forest there. It's bad enough when people cut off the branches of living trees because they've run out of firewood, but I tell you, this other business is organized deforestation."

Chun-t'ae was reminded of his friend's story about the theft of the trees in Kyerim, near Kyŏngju. "It's not just deforestation," he said.

"That's why it's a headache. They say in Germany they care for trees as if they were people..." Pak removed his glasses and wiped them roughly several times with his crumpled handkerchief. "Somebody told me there was a foreigner who was out hunting, and one of his shots landed in a tree. When he got back down the mountain, a ranger came up and said he'd have to pay since he'd injured tree number so and so. They stick a number on every tree. You just wouldn't believe how well those Germans take care of their trees. And it's not just trees but their towns that they take good care of. 'Cause if their towns get stripped of trees then they'd get to feeling empty, and if they were to get to feeling empty then they'd abandon their towns, right? Here I am getting carried away again. Whenever people start talking about trees I feel awful."

Chun-t'ae had often heard people talk about trees, but when the subject passed Pak's lips he was affected more deeply. The last time they were drinking Chun-t'ae learned that Pak had been born in a place called Hoenggye, which wasn't far away. He'd been working for nearly twenty years at the testing station here in Taegwallyŏng, which was very similar to his hometown. He had devoted much of his time to studying the spores of potato blight, and the years of peering into a microscope had damaged his eyes. He deplored the stripping away of the natural surroundings of his town, and perhaps that was why his stories moved Chun-t'ae so deeply.

As the two men exchanged glasses, a truck slowly went by on

the highway. Crawling along, its feeble yellowish headlights lighting up the pellets of snow, it resembled a decrepit animal.

"What's on your mind?" Pak asked, looking into Chun-t'ae's face. "Feel miserable thinking about spending the winter in a place like this?"

"It's not that..."

"It's too far out of the way, so..."

"I was thinking about something you said while we were playing *paduk*."[1]

"What was that?"

"You said that playing *paduk* was like living. In *changgi*[2] you can move a horse once and then move it again, but in *paduk* once you've put a stone down that's it. An interesting comparison, wouldn't you say?"

"I said that while I was playing *paduk?*"asked Pak with a laugh. "I'm afraid I don't remember."

"And doesn't the administration of a country tend to be more like *paduk* than *changgi*?"

After they exchanged several more glasses of *soju*, the glass-paned door lurched open and an elderly man with a bundle under his arm stepped in. The bus for Kangnŭng had apparently arrived. The elderly man and Pak exchanged simple greetings and then, just before the proprietor came out of his room, Pak turned up the wick of the kerosene lamp. The man bought a large box of matches and went out, and the proprietor went back to his room.

Several circles appeared on the thick lenses of Pak's glasses in the light cast by the slightly raised wick.

"Mr. Ham," Pak said, but instead of looking at Chun-t'ae he

---

[1] *Paduk:* a game for two players on a board on which black and white stones are alternately placed, the object being to block and surround the opponent's stones and thereby control the larger part of the board; it is called *go* in Japan.

[2] *Changgi:* a game similar to chess; it originated in India and came to Korea by way of China.

lowered his head as if he wanted to remove the circles from his glasses. "Who's supposed to take care of their hometowns? It's the young people, isn't it? Yet they continue to leave. There's nothing else they can do. But you know, they'll have to return someday. And when they do, they'll have to take an interest in the deforestation of their towns. They've got to."

Remembering that the son of the farming couple with whom he was boarding had also gone elsewhere, Chun-t'ae said, "If I may ask, have you ever thought of leaving here?"

"Why shouldn't I have?" Pak picked up a strip of squid and chewed on it. "And not just once or twice. When the time came, though, I just couldn't do it. You see, I had this thing called a microscope. Those potato-blight spores got into me and they haven't let go. Anyway, did I hear right that you came here on your own?"

"Has that been going around?"

"Well, now that would be more of a riddle than why I can't leave. Don't you think?"

One of Chun-t'ae's colleagues in Suwŏn had been transferred to this testing station, but Chun-t'ae had come instead. Pak didn't seem interested in unearthing more than that, and Chun-t'ae remained silent, as if there were some mutual understanding between them.

"So this is where you've been," the guard from the testing station said after opening the sliding door with a lurch. It seemed the snow had changed, as flakes and not pellets spotted the guard's hair and shoulders. "You have a visitor, Mr. Ham. I thought you'd gone home, so that's where we went."

"Is that so. Well, I appreciate it." Chun-t'ae accepted the message calmly, even when the guard said, as if appending a footnote, that the guest was a woman. It was as natural as he and Pak emptying and filling their glasses, as natural as the kerosene lamp becoming a bit brighter as the surrounding gloom deepened, as natural as the room becoming more drafty despite the earthen stove.

"Well, I guess you'd better go," Pak said, adding the finishing touches to the atmosphere in the shop.

Not until it was completely dark did Sŏng-ho close up the barrel-shaped stove in which he baked sweet potatoes over charcoal briquettes. After leaving the ministry he had sold cement blocks that he had stamped out himself with a mold beside the ditch that ran by the settlement of shacks where he was now living. But with the advent of winter he had become a vendor of baked sweet potatoes.

Sŏng-ho enters the alley leading to his shack. The shanties lying jumbled together to his right and left are bristling with vitality. Having scattered in the morning to make their living, the people have converged on the neighborhood again.

Upon reaching his shack, the very last one in the alley, Sŏng-ho looks into the hole where the charcoal briquettes are burning in his open-air cooking range. Before leaving the house that morning he blocked up the vent as much as possible without extinguishing the fire, and the briquettes are still burning as they were then. With the onset of evening, the air has suddenly become colder, but Sŏng-ho leaves the stove as is and enters the shack. The interior is about seven feet square. Sŏng-ho makes do with the rice he prepared for both breakfast and dinner. Then, taking a parka out of the bundle on the shelf and putting it on, he goes out carrying a sack. He must buy some sweet potatoes.

Just before he slips out of the alley, he hears a man's rough voice entangled with the squalling of a woman coming from one of the shacks. At the side door a boy squats, sniffling. It's almost an everyday scene. Sŏng-ho walks faster.

He steps out of the alley, and a street opens before him. It marks one end of the shanty neighborhood and the beginning of a residential area.

As Sŏng-ho crosses the street toward a store that sells sweet potatoes, a woman darts out of the gloom and approaches him. "I've got a pretty girl for you," she says in Chŏlla Province dialect. It's a woman who has accosted him several times at about this hour. Realizing that he's the man who never responds to any of her proposals, she doesn't use any of her tricks but disappears, arms folded, into the darkness. Sŏng-ho walks a little faster. He doesn't know that she's the woman who caused him to regret his insincerity some time ago — the woman walking down the middle of the road to Stone Village, her entire body drooping, unconcerned that her limp, rain-soaked *ch'ima* had slipped down so low that her dragging feet were about to tread on it; the woman who didn't get out of the road when a truck was bearing down on her, its horn blaring, until Sŏng-ho pulled her to the side. For some reason she had worn an expression of deep pain. Sŏng-ho had heard the following day that she and her son had been poisoned by gas from their charcoal-briquette stove and had been taken to the hospital that night. He had interpreted it as a suicide attempt rather than an accidental gas poisoning. He had regretted not having helped the woman the previous day. The woman had survived, and here she was. Even if Sŏng-ho had recognized this pandering woman, he could only have regretted that he was now unable to help her, much less make up for his previous insincerity.

Leaving Sŏng-ho, Chŏnju Auntie concentrates only on catching the next customer. Another big fat zero today, she thinks. What's gonna happen? I've gotta get at least one customer back to the hotel. Her job is to guide customers to one of the shacks or to the hotel, according to their desire. If it's one of the shacks she receives a tip of fifty *wŏn,* if the hotel then one hundred *wŏn.* Chŏnju Auntie shivers. She approaches Uk-i's mom, who has been hanging back in the darkness, and says in her Chŏlla accent, "It must be snowin' somewhere, it's so cold here." Uk-i's mom takes the baby she's carrying on her back and gives it her breast.

Chŏnju Auntie walks past Uk-i's mom and takes a cigarette from her waistband, lights it, and takes three or four drags before extinguishing the match. She walks a short distance, stops, and looks below a street light—Kŏl-i has hooked onto a customer.

Kŏl-i goes into his spiel: "She's brand new, mister, a virgin just off the train this mornin'. If I'm tellin' a lie you can rip my mouth out." Please, Chŏnju Auntie thinks, if the kid can only get him to one of the shacks, it'd be the first break we've had today. As a matter of fact, Kŏl-i's score is better than hers. However, the man shakes Kŏl-i off. Chŏnju Auntie is disappointed, but Kŏl-i hums a tune:

> I'll never want it
> Never even wanna laugh...

Some time before coming to the alpine testing station Chunt'ae had gone to Seoul and met Chi-yŏn. It was a blustery afternoon. They met at a tearoom in Sŏsomun and then strolled along behind Tŏksu Palace. Frail sunbeams slanted over the high stone wall running in back of the palace. I don't know how many times I've walked along this street, Chi-yŏn said, brushing back the hair streaming down her face. Chun-t'ae was not familiar with it, but Chi-yŏn had had to walk it morning and evening to attend a girls' high school in the area. I enjoyed it especially in the evening, she added. It was not quite evening, and Chun-t'ae felt that although they had no destination they had come here on purpose. His eyes traveled again to the high stone wall rising up against the wind. The stones had been set elaborately, and their facing was square and straight. In places the joints between the stones were new. When I passed by here, said Chi-yŏn with a laugh, I always thought I'd like to use this wall as a net and try hitting the ball against it. Chun-t'ae also laughed, saying, That's pretty greedy. The way you talk, it sounds like you'll take over everything under the sun. Do you still get the urge to play tennis? A while back, Chi-yŏn answered, I started playing every morning again. What, you've got something on your mind and you use tennis to get rid of it? Chun-t'ae asked. No, it's something I enjoy doing after I've cleaned out my mind. So if you get those complicated thoughts again you'll quit playing? No, I don't think I'll quit because of that—I made up my mind about some things

I've been mulling over. They walked past Kyŏnggi Girls' High School and reached the foot of a pedestrian overpass in Kwanghwamun. Chi-yŏn hesitated momentarily. You go first, Chun-t'ae read in her smiling eyes. Listening to the fluttering of her coattails as they crossed the overpass, Chun-t'ae swallowed the thought that he ought to be acting as a windbreak for her. When they parted that day, Chun-t'ae had still not told her that he was thinking of moving. I haven't decided where to go yet, so why not inform her when I've settled in a new place? he had thought. But it was now a full ten days since he had come to the alpine testing station. To notify her with a letter would have left something to be desired, so he had made up his mind to go to Seoul and meet her. In the meantime, Chi-yŏn had come to see him in this out-of-the-way place. He had not expected it. But he wondered how it was that he could accept this surprise so calmly. Perhaps some intuition, difficult to explain, had taken root in his mind.

Chi-yŏn merely said she had heard that the testing station was in Hoenggye and thus had gotten off the bus at the wrong place—she was late because she had come on the following bus. She didn't ask why there had been no word from Chun-t'ae, nor did she mention that she had gone all the way to Suwŏn, only to find that he was here. She seemed to be able to fathom what Chun-t'ae had been doing in the meantime. She knew that Chun-t'ae's failure to communicate wasn't a sign of disinterest or a means to an end. It was just that he wasn't as sophisticated as others in expressing his feelings, and this lack of sophistication was as much a part of him as the smell of his body. Chi-yŏn couldn't help feeling more intimate with Chun-t'ae because of this. Mutual exploitation did not figure into their relationship. In the darkness redolent of mud-plastered walls they entwined their bodies, licking each other's hidden wounds.

The next day was cloudy. The snow had stopped and the temperature was pleasant.

Even without the sun the scant snowfall of the previous night started to melt, and during the morning it vanished, leaving the ground moist.

"I'll take over for you tonight," Pak said as he came over to Chun-t'ae, who was cleaning up his desk. Since it was Saturday, work was over at noon, but it was Chun-t'ae's turn to remain on night duty at the office. Pak hadn't asked who Chun-t'ae's visitor was. He hadn't even seemed curious. "If you want to go on a short trip you ought to go to Wŏlchŏng Temple," Pak said matter-of-factly. "It's not the right time of year to go to Kyŏngp'odae in Kangnŭng. It'd be better to go to the temple. In its own special way that area still has a kind of old look about it. And it's not far from here. If you call Kangnŭng, a taxi'll come right away."

The taxi sped along the road to Hoenggye. Though not overly rough, the road was slightly muddy from the melted snow.

After crossing several hillocks and arriving at a bridge, the taxi turned right and began traversing the side of a valley. Linked fields of mulberry trees lined both sides of the road for tens of meters. The skies cleared and the sun lit up the peaceful valley. Wet with the melting snow, the moss on the rocks had become bright green. When Chun-t'ae or Chi-yŏn looked somewhere, the other would instinctively look there too. Both were in high spirits, as if they were going on a picnic.

At last a forest of firs appeared through the windshield. Just before the road entered the forest, the taxi stopped beside a building. The driver tells Chun-t'ae and Chi-yŏn that they have arrived. Seeing a hotel sign through the window, they think he has selected this particular hotel for them, but then he tells them it is the only hotel in the area. Indeed, no other dwelling could be seen.

There was neither fence nor gate to the hotel. Rounding a corner of the building and entering a spacious yard, Chun-t'ae and Chi-yŏn discover a second building facing it. Each building has four or five rooms. All of them appear to be empty.

They call for the proprietor, and a middle-aged woman emerges from the cloud of vapor rising from the kitchen of the building closer to the road.

After settling on a room, the two of them ask directions to Wŏlchŏng Temple and go outside.

Both sides of the road were occupied by bosky stands of firs, unmixed with other trees. Two arms joined could barely encircle any of them. As Pak had said, there was a look of antiquity here—no trace of logging caught their eyes.

The gloom created by the shade of the trees filled the surroundings except for the occasional places where the rays of the setting sun feebly broke through the thick, heavy branches. It was a cozy dusk. Chun-t'ae and Chi-yŏn looked at each other and smiled. It was good they had come here, their eyes said.

The road remained wet. It appeared to be because of the shade, not the snow. Though they had no idea how much snow had fallen here last night, they could see that the treetops were wet, as if they had absorbed it all.

After walking for five or six minutes they arrived at the foot of the steps leading to the temple. A map showing Wŏlchŏng Temple and all the other temples on Odae Mountain was displayed on an information board.

Upon climbing the steps they were surprised to see only the foundation of the temple. The temple was being reconstructed, and building materials littered the courtyard. Although it appeared the monks were being quartered temporarily in a barracks at a corner of the courtyard, not a soul could be seen. Chun-t'ae and Chi-yŏn realized that they hadn't met a single person on their way here.

After they descended the steps, their feet seemed to develop their own momentum, taking them where they pleased. The forest gradually thinned, and they saw many stumps. This was clear evidence of logging.

The twisting road coiled around the side of a mountain. To their left, the stream embraced by the bends in the road alternately withdrew and approached.

Lacking a destination, they were about to turn back at a spur of the mountain when Chun-t'ae saw a squat, thatch-roof hut in a clearing about two hundred meters from the other side of the stream. The hut and its surroundings, shaded by the mountain, were engulfed in a gloom deeper than that of the forest. Chun-t'ae glued his eyes to the hut. Whether from suffering or from ecstasy—he couldn't tell which—his chest began to throb. He didn't care who lived there. Strangely, he was disturbed by the notion that the hut wasn't old, and would not become a fixture there.

"Do you suppose it's a slash-and-burn farmer?" Chi-yŏn asked, her gaze overlapping Chun-t'ae's.

"Hard to say..."

"Or an herb gatherer?"

"Hard to say..."

"It looks lonely."

Whether it looks lonely or not isn't the question, thought Chun-t'ae. At the same time he couldn't understand the throbbing in the depths of his heart. He turned to Chi-yŏn. "What was that you ended up saying about colors?"

"Oh, then you heard that?" Before being cut short by the sight of the hut, Chi-yŏn had been saying that she always described life in terms of colors.

Chun-t'ae nodded. "First of all, I think it was black for the Korean War, white for the time you were playing tennis, and then ash-gray for..."

With a look of concentration radiating from her dark brown pupils, Chi-yŏn replied, "Do you know that Giacometti sculpture *City Square?* I've got a print of it hanging in my room..."

Even while Chun-t'ae listened to Chi-yŏn, the image of the hut remained in a corner of his mind.

"The people in the plaza are walking toward the center, but they aren't gathering in one place and they aren't meeting to talk with each other."

Chun-t'ae had to force himself to pay attention to what Chi-yŏn was saying.

"Every time I used to look at those sticklike people oppressed by solitude I felt ash-gray." Chi-yŏn paused for a moment. "But some time ago it began to look different. At some point those people in the plaza would surely group together and begin talking. I didn't feel any color from then on."

"That's kind of like girl talk."

"Infantile, isn't it? I'll tell you something even worse."

Chun-t'ae waited expectantly.

"I was in that kind of mood—colorless as the air—when I made up my mind about something I'd been hesitating about."

As Chun-t'ae looked at Chi-yŏn a gentle smile floated over her face. Her profile is beautiful, Chun-t'ae thought. Her face was telling him something—that's the way we met, and now we can talk like this—and Chun-t'ae realized that these words were dissolving him. That feeling I had when I was looking at the hut was merely an illusion. Why should I have to avoid what I am now? Like breath finally released, happiness washed over him, enlivening him. He placed his arms on Chi-yŏn's shoulders. Immediately her body drew close. Chun-t'ae's chest tightened and a spasm of coughing overwhelmed him. Exhaling became difficult, and he squatted down in a ball, his fingers raking down Chi-yŏn's body. Surprised and bewildered, Chi-yŏn began to rub Chun-t'ae's back, which was jerking as he tried to free himself of the continuous coughing and choking. She rubbed more and more vigorously. The knotting in Chun-t'ae's chest became unbearable. He wanted to tell her to stop rubbing, but the words wouldn't come. Finally extricating himself from her, he staggered to the base of a nearby tree. Wrapping an arm around the trunk, he leaned forward as the choking continued. Chi-yŏn approached, wondering what to do, but Chun-t'ae motioned stiffly to keep away. Hearing the gasping noise being wrung from his throat, Chi-yŏn realized she was powerless to help him. Frustrated and perplexed, she could only look on.

The fit ended. Exhausted, Chun-t'ae remained motionless,

his head touching the base of the tree. Chi-yŏn took out a handkerchief and dabbed at the perspiration dripping from his face. His lips and the tips of his nose had become pale and cold. She gripped his hands. Even his fingertips had become white. The heartache was too much for her, and she closed her eyes.

When she opened them they were filled with tears. "Are you all right? Has this kind of thing ever happened before?"

"Yeah. It's the second time." But Chun-t'ae didn't tell her that this time it was more severe.

They returned to the hotel and saw several pairs of men's and women's shoes lying outside the door of a room in the building farther from the road—more guests.

"Been looking around the temple?" asked a middle-aged man they had not seen before. He was sitting beside the kitchen on the wooden platform at the entrance to the rooms. "There's nothing to see here, unless maybe you go to Sang-wŏn Temple. I dunno, it got burned down during the war and I thought they'd finally gotten their asses in gear and started rebuilding it, but then there were foul-ups, and now look at the shape it's in, things laying around every which way. Can you believe it?"

Annoyed by the man's blather, which seemed about to spread, Chun-t'ae pretended not to listen.

Chun-t'ae and Chi-yŏn went into their room, and before long their dinner table was brought in. The side dishes were primarily mountain vegetables, such as *tŏdŏk,*[1] aster, and fiddleheads. Tucked among them was a bowl of soft bean curd. Perhaps the steam that had been rising from the kitchen when they first arrived had been produced during its preparation. But Chun-t'ae's appetite had forsaken him and he merely picked at the food.

Not long after the kerosene lantern had been lit, Chi-yŏn laid out a bed and made Chun-t'ae lie down. Sleep seemed to

---

[1] *Tŏdŏk: Codonopsis lanceolata,* a vine with thick roots that are used for medicine as well as food.

come easily to him. She put out the lantern, and in the darkness his outline was barely visible. It may have been just her imagination, but his chest, covered by the quilt, looked somewhat sunken. No matter what happens, she thought, we'll go to the hospital tomorrow morning and get him examined.

Sensing that Chun-t'ae was awake, Chi-yŏn discovered he was putting on his clothing piece by piece. His actions were cautious, intended not to disturb her sleep. Worried, she asked where he was going and whether she could light the lantern for him. It was all right, he replied; he was just going to slip out to the toilet.

The toilet was quite a distance behind the inside building. The sound of water washing against stones in the stream flowing down the valley behind the toilet was louder than in the daytime.

As Chun-t'ae was about to reenter the room, he turned toward Wŏlchŏng Temple as though drawn by something.

He groped his way along the dark road. A smattering of starlight hung from the tops of the trees in the black forest. Chun-t'ae passed the temple and kept walking. Finally he arrived. He gazed across the stream to where he guessed the apron of the mountain was.

The gloom of the mountain seemed to blend with the gloom all around, and from this blackness came a low, tiny light, tinged with yellow. For a long time he watched the feeble light, which made him feel that the surrounding darkness was even thicker. The light and the darkness advanced upon him. They became one with him and began moving. Somewhere he was crawling up a bare, desolate, rock-covered mountain, then he was staggering endlessly across a vast, barren plain. Chun-t'ae stood there, staring at the scene.

On his way back to the hotel he met Chi-yŏn, who had come out to look for him.

After changing into her nightgown and removing her makeup, Ch'ang-ae takes a bottle and a wineglass from the cabinet. Every night she relaxes over one or two glasses of wine before going to bed. Now that she is managing the dressmaking shop by herself, she is busier than before—serving the customers, looking after the workshop, and from time to time visiting the places in It'aewŏn and Hannam-dong where she obtains the foreign-made clothing demanded by her customers. She feels more zestful managing the shop alone, and the business has become more lucrative. Ch'ang-ae had gotten a good deal in buying out Mrs. O, and her half of the proceeds from Chun-t'ae's sale of the house had given her the wherewithal to carry on independently.

Ch'ang-ae takes another sip of wine. It appears Mr. Kang won't return tonight either. It's been almost twenty days since they began living together on the second floor of the shop. During that time Mr. Kang had been concentrating markedly on his work. Ch'ang-ae checks whether the maid has put Mr. Kang's rice bowl under a quilt on the heated part of the floor to keep it warm. Then it strikes her that with her husband she had never bothered herself with that sort of thing. In the end, living together isn't something that's done according to a formula. The day before, she had met Ŭn-hŭi on the street. Ŭn-hŭi had a particular interest in her and Chun-t'ae, and was startled when Ch'ang-ae told her of their divorce. So it finally happened, she had said, making no secret of her sympathy for Ch'ang-ae. Sure enough, Ch'ang-ae's husband hadn't severed his relationship with the other woman, and the marriage had broken down. Ch'ang-ae hadn't denied this, for to have done so would doubtless have been taken by Ŭn-hŭi as bravado. How much more difficult it is, Ch'ang-ae thought, for a third person to understand such a subtle state of affairs between a man and a woman.

Ch'ang-ae's thoughts expanded to the couple she had to visit in the foreigners' compound in Hannam-dong the next day. The man, an American, was easily fifty and the woman looked barely twenty. She was short, and her thick makeup gave her swarthy face a greenish tinge. But when Ch'ang-ae thought about this woman, what she remembered most was her feet. She was always barefoot, and her painted toenails were always bordered with dirt. And she chattered. In front of Ch'ang-ae she would talk spitefully about her husband in her Kyŏngsang Province accent, saying nothing of consequence. The husband, with his enormous body, silver hair, and blue eyes, would shrug his shoulders, smile awkwardly, and look at his wife as if she were cute. Perhaps she wants to show others their relationship, Ch'ang-ae thinks. Otherwise, why would she ask me to drop by only on Sunday, when her husband is home? In any event, it was clear that a third person could not criticize what went on between a couple. The prospect of visiting this woman the next day and having to haggle with her over every item made Ch'ang-ae gloomy. Promising herself that some day she would stop this sleazy business of going around to the foreigners' compound, she goes to the dresser and looks at herself in the mirror. Not too bad, considering how busy life has been. But then she glimpses a shadow of loneliness in her eyes. She looks squarely at her eyes, searching for any traces of the shadow, and then empties the wineglass.

The extension phone in the bedroom rang. It was the film company where Mr. Kang worked. "Something urgent's come up, and Mr. Kang hasn't been around since the day before yesterday," said the voice at the other end. "We're in a fix." Presuming he would be there at night, they had called late. "Isn't there anywhere we can reach him?" But Ch'ang-ae had no way of knowing where he was. She thought he had been busy at work.

After putting down the receiver Ch'ang-ae poured herself another glass of wine. It had become painfully clear to her that Mr. Kang had devoted no time at all to his movie sets over the past two days.

At that moment Mr. Kang was with Miss Chŏn at a bar. Miss Chŏn was dipping a fingertip in a glass of *yakju*[2] and doodling

[2] *Yakju:* a slightly refined rice wine, somewhat stronger than *makkŏlli.*

on the table. Because of her tipsiness her eyes had become ringed with light purple. One or two glasses of beer was her limit, and this was the first time Mr. Kang had seen her drink several glasses of *yakju*.

Miss Chŏn suddenly lifts her head. "Take a guess what this masterpiece is."

Mr. Kang sucks away at his pipe without listening.

"A snail. It's a drawing of that man sitting way over there. The one who looks like he's bearing the pains of the whole world all by himself. Thinks he's a Socrates. I like Clint Eastwood better. Simple, no aftereffects."

Mr. Kang silently blows smoke in Miss Chŏn's face. Miss Chŏn purses her lips and blows the smoke upwards, and after stirring her *yakju* with a chopstick she tosses it down. Mr. Kang tells himself that the way she drinks is better than he expected. There is a trace of bitterness in her smile.

"I'm gonna get drunk today. Drunk as a skunk. Liquor doesn't ask any questions. I like it like that. Only liquor understands how I feel."

"Are you going to be all right drinking like that?"

"Getting scared? Afraid I'll ask for a piggyback ride later on? Even though they flunked me, I won't give you a hard time about it. I've got enough class for that. So the cast is all filled. I'm not good enough." Miss Chŏn snorts. "They don't know a big star of the future when they see one. That scummy director, when he met me he looked me over like he'd taken all my clothes off, drooling..." Her voice is clear, considering the amount she has drunk. "I know, we're taught that whatever the competition, it's more important to play fair than worry about winning or losing. But that's just a way of patting yourself on the back when you lose. First of all you have to win. Win at everything. Losers don't get anything, except maybe darkness. Grownups make a big deal about how you have to have the right attitude and do your duty, but you can't see anything in the dark. Losers try hard to show they've got something, but—"

"What's your problem? Who're you trying to lecture?"

"So my performance is clumsy. You're gonna give me the thumb's-down, is that it?" Miss Chŏn laughs mischievously. "Would you be so good as to allow me one more word, Your Excellency? I wanna win. Win, I said. I'll win no matter what it takes. Okay, in order to boost my morale I'm..."

Mr. Kang persuades Miss Chŏn to leave, and they slip down a narrow alley. Miss Chŏn scuffles along, one arm entwined in Mr. Kang's, the other holding fast to the bag slung over her shoulder.

"You'll be okay if I get a taxi for you, huh?"

"Where to?"

"Whaddya mean 'Where?' To your house."

"No. I don't wanna go home. Anywhere except home. Take me along."

"Well, where're we supposed to go?"

By previous arrangement, the taxi that had brought Chi-yŏn and Chun-t'ae to the Wŏlchŏng Temple area picked them up the next day. But instead of getting out at the testing station they went straight to Kangnŭng.

After listening to Chun-t'ae's description of his coughing fits and giving him a comprehensive examination, the doctor said conclusively, "If there's nothing more than that, then it's asthma. Did you happen to have a bad cold before the first coughing fit?"

"No."

"How about soreness and swelling in the throat?"

"No."

"When you were little did you ever break into a rash after eating eggs, milk, fish, or anything like that?"

"Not that I can remember." Chun-t'ae had grown up not eating eggs, milk, and similar foods.

"Do you tend to smoke a lot?"

"About a pack a day."

"Now the first spasm you had, was there a smell—for example, a musty smell or a flowery smell?"

"Hard to say. I was out walking early in the morning, and suddenly it was hard to breathe...I can't remember seeing any flowers."

"And the second time—you said it happened in the mountains? Were you by any chance feeling uncomfortable because of the cold air?"

Recalling that there were no problems when he returned to see the hut at night, when the temperature had fallen, Chun-t'ae said, "No. Can't say that I was."

"It looks like asthma resulting from an allergy. We'll have to find out the cause. From now on, if you feel you're about to have a spasm, look over the surroundings real carefully. We can't fix you up until we find out the cause and get rid of it."

"I see," Chun-t'ae responded inattentively. He had his own vague hunch as to the cause. But he couldn't put it into words, nor did he want to. At the same time, he caught a glimpse of something frightening—a thick shadow blocking his vision.

"I'm going to give you a shot, and also some medicine. But unless we get rid of the cause we can't cure you completely, and in fact you'll get worse, little by little. And then..." The doctor wanted to say something but stopped.

After giving Chun-t'ae an injection the doctor asked him to cough up some sputum, but no matter how Chun-t'ae tried, nothing came up.

After obtaining some medicine Chun-t'ae left the hospital with Chi-yŏn, who had been sitting anxiously in the waiting room. To prevent her from worrying, he talked lightly about his symptoms.

Relieved to see Chun-t'ae's normal demeanor, Chi-yŏn dropped by a fruit store and bought some tangerines, apples, and other fruits. She then asked for a place where coffee was sold and went there and purchased a bottle.

At first Sŏng-ho couldn't hear it clearly, but then he detected the low, muffled voice calling him from outside. Since it was Sunday, he and the other vendors were taking the day off.

Sŏng-ho had returned from church, which was a considerable distance from the shanty neighborhood, and was reading a book.

He opened the side door and P'yŏng-i's father bowed in greeting. There was someone behind him. Sŏng-ho's eyes widened. It was Tae-shik. P'yŏng-i's father knew where Sŏng-ho lived, for he had transported his belongings here, but Sŏng-ho couldn't help being astonished at the sight of Tae-shik: How clever he was to follow P'yŏng-i's father here.

Chapter 2

"Can you guess who sent mother's journal to the Council of Elders?" Tae-shik spat out defiantly. "It was me. I'm the one who gave it to them."

P'yŏng-i's father had left when Tae-shik entered the room. Thinking he had been too indifferent to Tae-shik all along, Sŏng-ho asked him if he had finished his military service, to which he curtly answered "Yes." When Sŏng-ho said he must have had a hard time of it in the service, Tae-shik just sat silently for a while and then burst out.

"What did you say?" Sŏng-ho raised his voice in spite of himself but soon regained his composure. In fact, when the journal was first brought to light, he hadn't ruled out Tae-shik. After all, he was the one most likely to have seen it first. Even so, how could he have revealed his mother's secret to the world by sending that notebook to the council? Besides, what was the need? Sŏng-ho immediately put aside his suspicions.

"It was a bad thing to do, wasn't it?" said Tae-shik.

Sŏng-ho looked directly into his eyes, which were bordered with thick lashes. Two of their features were more prominent today: their size, inherited from his mother, and their gleam, inherited from his father, Pastor Chŏng. Sŏng-ho had always delighted in those eyes when Mrs. Hong was merely the wife of his respected minister and Tae-shik their cute little son, but after those boundaries were destroyed, it was with anxiety that he was forever having to confront them. Now they were faintly bloodshot, as they had been since he began talking.

"I'm sure you're cursing me, wondering why I didn't get rid of the thing instead of pulling something like this," Tae-shik said. He looked at the floor. "When I first discovered it among

264

Mother's belongings I thought I'd burn it, but after reading the whole thing I decided I'd have to do something else with it."

What could have made this young man come to such a conclusion? wondered Sŏng-ho.

Tae-shik's eyes bored right through Sŏng-ho.

"The two of you loved me very much. No other parents on earth could have loved me as much. And I was aware of it. I've known all about your suffering ever since I started to grow up."

Even though Tae-shik was now referring unhesitatingly to his mother and Sŏng-ho as a pair rather than as separate individuals, it didn't make Sŏng-ho uncomfortable.

"Mother's efforts not to damage Father's reputation or yours, or mine either, and your choosing divinity school to expiate your sin—I knew everything. But I didn't stop with just knowing. I tried to understand the two of you, even though you didn't bother even to confide in me. But what was the idea behind that confession of hers? Didn't Mother leave that journal behind so that she'd have a heavier cross to bear? I know the record she left in that journal must have been torture. I felt pity for her while reading it. But you know what I thought when I finished? Why wasn't Mother a little more candid with herself? Why not a little more humane? How could she dare try to bear a cross that a human could hardly bear? When I thought about such things I got angry. I couldn't stand it. Maybe I was too young. Or maybe I just didn't know anything about the world."

So he got angry? And his mother's penance seems like mere sentiment to him? Sŏng-ho wanted to shake his head in denial, but instead he said, "What your mother did redeemed her completely."

"Redemption? Did she have to redeem herself to the point of hastening her death? Was it what God wanted? To me it was nothing but vanity. So I sent the notebook to the council to satisfy your vanity."

In Tae-shik's tone Sŏng-ho sensed a rage he had never seen in him before. Already the look of his mother's eyes and the gleam of his father's had vanished; Sŏng-ho felt only unfamiliarity entangled with the rage and pain.

"At any rate, that notebook woke me up, and it changed me," said Sŏng-ho in an undertone. "It saved me from being a coward. I guess I've been redeemed as well." Unfazed by the glare of Tae-shik's bloodshot eyes, he concluded, "It's been a priceless experience."

"What a bunch of hypocrites!" Tae-shik stormed out of the house. Seeing the ditch running beside the shanty neighborhood, he took out the notebook, which Pastor Shin had returned to him, and without regret hurled it into the water with all his might.

Ŭn-hŭi frames her body in the mirror. As she expected, the dress from Ch'ang-ae's shop appeals to her. Picking up her handbag, she looks at her reflection from various angles. The face in the mirror smiles subtly at Min-gu, who is standing to the side. For several days Min-gu had been busy with something, but they are finally taking some time before the evening service to go house hunting.

Ŭn-hŭi locks the door to her room and sticks her head into the living room. "I'll be back, Father." But then she hesitates.

There's a visitor in the room but that's not the cause of Ŭn-hŭi's hesitation—it's her father's expression. Her father's usually gentle face, which is always smiling, is now stern and cold. He's frightening when he's like this. Thinking she ought to protect her father from the visitor who has made him that way, she suddenly gestures to Min-gu to step inside the room with her.

Taking no notice of her, her father speaks to the thirtyish man kneeling before him. "Do you know what kind of money it is? It's God's money. Not my money, I tell you, but God's money."

"Please look at it as if you were saving this young guy's life and be patient a little while." The man kept his reddened face lowered. "I'll get it back for sure, and repay you right away."

"Uh-uh. How many times do I have to tell you before you

understand? That money's only what God entrusted to me. God doesn't want it to be returned late. If I don't receive that money on time, God'll become angry and take away everything he's entrusted to me. And you think that's all right? Nonsense! If you don't repay me on time I'll have no choice but to take care of it legally."

"I'm doing this because I see some good prospects once I've gotten over this crisis. Please be patient a while."

"What can I say? It's God's affair, not mine." Her father's voice was harsh.

"First clear up the debt and then use what's left to try to get back on your feet."

"But if I settle the debt now, there's no way I can get back on my feet. Please, just this once..."

Paying no heed, Elder Han says to Ŭn-hŭi in a gentle voice, "Don't make a rash decision after seeing only one or two houses. Tell me about them first."

"All right."

Making Min-gu go first, Ŭn-hŭi withdraws from the room.

As they are leaving the house Min-gu says, "I wish he'd help him out a little."

"What are you talking about? Father's right," replies Ŭn-hŭi in a cutting tone. And even the change in his expression, which I've never seen before, was proper, she thinks.

Min-gu refrained from speaking his mind as they looked at houses that day. Although he tended to favor a wide yard over a large house, he allowed Ŭn-hŭi's taste for an attractive residence to become the prime object in their search.

By deciding to follow Ŭn-hŭi's inclinations as much as possible, Min-gu meant to offset his regret at being bound in a relationship that involved more than just Pyŏn and the recording of shaman customs.

After looking at several houses, they stopped simultaneously, charmed by three climbing gourds hanging from the second-floor veranda of a Western-style house removed from the main road. If it hadn't been winter, they would have taken the gourds for living plants. The hairlike projections from their stalks were visible, as were the veins of their leaves, and the greenish color around the stems descended to the bellies and gradually lightened to a natural tone, as gourds do in season.

"I feel strange when I see fresh-looking gourds like that at this time of year," Ŭn-hŭi said as she gazed at the plants.

"Yeah."

"And isn't it marvelous the way they're made? I can't distinguish an artificial flower from a real one these days. If things keep going on like this, I'm afraid the fake'll be the real thing, and vice versa."

"Anyway, isn't it good that we can see flower during any season?"

"Artificial flowers are good like that, but it's different with people. We have to distinguish clearly between the fake and the genuine. But men are all idiots—that's what I say. They can't distinguish correctly, so they end up straddling a fence, unable to jump one way or the other. Someone like Mr. Ham's a good example. He must be out of his mind. He couldn't even recognize the real thing. How on earth could he have let that chic wife of his get away?"

Ŭn-hŭi passed on to Min-gu what she had heard from Ch'ang-ae upon meeting her on the street. Min-gu was shocked, having heard nothing about the divorce. Ŭn-hŭi regarded Chi-yŏn as the cause of the divorce and accordingly blamed Chun-t'ae for his failure to judge people correctly. Min-gu agreed, telling himself that Chi-yŏn had cast a pall over Chun-t'ae and Ch'ang-ae. But on the other hand, there may have been something else involved, and he wasn't ready to blame Chun-t'ae unconditionally. Anyway, he would soon visit his friend whose marriage had ended in pieces.

"And Mr. Ham isn't the only one," Ŭn-hŭi said suddenly. "How about Reverend Yun? I heard he was fired from the ministry. If he hadn't stepped out of line, Father would've arranged a good position for him..."

Min-gu prickled. Everything around him was upside-down.

Sŏng-ho, suspecting Min-gu might be wondering about him, had called to tell him of his whereabouts before telling anyone else, and Min-gu had payed him a visit. He was utterly unable to understand Sŏng-ho. It seemed he was trying to atone for everything through a new life of penury. "Doesn't your father have a large business in Pusan? If you feel uncomfortable speaking to him directly, I could go see him for you," he had offered, but Sŏng-ho had stubbornly refused.

"And by the way, your speaking up for Reverend Yun before the Council of Elders—what was that all about?" asked Ŭn-hŭi.

Min-gu prickled again. Perhaps I did overdo it a little that day, he thought. Well let's forget about it. Elder Han didn't send me to the Council of Elders to help Sŏng-ho. He wanted to warn his future son-in-law to watch his step by having him witness Sŏng-ho's predicament. And then there was the scene he had just witnessed at Ŭn-hŭi's house. Min-gu told himself again that he would have to be a bit more careful in his dealings with Elder Han.

"In any event, men are not to be believed." Ŭn-hŭi declared, as if handing down a judgment.

"Including me?" Again Min-gu prickled, but he smoothed over the situation with a laugh from his big mouth.

Min-gu's attendance at the Sunday evening worship was another way in which he acceded to Ŭn-hŭi. But today he took her home by taxi as soon as the service was over, and after refusing her invitation to come inside for a short rest by saying he was late for an appointment he couldn't avoid, he had the vehicle turn around and take him away.

Ŭn-hŭi stood there. Shutting the door of the taxi and taking off like that was no way to see her home, she thought. Before the taxi had disappeared down an alley, something occurred to her and she looked around almost absentmindedly. At that moment an empty taxi came toward her from the alley. She hailed it and climbed in. Not caring what the driver might think, she urges him to hurry, saying she is chasing someone. But her taxi can't catch the yellow one carrying Min-gu. After three or four more blocks of vain pursuit, Ŭn-hŭi listlessly directs the driver to turn around and take her home. She pays no attention to the driver's searching gaze in the rearview mirror. All that talk about being busy is just a cover-up, she thinks. He's hiding something from me. I'm sure of it. And it's not just one or two things I can't figure out. He avoids my eyes when I look him in the face. He never used to do that. And that crazy laugh of his when I least expect it. Nothing makes sense. He makes me sit there in a tearoom twiddling my thumbs for oh so long, then tells me it's nothing when he finally comes in, but then he can't sit still. And the more I think about it, it's strange the way he concedes everything to me—no strings attached—and follows my suggestions. And today, when we were looking at those houses he didn't have anything to say at all. Sure men change just before they get married, but this is too much. I think he's hiding something...Men are not to be believed, they just can't be believed.

That night Pyŏn, his bluish upper gum disclosed by his smile, greeted Min-gu in a yellow-green *chŏgori* and *ch'ima*. The cuffs and collar of the *chŏgori* were trimmed with purple, and a purple bow hung from the front. Pyŏn never failed to impress Min-gu as a woman welcoming a man she had been waiting for.

A bottle of Western liquor and some snacks had been set out for them, and after a couple of rounds they began performing the music and dances of a *kut*. Min-gu was excited to have started, two days before, to learn the ceremony by practicing it.

Having finished the *pujŏng kŏri*, the first of the twelve stages of the ceremony, they were to turn to the second stage, the *kamang kŏri*. In the *pujŏng kŏri* they had ritually cleaned the area where the various spirits would descend and sit, and in this next stage they would pray for a response from the spirits.

Min-gu sits and taps the hourglass drum, following Pyŏn's chants and movements. Pyŏn begins with a recitation and eventually changes to song. Spreading his arms wide, he dances to the rhythm.

The phrases of the song are beautiful:

> With a *kayagŭm* we'll prepare a bridge for you to your hometown of Yangsan,
> Which of the twelve strings of the *kayagŭm* shall you cross?
> We'll make it pleasant for you with a *tŏnggidŏng* sound on the string...

Flushed with excitement, Min-gu puts down the drumstick and rises. Pyŏn immediately takes over the drum—*ta'anggidagi, tangttagda'agi, ta'anggidagi, tangttak...*

Min-gu opens his arms, bends and then straightens his knees, makes circles to the left with his bottom, folds his right arm toward his chest, raises one shoulder then the other, bows and twists his head, quickly straightens his right arm to the outside and folds his left arm toward his chest, makes circles to the right with his bottom, and repeats these movements, concentrating all the while on his knees and shoulders.

"*Ŏlsshigu!* There you go!" Pyŏn shouts, trying to spur him on.

Feeling his hardened body relax more and more, Min-gu becomes elated. Not long before, he had been singing a hymn with Ŭn-hŭi in church, and now he was singing a shaman chant and dancing—but he had no second thoughts about it. He felt only that his performance had become natural and convincing.

Pyŏn flung more praise: "Great! That's the way to dance!"

Min-gu worked his body more feverishly.

After the performance they again shared some drinks, and then Pyŏn prepared a bed in the room where Min-gu had stayed the first time.

That night Pyŏn came and performed the same act and then left as soon as he had finished. Again Min-gu couldn't fathom Pyŏn's secret, and with lingering regret he fell asleep.

The next morning, as before, he is awakened by Pyŏn's voice as he consults with people who have come to have their fortune read. Lying prone, he lights a cigarette. Inhaling deeply, he thinks how he has become addicted to the world of shamanism.

It's cold, so the children from the shacks are gathered as usual in the sunniest spot—in front of the barbershop at the corner of the main road, at the end of the shanty neighborhood. While they are jabbering over what sort of game to play, the barbershop's patchwork wooden door flies open. Clippers in hand, the barber scowls at the children and shouts, Goddamn sonsabitches, everyday makin' a racket, you'll be the death o' me yet. Why cantcha get lost!

The children run off in a herd. Kŏl-i alone remains, staring the barber in the eye. Whaddya have t' get all red in the face for? he says. You blind, ya goddamn sonofabitch? asks the barber. He makes as if to give chase, crippled leg and all, but merely goes back inside.

Having discovered a source of amusement, Kŏl-i rips open the door of the barbershop. Hands in his pants pockets and chest out, he shouts, Hey Lame-leg! Us kids are playin' out there. What's the big idea, goin' nuts like that? Then Sung-i, who had run away with the others, comes up beside Kŏl-i and joins in: Hey Lame-leg, give us a lurch. Lurch for us, Lame-leg... Among the children, Kŏl-i and Sung-i are always the leaders; whatever the game, they're the ones who divide the others into opposing teams. At the same time, they're close to each other.

The man in the barber's chair smiles and reasons with the boys, asking them to behave. The barber merely looks askance at the two of them in the cracked mirror.

Kŏl-i becomes more furious: C'mere Lame-leg! Why no answer? Ya dead or somethin'?

Feigning indifference, the barber finishes trimming the customer's hair and brushes him off. Then suddenly he comes alive and starts after the two boys. They nimbly avoid him. The barber lurches in pursuit, but every time he tries to grab Kŏl-i, the boy runs just far enough to avoid his hand.

Sung-i remains some distance off, imitating the gait of the

barber and shouting, Lurch, lurch...

The more vexed the barber becomes, the more he lurches. Lurch, lurch... Sung-i runs circles around the barber, continuing to imitate him, but then he trips on a stone and falls. The barber jumps on him. Grabbing him by the scruff, he twists and shakes him unmercifully. Goddamn sonofabitch, I been waitin' for this, yessir! The barber begins to strangle him. Sung-i's face reddens and his breathing becomes choked. Unable to stand it any longer he wrings a plea from his throat: I promise I won't do it again. There's a thunk and the barber falls—Kŏl-i, who had been biding his time, had butted him in the side.

The barber struggles up and hefts a rock, but someone is standing in his way. A man fightin' with kids—what's goin' on here? says the newcomer. The barber glances at the man and then disappears inside his shop without a word.

Medalman sure showed that guy who's who, Kŏl-i thinks. He grins at Medalman in his black suit and red tie—his clothing is always neat. The man approaches Kŏl-i and gestures to him. The children watch in envy as Kŏl-i walks toward the man and looks up in elation at the long vertical scar on his left temple. It's because of the decoration awarded him for that scar that Medalman's been tagged with his nickname. Kŏl-i is proud that he's close to him.

You'll hafta go another round, says Medalman. After leading Kŏl-i around the corner, he gives him a piece of paper and quietly explains the map that's on it. Then he takes a small envelope from his pants pocket and gives it to Kŏl-i. Tonight, eleven o'clock. Got it? he says once more to make sure.

"That was a long phone call. What's going on?" asked the old vendor. Sŏng-ho had been calling the hospital about Myŏng-suk. "In the meantime, I flipped over the taters a couple o' times. It mustn't 've been very pleasant. You look worried."

"Yeah, well..."

Even after Sŏng-ho had suspended all his previous affairs and begun his present life, one thing continued to tie him to the past—Myŏng-suk's illness. Regularly he visited the hospital or called to check on her condition. She had been all right the last time, but the news today wasn't good at all. There were new symptoms involving flowers. An incident from Myŏng-suk's days of selling flowers with her mother appeared to have worked its way up from her subconscious, the head doctor had explained.

Repeatedly muttering something about flowers, Myŏng-suk had taken a chrysanthemum that someone had given her, laboriously picked the petals off one by one, filled the floor of the ward with them, and then, sitting amidst them, mumbled for half a day or so, "It's my money, my money. No one can touch it." Then she had suddenly thrown off her clothes, lain face up, and inserted the denuded stalk of the chrysanthemum into her vagina. No matter how the nurse attempted to dissuade her, she lay there unconcerned, mumbling "It's spring now and I'd better grow the plant again. Mommy'll come then and it'll have lots of blossoms."

Even after the doctor had finished his explanation, Sŏng-ho remained beside the telephone. Since the symptoms of mental illness cannot be predicted, it's not impossible for improvement to occur even after a regression, the doctor had said almost consolingly. Yet his cool voice left Sŏng-ho with a sense of foreboding.

A feeling of helplessness tugged at Sŏng-ho until he went to bed that night. He'd given Myŏng-suk too much of a shock the day he'd rushed over to her house after hearing she was being initiated as a shaman, and he was besieged by remorse over the fateful mistake.

He tried his best to sleep, but was drawn to the voice of a drunken man in the shack behind. Sŏng-ho guessed from the sound of the door opening and closing that the woman living there had latched onto a man and brought him back. The woman looked well over thirty. Thin wrinkles scored her forehead and the corners of her eyes.

—— Hey young stuff, who're you talkin' *panmal*[1] to? the woman said rather forcefully.

The man said something in a low voice.

—— Cantcha see? I'm pro'bly ten years older, said the woman with a low laugh.

—— Don't show off.

For the first time Sŏng-ho could understand the man. Perhaps she's right, he thought. His voice has a boyish pitch.

On other nights when she had brought men home, Sŏng-ho had paid no attention and fallen asleep. Because of the proximity of the walls of the shacks, sounds carry well from one to the next on a quiet night, but little by little Sŏng-ho had ceased being concerned about this. His thoughts returned to Myŏng-suk. There she was, staring at him, the stalk inserted in her nude body. Sŏng-ho avoided her gaze. Again he tried to sleep, but the clear voice of the man in back pulled at his ears.

—— Don't you wanna die with me?

In spite of himself, Sŏng-ho listened attentively for the reply.

Without giving the woman time to answer, the man spoke in a slightly louder voice:

—— You don't wanna die, is that it?

—— I've done died several times already.

—— Do it once more.

—— How come you wanna die?

Her tone told Sŏng-ho she thought the idea was ridiculous.

—— Life is tough.

The man's voice trailed off.

—— You think everyone's alive 'cause that's the way they want it?

—— That's why I'm sayin' let's die together.

—— Now look here. Take a look at me. Even the likes o' me is still alive, right?

—— You never wanted to kill yourself?

---

[1]*Panmal:* A low form of speech, used between intimates, by parents to children, by superiors to subordinates, and so forth.

—— Didn't I say I've already done it several times? But I'm gonna try like hell to keep on livin'. I'm gonna fight to the end with this damn' world that made me like this.

The man's voice was too low to be heard.

—— What the hell. It's better than robbin' people. 'Cause even though I'm sellin' my body I'm makin' a livin' with my own sweat.

Again the man's voice was inaudible.

—— I thought as much. Okay, there's some water. Take 'em and go ahead and kill yourself.

For a while Sŏng-ho could hear nothing. He sat up, afraid something had happened.

At that moment the woman spoke in a loud voice:

—— Whaddya doin'! Don't act like no damn idiot. I'm still livin', and look at me. Like I said, we gotta be tough and keep on goin'.

Then there was the stifled sound of the man's sobbing.

—— Okay, c'mon over here. I'll get you a good night's sleep.

There were no more words from in back.

Sŏng-ho put his mind at ease. There's no readymade solution to life, he reflected. The only way is to connect the links of the chain, one at a time, toward a solution. The sincerity of a woman, artless to the point of pity, has made a young man connect one humble link to the chain. Could I have done the same thing for him? Sŏng-ho didn't feel confident. Countless unconnected links floated here and there in front of his closed eyes. Can I find the links for Myŏng-suk? For a while longer Sŏng-ho couldn't sleep.

Kŏl-i easily finds the house to which Medalman's map directed him. As he reaches the wall of the house, a dog on the other side barks. But Kŏl-i is composed, having just gulped a bowl of *makkŏlli*. When no one is around, the proprietor of the Mini Taep'ojip[2] pours Kŏl-i a bowl without a word and Kŏl-i

[2] *Taep'ojip:* a drinking place featuring inexpensive food and liquor.

drinks it on the spot, but when other customers are present, he pours the bowl saying, "Your mother must have an upset stomach again," and Kŏl-i takes it outside and drinks surreptitiously. For as long as Kŏl-i has been pulling customers off the streets at night he has been hoodwinking his mother by deducting some of the tips.

Kŏl-i opens the envelope he received from Medalman and takes out a cotton ball with a piece of string attached to it. Holding the end of the string, he tosses the cotton ball over the wall. Shortly the barking stops. Kŏl-i knows. The cotton ball has been smeared with fluid from a bitch in heat.

Kŏl-i pulls gently on the string. When he guesses the cotton ball is about halfway up the wall he begins to pull it up and down. He hears the dog jumping up after the ball, and he concentrates on that sound. When he's worked the dog to a fever pitch he gently pulls the cotton ball back over the wall. As he expected, the dog quickly leaps over the wall after it. It was a large black mongrel. It's in the bag, Kŏl-i thinks. He throws beside the cotton ball a piece of pork with a fishing hook inside, which he had taken from the envelope. The dog nuzzles the cotton ball for an instant and then moves its snout to the piece of pork and devours it. Kŏl-i immediately jerks on the line to which the hook is attached. The dog flinches and holds back, stretching out its front legs, but then walks toward Kŏl-i, its neck extended. The fishing line is not thick, but a dog whose throat has been hooked can't resist being pulled by it. Kŏl-i quickly puts the cotton ball back in the envelope and stuffs it in his back pocket. There's no need to keep to the alleys now. Any street will do, as long as there aren't too many passersby. Though the fishing line wouldn't catch anyone's eye at night, Kŏl-i still takes this precaution. Occasionally the dog balks, but then with a low whimper of pain, it follows more docilely. Kŏl-i merely walks on coolly, not even looking back.

The bridge over the large ditch next to the shack settlement comes into sight, and then the shadows of two men, one atop the bank and one at the bottom. The one above is Medalman and the one below, Highpockets.

To keep the dog in tow, Kŏl-i walks slowly as he descends a set of steps to the stream at the bottom of the ditch. He whistles twice toward the bridge—the signal for success. The shadow atop the bank doesn't move; the shadow below bends over and then straightens up as before. Kŏl-i walks more slowly toward the underside of the bridge. Highpockets stands motionless, like the trunk of a tree. Kŏl-i passes in front of him in a stately manner. Just then he hears the sound of a heavy object colliding with something, and a single yelp soars up from the ground. Highpockets has flung the large rock in his arms directly atop the dog's skull. Kol-i turns around just in time to see Highpockets pick up the rock and smash it down again on the skull of the wriggling dog. Without pausing, Highpockets begins to roll the dog up in a straw mat. Oughta be worth four or five thousand *wŏn*, he mutters.

Happy to have safely completed the adventure, Kŏl-i looks back again at Highpockets and then climbs the bank. Medalman stands as still as before. Kŏl-i takes the envelope out of his back pocket and hands it to him. Unable to contain his pride any longer, Medalman tousles Kŏl-i's hair. Kŏl-i titters in satisfaction.

Chapter 3

Chi-yŏn couldn't believe her eyes. At first she couldn't recognize the man in the drab quilted clothing standing next to the barrel-shaped stove. His face, darkened by the sun, had grown haggard and thin—he was altogether a different man. It was only the ambience of his body—and that barely—that told Chi-yŏn it was Sŏng-ho. Her astonishment and pain upon learning of the change in his life were revived by the sight of him. She just stood where she was, her throat tightening.

Sŏng-ho turned around, as if nudged by ripples generated by Chi-yŏn's breath.

"Whoa, now who's this?" It was the same unreserved tone as always. "You know, I was about to try calling you again. You went on a trip somewhere, didn't you?"

At Sŏng-ho's cheerful welcome Chi-yŏn smiled and approached him.

"How did you find out I was here?"

"From Mr. Song just now. Why didn't you tell me earlier, so I could have come before now?"

"I guess it just worked out that way. Anyway, is this your first time to visit an area like this? Now let's see...they don't even have tearooms around here," Sŏng-ho said, looking around.

"That's okay. The first thing I want to see is an example of your baking skills."

The two of them could not have exchanged smiles more easily.

Sŏng-ho selected a sweet potato from the stove, expertly transferred it from one hand to the other until it was cool, and handed it to Chi-yŏn. Fearing that she would be uncomfortable eating alone, he picked one up for himself and said, "You know, someone who hasn't baked a sweet potato can't appreciate the way I feel when I cook one evenly so that the inside's light yellow and the outside's slightly burned." He chuckled.

Chi-yŏn swallowed the warm sweet potato. Her heart had also become warm. What in the world does the church do? she asked herself. Is it a place where people's inner selves are judged right or wrong, with nothing in between? Yet it wasn't these questions that had warmed Chi-yŏn's heart but Sŏng-ho's having stood strong after absorbing an enormous bruise.

"Your face seems a little pale," said Sŏng-ho.

"I haven't been feeling so good the last few days."

"Better take care of yourself. I myself haven't been sick, and thanks to that I can put up with everything... Hey, here comes Yŏng-i."

A girl with her fingers in her mouth comes to a stop in front of the stove. She's four or five, with round eyes and an oval face. The sky-blue sweater she's wearing isn't overly worn.

"Didn't I tell you it's no good to suck your fingers?"

The girl promptly removed her fingers from her mouth.

"Yŏng-i likes the ones that've cooled off." Sŏng-ho took one of the sweet potatoes on the edge of the stove and gave it to her.

Without a word the girl turned around and went hop, hop, hop into an alley.

"I can't believe how happy she is..."

"She's a sad case," said Sŏng-ho.

"When she got that sweet potato... How can someone be that happy?"

"I just wish I could solve all her problems with one or two sweet potatoes... Well, Miss Nam, as long as you're here, why don't we go to my place? Then you can see how I get along these days."

"Fine."

"Grandfather, could you keep an eye on this for me again?" Sŏng-ho said to the old vendor next to him as he removed his gloves.

Chi-yŏn followed Sŏng-ho into the shanty neighborhood. They walked down a narrow, twisting alley strewn with charcoal ash and other rubbish. Chi-yŏn brushed past a woman; without intending to do so, they had looked into each other's eyes. The woman's face was expressionless, yet it made Chi-yŏn all the more aware that she wasn't a resident of this area.

In the distance, Yŏng-i was eating her sweet potato and touching the stovepipes she passed.

"The people here are worse off than the people in Stone Village. I feel fortunate that I came here. If I hadn't, then I would've missed out on too many of the realities of life, realities that I never would've imagined. I got kicked out of the church, but I should've left long before. The people here are fighting their way through the pits of existence, and I didn't realize till coming here that to them religion is a luxury. I've decided not to do any mission work. First of all, it doesn't sink in, you know?"

Yŏng-i touches every stovepipe she passes. Most of them are rusty, crumbling affairs made from crushed cans connected together and in some cases overlapped with the flattened casings of artillery shells.

"You wouldn't believe her family background—a real hard-luck case. There's just her and her mom—they came to this slum after I did. A day doesn't pass that she doesn't come see me. Sometimes she has a five-*wŏn* piece in her hand, but usually she's just got her fingers in her mouth. One day she came running over, crying her heart out. 'Mommy's dying,' she says. So I went with her—it was the only thing I could do—and there was her mom clutching her stomach and rolling around on the floor. It was terrible. I found out later she'd been beaten, pregnant and all."

Yŏng-i only touched some of the stovepipes but rubbed her hand back and forth over others.

"When Yŏng-i's mother told me her story, I was amazed. Yŏng-i's dad lives in Japan, and the kid her mother's pregnant with is his son's. You got it? It seems Yŏng-i's dad is a well-known businessman among the Korean residents there. For a while he was going from Seoul to Japan and back almost every month. He struck Yŏng-i's mom as being resourceful and warm-hearted. She got to know him at the nightclub where she used to work—he probably flashed his money around. About a month after Yŏng-i was born he came for a visit, and not long after he left, a young fellow arrived. He told Yŏng-i's mom that he was the son. He could roughly understand what people said to him, but he couldn't speak Korean very well. He said he'd come to Seoul and gotten into college, and that he'd been on the baseball team since high school. And then the trouble started. They hadn't been living together for even half a month when he raped Yŏng-i's mom. His father hadn't sent any money for his tuition, not to mention living expenses, and now the kid had gotten her pregnant. She made up her mind to kill herself."

"That's too much, really... But tell me, why does Yŏng-i brush her hand along all of those stovepipes?"

"She's looking for a warm one... Her mom wasn't a bit scared of dying, she said." I know a little about that too, thought Sŏng-ho. Far from being fearful, the thought of lying dead in a grave in the mountains was very peaceful. "So one night she went out, cool as could be, and went around to all the drugstores buying Seconal. When she got back home and was about to take the stuff, though, it occurred to her that it might be too bitter to swallow. That would've fouled up everything, so she had the presence of mind to go out and buy a bottle of orange juice and take the Seconal with that." Sŏng-ho remembered how he had lain down, wrung out and languid. Thinking he had better use a pillow, he had crawled over to the cabinet and barely pulled one down. But he was unable to position the pillow under his head. So he had tried to put his head up on the pillow, but despite his best efforts, he couldn't get it at the proper angle, and the pillow ended up under his shoulders. He had moved his body around straining to get his head square on the pillow and then lost consciousness. "She woke up three days later in the hospital, and somewhere along the line she had a miscarriage."

"Seems people can't die even when they want to."

"They sure can't... So to make a living, the only thing she could do was go back to work in a beer hall. At the same time, she had a change of heart; she'd have a child, but this time it would be a son who would get revenge for her. Isn't that silly? She must have wanted it badly. So this past summer she got pregnant by the young fellow again. He was dead set against her having the child and told her to have an abortion, but she wouldn't listen. And that's when the beating started. His excuse was that it was enough of a burden to have one child underfoot, but a second one would hinder her from going out and making money. She couldn't stand it, so she sneaked out and ran away. After hiding around she ran out of money and ended up here."

"It's hard to believe... The father and son must've cooked it up."

"Exactly. The son'd brag that his father was a smuggler and that he was a hoodlum. He said his father had been deported from Korea and had gone to live in Japan, and that if he couldn't make a living there, then they'd go to another country to live."

"So what's going to happen to Yŏng-i and her mother?"

"Hard to say... You know, they're not the only ones with a checkered past. Once I get going on this I can't stop... Okay, we're here." Sŏng-ho opened the side door and went in first, bending at the waist. "You can bring your shoes in with you."

Chi-yŏn hesitated.

"You must be surprised," said Sŏng-ho with a laugh.

But it was just that Chi-yŏn's eyes hadn't yet adjusted to the darkness of the room after the brightness of the outdoors.

"There has to be a special reason for someone to come to a place like this. Come on in."

Chi-yŏn stepped into the room.

"I couldn't come inside right away either, the day I moved here. But it's okay—it's livable. When the people here were born, they were no different from you or me. There's a saying that poverty's a sin. But being poverty-stricken isn't entirely the fault of the people here."

The room had a low ceiling but fresh wallpaper that made it more tidy. On a shelf on the warm part of the floor was a folded quilt and next to it a bundle of Sŏng-ho's belongings. There were more than thirty books, piled up in two stacks. Four apple crates filled with dirt took up a large space on the cold part of the floor.

"Miserable to look at, isn't it? But you wouldn't believe how peaceful I feel here." Noticing that Chi-yŏn had focused on the apple crates, Sŏng-ho said "They're plant beds. First I'm going to grow pepper, cucumber, and tomato sprouts in them. Then I plan to make a greenhouse out of plastic next to the ditch where I used to make cinder blocks. There are so many kids here who have nothing to do but play, and they only end up learning how to get into trouble. I'd like to put them to work with me on the greenhouse. Like I said before, the first thing is to make a living, and then we can turn to religion or whatever. Gee, am I pretending to be a frontiersman? I guess I'm chattering like this because it's been a while since I've seen you. Now it's your turn. I haven't heard anything about your trip yet."

"I went to the Taegwallyŏng area."

"Huh? Taegwallyŏng? When it's this cold?"

"I guess you didn't know that Mr. Ham was transferred to a testing station there."

"Oh?...Well, how about that. I see, I see."

To Chi-yŏn the words "I see" carried many implications. For a time the two of them remained lost in thought.

"By the way, Miss Nam, there's something I have to apologize to you for." After a pause Sŏng-ho continued. "You probably don't know that I went to see Mr. Ham about you. I went so far as to advise him to think over his relationship with you—can you believe that? Perhaps it was because I didn't want the two of you to end up like me."

Chi-yŏn suddenly lowered her head, feeling she was about to cry. First there was Sŏng-ho's consideration—he always seemed to be revolving around, protecting her. And then there was Chun-t'ae—although he had listened to Sŏng-ho he had given Chi-yŏn no indication that they had talked. At last Chi-yŏn said, "Actually Mr. Ham and his wife had already ended their relationship."

"You don't have to tell me about that now. I regretted going to see him as soon as I'd done it. No two relationships are the same. And I think that's even more true of the relationships between men and women. When I looked at your situation in terms of my own, I realized it was absurd to do what I did. Anyway, did you inform your parents?"

"Not yet..."

At that moment the door was ripped open and a young woman came tumbling in.

"Help me, please."

Startled, Chi-yŏn looked at Sŏng-ho.

Sŏng-ho seemed unperturbed, as if he knew what kind of woman she was and why she was asking for help.

"Quick! I said I need some help."

Only then did she realize she had come in the room with her shoes on. She took them off and placed them in a corner.

Sŏng-ho took a Bible and hymnal from the top of the piles of books. After opening them and putting them on the floor, he began singing a hymn.

"Not that one. One that I can sing along with. I know a few of the ones they sing at Christmas," the woman said hastily. Then, without waiting for Sŏng-ho to reply, she began singing,

"Joy to the world, the Lord is come..."

Sŏng-ho switched to that hymn.

"Let earth receive her King..."

The woman knows no more words, and as Sŏng-ho's voice gradually takes over she merely mumbles along, following the melody. Sŏng-ho picks up the hymnal, finds the song, and places the book in front of the woman.

The woman looks at Chi-yŏn, who is still somewhat bewildered. Her gaze is intense. Chi-yŏn begins to sing in spite of herself.

There's murmuring outside, and then the door is flung open and a man's head is thrust in.

"And heaven and nature sing..."

For an instant he sweeps the room with his eyes. Then he slams the door shut, muttering "What a bunch—so crazy about Jesus they think Christmas is right around the corner."

As soon as they finish the hymn, the woman peers at the Bible, which Sŏng-ho had opened randomly, and reads in a faltering voice:

By the waters of Babylon,
There we sat down and wept,
When we remembered Zion.
On the willow there
We hung up our lyres.

Looking up from the Bible the woman says, "I don't get what they're talkin' about."

For a while she listens attentively for movements outside. Then she stands up, saying "I've gotten rid of 'em, the sonsabitches! They don't even feed me." And with scarcely more than a thank you she picks up her shoes and disappears.

"Pretty bold," said Chi-yŏn in amazement. She finally understood what kind of woman this was.

"It's because they have to get by any way they can... They even rush in in the middle of the night." Sŏng-ho searched in the Bible for the verse following the one the woman had read.

For there our captors
Required of us songs,
And our tormenters, mirth...

Overlapping the words on the page was the scene of a

woman inching her way through the muddy wastewater in a dark sewer pipe. Two days before, the newspapers had reported that upwards of twenty people had escaped from Hope Farm, a detention camp for wayward women; less than ten had been captured.

"I guess I'll leave now." Chi-yŏn stood up.

"I'll go with you. By the way, you said you hadn't informed your parents yet?"

"My father looks quite upset. Maybe he suspects something..."

"If that's the case, you'd better hurry up and tell him. Would you like some help?"

"No, don't worry. I'll take care of it somehow."

Chi-yŏn got in the car and began a long wait for her father. True, she'd had several X rays taken, and it would be a while before he could find out the results of her examination. But Chi-yŏn was seized by the unpleasant suspicion that this was not the only reason for the delay. The endless stream of people looked especially healthy. Chi-yŏn took her eyes from them, stretched her legs to the side and leaned back.

The day she returned from seeing Sŏng-ho, she had unburdened herself to her parents about Chun-t'ae—something she had long wanted to do. Until then, it had been too difficult to broach this subject. But she had also wanted to order her thoughts some more. Does Chun-t'ae really need me, and am I being honest with myself about my feelings for him? she had wondered. It was while she was trying to settle such questions once and for all that she had visited Sŏng-ho, and it was during their conversation that she had obtained some confirmation. I guessed that, her father had said, as if he had sensed her inner change and emotional travail—something Chi-yŏn had suspected. It's kind of late to be telling us, he'd continued, but I'm glad you've spoken candidly. Chi-yŏn had thought he would be very upset, but instead he had been generous toward her. That had made her feel worse. Her mother, however, was a different story. After all, we parents just give birth and raise our children, and they go one way and we go another, she had said. Then she had left the room. Chi-yŏn had taken these grievous words rather lightly, though. That night her mind was full of dreams she couldn't single out, and the next morning she couldn't get up. For several days she felt generally indisposed, and had a dull headache combined with a chill. At first she had thought it was the mental and physical fatigue that follows the release of tension. But on the second day she was bothered by the same symptoms. On the third day, when she felt slightly better and was about to get up, her father came up to her room wearing his usual expression and without saying anything else suggested that she go to the hospital for a complete checkup. So here she was at the same hospital she had always come to.

Her father finally came out of the hospital. As soon as he got into the car he told the driver to go to the Secret Garden. It's a fine day, and as long as we're out we might as well get some fresh air, he said to Chi-yŏn, who studied his face and wondered why the Secret Garden all of a sudden. She remained silent, having concluded that the results of her checkup were probably bad.

There were few people to be seen in the Secret Garden, whose vistas had opened now that the trees had shed their leaves. Three Westerners photographing each other in turn caught their eye, as did a young man in a Western suit ambling about a pavilion with an old man in traditional clothing.

Chi-yŏn's father walked along quietly, looking in all directions. "It's so nice," he murmured.

The two of them walked without speaking along a path strewn with leaves. Then her father said, "I do believe I hear a tiger roaring."

Ŭŏhŭng, ŭŏhŭng. The roar carried to them from Ch'ang-gyŏng-wŏn through the transparent air.

Again her father was silent. After walking a bit further, he fixed his eyes on a sign and laughed. "Ha, really now—how could that be three thousand *ch'ŏk*?[1] It's not even three *cha.*"[2]

Chi-yŏn had come here with friends and had also seen this sign and laughed. Carved on a rock barely three *cha* high was "Three thousand *ch'ŏk* straight down flies the water" in Chinese characters. When Chi-yŏn was here before, there was at least some water purling along and dropping over the rock, but now even that bit had dried up and the place looked the worse for it. Although it may have been this baby waterfall, which Chi-yŏn's father wasn't seeing for the first time, and the exaggerated line inscribed beside it that made him laugh, there was a tinge of emptiness to the laugh that didn't blend well with the scene.

"Whatever you have to say is all right, Father, so please tell me," Chi-yŏn said at last.

"It's not very good news."

"I know." Chi-yŏn's voice trembled even though she had prepared herself for this. Controlling her breathing, she continued, "Tell me in detail."

"Mmm...they say you're in danger of having a relapse of your caries. It's not a certainty but a possibility. Of course it's also possible that you won't have a relapse."

"Did they say, then, that I shouldn't get married?"

"No, they didn't come right out and say that, but..."

"But what?"

"They said you couldn't have children."

Although Chi-yŏn had expected unpleasant news, she couldn't help feeling heavyhearted upon hearing this.

"I'll meet young Ham," said her father, as if ending the conversation.

Again they heard the *ŭŏhŭng, ŭŏhŭng* of the tiger.

They left the Secret Garden and got in the car. Because of

---

[1]*Ch'ŏk:* a measure of length equivalent to 30.3 centimeters or 0.944 feet.
[2]*Cha:* a pure Korean word having the same meaning as *ch'ŏk* (a Sino-Korean word).

her father, Chi-yŏn strained to keep composed and stared out
the window. Seeing a sidewalk newsstand, she asked the driver
to stop and buy one of each newspaper. She scanned the movie
sections and then, tracing a small advertisement with her
finger, said, "Why don't we go see a movie. It's something we
haven't done for a while." There was a Western playing at a
third-rate theater.

Chi-yŏn rarely went to Westerns, even if they were appearing in Seoul for the first time. And the film was in poor condition, scratched and cut. But as she sat in the hard, uncomfortable wooden seat, her eyes on the screen, she thought it
was time for her to do what her father had done at the Secret
Garden. So she laughed or gasped in surprise at unremarkable
scenes and occasionally whispered to her father: "Isn't he marvelous with that gun?" "Wow, how'd he manage to save his skin
that time? I thought he was done for." Then the screen curled
up before her eyes and she could see nothing. It wasn't the film
but her eyes. It wouldn't do to dab at her tears with her handkerchief or the back of her hand because her father would see.
Let them dry up by themselves, she thought. I want to see
him. I want to see him more than Father does. I want his decision.

Why would he want to be transferred to such a remote area?
Min-gu wondered. But that's Chun-t'ae for you. Could it be
he's trying to experience the nomadic mentality of Koreans he's
always carrying on about? Or is he running away with that
woman Chi-yŏn? Hell, I don't care. All a person can do is get
along the best way he can, and it's no concern of mine.

His trip to Suwŏn to see Chun-t'ae had been a wild-goose
chase, so Min-gu was now going to visit Sŏng-ho on his way
home. Only by venting his feelings to someone could he begin
to unburden himself. Ŭn-hŭi had apparently called his apartment twice—once last Sunday night, when he had gone to
Pyŏn's, and then again early the next morning. He had said
he'd slept at a friend's because it was late, but Ŭn-hŭi didn't

believe him, and besides, their cold war of several days had not yet lifted. He had hoped Chun-t'ae could sympathize with him, but he had also thought he could dispel his gloominess over drinks with his friend. But that plan having fallen through, he decided he might as well visit Sŏng-ho, for he couldn't bear the thought of keeping his feelings bottled up.

"Always searching for enlightenment, even this late in the day."

"Hey, step right up. Now you're just saying that because you've never tried to sell anything. You'd think otherwise if you actually tried it."

"You'd even *buy* trouble, and feel you were getting something out of it."

"Wanna try one?"

"Why don't you save it? The kids'll give you some snotty money for it. Why in the world do you make a point of buying trouble for yourself? If you go on like this, we'll have Jesus being born in Korea some day."

"There you go again."

"I'm afraid you've got the wrong idea about Jesus."

"What's this all about?"

"I decided to get in an argument today. So don't hassle me and just answer the questions, okay?"

"What do you want me to answer, Pal?"

"I think the life of Jesus is just a symbol."

"Go ahead. I'm listening."

"Yessir, just a symbol. I say some people misinterpret this symbol, and you're one of them."

"Keep going."

"You listen now. If it isn't a symbol, then why would God have his son Jesus born in a manger of all places? Why did Jesus have to fast in the wilderness for forty days before he could win his trial with Satan? And why did he end up having to be nailed to the cross? Why? Why? He's the son of the Almighty God and no one else, you know. In other words, God's love for humans was shown through the symbol of Jesus.

Isn't that it? Therefore, people are feeling God's love through the symbol of Jesus, and at the same time they're getting consolation and sympathy, and that's all there is to it."

"And so?"

"In spite of that, there're many humans who voluntarily undergo penance, figuring that if Jesus suffered those tribulations then shouldn't they suffer them more? Just like you. So what's the point of using Jesus to symbolize God's love for humans?"

"What if my present life gives me consolation and enjoyment?"

"Don't make yourself say that. You make yourself think it's consolation and enjoyment, but they can't be the real thing."

"It's going a bit far to say I'm making myself think that," said Sŏng-ho with a smile. "Actually it's difficult for one person to understand another. Everyone has a different way of thinking. And it helps if people can feel they've gotten something out of their thoughts."

"At any rate, if you really believe in Jesus, then change your attitude toward the way you live."

"What's the point? Why're you saying all this?"

"First of all, there's no need to bind yourself to the church's decision. It's all right if you have another love affair like the one with that minister's wife."

"Are you in your right mind today?"

"Take this fellow Chun-t'ae. He got divorced without blinking an eye, and now he's run away with another woman... Don't you envy his attitude? Just getting along in life the best way he can?"

"He's been suffering too."

"Do this and it's suffering, do that and it's suffering. Why don't you knock off all this business about suffering?"

"You talk like that, but you look like you've got some troubles of your own today."

"Are you kidding?" But inside Min-gu starts. "I don't know why, but I really feel like tying one on today. So how about keeping me company? But I guess that's no good either, since you're an ex-minister."

"I'm willing, if I can lessen your suffering a little. It appears the shaman gods you look up to can't do that, kind sir."

Instead of answering, Min-gu opened his big mouth and laughed so openly that Sŏng-ho was startled.

The next day, while Min-gu was home from school recovering from a hangover, a telegram arrived. His mother had passed away. At first he blamed his older brother for not notifying him before her demise, but then he changed his mind; since she had always been troubled with a minor ailment, perhaps his brother had missed the opportunity to inform him when the time came.

For some reason he was not especially sad. Seized with the irrelevant worry that he might not be able to cry when he returned to his hometown, he reiterated to himself, You've gotta cry, you've gotta cry, and the tears welled up in his eyes.

After notifying Ŭn-hŭi and the school of his impending absence, Min-gu thought of informing Pyŏn. But what if Ŭn-hŭi and Pyŏn met at the station while sending me off—it'd be a pain in the neck. He dismissed the idea. At the same time, he considered it extremely fortunate to have the opportunity to go down to his hometown as well as to alter his present mood.

"Did you get a warnin' or somethin'?" the old vendor asked Sŏng-ho with a dissatisfied look.

"Yes, I did."

"There've been several of 'em this autumn."

Sŏng-ho had paid fifty thousand *wŏn* for the shack he was living in, unaware that the residents of this area had been warned to move out.

"Durin' the election there was a lot o' big talk about legalizin' the shacks in this area, or somethin' like that, but now they're raisin' a big stink and tellin' us to clear out. God! I dunno which tune to dance to."

"They're saying we have to be out by December thirtieth,"

said Sŏng-ho.

"That's right. But where're we gonna go, and this winter cold ain't lettin' up none. We gotta stick it out 'till spring—ain't no two ways about it."

"I heard they've decided to flatten this area over the winter and then put up a row of shops with apartments over them starting early in the spring. Do you think they're just going to forget about it?"

"Who knows. Apartments, shops...what's next? If they ain't figured out a place for us to go, what the hell are they gonna do? At any rate, all we can do is stick it out. It's the only way."

Sŏng-ho agreed.

"It's my fate. I lost all my money. What kind o' fate is that?" The old man sniffed, though his nose was dry. "Luck only comes once, and I just let it slip by, and now look at the shape I'm in." Again he was bewailing his lot. Sŏng-ho had heard the story several times. The old man had done his best to save money as a day laborer, one copper at a time, and had set up a tiny variety shop. He put away several hundred thousand *wŏn* and went along without any worries about making a living. But then a young wholesaler of cookies persuaded him to try for larger profits, and before he knew it he had thrown everything away and gone into debt. That was his fate, he complained. "Luck don't come twice. It only comes once. And it'll only visit you once too. So keep your eyes open, grab right onto it, and don't share it with anybody—that's what I say." He always came to the same conclusion.

"Thanks for the advice." At the same time, Sŏng-ho thinks that even if there is this thing called luck, as the old man says, he too let it slip by a long time ago. But he had no regrets—it was a fait accompli.

As Sŏng-ho was selling fifty *wŏn* worth of sweet potatoes to a young day laborer, Yŏng-i came running over in tears. "Mommy's dying, Mommy's dying," she cried over and over.

Sŏng-ho immediately left with the girl. But in front of their shack he found Yŏng-i's mom being beaten by a young man.

Sŏng-ho didn't have to guess who he was.

As Yŏng-i's mom lay curled up on the ground, the young man shouted, "You not goin'? You not goin'?" and kicked viciously at her sides and shoulders. The women of the neighborhood expressed their disapproval but the young man ignored them. He seemed intoxicated. He was well built, though not tall, and his head was large. His whole face was red, and his thick lips even redder.

Curling up her small body, her unkempt hair touching the ground, Yŏng-i's mom wrapped both hands around her stomach, and with every vicious kick she gasped. The young man grabbed her by the scruff and began dragging her away. She tried to plant herself in the ground with her fingers, but the young man's strength was too much for her. As he dragged her along, little by little, her fingertips dug up the earth.

Two of the children who were looking on suddenly came forward and took hold of Yŏng-i's mom to try to stop her from being hauled further. It was Kŏl-i and Sung-i.

The young man easily kicked them away.

"Now look here schoolboy!" Sŏng-ho stepped in front of the young man.

The young man glared up at Sŏng-ho. "Schoo-ool-bo-o-y? Whatcha keer if I'm a schoolboy or not?" His thick red lips spread in a mean smile.

"What kind of behavior is this? You ought to be talking to her instead."

"My wummun, so whut's wrong wi' takin' her away?" Although the young man's speech was not so unnatural, some clumsiness was evident in his pronunciation and intonation.

"Put her down and talk to her!" Sŏng-ho said, snatching away the hand that was holding Yŏng-i's mom by the scruff.

"Okay. So whut now?"

"I'm telling you, schoolboy, to stop being mean!" Sŏng-ho's voice was rich with rage. "Being mean is the most shameful thing in the world!"

The young man snorted and smiled stupidly, then grabbed

Yŏng-i's mom by the scruff and roughly dragged her a short distance.

Yŏng-i's mom's weeping grew louder and her curled-up body trembled. She planted her bleeding fingertips in the ground once again.

While Sŏng-ho was hesitating over how to make him stop, the young man let go of Yŏng-i's mom and jumped back. Kŏl-i and Sung-i, holding cans of excrement, were standing ready to splash him.

Although the young man poised himself to pounce on the two boys, they only waited for him to approach and then made as if to splatter him. The young man retreated. The two boys followed, aiming the cans of excrement at him and narrowing the distance between them. Finally the young man muttered something and began to run. As the two boys gave chase, the women gathered about burst into laughter.

Yŏng-i's mom remained curled up and she trembled even more. Sŏng-ho approached and helped her to her feet, and she staggered away weeping soundlessly, her disheveled hair falling about her.

Sŏng-ho left, steeped in the feeling that he had received an awakening from driving the young man off, together with the two boys. He felt he had gained a firm belief in a thought that had been vague until then.

Chapter 4

Every passenger on the bus is seated. They are all chilly, and white vapor is coming from their noses. A mix of cigarette smoke and vapor veils the face of a man smoking in one of the front seats.

Vapor also rises in puffs from the mouth of the conductress when she shouts out the stops. The girl is wearing so many undergarments her slacks are tight. She's sorting out the fares she's received. The thumb and index finger of her gloves have been snipped off at the middle—the thumbtip and fingertip wiggle like animate objects separate from her hands. She has to wear the gloves because her hands are cold, but it's annoying to have to remove them to sort the money and then put them back on, so she's cut away the fingertips to make it easier. Although Chun-t'ae knew she was merely adapting to the circumstances the best she could, he couldn't quickly rid himself of the unseemly impression the gloves gave him.

Outside the bus a man walks by as quickly as he can. Shopkeepers have closed their doors tightly to block out the cold air. In front of a bicycle shop a youth is pumping air into a tire, and even his herky-jerky action is faster because of the cold. The iron reinforcing rods rising in uneven lengths from buildings under construction look bleak, like branches that have shed their leaves. It's a frigid day.

Chun-t'ae got off the bus and walked through the main entrance to the university hospital. He looked all around, but his view was obstructed by the evergreens lining the cement driveway. She said the tearoom's on the right, he thought. He considered asking the guard at the entrance, but began walking down the driveway instead.

Rounding a turn, he spots a woman in a navy-blue coat, her hands in her pockets, walking about ten meters in front of him. As the driveway descends the woman leans slightly forward, and as she walks each foot seems to imprint itself on the cement.

Chun-t'ae stifles an impulse to simply call her name, and, quickening his step, moves ahead of her and then resumes his normal pace. Shortly thereafter the woman moves ahead of Chun-t'ae. Chun-t'ae again hastens forward and just as he's about to move ahead of the woman she stops and slowly turns around. A full smile forms on her closed lips.

"So you got to Seoul this morning," Chi-yŏn said, retaining the smile.

Chun-t'ae also smiled. Nodding in reply, he moved next to Chi-yŏn. "Where might the tearoom be?"

"Isn't this it?"

They were standing directly in front of a green, two-story wooden building. "Cafeteria" had been painted in black beside the entrance to the lower level and "Tearoom" next to the windows on the upper level. Two men, one in a hospital gown and the other in casual wear, came down the wooden steps leading from the upper level. They shook hands and parted.

"What did you do about breakfast?" Chi-yŏn asked, hesitating in front of the steps to the tearoom.

"I ate at a place in front of the train station."

"I was wondering if you'd come yesterday afternoon, since it was Saturday."

"There's no bus to Seoul in the afternoon, so I went to Kangnŭng and caught the evening train. By the way, was somebody hospitalized?"

"No."

"I thought that since you suggested meeting here..." Chun-t'ae had expected to meet Chi-yŏn and her father, but since she had come alone, he wondered if he was here in the hospital.

"I don't know of any other tearooms around here, so I decided on this one."

If that's the case, thought Chun-t'ae, why should we be meeting around here?

"You know what?" continued Chi-yŏn. "I'd like to go to Ch'anggyŏng-wŏn today."

Ch'anggyŏng-wŏn?"

"Sure, Ch'anggyŏng-wŏn in the wintertime. And not only that, Ch'anggyŏng-wŏn on a winter morning. I think it'll be fun."

"Boy, you're just full of great ideas today."

"Okay, I give up. You're probably tired, coming over on the night train."

"Just because I'm tired doesn't mean we can't go."

After arriving at Ch'ŏngnyangni Station about half past six that morning Chun-t'ae had gone for a bath to pass the time, and now his body felt light. He looked calmly at Chi-yŏn's face and said, "You seem more done in than me. Have you been sick?"

The fold between Chi-yŏn's double eyelids was recessed more than usual.

"Yes, a little. And how about you? Have you been all right since last time?"

"Mmm." Since their last meeting Chun-t'ae's asthma had flared up twice, but neither occasion was serious. "Well, now that I'm here, I'd better do what the young lady desires." Chun-t'ae put his arm around Chi-yŏn's shoulder and led her toward the main entrance to the hospital. Placing her hand in the small of Chun-t'ae's back, Chi-yŏn began rubbing it in response.

Sunday may have been the reason. They had expected to see no one in Ch'anggyŏng-wŏn, but after entering the park they occasionally glimpsed other sightseers.

And now that the sun's rays had diffused the air, the day seemed milder.

"I wonder why they start with the birds," Chi-yŏn said as soon as she reached the bird cages. She spoke less from inquisitiveness than from a desire just to say something.

"Who knows?...Maybe they figure it's more exciting to see the big animals later on."

"Now that I think about it, the birds of prey are the first ones. They probably do that to attract our interest right off." Again Chi-yŏn had said something in order to hear the sound of her voice.

Chun-t'ae stops momentarily in front of the hawk cage. The flitting eyeballs, always watching for something; the claws, unlikely to release the prey once it is caught; the beak, rending the prey thoroughly, piece by piece. Probably those falcons P'il-jae's training are able to hunt now. P'il-jae appears in his mind, making the falcon fly after a pheasant and then chasing it by the sound of the bell attached to it. Chun-t'ae watches P'il-jae run over, expecting to see the pheasant beating off the falcon with its wings rather than the falcon swooping down and hooking the pheasant. For some reason Chun-t'ae hopes that P'il-jae's unusual expectation is met.

Several people have gathered in front of the cage of a white peacock. Chun-t'ae guesses they're waiting for the bird to spread its tail. Chi-yŏn too is prepared to wait, but noticing that the peacock's tail is soiled from being dragged along the ground, she thinks how cumbersome it must be and decides not to stay longer. She and Chun-t'ae walk on.

The black swans are more worth seeing. Their bodies clean and black all over, their beaks bright vermilion—they could actually be called beautiful, they thought. One is floating in the water, and another standing on the bank. Both are dipping their beaks in the water. Every time they do this their short tails wiggle charmingly.

Inside a spacious wire-mesh aviary in which a roundish trench had been dug and supplied with water, geese, cranes, storks, seagulls, night herons, and other birds are flying, swimming, or standing poised on the banks. Some of the seagulls are calling, but Chun-t'ae and Chi-yŏn can't tell which ones. A crane flies over and settles on a bank near the mesh where Chun-t'ae and Chi-yŏn are standing, and they can see a mud-fish in its bill. The crane walks on its long, thin legs to a pool of water, rinses its catch, and promptly gulps it down.

"Did you know that those fellas have straight innards?" asked Chun-t'ae. "So when they swallow a snake it comes out the other end still alive. They have to swallow it over and over, and when it's completely dead, then they can eat it up."

"You're kidding!" Chi-yŏn said with a snort. She laughed, not caring whether the story was true or not.

Chun-t'ae also laughed, not pushing the story further.

More than anything else Chi-yŏn felt it was fortunate that Chun-t'ae didn't appear bored. After hearing he would be coming to Seoul she had racked her brain over where and how to bring up what she had to say to him, and, recalling her visit to the Secret Garden with her father, she had come up with the idea of going to Ch'anggyŏng-wŏn in the morning. But now, surprised that Chun-t'ae was happy, she decides to enjoy herself with him at this stage rather than speaking her mind.

Just when they were noticing that fewer animals than usual were about, they came upon the tropical zoo, where the animals vulnerable to the cold had been transferred, and went inside.

A turtle almost a meter in diameter lay still like a broad, round rock lined with cracks. With its head and tail retracted into its shell, it looked even more like a rock. Two such rocks were in the cage, a slight space between them.

"My goodness, look how big they are! We could ride turtles that big to the dragon king's palace," said a middle-aged woman from the countryside who had been standing alone in front of the cage sighing in admiration. For a while she'd been alternately following and preceding Chi-yŏn and Chun-t'ae.

Pressing her face against the glass of a cage containing a large yellow snake, the woman cried out in surprise. Chi-yŏn and Chun-t'ae walk past her and cross to the row of cages opposite.

An orangutan was sweeping together fragments of cement from the floor with the backs of its hands. Another orangutan was picking up the larger pieces with its long hands and trying to match them and rub them together.

"Sure enough, that's just how people do it," remarked the middle-aged woman, who had come over before Chi-yŏn and Chun-t'ae realized it.

The orangutan that had been gathering the cement fragments picked at its body, as if trying to catch lice. Then it extended its long arms toward the other orangutan and began groping at its body. At first the nature of this action was unclear, but suddenly the other orangutan squealed—*kkik, kkik.*

"Will ya look at that—it's feelin' the female's tits," the woman cried in a loud voice, as if she had discovered something miraculous.

Chi-yŏn quickly stepped away from the woman. The huge stomach of the orangutan that squealed was imprinted in her mind.

She and Chun-t'ae walked past a large cage in the corner in which an elephant was standing, moving its mouth back and forth as it ate. They ascended to the second floor, where they found some bird cages. In the tropical zoo, unlike in the other zoo, the large animals were displayed on the lower floor and the birds on the upper floor, for it would have been difficult to move the large animals to the upper level.

Chi-yŏn whisked by the mandarin ducks, the Japanese crested ibises, and the parrots, and after pausing for a moment before the hornbills, whose long orange horn protruding like an ornament from their large bill gives them a strange appearance, she went out the back door. She mistook for eyes the white spots on the upper eyelids of the black bears lying in a cage at the bottom of a hill, and she passed by the black leopards as if she could see only the yellow centers of their eyes and not their bodies. A huge brindled tiger pacing to and fro reminded her that for a while now she had been hearing its *ŭŏhŭng* from time to time. It was the sound she had heard at the Secret Garden with her father. Suddenly she looked to her side—Chun-t'ae wasn't there. Only then did she realize that since leaving the orangutan cage she had gone ahead of Chun-t'ae and hadn't been paying much attention to the birds and animals.

As Chun-t'ae was approaching Chi-yŏn he stopped and questioned a janitor who was sweeping the grounds: "Where are the camels and giraffes and things like that?"

"Way over there." The janitor pointed in the direction from which Chun-t'ae had come.

"Let's stop for a while," said Chi-yŏn as Chun-t'ae caught up with her.

"Tired?"

"I'd like to take a rest."

The two of them went to a snack shop not far away. The interior was quite roomy, and the center was occupied only by a stove—there were no other customers.

Chi-yŏn took a seat next to the stove.

"Just like I thought," said Chun-t'ae, "the animals aren't very active in winter. Except for the ones that prey on others."

"Yes, I feel the same way."

A girl came to take their order.

"Would you like some lunch?" Chun-t'ae asked. "It's a little early, but..."

"How about a hot drink now, and then we can have lunch a little later, after we leave," Chi-yŏn replied. It didn't seem fitting for them to be eating when she said what she had to say.

After ordering, Chun-t'ae looks quietly at Chi-yŏn, his chin propped up with his palm. Again it occurs to him that her complexion isn't good. The brown centers of her eyes are enveloped in shadow. He wonders whether she is sick, or whether she's having disagreements with her parents because of him, and then asks, "Didn't you say in your letter that your father wanted to see me?"

"Yes, but something came up and he had to go down to the countryside on business," Chi-yŏn replied, avoiding Chun-t'ae's eyes. This was a fabrication. Chi-yŏn wanted to have some time alone with Chun-t'ae. She might not be seeing him again because she had decided to tell him about her checkup, no matter what might happen. Wanting only to extend these precious moments a little longer, she again put aside what she had to say. Straightening up, she took in Chun-t'ae's gaze, which she treasured so much.

As Chun-t'ae and Chi-yŏn were leaving Ch'anggyŏng-wŏn quite a few people were entering. Just before the main entrance they ran into Ŭn-hŭi and Min-gu, who were on their way in. So unexpected was this meeting that except for a cry of surprise the two men momentarily lost their tongues. Then all at once they burst into laughter, as if they had planned it that way.

"What a strange coincidence. Looks like I'm trapped," Min-gu said heartily as soon as the women had exchanged perfunctory greetings.

"I guess the latest fad among the gentlemen of Seoul is going to Ch'anggyŏng-wŏn in the winter," said Chun-t'ae.

"Hey, pipe down. You ran away to the boondocks without a peep. What gives?"

"Actually I was thinking about dropping by your place today."

"Only if you had a few minutes to spare, right?"

"There you go again."

"In any event, it's been a while since I've seen you. How about going somewhere? These days I've been thinking about writing an essay, so I came here to get some material for it, but what the hell, I can always come back." Min-gu was considering writing about birds and had stopped by Ch'anggyŏng-wŏn to observe some of the birds there. He and Ŭn-hŭi were then going to go to the area around Myŏngnyun-dong and Hyehwa-dong to do some house hunting.

But Ŭn-hŭi's expression showed that she didn't agree with Min-gu's suggestion.

Chi-yŏn looked at Chun-t'ae.

"Let's just go our separate ways for today," Chun-t'ae said. "I don't know what your paper's on, but we'd just be interfering. Why don't you come out to where I am sometime? You can

gather some stuff about shaman culture while you're there."
Chun-t'ae took out a pen and some paper and jotted down his
address for Min-gu. "Go a little ways past Hoenggye, and then
ask where to get off for the alpine testing station."

"When're you going back?"

"On the train this evening. Well, take your time here."

The two couples parted.

"What did you want to go out with them for? There's no
reason for us to interfere with them," carped Ŭn-hŭi as she and
Min-gu moved toward the bird cages.

"Yeah, that makes sense," Min-gu agreed. Taking advantage
of the thaw in their cold war that had occurred after he
returned from his mother's funeral, he had been even more
careful than before to avoid upsetting Ŭn-hŭi.

"I wonder what's wrong with her face. It's all blotched up."

"Yeah, I saw."

"I tell you, I'll never be able to figure men out. She's not in
the same league with his ex-wife."

"I agree," Min-gu replies unconcernedly. Here comes that
same old comparison theory, he thinks.

While Ŭn-hŭi carried on about Chun-t'ae's shady expression
and his conscience, Min-gu continued his ritualistic responses
and looked into the eagle cage. An eagle is crouching fiercely,
blood staining its beak. It appears to have just finished a meal.
Min-gu sees from the signboard that it feeds on rabbits and
chickens. It would be something to see, he thought, if it were
given something to eat that was still alive. It's exactly this kind
of eagle that's been sanctified in eastern Siberia. In Korea too
there's an important relationship between shamans—and in
particular almost all *myŏngdo* shamans[1]—and fowl, but it's the
birds that are weak and beautiful that are the center of attention. One *myŏngdo* shaman reported that one day a green bird
came without warning and settled in her hair as she was

---

[1]*Myŏngdo* shaman: a shaman possessed by the spirit of a young girl who
has died of smallpox or some other contagious disease.

standing in her yard. Even when she grabbed it, it didn't try
to fly away. So she threw the bird up toward the sky, and from
then on she was afflicted with possession sickness. She was possessed by the spirit of a daughter who had died of measles the
previous year and turned into a bird. When she told fortunes
the *su, su, su, su* sound of a bird would come from her mouth.
Another *myŏngdo* shaman said that her four-year-old daughter
died and became a yellow bird that flew to the top of a tree and
nested there. She told it to come down and it provided her
with divine inspiration. While reporting this, the shaman was
worshiping a yellow toy bird in her shrine and telling fortunes.
This shows that Koreans consider birds to be incarnations or
messengers of spirits. Could it be, thought Min-gu, that this
awe of birds that fly around in the sky is an expression of our
worship of heaven? Min-gu's spirits lifted considerably as he
outlined the direction he would take in his paper, to be called
"Birds and the Characteristics of Koreans."

   After having lunch, Chun-t'ae and Chi-yŏn looked around in
several bookstores that they happened upon as they walked
along Chongno. In one of the stores Chun-t'ae picked up an
atlas and began leafing through it.
   "What are you looking for?" asked Chi-yŏn.
   "Nothing. Just looking."
   "Dreaming of conquering the world?" Chi-yŏn whispered
with a mischievous smile.
   "At least that's better than your having an interest in books on
agriculture." Chun-t'ae also spoke in a low voice and smiled.
"Look here. It's beautiful, no matter where I open it. Here're
plains, here're mountain areas, and here's the sea... The fields
are all the same color—green—but the mountains and oceans
are different colors, according to their altitude or depth. The
colors are the same all over the world, no matter what plain,
mountain area, or ocean it is."
   "But the story of you and me is included in those agriculture
texts, not in the atlas."

The two of them faced each other and smiled through their eyes.

They left the bookstore and went to a nearby tearoom, which, according to Chi-yŏn, served delicious tea and coffee.

The tearoom was not large and rather quiet. The interior, not too dim and not too bright, made them feel cozy.

Their coffee was served in cups of high quality.

"Tastes pretty good, doesn't it?" said Chi-yŏn.

"Well, I'm not sure. I don't know much about coffee, but I don't think this matches yours."

Chi-yŏn chuckled.

"Am I wrong?" asked Chun-t'ae.

"I'm afraid you're not cut out to flatter women. You're too stiff."

"Really." Chun-t'ae joined her in laughing.

It was easy for them to laugh over and over that day.

Suddenly they heard the thunderous sound of psychedelic music. But the booming music merely made them feel they were in a world of their own, separate from the others in the tearoom.

At times they remained silent, but even then they weren't uncomfortable. They could gaze at each other, satisfied simply with being together.

Sŏng-ho came up in their conversation, and Chi-yŏn summarized his recent activities. Chun-t'ae listened without a word, merely nodding his head. Chi-yŏn was gratified that he could understand Sŏng-ho so easily.

"You're really loaded!" said Ch'ang-ae to the bleary-eyed Mr. Kang when he entered the bakeshop. It was well past their appointed meeting time.

"I had to loosen up a little."

Sensing some irregularities in Mr. Kang's life since his two-day absence, Ch'ang-ae had been advising him to return to serious painting. He had appeared to agree, but it was only after procrastinating at length, fashioning this excuse and that,

that he had finally decided to replenish his art supplies. Today they had decided to meet and go buy the materials he needed.

"You're not too drunk to choose your art supplies, are you?"

"It's not my eyes that are drunk, just my mind. Now c'mon— gimme a break from this painting business!"

"Didn't you promise me only yesterday?"

"I'd better think it over a little more."

"What's there to think over? Have you gotten sidetracked, pulling out like this?"

"I don't have any enthusiasm. What am I gonna do?"

"That's what happens when you don't use your brushes for a while. Just get started and your enthusiasm'll pick up."

"The more I think about it, the more I lose my confidence. I just get scared."

"It's too bad. Even though you look like you have a strong will, you've got some weaknesses. Aren't there some other things on your mind these days?"

"Other things?"

"When men have other things on their mind, it's usually connected with women, isn't it?"

"You're a frightening woman."

"Is it that girl Miss Chŏn? The one with the long hair who got it cut short?"

Mr. Kang lit his pipe noisily and said, "I won't deny it. But she's a nuisance."

"I think you're the problem, not her."

"What?"

"Well, do you like her?"

"There's nothing I particularly like about her, and nothing I particularly dislike."

"I get it. You mean you don't dislike her. Okay. When you have a complete outline of your feelings toward her, tell me, without hiding anything. Because I don't want to interfere with anyone. And when you've found out, don't meet her and then pretend to me you didn't. It's okay if the two of you come by my place."

"You're a frightening woman."

"You already said that. What do you mean?"

"You're too thorough. There's nothing naive about you at all."

"That's probably relative."

"I don't know about that man Ham, but I can see why he put up his hands and surrendered."

"Don't bring him up unless you know what you're talking about. He has some good qualities. It's just that we were each so stubborn—right up to the end. We couldn't fit in with each other."

"How about me?"

"You look stubborn, but you're full of weak points. Maybe I act the way I do because I want to shore up those weaknesses. Now why don't you straighten out that beret. It's about to fall off. You're dozing—what am I going to do with you? Okay then, let's forget about the art supplies till next time and go home and get some rest."

Ch'ang-ae closed the dress shop early that evening. It was Sunday, and Mr. Kang was home early for the first time in a while.

Mr. Kang was in bed.

"Are you sobering up a little?" Ch'ang-ae asked as she changed her clothes.

"I had a good nap."

"Seems like I push you too much—telling you to start painting again, I mean."

Mr. Kang is lying on his stomach and slowly packing his pipe with tobacco.

"No?" Ch'ang-ae begins to remove her makeup.

"I don't know."

"You don't know?"

"I mean I don't know what to do."

"You probably ought to do some serious thinking about that."

"I don't want to be serious. It's not good for my mental health to put a wet blanket on it." Mr. Kang sighs, producing a cloud of smoke.

"Maybe you're right. People have to think for themselves and choose their own path—that's the only way. Anyway, that's enough talk for today."

"Agreed."

Ch'ang-ae takes a bottle of wine out of the cabinet and pours a glass. Taking a mouthful of the wine, she walks over to Mr. Kang. Propping up his chin with her hand, she joins her mouth to his. Mr. Kang waits for all the wine to jet into his mouth, but Ch'ang-ae shakes her head. Finally Mr. Kang transfers the wine he has received back to Ch'ang-ae's mouth. Ch'ang-ae again transfers it to Mr. Kang. As it is transferred back and forth, the liquid gradually disappears down their throats. Ch'ang-ae realizes that she is performing these actions without any feeling. *Why would my vitality run away from me like this?* she wonders. *Or could that be something relative too?* Ch'ang-ae lifts herself up and refills her glass. This time she drinks the wine herself, downing it in a gulp.

Chun-t'ae and Chi-yŏn remained on the platform after most of the passengers had boarded the train. Chun-t'ae had unabashedly clasped Chi-yŏn's hand tightly and inserted it in his pocket.

"You said this morning that my face didn't look good." There was no anxiety or hesitation in Chi-yŏn now. *I have to tell him, even if it means I lose him.* "Everything's gone wrong. Ever since I came back from the testing station I haven't been feeling right. Finally I had a checkup, and..." Despite her intentions, she cut herself off. *What she had to say was not short. I had the checkup and found I probably couldn't become a complete woman. Before, because of the caries, I gave up being a woman—but no, I wasn't giving up, I was losing interest. I could live on, being disinterested, and even after I met you I felt the same way. But then I became infused with you, and from then on it was different—I wanted to be a woman, and I thought I could be a woman.*

"Your caries has taken a turn for the worse, hasn't it?" Chun-t'ae asked quietly.

"It's more than that—I probably can't be a mother." Chi-yŏn repeated it to herself. There's a difference between not being a mother when you're able to, and not being a mother because you can't; it's not just my problem, it's our problem. Chi-yŏn bit her lips.

"I'll tell you just what I think. This seems to be a good time for it," Chun-t'ae began slowly. "Actually, I've been afraid that you wanted to have children. You see? I'm not saying this just to console you. I've been that way for a long time now. I hope you understand."

Chi-yŏn dropped her head slightly and held her breath. Tears were about to run from her eyes; she swallowed.

Calmly and unselfconsciously Chun-t'ae lightly raised Chi-yŏn's forehead with his own. Their eyes were almost touching under the dim lights on the platform. The gaze of each became entwined in the eyes of the other. With their eyes they spoke to each other. I love you—that's all that matters. I love you too—really.

A bell sounded. The train was about to depart.

The two of them smiled, mouths closed, and parted. Chun-t'ae went up the steps to the entrance at the end of his coach; Chi-yŏn remained where she was, not lifting a hand in farewell.

When Chi-yŏn's stationary form became too small to see, Chun-t'ae turned around and grabbed a handrail, intending to enter the coach. His breathing suddenly became heavy. For a short time, actually, he had been feeling it coming on. He crouched, his hand about the railing, and thrust his head and chest forward, waiting with a searching look for the suffering to come.

Chi-yŏn looked at the red taillights of the train. Her chest began throbbing. She thought she saw Chun-t'ae looking back at her from the entrance to the coach as it receded from her. He seemed to be suffering. Does he look that way because the taillights are so dim? I should be next to him on that train, no matter what, she repeated to herself. She blindly walked after the taillights, which had long since faded from view.

After returning from his mother's funeral Min-gu went to Pyŏn's, having first tried to appease Ŭn-hŭi. That night a young man was there whom Min-gu had not seen before. Pyŏn introduced him as a cousin on his mother's side who had been dispatched to Vietnam and was now taking his last furlough before being discharged from the army.

"I've already learned a lot about you from my cousin," the young man said unreservedly. He gave Min-gu a meaningful smile.

"From now on he'll be helping you practice the stages of the *kut*," Pyŏn added.

The liquor tray appeared. The young man Pyŏn called his cousin wasn't a drinker. He couldn't even keep up with Pyŏn. Although he merely touched his glass to his lips a couple of times—and even then, only at Min-gu's insistence—his throat became red and he began to pant.

"You've come a long way," the young man said to Pyŏn. "You can drink now."

Pyŏn looked askance at the young man.

"In Vietnam—"

"Vietnam, Vietnam—I told you to stop talking about that," said Pyŏn spitefully.

The young man grinned at Min-gu and then said to Pyŏn, "Who said I was going to talk about war?" Then he turned back to Min-gu. "He hates to hear war stories... When I saw that dried meat there on the tray, it reminded me of something. Compared to beef, you wouldn't believe how expensive vegetables are in Vietnam. If you sold a cow down there, you could only buy maybe a few cabbages. Wouldn't it be great if we could trade 'em our cabbage for their beef? But I guess that's not the only thing that's unfair in the world."

"I'll say." Min-gu thought the young man was quite amiable considering they had just met.

As soon as they began practicing the *kut*, Min-gu noticed that the young man's hand movements as he played the hourglass drum were extraordinary. He had suspected as much from what Pyŏn had said. Though Min-gu had not practiced for a while, his dancing was not unbecoming. He was able to follow the drum correctly. He became excited once again and lost all track of time.

That night Min-gu solved the puzzle of Pyŏn. He had thought about leaving after the practice session, especially since the young man was there, but sensing that Pyŏn wanted him to stay and that he had explained everything to the young man, he ended up settling in for the evening. It was in bed that he came to know Pyŏn's secret.

Min-gu had virtually no time to become the rock of resistance while his manhood was being uncompromisingly buffeted and sent drifting here and there by the strong waves, and at the moment he broke to pieces he unknowingly pushed Pyŏn to the side. At the same time, he slid his fingers along Pyŏn's crotch. Taken aback by this unexpected behavior, Pyŏn tried to defend himself, but Min-gu had already touched the strange thing. It was a tiny, insubstantial, shriveled thing, like a piece of leather. But it was unmistakably the emblem of manhood.

After releasing himself from Min-gu, Pyŏn made no attempt to escape, as usual. Instead, he turned around and, covering his face with his hands, mumbled an appeal through his fingers. "You don't like me, do you. You don't like me now. But please don't get rid of me."

Min-gu was at first astonished by Pyŏn's strange organ, but he wasn't repelled by it, maybe because he had sensed there was something abnormal about Pyŏn. Indeed, he had gotten used to thinking that this abnormality might be greater than he imagined. Min-gu reached out and gently rubbed Pyŏn's back. "All right, go to sleep now and don't worry."

In the morning Yŏng-i's mom had a miscarriage. The obstetrician Sŏng-ho had summoned motioned him outside. He shook his head. He had applied an agent to stop the hemorrhaging, but Yŏng-i's mom had lost so much blood that there was no hope for her. After saying he would give her some Ringer's solution as a last step, he went away, leaving a nurse behind.

Yŏng-i's mom's dark, dying face didn't show the slightest movement. Yŏng-i was not there, Sŏng-ho having left her with a neighbor before the doctor arrived.

"Mother," said Yŏng-i's mom, as if the injection of Ringer's solution had revived her. Her eyes remained closed, and her voice was pinched and faint. "Water…"

Sŏng-ho spooned some water between her lips. What she couldn't swallow trickled from the corners of her mouth. At the third spoonful Sŏng-ho was barely able to distinguish a shake of the head indicating she didn't want any more.

Sŏng-ho lifted the arm that had not received the injection and wrapped the deathly cold hand in his own. But he wasn't able yet to produce a prayer.

"Mother," she called, and in just a short time she opened her eyes and looked at Sŏng-ho. Then, as if she had regained her senses, she said, "Don't pray for me to go to heaven… I don't want to go to heaven."

Sŏng-ho strengthened his grip on her hand.

"I have to go to hell," she said in her faint, dragging voice. And then, after a pause, "That guy'll go to hell, won't he…I can't get even with him in this world, so I'll do it there."

"You shouldn't think like that," said Sŏng-ho.

"What am I going to do with Yŏng-i?…" Her eyes closed again, and tears squeezed out between the lids.

"You don't have to worry about Yŏng-i."

"I *have* to see that guy while I'm in hell… But…when I took that medicine and tried to kill myself I was so comfortable…why isn't it like that now…" She turned her head away from Sŏng-ho, and tears ran down her face.

Sŏng-ho sat there vacantly, unable to stanch her tears.

Within a few days of his visit to Seoul, Chun-t'ae received a letter from Chi-yŏn.

"...I've never felt as keenly as I do these days the distance that separates us. I want to be by your side, whether it's helpful or not..." Chun-t'ae read this passage over and over.

At the end of the letter Chi-yŏn added that her father had decided to go meet Chun-t'ae at some convenient time.

Chapter 5

Chi-yŏn turned off the light in Sŏng-ho's cramped shack and lit a candle. As the flame expanded, the outlines of the people hidden in the gloom resumed their normal appearance. In addition to Chi-yŏn and Yŏng-i, whom Sŏng-ho had taken custody of upon her mother's death, the woman who had come rushing to Sŏng-ho's that day had been invited, together with two friends, and the three of them were sitting in a row. Everything had been arranged by Chi-yŏn.

A white Christmas had been forecast, together with a comparatively mild and clear Christmas Eve. The stars were vivid in the sky.

The plastic over the small window glowed red in the candlelight, and the Christmas carols and children's songs flowed on and on. The six ate cookies and fruit, and their conversation and occasionally their soaring laughter carried far beyond the shack.

A longing to have Chun-t'ae with her flashed through Chi-yŏn. I wonder if he's in good health. His appearance as the train left Ch'ŏngnyangni Station had weighed heavily on her mind, and when she told her father about Chun-t'ae's coughing fit at Wŏlchŏng Temple he had immediately said that it was asthma. She had then looked through a medical encyclopedia and had come to the same conclusion. Her father's voice had been tinged with concern, and the encyclopedia said the disease was not a simple one to treat. Perhaps Chun-t'ae had kept the disease a secret, afraid that she would worry. Anyway, she thought, Father said he would visit him before the year is out, and after that I'll have to find some way to look after him.

There's a knock at the door.

Sŏng-ho gets up and opens the door. "Hey, come on in. What took you so long?" It's Kŏl-i and Sung-i.

"We hafta go." Kŏl-i tells the three women sitting in a row to come along quickly.

The three women get up at the same time, as if by prearrangement. Chi-yŏn suggests that they stay a little longer and then leave with her. The women merely smile, but their smiles are somehow awkward and cheerless. Chi-yŏn realizes that though she had been singing and laughing with them, they had not completely yielded to the mood of the evening. She felt she understood why. It was time for them to start their evening's work. There was to be no curfew that night, but for them it was business as usual. A woman like them, Chi-yŏn ached inside. She wrapped up some cookies and fruit, piece by piece, and forced them on the two boys, who had remained standing at the door.

Yŏng-i, who had been enjoying rubbing the toy puppy Chi-yŏn had bought for her, had fallen asleep before the adults realized it.

"Next May, by the lunar calendar, looks like it'll be a dry month." A colleague sitting opposite Chun-t'ae was taking a break and, with a cigarette in his mouth, was looking out the window and talking to himself.

"Why is that?" asked a young temporary employee who was sitting next to Chun-t'ae and helping him organize two reports, one on operations and one on experimental research, that were to be submitted to the main office.

"No snow in November. There's a connection between the amount of snow we get in November and the amount of rain we get the following May. It's the same with December and June."

"I've never heard that. But speaking of snow, I've got this unforgettable memory." The temporary employee wore a faint smile at the corners of his mouth. "It was when I first started teaching at an elementary school, on a day when there was thick snow coming down everywhere. I'd sent the kids home and I was sitting in the teachers' room looking outside, having all kinds of strange feelings. I imagined that a close friend of mine suddenly showed up and gave me a tap on the shoulder, or I felt like tapping someone else on the shoulder—things like that. There was a woman teacher next to me who hadn't gotten married yet, and as luck would have it, she was looking outside too, watching the snow come down, so I wrote something on a piece of paper and slipped it over to her—'I'd like to walk with you in the snow forever.' Now take a look at what she wrote at the bottom of the paper: 'There's too much snow'[1] —just like that. Snow from the sky, and people's eyes—she included them both."

"What a great way to get shot down."

"But it didn't bother me."

"Oh no, of course not."

Everyone laughed.

Chun-t'ae was putting the finishing touches on the two reports. They had enabled him to obtain an understanding of the present operations of the alpine testing station.

Its principal research projects included improved plant breeding, better methods of cultivation, prevention of damage by blight and harmful insects, and better methods of livestock breeding—all for high, cold areas. The most important of these projects were the ones involving potatoes.

First of all, the report encourages the adoption of a variety of seed potatoes from this alpine area in every region of the country. This is because in cold, high areas potatoes are planted in May, and in September or October the crop is stored as seed potatoes—an advantage over the lowland plains, where potatoes are planted in early spring and harvested at the beginning of summer.

These days the standard variety of potato in Korea is the *namjak*. Roundish and oval, with deep eyes and crisp flesh, it

---

[1]The woman was punning on the Korean word *nun,* which means both "snow" and "eye."

suits the taste of the everyday citizen. Statistics show that it has a higher starch content than any other variety.

Although there are experiments to make various improvements in the new varieties introduced from abroad, the emphasis now is on adding to the *namjak's* superior qualities an increased yield and a greater resistance to disease.

Since Chun-t'ae had begun organizing the two reports, one thing had drawn his attention time and time again—whether it might be possible to obtain a potato as good as the *namjak* that could be planted in the fall.

It would be very desirable to use the *namjak* as a seed potato for autumn planting, but because of a variety of problems it's not possible. Although the planting and harvest periods for potatoes differ with the climate and environment of each region of Korea, we can take as a frame of reference the central region of the country, where in the case of the *namjak*, planting is done at the end of March and harvesting at the beginning of July. There follows, however, an especially long fallow period of more than four months. But keeping in mind the climate of the country, we can't expect the potato to grow properly in any region if it is planted in November, at the end of that period. True, the natural fallow period can be shortened by artificial means. Several such methods have been contrived and tested—among them, treatment with heat and cold at fixed periods, removal of the skin and application of a stimulus, and the use of drugs—but there have been problems in spreading and promoting them among farmers. Of these methods, the use of the drug gibberellin is the simplest, but according to the experience of Chun-t'ae's testing station and experimental results from other countries, the yield cannot but be smaller due to damage from its use.

Chun-t'ae had talked about this with his co-worker Pak.

"Have you ever experimented with ways of planting the *namjak* in autumn? For example, by shortening the fallow period?"

"No, I've never tried it that way."

"Suppose you were to crossbreed it with the variety that requires the shortest fallow period—the *tachi bana*—what do you think would happen?"

"You're suggesting something with a shorter fallow period than the *namjak*? Sure, we could probably come up with a variety like that, but I'm afraid the disadvantages would outweigh the advantages."

Chun-t'ae understands. The *tachi bana* has been promoted to some extent for autumn planting, but due to its poor marketability, it has not been welcomed by growers. It is long and whitish, and the eyes are few and shallow. The flesh is soggy and insipid, so it is virtually unsuited to the Korean palate. If the *tachi bana* were crossbred with the *namjak*, the fallow period might be shortened, but other than that, the disadvantages were apt to reappear, Pak was saying.

"But don't we actually have to test it? When you say that it's difficult to obtain a good variety, isn't that just a theory?" Chun-t'ae's tone became more inquisitive.

"That's correct. Theory alone won't do. We get solid results only by being patient and testing over and over again for a long period of time."

It normally takes more than three years to come up with a new variety from seeds gotten through crossbreeding. What appears after the first year is the size of a bean, and from then on, enough time is required for it to grow year by year until it's the size of an average potato.

Pak pushed up his glasses and resumed. "As you know, we have to have money to conduct tests like that. If there's no support in the budget, we can't even think about running those experiments, and so we can't expect a whole lot of progress."

Although Chun-t'ae understood, he was left wondering whether something ought to be done.

"Isn't there any way to get rid of that damned virus or wipe out those aphids? I tell you!" The temporary employee was indignant.

There is an incurable disease of potatoes that is caused by a virus. The virus is transferred by aphids. The most numerous aphids inhabiting each region of the country are the peach-knob aphids; next come the cotton aphids; and the least numerous variety are the bush-clover aphids. The testing station was endeavoring to find ways of controlling them.

"If you look at these reports you'll see that the distribution of aphids is greatest in the Kangnŭng region and smallest in the Kimje-Okku region. What's the reason for that?" The temporary employee, transcribing the manuscripts of the reports into their final form, did not pose the question to anyone in particular.

The worker opposite him replied, "A phenomenon like that depends on whether the plants the aphids feed on are numerous or scarce. The more rice you plant, the less plants you have, so naturally the fewer aphids you have."

Chun-t'ae had almost finished organizing the report when Chi-yŏn's father arrived. The older man had been attending to some business in Kangnŭng.

The two men exchanged greetings in the reception room. There was a short pause. "The building's clean and the surroundings are quiet—I like it," said Chi-yŏn's father as he looked around the room.

"They tell me this building went up last year."

"At this testing station you're working mainly on improving the varieties of potatoes?"

"That's right."

"I think our people should have a different opinion of potatoes. We think that hardly any other crop can be grown in the mountain areas, and that the people are forced to grow them there for food. We have to start by correcting that assumption. Apart from being highly nutritious, potatoes, I believe, should be grown and promoted by our country as a major food item since we aren't even self-sufficient in rice and barley. But it'll be difficult to correct in one morning something that's been rooted in tradition for so long. Do you know how useful they are? They're an everyday food in every country of the world."

"That's a fact."

"Granted, even the Westerners appear to have tried every means possible when they were first popularizing the potato. Didn't Napoleon have his army stand guard over potato fields? Because of that, people couldn't help looking at potatoes as a valuable crop. During the day he had soldiers guarding the potatoes, but at night he removed the soldiers and let the people take them away. A strange method, but it seems to have popularized potatoes."

Chun-t'ae thought the story was plausible, whether or not it was based on fact.

From outside the reception room came the *tchigŭdŭk*, *tchigŭdŭk* of someone working the empty water pump, which was always on the verge of breaking down. It must have been the errand boy trying to draw water.

Chi-yŏn's father took the square package that he had set atop the coffee table and handed it to Chun-t'ae, saying, "My daughter sends this. She says to try it, and if it's effective she'll send some more."

Although he knew his illness couldn't be cured by medicine, Chun-t'ae said nothing and bowed in appreciation.

"By any chance..." Chi-yŏn's father took out a cigarette and struck a match to it. "...have you ever thought about leaving this place? I know the air's good here and it's probably better for your health, but the hospitals are far away, and..."

Chun-t'ae didn't know a good way to answer this sudden question.

"If you had a mind to, I could look around and try to get you a job somewhere in Seoul..."

Thinking that he must have good connections since he was the assistant to the president and vice-president of a textile company, Chun-t'ae replied, "I appreciate your concern."

"It's not a simple matter to switch jobs, so give it a little thought... Well, I guess I'd better be on my way. If I leave now, I can get back to Seoul late tonight. It's nice to have met you."

The sound of the empty pump had ceased. Perhaps the errand boy had inserted some rubber packing and fixed it.

Chun-t'ae stood in front of the entrance to the building until Chi-yŏn's father had gotten into the car parked outside and been driven into the distance. His interview with him had been extremely short. It was a process he had had to undergo, and it seemed to have ended without complication or difficulty. The interview gave him the feeling of being wrapped up cozily in a thin layer of cotton. It was a gentle, unburdensome sensation. But then the cotton started to slowly fill with moisture. He could endure it, though. But when the cotton became completely soaked, it was heavy and clinging and it began to constrict him. Now it was unbearable, and he felt congested. This was not the first time he had experienced the sensation of moistness that followed the coziness of the cotton. It had risen from time to time when he thought about Chi-yŏn, but he had always ignored it. Chun-t'ae turned around, expecting the usual spasms. His legs trembled.

The young man whom Pyŏn called his cousin was passable in the role of shaman, and with his help Min-gu easily made progress in his performance of the *kut*. Moreover, because the young man was not only enthusiastic but easygoing as well, the practice sessions were not especially stressful. And if the hour was late, Min-gu would not hesitate to spend the night.

All the while, Min-gu was attributing a certain value to his having met Pyŏn. He had told himself that the research he was now doing was something that no student of shaman culture could set his hand to blindly, and even if he strayed a bit from the path of common sense in order to finish it, he had to push on. There was just one thing—discord might arise between him and Ŭn-hŭi as a result, but he had tried his best to be careful, and believed there was nothing wrong with it.

On this particular night Min-gu again exercised great caution in going to Pyŏn's house. Not only did he pay attention to his behavior, he asked the switchboard operator at his apartment building to tell anyone who called that his receiver was out of order.

Only the young man was home. Pyŏn had gone out on some pressing business. "He said he'd be back for sure, but it might be a little late," the young man said in an apologetic tone. He then guided Min-gu inside.

Once he was at Pyŏn's, Min-gu didn't bother keeping track of the time. If it was late, he would sleep there and then leave, and that would be that. But something told Min-gu not to stay at Pyŏn's that night. Nowadays a mysterious anxiety sometimes swept through him, and even now he suddenly began to suspect that someone was pursuing him.

"Let's take the evening off," said Min-gu to the young man.

"Now why do you say that? Can't we practice by ourselves until my cousin arrives?"

Min-gu agreed that he ought to do that as long as he was here, but somehow he was not in the mood.

"Well, how about a drink or something?" continued the young man. "I'm not too good at drinking, but I can keep you company. And I've got a lot of good stories about Vietnam."

"I'm sure you do, but I think my best bet would be to go home."

Min-gu ignored the young man's attempts to detain him and left. After scrutinizing the surroundings under the dim street light, he began walking briskly. Regret at not having waited for Pyŏn and satisfaction at returning home like this crisscrossed his mind.

Min-gu had no way of knowing that Ŭn-hŭi was peeping out at him from a shop about fifty meters from Pyŏn's. She then went to see the young man whom Pyŏn called his cousin.

Two days later, Min-gu was at Pyŏn's house again.

Today he was practicing the *taegam kŏri*.[2]

---

[2] *Taegam kŏri*: a *kŏri* performed in honor of *taegam* ("great overseer" or "excellency"), a spirit who is responsible especially for safeguarding houses and other buildings.

It is a full-scale performance. Min-gu, wearing a *k'waeja*, holds up an *anollim bŏnggŏji*[3] and steps deliberately front and back while following Pyŏn in reciting a chant. At the same time, he hears the *tŏ'ŏng, tŏ'ŏng, tŏngdŏkk'ung* of Pyŏn's hourglass drum and the *ch'ŏ'ŏng, ch'ŏ'ŏng ch'ŏ'rŭrŭ* of the young man's cymbals. Min-gu circles the room, stepping forward and back, and then places the *bŏnggŏji* on his head. As soon as Pyŏn completes the invitation to *taegam*, the rhythm of the drum and cymbals accelerates a bit. *Tangdang tangdak'kkung, ch'angch'ang ch'a'rŭrŭ...* Min-gu begins jumping lightly in the air, in time with the quickened tempo. After a series of jumps, Min-gu makes one turn to the left and stops, drawing himself up to his full height. The drum and cymbals immediately stop.

"The line of long life and the line of good fortune, coming down from the green water and the blue mountain, bend them to the children of this family so that they may inherit them." As soon as this message from *taegam* is delivered by Pyŏn, the *tangdang tangdak'kkung* of the drum and the *ch'angch'ang ch'a'rŭrŭ* of the cymbals resumes. Min-gu begins jumping lightly again. The drum and cymbals accelerate. *Tangdang tanggidang, ch'yangch'yang ch'ya'rŭrŭ...*Min-gu soars higher and higher. *Ttangttang ttangttang, ch'yangch'yang ch'yang-ch'yang...*Becoming less and less aware of the movements of his body, Min-gu gives himself up to the drums and cymbals. Whether or not his feet are touching the floor, the scarlet carpet is the curtain or the sunflowered curtain the carpet, up is down or front back—all is mixed up. Min-gu knows only that he is fluttering and floating formlessly in the air. The cymbals stop, but to Min-gu it means nothing. He doesn't even know that the young man has released the shutter of a camera. For a while longer Min-gu continues to jump, but then, unknown to him, the jumps become shorter and less frequent, and after

---

[3]*Anollim bŏnggŏji:* a hat worn by high military officials, the inside of which is painted.

pacing off a circle to the left he comes to a halt, as does the drum. "Boy, you really surprised me," said the young man. He swaggered toward Min-gu. Then, as if he has inherited Min-gu's ecstasy, he sways his shoulders rhythmically and begins murmuring, attaching a tune and rhythm to the words:

A lonely orphan, with no place to fall back on
Wandering all the way to the soil of Vietnam
Only today did I meet my excellency.

The narrative isn't part of the *taegam kŏri*. The young man continues to sway and, folding his hands and then raising and lowering them, begins to walk in circles around Min-gu.

From the haze of the ecstasy that still enshrouds him, Min-gu looks blankly at the young man, who murmurs another narrative that departs from the *taegam kŏri:*

Spirit in the heavens, spirit in the earth
Take a personal interest in him
Bestow on him
Your magical powers.

At the same time, the swaying of the young man's shoulders, the motion of his folded hands, and the movement of his feet around Min-gu accelerate. Carried away by the scene, Pyŏn again sounds the *ttangttang ttangttang* of the hourglass drum.

Bestow on my excellency, Excellency Song
All the powers you can.

Finally Min-gu joins the young man, responding to the movements of his shoulders by swaying his own. For a while they attempt to move in circles about each other. Then with an attenuated swaying of his shoulders the young man quickly makes circles around Min-gu, pretending to shake a *shinjangdae*,[4] and then prostrates himself in front of him, saying, "The spirit of the heavens and the spirit of the earth instruct

---

[4]*Shinjangdae:* a wand used by shamans for invoking spirits.

you to establish a religion." Even though he is panting, he pours out these words, in tune and in rhythm, in a breath.

"A religion?" says Min-gu from within the haze that continues to shadow him.

"You know—a religion."

"Oh yeah, a religion."

"They instruct you to establish a religion. You're the founder. You must write a book and make it the gospel. It will include all the various chants of the *kut*. And we are the followers. It will be a splendid religion. As for the name of the religion—"

"The name of the religion," Min-gu interrupted, excitement penetrating his haze. "What if we call it Tanggul?"

"Tanggul? What does Tanggul mean?" the young man asked.

"It's the same as Tan-gun."

"Fine. Tanggul it is. Now that I think about it, you've been considering establishing a religion anyway, haven't you?"

"Well..." Indeed, Min-gu felt that to unify shamanism under a single religion wouldn't be a bad idea.

The young man turned to Pyŏn. His eyes said, Of course you'll approve, won't you?

Pyŏn nodded, but sent the young man a dubious look.

"Well then, again I congratulate the founder." The young man prostrates himself before Min-gu.

All of this fit perfectly, as if it were an extension of the chants and dances of the *kut*.

When Pyŏn and Min-gu were alone, Pyŏn said in a low voice, "He's kind of a braggart, isn't he?" He seemed afraid that the young man's words and actions might hurt Min-gu's feelings. But instead, Min-gu, ruminating on the tiny aftertaste of ecstasy that still remained in some nook in his body, attached an amorphous expectation to the religion the young man had advised him to establish.

In another room the young man turned off the light and lay down. He chuckled softly. I didn't expect such a good opportunity to come so easily. It won't be long before Pyŏn is all mine, just like he was before I went to Vietnam. In the darkness the young man searched for the kettle of water near his head and, putting the spout to his mouth, swallowed *kkulkkŏk kkulkkŏk*. The taste of the water relieved the frustration that weighed on his heart.

Kŏl-i opens the door of the Mini Taep'ojip and steps smartly inside; Sung-i quickly follows. As Kŏl-i had determined from scouting the premises, there's not a single customer. Without a word the proprietor pours two bowls of *makkŏlli*. Kŏl-i lifts his bowl and drinks it, pausing only a few times along the way. Sung-i equivocates, however, and after taking a sip, his face wrinkles and he shudders. Asshole, Kŏl-i says, glaring at him. Come on, the proprietor says, flinging the words at Sung-i. You look like your balls've ripened—can't you handle a thimbleful o' *makkŏlli*? Sung-i clamps his eyes shut and, bearing up to the sickening stuff, barely manages to toss off the bowl. In the meantime Kŏl-i easily empties a second bowl.

Satisfied with this show that he is more grownup than Sung-i, Kŏl-i keeps himself straight and walks with dignity as they leave the place.

Sung-i also tries to walk as if nothing has happened, but he can't carry it off. His head is spinning and his stomach's queasy. He feels like vomiting. He clutches his stomach. Asshole, you look just like a two-year-old, says Kŏl-i. He thinks of leaving Sung-i behind, but wanting to show how much more mature he is, he goes to Sung-i's side and grabs him by the arm.

Sung-i begins to vomit. Kŏl-i supports him and, avoiding the eyes of the people nearby, takes him to the bank of the ditch that runs by the shanty neighborhood. The midday winter sun is shining brightly on the filthy bank.

Sung-i continues to vomit the sour liquid. Asshole, puttin' on such a show after chuggin' one measly bowl. Kŏl-i pats Sung-i on the back, as an adult would do.

After vomiting for some time Sung-i turns around, as if to escape the sunlight in his eyes, and begins to sniffle. Asshole,

you're cryin'. Did yer dad kick the bucket or somethin'? Between the sniffles Sung-i murmurs, Bok-i, Bok-i. So what happened to your little brother, asshole? says Kŏl-i. Bok-i asked
me for some rice…rice…and I gave him a cuff, and then Bok-i,
Bok-i—

They suddenly heard a voice coming from a loudspeaker
somewhere in the shanty neighborhood: "Come out quickly
with your belongings! Right away! Come out quickly with your
belongings!" Straining to hear, Kŏl-i pulls Sung-i up by his
armpit.

A squad of government officials are invading the neighborhood to remove the shacks. A loudspeaker in a midsized truck
parked at the entrance to the neighborhood repeatedly blares
out the command for the inhabitants to come out with their
belongings, and upwards of ten squad members carrying pinchbars, crowbars, and sledgehammers are standing ready to
demolish the shacks once the order is handed down. The
inhabitants who had not gone to work are rushing outside and
squaring off against the squad members. "We assume you are
now coming out with all your belongings!" blares the
loudspeaker. "It's a hard winter—where're you tellin' us to go?"
shouted someone from the neighborhood. "We assume you are
now coming out with all your belongings!" "Give us a place to
go and *then* kick us out!" "Squad members ready!" "You'll have
t'kill us first—then you can do what you want!" "Demolish the
houses!" The moment the squad members move into action,
the people from the neighborhood surge forward and block
them. "Capture those who are interfering with the execution of
official duties!" But the inhabitants do not retreat. "Demolish
them, quickly!" The squad members wade through the people
and demolish one of the shacks. Pounding with sledgehammers, overturning with crowbars, puncturing with pinchbars…
"What about our kids!" "Quickly, quickly, demolish them!"
"Bastards—you're gonna die before your time!" "Quickly,
quickly, demolish them!" "You'll hafta kill us first, kill us!" In
an instant, some more of the shacks are made rubble. The inde-

cipherable clamor, the crying of the children... "Quickly, quickly, demolish them!" But then the squad members jump back. Rocks and excrement are flying down on them. Kŏl-i and Sung-i bring can after can of excrement to the front, and the neighborhood women supply the rocks. A police unit waiting nearby surges forward. As soon as they start swinging their billy clubs, the inhabitants fall back, and as soon as the rocks and excrement start flying, the policemen fall back... "Capture the ringleaders! Capture the ringleaders!" the loudspeaker blares. In the midst of this, Sŏng-ho springs forward and shouts to the shanty people to calm down. He too is hit by rocks and splattered with muck. But rather than dodging he shouts, "It's not them we have to deal with, but their superiors." Someone emerges from the crowd with a towel and wipes the excrement from his chest. The muck and rock throwing come to an abrupt halt. Sŏng-ho turns to the demolition squad and shouts, "Let us meet with your superiors!" "Ringleaders, come forward!" the loudspeaker responds. "Keep in mind that if things go on like this and the situation gets worse, the responsibility is not ours!" Sŏng-ho shouts. "Ringleaders, come forward!" Perceiving the support of the people of the neighborhood, Sŏng-ho slowly but willingly walks forward and climbs into the truck.

The next day the shanty people, taking with them whatever they could peel from their shacks, are transported to an area near Namhan Mountain Fortress.

"Goodness, I can't believe how high up you are on this ridge." Chi-yŏn retied her flapping scarf.

"That's why we decided to call it Starland Village," said Sŏng-ho. The sound of his laughter was whisked away by the wind.

"Where's Yŏng-i?"

"Asleep inside. Even with the wind blowing she sleeps like a log. But this is the way the wind usually is."

"It looks like people used to live over there. What happened?"

"From Starland Village they went down to the nether realm—back to Seoul. There's no place for them to work as day laborers here, so they sold out and left. But they didn't get a very good price. Brokers bought up their lots."

"Where did those women end up?"

"Those women? Oh yeah, they were left back in Seoul. Because they were renting. They didn't even own the shack they were in... It looks like they were thinking about all sorts of other jobs, but I don't think they'll be able to change their occupation for the time being. They felt sorry about us leaving—they said they'd find time to come by sometime."

Because Kŏl-i and his mother, like the women, had been renters, they too were not apportioned land here and were left behind in Seoul.

Chi-yŏn looked at Sŏng-ho, smiling despite the strong wind in her face.

"My life must seem ridiculous to you," said Sŏng-ho. "I still haven't decided what to do here. The greenhouse won't work, so I'm thinking the first thing I'll do is plant bellflowers around the outside of the neighborhood. If I have the chance, I'd like to ask Mr. Ham what'd be the best thing to do."

At the mention of Chun-t'ae, Chi-yŏn was overwhelmed with thoughts that she should be by his side. Whether or not he moved to Seoul, as her father had recommended, she had to be by his side. She stood in the cold wind a moment longer and then followed Sŏng-ho inside.

Chun-t'ae visually traced his route on the map attached to the back of his engagement book. He had left on this trip after several days of thought.

Where would the bus be on the map now? he wondered. And the plain outside the window? Though he called it a plain, it was more a basin surrounded by the mountains, which weren't far away. Probably here; after taking a rough visual measurement and noting that the area was colored green, he marked the point in his mind. The green area on the map was the dark red earth that appeared outside; under the wheels of the truck up ahead it was being changed to a whitish dust and dispersed.

Villages come into view. As soon as the bus passes one, another appears. Willows and zelkovas stand at the entrance to most of them, and the shapes of their houses are similar. Chun-t'ae occasionally sees a brick or stone building occupying the highest location in the village—it is a church with a cross on the roof. Looking absentmindedly out the window at the modern church buildings, Chun-t'ae feels they are quite out of place in the villages. He wonders what it would be like if they were used as schools for the village children on weekdays and places of worship on Sundays.

Mountains approach from both sides, and the bus enters a gorge. The bus bumps up and down—*t'ŏllŏk, t'ŏllŏk*—on the stone-flagged road. Just as he thinks the bumping is about to die down, the head of the bus lifts a bit and the bus slows down—they are crawling up a slope. At every turn in the road the driver sounds the horn. Then, just when the bus is leveling out, the front goes down and the bus accelerates. A woman sitting across the double seat in front of Chun-t'ae retches. With a cranky expression the conductress pushes a rusty can under the woman's feet. The woman rests her forehead on the back of the seat in front of her and vomits. Glancing at the suffering woman, Chun-t'ae guesses that the regurgitated, half-digested contents of her stomach might be corn and potatoes.

At Wŏnju Chun-t'ae transfers to a bus for Ch'ungju, and from there to Ch'ŏngju, and then to Taejŏn, where he spends the night.

Early the next morning he catches a train on the Honam line and gets off at Kimje. It's a much larger town than he had thought. His plan is to walk as far as possible, starting here. Having asked directions to the highway leading to the Okku area, he left Kimje. The climate's certainly warmer here than in Taegwallyŏng, he thought.

As he walks along he examines the topography and general

aspect of the surroundings. Fields stretch out on both sides. Villages are scattered sparsely among the plains. He stops by the villages that are surrounded by dry fields rather than paddies. Not caring how far they are from the highway, he enters even the villages of only two or three houses that have caught his eye, and after scrutinizing them he leaves—all the while taking the necessary notes.

Not until midafternoon, after he visited a place called Man-gyŏng, does he stop at a corner inn for a meal of bean-paste soup and rice, with a side dish of dried radish that had been spiced and salted. After emptying his rice bowl he checks the time and boards a bus for Okku. Even then he continues his observation of the countryside. He gets off the bus in Okku County and once more begins walking.

Chapter 6

As soon as she read the letter that came from Chun-t'ae that afternoon, Chi-yŏn went straight to her mother and spoke to her, packed lightly, and left the house. Since her mind was always on standby status these days, she was like an athlete in motion who, fully prepared, performs without a slip.

Her movement, however, was arrested at the airline ticket counter. Although the weather in Seoul was fine, the forecast for Kangnŭng was not good and the flights heading there had been suspended since morning. Without hesitating she rushed to the bus station, but the last bus for Kangnŭng had long since departed.

She had no choice but to go to Ch'ŏngnyangni Station and purchase a ticket for the night train. She was too impatient to return home and wait quietly until departure time so she caught a taxi. She got out at a stoplight just before Tongdaemun and began walking. Her bag wasn't very heavy, but she frequently changed it from one hand to the other. Her hands became cold and her shoes heavy. Such annoyances, though, seemed to reduce her anxiety and fretfulness.

Before she knew it she'd arrived in front of the Hwashin Department Store. A few steps beyond, a beauty shop caught her eye and she dashed inside. Chi-yŏn rarely visited beauty shops, for she had little interest in making herself up, and she could not stand the drudgery and vacuity of sitting in a chair and looking in a mirror while entrusting her hair to someone. "How long does it take for a permanent?" she asked. One of the beauticians said, "An hour and a half'll be plenty—come sit down here." Thinking she wouldn't mind if it took even more time, Chi-yŏn put down her bag and sat down. "Cut it the way you want," she said as the beautician tied a bib around her neck. Then she closed her eyes. Today, unlike other days, she was anticipating the repulsive smell of the chemicals applied to her hair and the unpleasant feeling of being strait-jacketed while the curling pins were inserted through the curlers.

Ŭn-hŭi had said she would not visit Min-gu's apartment until the wedding, but here she was, unannounced. Min-gu was ready to welcome her with a smile because of this unexpected visit, but his face hardened when he saw her grave expression. Remaining standing, Ŭn-hŭi took something out of her handbag with the tips of her thumb and forefinger, as if it revolted her, and held it out to him.

Min-gu cringed as soon as he saw it. It was a large photograph. The entire picture was blurry, giving the impression that the subject was trembling, but even though the person's features were unclear, it was no doubt Min-gu. The photograph showed him wearing the *an-ollim bŏnggŏji* and performing a leap, his *k'waeja* trailing in the air. How could such a scene have been photographed? Min-gu wondered. Upon tracing the events of that day he realized, as if the memory were jutting out before him, that at the climax of his leaping, when he had been oblivious to almost everything, the young man whom Pyŏn called his cousin had been playing with a camera. Even so, how could Ŭn-hŭi have gotten this photograph? Min-gu strained to compose himself, but he couldn't help asking, "Where'd this come from?"

"Do I have to tell you? And what does it matter? The important thing is whether this is for real or not." Ŭn-hŭi spoke coldly. "In any event, it's you for sure, isn't it."

There was no way for Min-gu to escape.

"Look at the back, too."

Min-gu turned over the photograph with trembling fingers. The small, precise letters written in ball-point pen lanced his eyes, and he felt he'd received a blow to the back of his head.

"To the Founder of the Tanggul religion," it read. "You

would be wise not to distinguish what is right or wrong. Not disclosing any of this to anybody (including Pyŏn, of course) would be a way to avoid the consequences. I hope you will bear in mind that if you do not do this, things will escalate into an uncontrollable situation. I state positively that I will say nothing further of this to anyone. I will simply entrust the future course of action to the judgment of the wise Founder. From one of the faithful."

Min-gu felt dizzy. He outlined the true character of this young man whom Pyŏn called his cousin. So that was it after all. The young man and Pyŏn were not relatives, nor was their relationship a casual one—the relationship between Min-gu and Pyŏn was what the young man had enjoyed until he went to Vietnam. These facts were more than enough to confirm Min-gu's hunch that Pyŏn had been sincere when he first appealed to him, saying he couldn't endure his need for a man. The young man, on the other hand, couldn't tolerate Min-gu's presence upon his return from Vietnam, but being dependent on Pyŏn, he disguised himself and waited for his chance. In the meantime he was able to make contact with Ŭn-hŭi, whom Min-gu had sensed was following him.

"I hate to bring this up, but I will. What on earth is the Tanggul religion?" Ŭn-hŭi asked in a standoffish tone.

Suddenly twitching his thick eyebrows, Min-gu laughed as loudly as he could. The laugh was so loud that it startled even Ŭn-hŭi, who heard his boisterous laughter all the time.

"He's just playing around," Min-gu said. "He wants to give me a hard time. I'll get back at that guy some day."

But Min-gu felt that his laughter and speech had no efficacy and were returning, hollow, to him. The young man was really harrying him; the threat was a faultless piece of work.

"Who's Pyŏn?" Ŭn-hŭi asked insistently and in the same standoffish tone. She stared at Min-gu, who appeared to have lost his composure.

"Huh?"

"I asked you who Pyŏn is. Is it true he's an expert at telling fortunes?"

"That's right, he's a fortune-teller. A fortune-teller who's been a great help to me in my research."

"The one who gave you the colorful necktie at our engagement ceremony, right?"

"That's right. I remember."

"And he looked pretty, like a woman."

"Like a woman?" Startled, Min-gu wondered how much Ŭn-hŭi knew.

"What have you been up to with this Pyŏn? Tell me frankly."

"You think I haven't been frank? Like I just said, he's been helping me a lot in my research."

"Is that all there is to it?"

"What else should there be? If you don't believe me, you can check with the fellow who gave you this photo." It was a flat denial. Under the circumstances, Min-gu had no other choice. On the other hand, Min-gu had grasped the meaning of a sentence in the young man's message that gave him confidence: "I state positively that I will say nothing further of this to anyone."

"Fine. This time I won't tell Father. Because I'm ashamed of this too."

Although Min-gu sensed something explosive within these seemingly generous words, his first response was to try to hold Ŭn-hŭi's hand, heaving a sigh of relief now that he was over the hump.

"Get away from me! I don't want it!" Ŭn-hŭi slapped away his fingers with the back of her hand and said, "Instead of telling Father, I'm giving you a condition."

"A condition?"

"From now on, you wash your hands of this kind of thing."

"What's that...All right, all right, I will."

"It's not enough just to say it."

"Then what? Do I have to write it in blood?"

"You'll have to show me."

"How am I supposed to do that?"

"That's for you to find out. Why should I have to spell every-thing out for you?" she asked spitefully. Then she whipped her-self around and walked briskly out the door.

Dumfounded, Min-gu chases her outside, thinking he should do better, but as Ŭn-hŭi descends the stairs her back leaves him with the impression of stout resistance.

Chi-yŏn attempted to calm herself once she boarded the train. She wouldn't be arriving in Kangnŭng until eight the next morning, eleven hours from now.

She tried to forget the time by sleeping. But although she closed her eyes, she couldn't fall asleep, and ominous thoughts forced themselves into her mind again and again. She tried to focus on the sound of the wheels screeching along the rails. Still the ominous thoughts edged themselves into the crevices of her consciousness, so in the end she concentrated on the *kadakkadak kadakkadak* of the wheels striking the rail fasten-ings.

Much later a *ssi'ik ssi'ik* opened her eyes. It was steam escaping from under the stopped train. The appearance of sev-eral passengers boarding and leaving the train, and especially their slow movements, glimmered in her eyes. Over and over she heard the *kadakkadak kadakkadak* and *ssi'ik ssi'ik* of the train, and although she kept her eyes closed, she knew when the train was moving and when it had stopped. In this state, closer to wakefulness than to sleep, the image of a throng of people was mirrored in her eyes. They are each looking for someone as they gather in the city square. Though all of them bustle about they make no sound—all is silence. Those who find who they are seeking walk off somewhere arm in arm, arms around shoulders, or simply side by side. After the people have departed, a lone figure remains. Tirelessly the figure wan-ders about the square, but the person being sought doesn't appear. A foglike gloom begins to fall upon the ever-mute square. The figure wanders about fretfully. How I wish he'd appear. How I wish it. The outline of the figure becomes obscure in the gradually thickening gloom, and finally blends into it. Again Chi-yŏn heard the *kadakkadak kadakkadak ssi'ik ssi'ik,* then she woke up as the train alternately fell back and leaned forward while passing over high ground, and then once more she was floating between wakefulness and sleep. Even in this state, the tentacles of her anxiety kept guard, gripping persistently at her nerves.

Awakening in the predawn darkness, Ch'ang-ae got up, clutched her nightgown about her, and went to the next room. Light was streaming from under the door.

She quietly opens the door. Mr. Kang is asleep, the base of his head against the back of the chair in which he sits. His head is tilted back as far as it will go, and as Ch'ang-ae looks down at his sleeping face—the mouth half open and a faint sound issuing from the nose—she experiences a strange illusion. It seems to be a face she has seen somewhere, yet it is unfamiliar. He appears to have aged so much she can't determine his age, yet he appears rather boyish. It is obvious only that he is quite fatigued. For several days he didn't even touch the art supplies he had bought, but then three days ago he started taking catnaps during the day and staying up all night wrestling with his paintings. He must have worn himself out, Ch'ang-ae tells herself.

Ch'ang-ae silently spreads a blanket over Mr. Kang and turns off the light. Muffling her footsteps, she returns to the bedroom, looks toward the window, and slowly approaches it. She touches her forehead to the glass.

Speckled things are flying by outside. The darkness has become milky, as if it is being washed away by them. Ch'ang-ae remains with her forehead against the window. But no matter how the speckled things wash away at the darkness, it becomes no thinner. The darkness is lovely. Things are lovely when, as now, no meaning is being forced upon them. But to expect that kind of beauty in the lives of humans is to overdo it, she thinks.

The speckled things are inside Ch'ang-ae as well, but they're gradually being darkened by a shadow. How could I have wanted these sticky entanglements? she wonders. Why can't I keep my distance from people and let them go their own way? For some reason she feels wretched. Can't we live so that we don't idle away the present while thinking about the past, or victimize the future on behalf of the present?

A chalky light, different from the light of daybreak, suddenly veiled the surroundings.

The passengers wiped the vapor from the windows with palms or handkerchiefs. Outside, snowflakes were fluttering by.

Chi-yŏn directed her eyes, dry from her fitful sleep, to the snow that had settled on the bare limbs of trees and blanketed the branches of the pines. Maybe because it was daybreak, she felt much less anxious than she had during the gloomy night. By midmorning I'll be seeing Chun-t'ae, she thought.

The farther the train sped, the thicker the snowflakes became. Outside, distances became blurred and elevations indistinct. The pine boughs drooped, unable to bear their loads of snow.

The sea, appearing to the right, swallowed the falling snow without leaving a trace. The passengers' view was blocked by the blur of the snow and then opened a bit, opened and then blocked. The train arrived at a station where men were pushing aside the knee-deep snow with wooden shovels. It's been coming down for quite some time here, Chi-yŏn thought.

The closer the train got to Kangnŭng, the thicker the snowfall and the heavier the accumulation. Chi-yŏn was seized anew by anxiety. She had been fretful before because she couldn't reach her destination instantly, but now she was apprehensive about nearing the place where she would find Chun-t'ae.

Even so, the train had no sooner arrived at Kangnŭng than Chi-yŏn was rushing to the bus station without even having breakfast. At the station several would-be passengers were pacing back and forth. They had found that the roads were impassable and the buses were not running. The situation again took on a growing urgency. The snow was still falling thick and fast.

Chi-yŏn grabbed a bite to eat and found a tearoom where she was able to hear the news over a radio. Transportation and communications in the Taegwallyŏng area and the greater Sokch'o area had been paralyzed by a heavy snowstorm in the Yŏngdong region. Chi-yŏn felt helpless.

A couple of hours later she returned to the bus station. Several buses sat empty, merely gathering snow—not a soul was to be seen.

Lunchtime went by and the snow stopped. Bored and impatient, Chi-yŏn listened to the news on the tearoom radio; the weather in the Yŏngdong region was gradually improving, and snow removal was under way. Chi-yŏn went to a public bathhouse.

Her hair still damp, she went to the bus station again, but the empty buses, wearing a heavy coat of snow, were still there. An employee told her the buses for Taegwallyŏng would run the next afternoon at the earliest, and if not, then the following day.

There was nothing for Chi-yŏn to do but spend the night at an inn. Mentally and physically tired, she slept more deeply than the night before. But still she woke up frequently, and every time she would examine the conditions outside. She could see that the snow had ended, but she wanted to be certain.

In the meantime, she dreamed she was outside in the falling snow. The snowflakes were feathery. She was trying to regain the dim romanticism of her high school days. But as soon as the snowflakes touched her they left black stains. Her clothing, face, and hands—all were stained black by the snow. Startled, she looked up at the sky and discovered that it was completely covered with black snow. But she wasn't displeased with the black snow that was extinguishing her romanticism. Instead she let it fall upon her, regarding it as something quite natural.

Before she knew it she was driving along at the wheel of a

truck. She was on her way to pick up a load of produce, though she didn't know where. She recalled a previous occasion when she had been on her way to pick up some produce. That time she had been dressed in blue denim work clothes and white sneakers, but now the clothing and sneakers were black. On and on she went, the truck slowly plowing through mountains of black snow, but no farms appeared. Even so, she kept on driving without a rest. But then ahead of her a sheet of paper had been spread out. The paper was darker than the black snow. She wondered whether to merely run over it, but then she looked more carefully and saw it was a letter she had received from Chun-t'ae. She quickly picked it up. She couldn't make out the writing because of the blackness of the paper. I *have* to read it, she fretted, and then she woke up. In the darkness she recalled the letter with much trepidation.

Chi-yŏn,

I'm not sure how to say this. I'm sick. What you've seen of my illness is only the surface. The cause is deeply rooted, and it's hard for me to explain. Though it's clear it can't be cured by medicine or the knife. I've been ignoring the disease for some time. To be exact, since I first started thinking about you. And the more I ignore it, the more out of control it gets. I've tried to make some compromises with it, but they've all been in vain. Finally I decided to obey its demands. Not because I've lost out to it, but because I realize it was me and no one else who planted and cultivated the cause of it. I may have to keep on living with the disease. Even if you criticize me for being incapable and cowardly, there's nothing I can do. Let me be. And it will be less painful for you that way. Chi-yŏn, I won't say any more. It might have been better if I hadn't said anything.

Chun-t'ae

At about eleven the next morning, sooner than Chi-yŏn had expected, the road to Taegwallyŏng was reopened. As soon as she arrived at the alpine testing station she went to the house where Chun-t'ae had been boarding. No path had been cleared through the virgin snow.

"Good heavens, in this snow, how..." Chun-t'ae's landlady could not conceal her surprise.

Chi-yŏn already knew intuitively that Chun-t'ae was no longer there. True, I suspected he'd left by now, but didn't I come to make sure? she reflected. Still, she was disheartened and depressed.

"Did he leave somethin' behind?" The woman apparently thought Chi-yŏn had come to retrieve something Chun-t'ae had forgotten when he left.

Feebly shaking her head, Chi-yŏn asked, "When did he leave?"

"Did somethin' happen to him?" With a worried expression the woman said, "It's been exactly four days now," as if she had been counting off the days in her mind.

Chun-t'ae had left two days before Chi-yŏn received the letter.

"He didn't say anything about where he was going?" Chi-yŏn asked.

Looking even more puzzled and concerned, the woman said, "No, nothin' at all. We just thought he was goin' to Seoul."

Chi-yŏn reiterated to herself the words she had been suppressing since she received the letter. Please don't say only the things you think will hurt me less.

"Are you all right? You musta had a devil of a time comin' up here in this snow."

Chi-yŏn was barely able to collect herself. She changed the subject, saying to the woman, "By the way, have you heard anything from your son?"

"Oh yes." The woman's face became smooth. "We had a letter two days ago. It was the first in five months and ten days. Can you believe it?"

"That's wonderful." Confused though she was, Chi-yŏn was truly happy that the woman had received a letter from her son. "It's the result of all your waiting." Chi-yŏn knew that at sunup every day the woman drew some well water and prayed fervently to the spirits, and that she was keeping in a separate crock a *mal*[1] of newly harvested rice to feed her son when he returned.

"He didn't say anything about when he'll be returnin'. But we'll just be patient and wait. And not just five months—we'll wait five years. If only he returns alive."

Suddenly it occurred to Chi-yŏn that from now on, she too had better develop that habit of waiting. But for me there'll be no letters. She quickly rejected the thought. I must find him, no matter what. And then I'll have to get used to his illness. But how?

"The night before Mr. Ham left I was drinking with him in that store out in front, but he didn't have much to say. We just drank, and when I asked him where he was going, he smiled and said he wasn't going to be a nine-to-fiver anymore—that's all." As Pak said this, he seemed to be staring into space off to the side of Chi-yŏn.

"Did his health seem all right?"

"Hard to say. He didn't look much different from usual... but while we were drinking he said several times that he was sorry he wouldn't be able to see some real snow."

Chun-t'ae had left so hurriedly that he had missed a real snowfall here. Where to? Chi-yŏn wondered. And what could he have meant by saying he wouldn't be a nine-to-fiver anymore?

"No, did he really? He didn't tell me anything at all." Mingu's voice on the other end of the line was unusually impersonal. "Even when he was transferred to Kangnŭng he didn't say a word to me. And then when we met at Ch'anggyŏng-wŏn he said to look him up there and he even gave me directions—I don't know what's going on. As a matter of fact, I've been kind

[1]*Mal:* a unit of liquid or dry measure equaling 18.1 liters or 19 quarts.

of confused lately and I was thinking of paying him a visit. He's really gotten strange. He wasn't like that before, but then he got divorced all of a sudden..."

Chi-yŏn hadn't expected much from talking with Min-gu, but she again realized that no one knew of Chun-t'ae's whereabouts. If I don't find him, if I don't find him somehow, she constantly reminded herself.

PART IV

Cornerstone One, Cornerstone Two

A long, vertical split had opened in the block wall plastered with cement. The place had been patched, but the crack had reappeared.

"I suppose it's no good plastering it over again. Once it's started to open up, it's no use, no matter how many times we plaster," the owner of the house said, looking with dissatisfaction at the crack running down the wall.

"On the contrary," said the plasterer. "Try having it well plastered just once. It'll be safe and sound." He taps the bottom of the wall. "The foundation's settled all that it's going to."

"Well then, should I have it done once more?"

"I'll take care of it, tomorrow at the latest."

"Let's do it when winter's over and done with. They say spring's coming early this year, but since it's only the middle of March, we might get another cold snap—who knows?"

"It'll be all right—it's sunny here."

"No need to hurry," says the owner. "Let's do it when spring's here to stay."

Ŭn-hŭi entrusted Ch'ang-ae with the selection and design of the material for her wedding dress, as she had with the outfit

Ch'ang-ae had made for her. She had been satisfied with the outfit. Strangely enough, in fact, she had covertly acknowledged Ch'ang-ae's talent as a designer the first time they met. And she had maintained her interest in Ch'ang-ae, sympathizing with her because of the breakup of her marriage.

After settling on a date for the first fitting of the wedding dress, Ch'ang-ae and Ŭn-hŭi left the dress shop for a tearoom. Again Ch'ang-ae led the way, though it was Ŭn-hŭi who had hoped they would have such an opportunity to talk.

"I'm glad your shop seems to be doing well," Ŭn-hŭi said, repeating what she had told Ch'ang-ae just before selecting a seat and sitting down.

"I'm almost out of debt now," Ch'ang-ae responded. Moreover, for some time now she hadn't been engaging in the humiliating business of buying and reselling foreign-made goods.

"You have a talent for your work and besides that you make a good impression on your customers."

"I just try to put my heart into it."

"But there's something I haven't been able to figure out. I just can't understand how your marriage fell apart. Don't you have to handle men just like you would children? Children are full of mischief, and so we always have to keep an eye on them and apply restrictions...Don't you have to treat a husband the same way in order to maintain a marriage?" The last time Ŭn-hŭi had sat across from Ch'ang-ae in a tearoom she had felt awkward, unable to steer the conversation in the direction she wanted, but today she felt she was succeeding beyond her expectations, and it made her feel mature.

Ch'ang-ae looked at Ŭn-hŭi as if to say that there was nothing extraordinary in what she had said.

"Of course, no matter how childlike they are," continued Ŭn-hŭi, "we have to make them as responsible as possible when it's necessary."

"If responsibilities like that linger in a marriage, then the couple only end up suffocating each other. And if you keep a marriage like that, then it couldn't have much meaning."

"Is that what you think?" Ŭn-hŭi took a match from the matchbox, and while breaking it into pieces said, "Now what if...what if you could start over again? What kind of marriage would you hope for?"

"I haven't thought about that, but..." Ch'ang-ae paused for a moment. "If by some chance I were born again, I'd probably take the path I'm following now."

Ŭn-hŭi was disappointed at this unexpected answer. So she'd take the road to failure again; I guess she doesn't want to swallow her pride, Ŭn-hŭi told herself.

"After all," Ch'ang-ae continued, "people live on with their regrets. It's only natural, isn't it?" She had come to view Ŭn-hŭi as very simple-minded.

A young man came in with a boy of six or seven and sat down next to them, saying to the boy, "I'll take you to the movies again, so if there's one you'd like to see, then mark it down." "Where do I mark it down?" the boy asked. "Where do you mark it down? Is that what you asked? You mark it down in your head," the young man replied. "Gee whiz, that can't be right. How am I supposed to see inside my head?"

The nearby patrons laughed.

Ch'ang-ae looked at the boy and continued to smile. With its longish countenance and the threadlike eyes in the narrow forehead, the face of the boy wasn't at all cute. If I were to have a child, how would its features be? she wondered. Like Mr. Kang's? Like mine? In neither case could she outline the face of the child in her imagination. But what's the use now of thinking about a baby's face being this way or that? she reflected. She removes her eyes from the boy, who isn't quiet for even an instant.

"You look like you enjoy children," Ŭn-hŭi said. Her smile was neither subtle nor overdone. "Why didn't you have one? It would have been a perfect baby...How many would you like to have?"

"One," Ch'ang-ae replied without hesitation. She was surprised—it was the first time she had clearly expressed her desire for a child.

"I'd have to have at least three."

Although Ŭn-hŭi proceeded to explain why she desired three children, Ch'ang-ae didn't listen attentively. She was absorbed in her own thoughts. Today was the first time she had ever said she wanted to have children, but hadn't such a desire been lurking in her mind for some time now? When she and Chun-t'ae were divorced her mind was light because there were no children, and later she had aborted the child she had conceived with Mr. Kang. I suddenly have this desire for a child—I guess there's no way I can get rid of a woman's mothering instinct, she told herself.

"Pardon me?" Ch'ang-ae had not caught what Ŭn-hŭi was saying.

"Has Mr. Ham shown up?"

"Shown up?" Ch'ang-ae tilted her head forward.

"Then you don't know that he disappeared? It's been more than two months...You knew he was transferred somewhere out in the sticks, didn't you? He was there, and then he left, covering up his tracks and everything."

"No...Why did he do that?"

"It's obvious—to escape from that woman."

"I don't believe it..." Ch'ang-ae was confident that Chun-t'ae was not a man to run away and hide from a woman. There must've been some pressing circumstances, something that made it necessary for him to do that.

"It's natural. He didn't realize how wonderful his wife was. And that other woman, what's so good about her? I just can't understand men."

Although Ŭn-hŭi's words were extremely galling, they were no longer a problem for Ch'ang-ae. Clearly some misfortune had befallen Chun-t'ae, and the cause of that misfortune, she believed, lay first with her. And just a month or so ago, Mr. Kang had given up his painting again and gone out wandering the streets, unable to put his mind to any work—wasn't I partly to blame for that? she thought. Why do the men I get involved with end up that way? Do I have some crucial defect that makes them like that? I've only tried to be honest with myself.

"I guess I'd better be going. The shop's been empty for a while now..." Ch'ang-ae didn't want to sit with Ŭn-hŭi any longer.

Outside, as they were parting, Ch'ang-ae said, "You told me the wedding was the twenty-seventh, didn't you? Oh, but you have to come for the first fitting."

"Yes, that's right."

"Since I didn't make it to the engagement ceremony, I'll have to go to the wedding."

Even while Ch'ang-ae was saying this, her thoughts of Chun-t'ae, whose whereabouts were unknown, were muddled with her thoughts of Mr. Kang, who was going around like a boat without its sail. She asked herself whether her fate was any better.

"I heard you might be leaving. It really surprised me," said the student to Min-gu while rolling and unrolling a paperback.

So there's a rumor's going around, Min-gu thought in alarm. Various possibilities played across his mind. Granted, he was in a tight position, unsure whether he would be able to continue his research on shaman culture. If in the end he couldn't, then it would be only natural for him to quit teaching, in which case he'd probably cast his lot with Ŭn-hŭi's father's pharmaceutical company. Ŭn-hŭi's attitude was that firm and obstinate. She had gone as far as to tell him, "Choose one or the other, me or playing shaman." Of course Min-gu couldn't help admitting that his conduct had exceeded the bounds of scholarly research. Among his difficulties, he had had to suspend work on his essay "Birds and the Characteristics of Koreans," not to mention his peculiar relationship with Pyŏn. These days he was barely able to appease Ŭn-hŭi by repeating his pledge to submit to any judgment she made in case of further aberrant conduct on his part. Realizing that she would constantly interfere if he continued his research on shamanism, he decided it might be better to establish a comfortable life by entrusting himself to the pharmaceutical company. But the decision did not come easily. He drank every day, and his large eyes had reddened. Having a great impact on this troublesome situation was Min-gu's belief that he loved Ŭn-hŭi and couldn't part with her. Even now this thought flashed through his mind. Then Chun-t'ae's face suddenly appeared. His tightly closed lips moved, and he said in a thundering voice: "Your situation is a direct result of having a nomad mentality, and you better be aware of that." Min-gu quickly averted his face.

"If you leave school, it will be a great blow to me, Sir. Your lectures are the most fascinating that I attend. And I've developed an interest in shamanism and have been wondering if I could study under you."

Min-gu examined the student's face once more. He had pleaded with Min-gu over the telephone for an appointment, and Min-gu had asked him to come here to the Uju Tearoom. But no matter how long he studied his face, he couldn't single it out from the others in his classes. In no mood to speak at length with the student about any aspect of shamanism, he merely told him matter-of-factly, "Researching shamanism is a tough business. It's not something you can do sitting in your study. You have to get right out and chase around for what you want."

"That's no problem. I've done so much hiking since high school that there isn't a mountain in the country I haven't been to."

"It's not the same as hiking." Min-gu had a hunch that this was a lazy student who disliked studying and was proposing that since he had to major in something he'd like to try a field that few others were involved in. Min-gu looked at his watch. He wished Ŭn-hŭi would appear. They had decided to look over the house they had bought in Tonggyo-dong.

"I've been thinking about this lately," said the student. "You know how women dye their fingernails with touch-me-not petals? Now it's developed into manicuring, but I've been wondering whether it was started in order to protect against evil spirits and misfortune more than to make people beautiful. It's the same theory behind hanging charcoal or red peppers over the door of a house in order to ward off evil spirits from a newborn baby. It's so easy for any kind of spirit to attach itself to a woman. And isn't it women who are possessed and become shamans? When I look at it like this, it seems that Korean women started using touch-me-nots and polishing their nails much earlier than women in other countries, and they did it to keep away those evil spirits. Don't you think so, Sir?"

Looking across at the eager expression of the student, who had unfolded his theory as if he had come across something new and wonderful, Min-gu recalled how he had behaved until a few months before and remarked, "As in everything else, a temporary interest isn't good enough. You have to resolve to marry yourself to shamanism."

"Ah yes. I have to put my heart and soul—"

In the middle of the student's sentence Min-gu got up. Ŭn-hŭi had entered the tearoom.

"From now on I think I ought to have some personal guidance from you, Sir." The student also stood up.

"You'll have to rely on your own efforts." With this blunt dictate Min-gu walked toward Ŭn-hŭi, who remained just inside the door. "At a time like this, when I haven't even made up my mind about my own affairs, how am I supposed to get involved with something else? No way," he grumbled to himself.

Chi-yŏn ascended the pass to which she had been directed in the village, and a thatch-roof hut lying at the foot of a hillock across a ravine came into sight. It was certainly a hut she had seen once before somewhere. When was it, and where, where? Ah, that's right. It's the hut I saw lying at the bottom of the mountain on the other side of the ravine when I went to Wŏl-chŏng Temple with Chun-t'ae. She hadn't known who was living in that hut, but she knew Chun-t'ae was in the one she saw now.

Forgetting the fatigue of several days of wandering in search of Chun-t'ae, Chi-yŏn began to drop down from the pass. She had gone to Kunsan upon receiving word from Pak at the alpine testing station that Chun-t'ae had had some seed potatoes sent to the train station in Kunsan, but Chun-t'ae had already left with the goods by the time she got there. Of course she hadn't been able to find his address at the station. She wished she could have gone to Kunsan before Chun-t'ae came for the potatoes, but Pak's letter had arrived much too late. Pak couldn't be blamed, however. For several days he had wondered whether to inform Chi-yŏn, and only when he had convinced himself that Chun-t'ae wasn't the sort to hide because of a mistake did he write to her. Having gone in vain to Kunsan Station, Chi-yŏn went next to Kunsan City Hall and the Okku County offices and asked which areas in the region were suitable for planting potatoes. After touring practically every town in Okku County, she had finally succeeded in locating Chun-t'ae's residence.

Chi-yŏn could hear the pounding of her heart. How will he treat me? she wondered. Will he be glad? Angry? Either way, the only thing I can do is face it. Whether this meeting is the end of everything or a new start comes afterward. The first thing is to see him.

Land reclaimed from the hill lay at the foot of the pass. The red earth, mixed with small rocks, was being cultivated extensively. Chi-yŏn stood atop a bank along one of the dry fields. There was nothing that looked like a path. Once again she thought it fortunate that she was wearing slacks and low-heeled shoes.

She reached a stream in the ravine. The shallow water flowed transparent over the bed of pebbles. The warm rays of the afternoon sun sparkled as the water reflected them. Snow remained in the shaded corners of her yard in Seoul, but she was further south here. The air felt different, and during her several days of wandering she had found that the warmth of spring had removed all traces of ice.

Chi-yŏn selected a large rock, and as she stepped on it to cross the stream the small fish among the pebbles flitted away in every direction. The image of the carps that she had seen in a dream long before dashed across her mind, but she was too occupied to reflect on it.

Across the ravine was another extensive field of land reclaimed from the hill. Again there was no path, so she ascended and then followed a bank that ran through the field.

The closer Chi-yŏn came to the hut the more her heart fluttered. I wonder what he'll say first. How will he react? Will his face be tanned? Bearded? Before she knew it her hands were patting down her hair.

Chi-yŏn walked toward the well in front of the hut. A woman who appeared to be a little over thirty was doing laundry, and a boy of five or six was squatting nearby. Composing herself, Chi-yŏn slowed her pace and approached the woman.

"This is where Mr. Ham lives, isn't it?"

The woman had paused to look at Chi-yŏn. Instead of answering she said "I guess you came from Seoul" in Chŏlla Province dialect.

"Yes...He's not here now?"

The woman merely stares up at Chi-yŏn. Her figure is rather full, and there's a luster to the sunken, unfocused eyes in her pale, haggard cheeks.

"He's not here now?" Chi-yŏn repeated.

"Tol-i's dad ain't here," the woman said, indicating with her chin the boy beside her.

"Pardon me?" Chi-yŏn looked around at the hut. Several straw sacks, covered with straw mats, had been piled against the near wall, and tags were attached to them. No doubt they were the sacks of seed potatoes, the very seed potatoes that had enabled her to find Chun-t'ae. She couldn't help asking again, "Isn't this Ham Chun-t'ae's house?"

"That's right. And I'm sayin' he's this here kid's dad. He ain't home just now."

Chi-yŏn was stupefied. Did she say Chun-t'ae's the father of

that kid? she asked herself. What on earth has happened? She
had thought that this woman with the boy was only someone
who looked after Chun-t'ae's meals and laundry.

"Hospital," said the boy to Chi-yŏn.

"Hospital?" Chi-yŏn asked the woman.

"He went to the hospital in town."

"What's the problem?"

"He's got this bad cough."

"Is it serious?"

"Can't say—sometimes it's real bad and sometimes it ain't so
bad..."

"When will he be coming back?"

Rapidly blinking her lustrous eyes, the woman replied, "It'd
prob'ly be better if you didn't wait. It'd be good for him, and
good for you too, lady." Having handed down this judgment,
the woman began to beat a violent tattoo on the washed clothing with her laundry sticks.

Chi-yŏn felt she was floating in space—there was no sensation in her hands or feet, and she couldn't locate them. She felt
only a continuous swelling in her head. Although she didn't
know the full story, she wondered if there wasn't at least a
conjugal relationship between Chun-t'ae and this woman. Chi-
yŏn stood there in a daze. There was only the cadence of the
laundry sticks ringing in her head. Her throat was parched. I'd
like some water, Chi-yŏn thought, but instead of voicing her
desire she turned on her heels and began to walk away. Her
eyes were swimming. She stopped and braced herself. Taking
her engagement book from her handbag, she tore off a sheet
and with an effort composed a short message.

"Please give this to him."

The woman took the piece of paper in one of her wet hands.

Chi-yŏn finally asked for water, and after taking several gulps
said goodbye and again turned around. She had gone but a few
steps when she heard the woman's voice.

"No matter how you try, the two o' you ain't gonna be able
to meet."

The woman's tone may have been calmer than before, but to Chi-yŏn it felt just like dry, cold sand sprinkled evenly over her naked back.

Chi-yŏn walked faster. She had no idea how to accept this situation.

She waited for the bus, unable to remember how she had found her way to the highway. In just two months there had been this much of a change in Chun-t'ae's condition—what am I going to do from now on? The only thing that was clear was that she had to leave at once, leave without seeing Chun-t'ae, leave without even knowing his condition now that he was in the hospital.

Searchingly Chun-t'ae read the note stained with the water-blotted ink.

> I came to see you, but I'm leaving. I don't know what's what. I'm worried about your health, but it seems best for me to just go back. Please take care of yourself.
>
> *Chi-yŏn*

"When did she come?" Lifting his eyes from the piece of paper, Chun-t'ae thrust the question at the woman. His feverish face was fraught with tension.

"Several hours ago," the woman replied in her Chŏlla dialect.

"Didn't you tell her to wait until I returned?"

Instead of answering directly the woman said, "I knew right away she was the lady you been close with for a long time. But I found out you and her can't meet again—it's your fate."

Disgust toward the woman swelled up in Chun-t'ae. He had never felt such a strong aversion to anyone. Determinedly he turned around. It's not too late to catch up with her. I have to see her, even if it means following her to Seoul. I can't bury myself in this empty life anymore. I have to follow her, even if it means my death.

After about ten paces he squatted. He was choking. He

knelt, overtaken by a long surge of uncontrollable coughing. He wanted to take hold of something, but there was nothing around him. He clutched at the soil. The damp spring earth lumped together in his hands.

Some time later the fit stopped, but Chun-t'ae's energy was gone. Unable to control his body, he couldn't lift himself from the ground. He felt the eyes of the woman ridiculing him, though he didn't look back. Perhaps she was thinking it was because he had disregarded her prophecy. The day after Chun-t'ae had settled here she had come to the hut in the deep of the night, carrying the boy on her back. She had said she'd been widowed long ago and had come here from far away because she had suddenly become a shaman and the spirit possessing her had directed her to such and such a place, where she would meet a noble man. Because of the child, Chun-t'ae felt compelled to take them in. The situation had dragged on until now.

Chun-t'ae got up with great difficulty. His mind and body seemed to be functioning separately. He thought of going to the well to wash his hands, but merely brushed the dirt from his palms and clothing and began to wobble along. His aversion toward the woman had already died out.

Chun-t'ae looked inward. Which side of me should I follow? The one that longs so much for Chi-yŏn, or the one that rejects her? Neither is a lie. The only thing is not to hurt her. I have to try to cope with my nomadic life in my own way, wearing these two sides of me just as I wear the smell of my body.

Reaching the stream in the ravine, he washed the earth from his hands and wiped the perspiration from his face.

After crossing the pass and entering the village, Chun-t'ae went to the home of Old Kwŏn. He wished to talk with him about how to distribute the seed potatoes, but at the same time, he didn't want to go home immediately. Kwŏn wasn't in. Thinking he might be at the inn, Chun-t'ae decided to go there. In any event, he had to kill some time. Even before looking inside the inn, he knew Kwŏn was there—his voice, higher and louder than usual, had reached all the way outside.

Kwŏn and two of the villagers were drinking *makkŏlli* in a room across from the inn's main room. They made space for Chun-t'ae and asked him to sit down. Chun-t'ae entered the room and took a seat.

Old Kwŏn emptied a glass of *makkŏlli* and passed the glass toward Chun-t'ae. Chun-t'ae waved it away.

"I see you've had a few drinks already," said Kwŏn in his Chŏlla dialect.

My God, Chun-t'ae thinks, my face is so feverish it must look like I've been drinking. He had a racking headache and his entire body was listless. He recalled what the doctor had told him that day. Asthmatics had to be careful or else they'd come down with bronchitis or pneumonia. And his heart had deteriorated terribly.

Chun-t'ae spoke briefly with Kwŏn, suggesting they divide the seed potatoes the following day. The other two villagers asked if they too might have a share, and Chun-t'ae assented.

Chun-t'ae felt that his eyes were popping out of their sockets. He wanted only to lie down. He gradually became more languid all over, and his head started spinning. After obtaining some water from the woman who kept the inn, he took the medicine prescribed at the hospital. Lacking an appetite, he had skipped lunch, and taking the medicine on an empty stomach made him unbearably nauseated. He felt uncomfortable sitting there and not drinking anything, but he knew some food would revive his energy, even though he would have to force himself to eat, so he asked the innkeeper to cook some rice gruel for him.

Upon seeing Chun-t'ae take the medicine and ask the innkeeper for some gruel, the villagers solicitously inquired if he was sick. Chun-t'ae said he seemed to have picked up a bad cold. He leaned back against the wall to make himself comfortable.

The villagers resumed their conversation. Their usual practice was to exchange several rounds of *makkŏlli* and then light up a conversation when they were tolerably intoxicated. Now they were telling stories about farming. So and so had sold his land to someone in town and was going to become a tenant farmer starting this year; he thought it was the smart thing to do, because when he farmed his own land the various expenditures mounted up while the price he got for his rice was generally too low and so he ended up in debt; anyway, they wonder if this year's fertilizer will be provided on time, and they hope to high heaven they won't have to take that stuff called *yongsŏng*, because even though government officials say it's good as a basic fertilizer, it actually isn't effective at all, and weren't they just shelling out money in vain to have it transported to their land, only to end up throwing it all away, and to top everything off, there weren't enough farmhands in the village—so and so had gone in the army, and this other fellow had gotten discharged and gone away to the city.

The innkeeper came in with an overly large bowl filled to the brim with gruel. Chun-t'ae could not finish a fourth of it, and even that bit he ate out of a sense of duty, all the time wondering if it was ever going to pass down his throat.

The three villagers had turned to wisecracking, and now they were caricaturing rustics similar to themselves. Chun-t'ae had heard the story when he was drinking with some of the other villagers. A backwoods fellow is about to begin a meal at his in-laws' house. The dinner table has been brought in, and as soon as he takes his first spoonful of rice he begins looking under the table time and again. When his father-in-law asks what he's doing, he replies that the rice he put in his mouth vanished so quickly he's trying to find out where it went. The villagers say that that's what happens the first time backwoods people eat glossy rice unmixed with other grains. By such caricaturing of farmers like themselves, Chun-t'ae thought, they're trying to lessen their anxiety that they might become like that man in the story.

Having taken in a few grains of rice and revived his strength somewhat, Chun-t'ae payed for the gruel over the protests of the innkeeper and left the inn. As always these days, the warm air of daytime had become chilly as evening set in. Chun-t'ae didn't mind the cold air, though he suspected it was not good for his health.

At home Chun-t'ae spread out his bed haphazardly and lay down, his clothing half on and half off. His knees stung and throbbed, and he felt he had sunk into a stupor in which his consciousness was slowly boiling away.

He was awakened by something grabbing and tugging on him. The surroundings had become faintly white. It's not dark anymore? he wondered. Is it already dawn? He soon discovered that moonlight was shining on the paper pane of the window. Feeling that his fever had ebbed and that his body was light, he closed his eyes.

Hands grasped Chun-t'ae's hands. They were the hands that had pulled on him in his dreams a short time earlier. The hands pulled on Chun-t'ae's and placed them on a voluminous expanse of skin. The woman's body was large, and her breasts especially so. They began near her shoulders, and when she lay down they projected from her chest. Chun-t'ae tried to remove his hands from the woman's, but she held them tightly and began rubbing her huge breasts with them.

After doing this awhile she gently releases his hands. She indicates that she wants Chun-t'ae's hands to move by themselves. His hands slide away feebly. Again the woman attaches her hands to the backs of Chun-t'ae's and massages her breasts. Then she gently takes away her hands. Instead of responding, Chun-t'ae weakly withdraws his hands. Suddenly the woman gropes for Chun-t'ae's crotch. You're not even alive. You're a carcass, a carcass! she spat. She gasps for breath, having worked herself into a passion.

Chi-yŏn had just given Sŏng-ho an account of her trip to Okku. "I wasn't going to tell anyone, and just put up with it myself," she added. "But it's not just me who's suffering. I'm sure something's going to happen to Mr. Ham."

"You should have told me before. There's no need to be like that with me."

"It was probably my last display of bravado. Anyway, I think I ought to hurry back there."

"For sure."

"Uh...couldn't we go together?"

"I was just thinking the same thing." Sŏng-ho was ready to take a day off from the brick-making operation that he had established near a somewhat distant residential district.

"Thanks, really. I was going to go by myself if I had to."

"No need to thank me."

"Can you leave now? We haven't got much time."

"Okay. Good thing I was a little late leaving for work—you almost missed me." The previous afternoon Sŏng-ho had gone to the hospital to see Myŏng-suk, who had not rallied from her relapse, and had bought some bellflower and cassiotora seeds on the way home. He had finished planting the seeds that morning, and had not yet left for work.

After asking the family next door to look after Yŏng-i, Sŏng-ho changed from his work clothes into some leisure clothes. After some coaxing he removed himself from Yŏng-i, who had slowly entwined herself about him, and hurried away with Chi-yŏn down the hill from Starland Village.

Although it took some time to get to Seoul Station, they were fortunate to be able to board a train on the Changhang line immediately. The coach was not very crowded.

"This'll be my first time in the Kunsan area. Anything worth seeing there?" Sŏng-ho began as soon as the train left. He was trying to turn Chi-yŏn's attention elsewhere, for she had become deeply depressed.

"I don't remember much about it, because I came and went with only one thing in mind." Chi-yŏn smiled wanly and then looked far into the distance. "Now I'm wondering how Mr. Ham is doing."

It had been a long time, but Chun-t'ae's head was clear and his body refreshed. He felt incomparably peaceful. How long could I have been lost in that nightmare? he wondered. Earlier his fever had abated and he was able to distribute some of the seed potatoes to Old Kwŏn and the others, but then the fever had flared up again and he had been afflicted with a severe headache and chest pains and had become comatose. Nevertheless, he had eventually realized that the woman had disappeared from the house and that Tol-i had been crying and looking for her. Now Tol-i was sleeping, his legs under Chun-t'ae's quilt. Chun-t'ae sat up, thinking he should cook something for the two of them.

"Oh no!" Chi-yŏn suddenly cried out.

"What's wrong?"

"We've got to get to Mr. Ham right away!"

Sŏng-ho looked more closely at Chi-yŏn's eyes. They were fixed on a point far off in space.

As Chun-t'ae was about to get up he became dizzy and his hands, which he had planted on the floor to support himself, gave way *ssuk*. He removed his hands from the *ondol*[1] flues and groped along the floor. There was nothing wrong with it: no trace of where he had sunk in. His right cheekbone tingled. Only then did Chun-t'ae realize that he had fallen forward while trying to prop himself up with his arms. He went back to bed and once more sank into a sleeplike stupor.

"I just remembered. You know Min-gu, right? He'll be getting married soon, and that'll be the end of his research on shamanism. He's trying to decide whether to go to work for his father-in-law's pharmaceutical company. He's practical, no matter what he does, so... Don't you think Mr. Ham ought to just make up his mind to move to Seoul and work there? How could he want to work in agricultural development when his health is so bad..."

Again Sŏng-ho was attempting to turn Chi-yŏn's thoughts to

[1]*Ondol:* the traditional heating system in a Korean home, consisting of heat from an external firebox (which is also usually used for cooking) radiating through stone flues beneath the floor of the home.

something else, but then he flinched. It wasn't just that she showed no signs of attentiveness; it had suddenly struck him that it should be him rather than Chun-t'ae that they were going to see.

Chun-t'ae's spirit rose, as if soaring up from underground. But his eyes didn't open. A boy of five or six appeared, shivering as he clings to his mother beside a frozen lake. The boy's mother grasps his hand so tightly he can't stand the pain. But the boy isn't upset. Then the mother lies down. The boy scratches at the frozen earth and begins to bury her. Every time he adds some earth his mother says, "more, more." The boy's fingertips are bleeding and sore, but he keeps scratching at the earth and piling it on his mother. He covers her body, and even when her face is about to be covered she only says, "more, more," as before. Chun-t'ae watches this spectacle without emotion. Before he knows it he's confined in a room about four feet square. He can't stand up straight or stretch out his legs and lie down. There are no windows. Even so, the room is filled with a dim light. He squats in the middle of the room and looks at a hole in the floor. It is a hole Chun-t'ae bored for eons with his own fingernails. He waits for a rat. Finally he hears it scampering toward him, and its feet appear from the hole. He caresses the feet. They are not the feet of a rat but Chun-t'ae's own hands. The two hands caress each other at length, as if soothing each other's loneliness, and finally they are removed from the hole. Chun-t'ae looks dejectedly into the empty hole.

Sŏng-ho searched his memory for Chi-yŏn's eyes; he had seen them several times before. Then Mrs. Hong's eyes confronted him, shivering in fright. Mrs. Hong has already died, and now Chi-yŏn is going to see the man she loves, worrying about his well-being. Mrs. Hong's face and Chi-yŏn's hovered one before the other, and then their eyes shivering in fright grew large and covered their entire face. These are the eyes of the Creator, Sŏng-ho thinks. They are the eyes of these women and at the same time the very eyes of the Creator. This revelation seemed to be the product of various thoughts that had long been clustering in Sŏng-ho's mind. No matter whose they are, such eyes are the Creator's. And why should it be just the eyes. It's everything that comes out of humankind: life, death, good, evil, and everything else are the Creator's. It is through humans, who in shape and mind are the image of the Creator, that the Creator Himself is thus able to carry out the struggle between thesis and antithesis. In order to achieve love—the synthesis in our earthly life—the Creator carries on the struggle in countless forms and without end. So Lord, I pray to you to realize this woman's desire, if nothing else—to allow this trembling young woman her desire on behalf of her love.

You don't know how to be loved or to love—you only know how to love yourself. Could it be? Something descends, flapping, in front of Chun-t'ae. Two things with wings are locked in a seesaw struggle. Looking closely, Chun-t'ae sees a hawk and a pheasant. A seesaw struggle: the hawk isn't winning, nor the pheasant. Over and over the same pattern—the hawk on top and then the pheasant. Hey, get out of here! Chun-t'ae yells.

"I should've gone earlier, earlier," Chi-yŏn murmured anxiously. The passenger opposite had been looking askance at her for some time, but this scarcely concerned her.

Chi-yŏn, you're here. Just in time. You're asking me to open my eyes? I can see well even though they're shut. You haven't changed at all. Let's leave, you say? All right, we'd better leave, anywhere. We'll take this kid Tol-i, too. I didn't want the little fellow, but now I've got him. Let's all go together.

"No matter what we do, it's already too late," Chi-yŏn murmured apprehensively. Her eyes became liquid as she stared into space.

Chi-yŏn, you're crying. Don't cry. You're not late. You're right on time. We'll never leave each other again. No way. Happiness saturated Chun-t'ae's body. At the same time, his breathing became labored and he erupted in a brief spasm of coughing. His chest was racked with pain. It would die down a bit and then flare up. The *sae'aek sae'aek* of his breathing became feeble and less frequent. Suddenly he cried out: Let's go, let's go right now!

Chi-yŏn's head abruptly dropped, and she covered her face with her hands. Far off a human form is walking. The swaying feet seem to barely touch the ground. It is a person drifting along with no destination.

Sitting in front of Sŏng-ho's shack in Starland Village, their backs to the wind, Tol-i and Yŏng-i are trying to fashion something out of a bunch of interlocking plastic chips. It's a toy Chi-yŏn bought for them. For the time being, Sŏng-ho is caring for Tol-i and Chi-yŏn is paying the expense.

Yŏng-i's creation is about to take the shape of an automobile, but it's hard to tell what Tol-i is making. He's tired of making houses, bridges, cars, and planes.

"Hey, hey, isn't this swell?" Yŏng-i thrusts her finished automobile in front of Tol-i's nose.

Tol-i concentrates on what he's doing and pretends not to notice.

"What's that?" Yŏng-i finally asks.

Tol-i merely screws up his mouth in a knowing smile.

After looking a moment longer at what Tol-i's making, Yŏng-i says, as if rapping him on the knuckles, "That doesn't look like anything."

"So what?" Tirelessly Tol-i fitted the chips this way and that.

August 1972